THE CURE

AN UNBOUNDED NOVEL

Books by Teyla Branton

Unbounded Series

The Change

The Cure

The Escape

The Reckoning

Under the Name Rachel Branton

Tell Me No Lies

Your Eyes Don't Lie

AN UNBOUNDED NOVEL

THE CURE

TEYLA BRANTON

This is a work of fiction, and the views expressed herein are the sole responsibility of the author. Likewise, certain characters, places, and incidents are the product of the author's imagination, and any resemblance to actual persons, living or dead, or actual events or locales, is entirely coincidental.

The Cure (Unbounded Series #2)

Published by White Star Press
P.O. Box 353
American Fork, Utah 84003

Printed in the United States of America
ISBN: 978-1-939203-30-4
Year of first printing: 2013

To my daughter Liana, who adores reading my books.
I love to hear you laughing and to watch your face while you read. Thanks for all the help with your little sister and for wanting to discuss all your great ideas.
Maybe someday I'll be reading

your

stories

in

a

book.

♥

I LOVE YOU!

CHAPTER 1

I PEERED AROUND THE TREE AT THE COUPLE WHO SAT ON THE PARK bench, their faces set, their bodies taut and anxious. The woman, Mari Jorgenson, had no idea what she was—what she had become. She spoke earnestly, but the man only pretended to listen. His eyes roamed the trees that dotted the area, stopping briefly on a grouping of three evergreens crowded by thick bushes.

What was he searching for?

I pushed my awareness out as far as I could, but nothing unusual registered on my senses. This area of the park appeared deserted, which was natural since November had slammed down on Portland like an iceberg from the Bering Sea, bringing a brutal cold spell the city hadn't seen in decades. Still, it was a nice change from the constant rain or the wet snowflakes that seemed to saturate every inch of every piece of clothing I wore. My hometown of Kansas City wasn't exactly warm in the winter, but the cold and wet had never been as penetrating. A twinge of nostalgia pinged in my chest when I thought about Kansas because I could never, ever go back to what I'd been. I was fortunate to have escaped mostly in one piece; others hadn't been so lucky.

Peering around the tree again, my eyes found Mari's small form on the bench. Even at this distance, I could see the Change that had taken place gradually over the two months I'd been watching her. I'd already sensed that she was Unbounded, though in the beginning it was hard to tell, even for someone like me. Complete confirmation had come last week after we'd gone skiing in Utah, and she'd banged up her knee so badly the doctors had told her she wouldn't regain full use of it.

A day later she was walking. With that single event, both her life expectancy and the likelihood of violent death increased by nearly twenty-four hundred percent.

I felt for my Sig tucked inside its holster at the back of my jeans, easing it out so my long jacket couldn't get in the way. It was racked, a bullet in the chamber. I'd double-checked before I followed them from work.

Crouching, I eased forward behind the bare bushes to the right of the tree, my muscles singing in relief at the movement. I'd trained vigorously for hours with the other Renegades before I went jogging in the park with Mari this morning, but I'd had all day for any strained muscles to heal. I felt as fresh as when I'd awakened.

My mind ran over what I would soon have to do. Mari and I had become friends, and I knew how betrayed she'd feel at the depth of my deceit. She'd figure it out quickly once it was all in the open. Her brain was already running at high speed because of the changes inside her. At the accounting firm where I worked with her under an assumed name, she'd begun to accurately calculate entire columns of numbers without the aid of a machine. Her Unbounded father had been skilled at engineering, and her great-aunt Stella was a technopath, so this ability didn't surprise any of us. It was only a matter of time until her co-workers noticed. There was no telling what else she might be able to do, and her very existence made her a potential danger. To us, to our enemies, to the entire world.

Mari jumped to her feet, hands in her coat pockets, her breath forming white clouds in the air, more visible now that the sun had set and twilight was deepening. Night came early on these winter nights, though it wasn't quite six o'clock, and some distance away, I could still hear the faint sounds of rush hour traffic on the main road. I couldn't make out what Mari was saying, but I knew her well enough to guess that she was giving Trevor an ultimatum. She wanted to see a marriage counselor and for them to work toward having a child. I wondered if he noticed the new sureness in her movements, how the blemishes in her skin had disappeared, and how thick her long, silky hair had become. Her heart-shaped face showed only a hint of her Japanese heritage, which was less than an eighth, but since her Change, I thought she was looking more and more like the small-boned Stella, whose mother had been full-blooded Japanese.

Trevor also came to his feet but didn't yell back at her, which made the fine hair on my body rise in alert. I'd been forced to get to know him somewhat over the past two months since we'd come for Mari, and this calm wasn't like him. He was a loud, opinionated man who liked his dinner on the table by six-thirty and his wife submissive at all times. He never planned dates, remembered her birthday, or sent flowers on their anniversary. She'd admitted to me once in tears that he only touched her with affection when he wanted her in bed—which happened less and less these days.

Trevor was another reason we had to act sooner than later. Unbounded had a high rate of fertility and most birth control methods failed. If she slept with him now, we might end up with more complications than we bargained for. Better that Mari first understood the consequences.

Trevor eased away from Mari, his hands in his jacket pocket. He darted a nervous glance in the direction of the trees behind her. Something was very wrong. If I were closer, or if I touched him, I might be able to sense what he was hiding, but the only thing I felt from him now was a tight nervousness. I almost hoped he'd turn violent. If he did, it would save us oceans of headache in the long run, though I wasn't about to let him have the satisfaction of hurting Mari.

A faint movement in the trees behind Mari caught my attention. Easing around the bushes, I paused at the edge of the sparse covering offered by an evergreen. To check out the movement physically, I'd have to expose myself by running across open space. Mari, Trevor, and whoever might be there would see me coming, and I couldn't have that. Being careless might cost more lives than just my own. The Renegades depended on me.

A breeze hit my face, soothing my fears. *Only the wind.*

The cell phone in my pocket vibrated, and I checked the caller ID before answering. It was Ava, the fearless leader of our little band of Renegades, and also my fourth great-grandmother. I wondered if she was calling about Cort, who was supposed to have taken over watching Mari after we left the accounting firm. Unfortunately, Mari had quit work early when her husband showed up without warning. Cort *should* be following the signal from my GPS chip now, and catch up to me at any moment, but he'd been known to become distracted with whatever scientific experiment he was working on in his lab. It was kind of getting to be a problem. As one of the newest Unbounded in our group, I was at the bottom of the useful list and tattling wouldn't earn any brownie points, but I'd endured the torture of the office all day and it was only fair that he and the others took their turns. Mari's Change affected all of us.

"What's up?" I asked, keeping my voice low.

"We have a problem." The tension in Ava's voice dissolved my concerns about Cort. She didn't stress over anything small.

"What is it?"

"You need to get back here as fast as you can. I'll explain later."

I glanced again at the bushes behind Mari. No more movement. Had it really been the wind? Regardless, I couldn't leave Mari alone with Trevor. "Is Cort on his way?" Okay, so I *would* rat on him. A guy who'd lived almost five hundred years should know better.

"He's on a plane to Mexico—as of nine o'clock this morning.

Dimitri went with him. I would have notified you sooner, but we've been a bit busy."

I gritted my teeth. We had only two main interests in Mexico, and problems with either would mean more deaths. Worse, her tone told me Mexico was only the beginning of what had gone wrong.

"I want you to bring in Mari," Ava continued. "We need you here. We should have brought her in last week when we were sure." There was no censure in her voice, though I'd sided with Stella in waiting. I knew how hard it was to have my life change from one minute to the next.

I was tempted to ask for backup, but I could imagine the fun my brothers and the rest of the Renegades would have if the movement in the trees turned out to be nothing more than the wind or a stray dog. I needed to be sure. I hesitated several heartbeats before saying with a slightly forced confidence, "I'll be there within the hour. Sooner if I can."

"Good." The line went dead.

How soon I'd actually make it depended on what I decided to do with Trevor and how good a fighter he turned out to be. Though I trained hard every day, my Unbounded ability had nothing to do with combat. I'd been weeks ahead of my brother Jace, and he'd surpassed me during his first lesson, his quickness immediately identifying his area of skill. Even so, they claimed I was progressing faster than most new Unbounded, and every now and then I felt I could almost see what my opponent would do next the way Jace could.

And Ritter Langton.

My stomach clenched. With the events in Mexico, would Ava call Ritter back from wherever he'd been the past two months? My pride hadn't let me ask, but she probably had some way to contact him.

I shoved away the unneeded distraction, though the tightness in my belly remained. Trevor was the main problem here. If it came to it, I could deal with him, but I didn't think knocking out her husband would go far toward lulling Mari's suspicions so I could more easily kidnap her.

First I needed to be sure about those trees. Pushing out my thoughts, I began searching, straining. A dull throbbing began at the base of my skull, my mind not at all appreciating the effort. Yet there in the trees where I'd seen the movement earlier, I now felt two faint life forces. They didn't glow as brightly as the average mortal, though they weren't as dark as someone who was experienced at blocking sensing Unbounded. So something in between, which could mean a lot of different things. From this distance, I couldn't pick up any thoughts or emotions. I fumbled in my pocket and came up with a tiny pair of binoculars that Stella had assured me were vital to my assignment. In the past two months, I'd used them exactly twenty-three times on mornings when Mari couldn't jog with me, when she'd run errands at lunch, or eaten out with Trevor. I was lucky not to have been arrested as a stalker.

I studied the trees, regretting the fading light. Someone was definitely crouching behind one of the evergreens, but I could see little more than a patch of green jacket. *Wait.* Between the branches of the bush next to the evergreen, where a few tenacious leaves clung to an otherwise bare limb, I spied what might be the black barrel of a rifle. I shifted to another position that was slightly more exposed and looked again. Another figure hunched farther to the left, the insignia of a hunter with a rifle standing out on his dark jacket. A jolt of emotion arrowed through me.

Hunters.

There are few things Unbounded fear, and Hunters are one of them. For over fifty years the society of Hunters has dedicated their lives to eradicating both the Renegades and our enemy, the Emporium, never differentiating between the two Unbounded groups. That many of the Hunters' older members began life as failed Emporium genetic experiments and were later abandoned, only makes their hatred that much stronger. Despite the fact that Renegades protect mortals from the Emporium, Hunters view all

Unbounded as false gods they need to depose and punish. Eradicate like vermin. Kill.

My first thought was that the Hunters had somehow tracked me, though I was new enough not to be in their database. The tightness in my stomach now extended to the tips of my fingers. Both my previous run-ins with Hunters had nearly ended in a date with a sharp blade.

My left hand slid to the cell phone in my coat pocket, pressing and holding the single button on the side. After the Emporium attack two months ago on our Renegade allies in New York, where nine Unbounded and a dozen mortals were murdered in a macabre slaughter, and several more had been taken captive, we'd begun carrying these altered phones.

With Cort and Dimitri in Mexico, Ritter gone, and Ava up to her ears in whatever she wouldn't explain over the phone, who would they send to answer my call? Stella wouldn't come, not in her condition, and my brothers lacked training. Chris wasn't even Unbounded. No, it would be someone from our mortal security detail, most of whom had served with the government in black ops. They were well trained and deadly. More than a match for any Hunters. Still, I'd try to mop up the Hunters before they got here—if only to prove to myself that I could.

I glanced at Mari, needing to adjust my position again to get a clear view. Trevor had moved several feet away from her, and now he dipped his head as he glanced at the trees where the Hunters crouched.

A signal.

I didn't know how he'd been contacted by them, but somehow he was involved—and he was giving them Mari. What was his price? Anger flooded me, and it was all I could do not to go running into the open and smash my fist into his face. Instead, I pushed partway through the bushes, forcing myself to wait.

Mari was still talking, her voice louder now. I couldn't quite make out the words, but her tone was pleading. I hurt for her, for what she was about to lose. It wasn't fair. Trevor had done a good job of isolating her in the three years since her mother's death, and lately she had no one to confide in except him—and me. I was about to betray her now. How long would it be before she'd trust anyone again? Ava had told me when I Changed that I'd been given a priceless gift or a great curse, and this was yet one more example. The necessity of sneaking around, of lying to people who would be your friends.

Somehow, I had to get us out of this situation. I couldn't depend on the others making it on time. *They won't shoot unless Mari fights them.* Except she probably would. She wouldn't realize that they didn't care how they managed to take her prisoner. A simple bullet to the brain or heart would temporarily stop any struggle—long enough for the cutting to begin.

Biting my lip until I tasted blood, I edged forward as far as I could without exposing myself, close enough now to pick out actual words.

The Hunters stepped from behind the distant trees, running toward Mari, as silent as wolves. Still only two. Good. A thrill of anticipation rolled through me. One man sported a ponytail, a grizzled beard, and wore a camouflage jacket; the other was clean-faced with stringy blond hair that emerged from his knit cap and fell to the collar of his brown coat. The older man would likely be more dangerous, especially if he'd dealt with Unbounded before. Neither was a match for me, though if they got off a lucky shot, they could immobilize me long enough that I might be in trouble.

Mari must have heard something because she glanced behind her. Seeing the strangers, she moved forward quickly to join Trevor, but he held up his hands and spoke loud enough for the oncoming Hunters to hear. "Nothing personal, Mari. You have too much of their blood. It's tainted. I can't be with you anymore."

"What are you talking about?" Mari sounded dazed. "Who are they? This has nothing to do with anyone but us."

Trevor shook his head like the dog he was. "They tracked your ancestry. It was a long shot that you were one of *them*"—he uttered the word with disgust—"but they assigned me to you to make sure.

Last week when your knee got better, and how you can add up those numbers. It all means something, Mari." He gave her a mean little grin. "It means you're a monster."

I was going to kill that man when I got my hands on him.

Mari reached for Trevor, but he shook her off as though she carried contagion. The other men laughed and lunged for her, securing her arms.

"Hey, I know you." Mari peered at the younger man. "You were at our wedding!"

He barked a laugh. "Ask Trevor how much bonus he got for that. Best way to see if you turned."

"Let me go!" Mari began struggling.

At the panic in her voice, Trevor hesitated. "Go easy on her now."

The older Hunter snorted. "You know what she is, and what you signed on to do. What you was *paid* to do. Now git outta here if you ain't got the stomach for it."

"You—you're not going to, uh, do it here, are you?" Trevor stared at his frightened wife.

"Of course not. Now git. Or have you changed your mind? Because you know what that means." The old man leveled his rifle at Trevor.

Trevor held up his hands, stumbling back a few steps.

"Trevor," Mari whimpered.

Without another word, Trevor turned and fled.

Mari's scream filled the park, and the grizzled Hunter shook her. "Stop that, or I'll shoot you right here. Ain't no one gonna hear you anyway. We got men making sure no one comes this way."

She didn't stop struggling. Fighting was against her docile nature—her former nature—but now that she'd Changed, the old Mari was gone.

The young Hunter pulled Mari against him, her back to his chest, and put a hand over her mouth. She promptly bit him, but he only laughed and stroked her neck with his other hand.

"She's a pretty one—and feisty. I want a go at her." Squatting slightly, he rubbed his groin up her backside. A terrified sob escaped Mari's throat as she arched away.

"There's no time," growled the old Hunter.

"Sure there is. It's not like I have to talk pretty to her. You said yourself they ain't human. What's it gonna hurt? I want to see what it's like. What Trevor's had all this time." His hand snaked to Mari's waistband.

The old man searched the growing darkness. "Be quick about it then. You know how the others are. They think it's a sin to touch one." He laughed hoarsely. "Like it's catching."

"Then hold this." The young Hunter thrust his rifle at his companion before turning his attention back to Mari, his hand slipping under her hip-length coat.

She struggled more furiously as he yanked open her pants. He turned her around, still pulling on the material, but Mari's fist caught him in the face. Shoving her at the old guy, he ground out, "Grab her. Keep her standing. Won't take but a minute. Smack her good if she tries anything. Might be true what they say about some of them being able to get into our minds." He emanated a wave of lust so strong, I could feel it from where I hid without even trying.

Tucking the rifles under his arm, the old Hunter complied, placing one big hand on Mari's stomach and pulling her to him, his other hand clapping over her mouth, jerking her head back until it hit his shoulder. Mari kicked at his leg, trying to free herself, but he shook her roughly. "Stop that, bitch, or he'll make it worse for you."

The young man laughed, his hand fumbling at his own clothing. "Just hold still and enjoy. I'm way more of a man than Trevor ever was."

Enough. It was tempting just to shoot them both, but I didn't want to alert the companions they claimed to have out in the darkness. If Ritter had been around, he'd have probably made sure I was carrying a silencer. But he wasn't. He'd abandoned me, and

I didn't need him to finish this task. Mari was my responsibility; I wasn't going to let them have her.

Slipping the gun back into my holster, I arose silently from my hiding place and sprinted toward the men, leaving a few strands of my blond hair on the bushes as I squeezed through. I'd traveled half the distance separating us before the old guy looked up and saw me, his face gray in the sparse light. He let go of Mari and tried to bring up his rifle, but he was clumsy with the added weight of the younger man's weapon.

I helped him drop both guns to the ground with a well-placed kick that even my brother Jace would have appreciated. The old man grunted as my foot continued on to connect solidly with his side. As he curled forward in pain, I followed with a left hook, striking him to the frozen grass and hopefully buying me a little time.

Mari screamed, and I turned to face her. The young man, his pants open and sliding down his narrow hips, had jumped behind Mari, his arm circling her waist.

"Mari, it's going to be okay," I told her. "But don't scream again."

The young Hunter peered into the night. "Help!" he shouted.

Great. I hadn't expected him to have that many cells left in his tiny brain.

Movement behind me signaled that the old guy had recovered. I whirled, slamming my elbow into his head as he tried to rise, a rifle clutched in his hands. I kicked the gun out of his reach.

The young man was backing away, dragging Mari after him. I took out my gun. "Let her go."

He shook his head, his knit cap askew. His breath came in fast gasps.

"Let her go, or when I get finished with you, you'll never touch another woman again." I took aim at the thin slice of his face that wasn't hidden behind Mari.

"You—you won't shoot her." His voice increased two octaves on the last words.

"Why not?" I took a step closer. "As you said, she's not human, so it won't matter if I shoot her. In fact, it'd probably be easier for me. I'll get you both with one bullet. It definitely won't hurt her as much as what you have planned."

The sound from his throat was half protest, half sob. His eyes grew impossibly wide. "You're one of *them,* ain't you?"

"One of who exactly?"

No answer.

I shifted my position so I could keep an eye on the old man. He wasn't moving, but cockroaches had a way of coming back to consciousness when least expected. Besides, there was no way to tell if anyone else had heard the commotion. I had to be prepared for the worst.

Mari was struggling again, her efforts loud in the quiet of the park.

"I'll give you to the count of three," I said to the Hunter. "One . . . two . . ."

The young Hunter's eyes went again to the blackness, where help had failed to materialize. With a whine, he pushed Mari at me and ran.

I sidestepped Mari and leapt after him. I didn't have far to go. His jeans slid further down his thighs and tripped him. I chuckled, kicking his sprawled body over with my foot, my eyes sliding down his nakedness. "So that's why you're a rapist. Can't blame a woman for not wanting any of *that.*"

Heat filled his eyes. He jumped up and lunged toward me, forgetting my gun and his bareness. Exactly what I'd hoped. I mean, how can you strike a naked guy lying on the ground?

I blocked his punch with my right arm, and hit him with two left jabs. He lunged at me again, and I heard a sharp click half a second before hot fire spread through my stomach.

A knife. I hadn't expected that. We trained with knives as we did everything else, and for an instant, I considered retrieving the one I carried inside my boot. Stupid when I had the gun.

I aimed the Sig. "Stop." I could feel warm blood leaking down my stomach, though already the wound would have begun healing. There were only two ways to kill Unbounded, and a scratch like that wasn't one of them.

"You ain't going to use that gun," the Hunter mocked. "My friends will hear. Then you'll be the one begging for *this.*" He felt his groin before hitching up his pants and rushing me. His movements were sloppy, unpracticed, but he had a knife and twenty pounds on me.

I turned to avoid the knife, hitting him at the same time with another left jab. He stumbled past me, pivoted on his heel, and dived at me again. I cracked the gun in my right hand down on his head. *Take that, idiot.* A pistol had more than one use.

He fell forward with a thump—and lay there unmoving.

Carefully I turned him over. He'd cut himself in the stomach with the knife, but unfortunately not deep enough to bleed to death. He still had a pulse, too, so that meant he'd recover from being pistol-whipped. For all that he was a scumbag, I was relieved. Since my Change, I'd shot people and fought a lot more, but I'd never killed anyone. Not permanently killed. Killing Unbounded didn't count if it wasn't permanent. At least that's what I told myself because in truth it was still horrifying.

No time to think about it. I had to get Mari to the safe house—and I still had to decide what to do with the Hunters. They could identify me now.

I turned, half expecting Mari to have collapsed in a sobbing heap, but she'd grabbed one of the Hunter's rifles and was pointing it—at me. She backed away, her eyes wild.

I put the Sig in my pocket and held my hands up to show I wasn't armed. "Put it down, Mari. We have to get out of here."

"You—how—why . . ."

"I promise I'll explain everything, but later, okay? Trust me."

"You killed him! You were going to shoot me!" Her face was flushed and her eyes wide, her hands shaking with fear. Fear of me, the person who'd gone to work at a boring accounting firm for months in order to protect her from people a lot worse than the Hunters. The person who'd brought her food when she was too depressed to eat. The one who'd urged her to start taking charge of her life.

The truth of it was that she had more than enough reason to be wary of me. I'd run myself if I were in her place—in fact, I *had* run, and my family had paid for that mistake with a life. Luckily, Mari had no family to endanger, except fourth cousins she didn't know and Stella, who was technically her fifth-great aunt but whom she hadn't seen since she was a little girl.

Mari looked ready to bolt, and I still didn't know what else might be lurking out there in the dark. "He was going to rape you," I reminded her. "Besides, he's not dead."

"How did you know I was here?"

"I followed you." The street lamps in the park chose that moment to go on, making me feel exposed. How long before the Hunters' backup arrived?

"You followed me?" Her voice rose to a pitch that hurt my ears. "Who are you, Erin? Who are you really? Because *normal* people don't follow their friends. *Normal* people don't know how to fight like that." Her eyes went to the sprawled Hunters.

"I told you I'll explain later. We have to get out of here. These guys usually travel in a pack."

Besides, wherever there were Hunters, the Emporium was never far behind. Hunters might hate all Unbounded, but Emporium agents had been infiltrating their organization for decades, using them as a weapon against us. That the Hunters had found Mari or knew to watch for her Change smacked of the Emporium more than the Hunters, who were too short-lived to think over generations. But no matter how they'd found her, if I didn't get Mari out of this situation safely, Stella might never talk to me again. Renegade Unbounded guard their family lines as carefully as any treasure—even from most fellow Renegades—and she'd been waiting more than a hundred years for someone in her family line to Change.

I sent out my mind, trying to determine if anyone else was

out there in the darkness, or at least within my sensing range. We needed to avoid running into anyone else. Mari was already spooked as it was without watching me fight again.

Someone *was* coming—and fast. Had to be Unbounded. No mortal could move that rapidly. No time to run.

I reached for my gun.

Mari gasped as a shadow appeared from behind her, yanking the rifle from her hand. Her eyes went to the man, as if she didn't know whether she should scream and run—or fall into his arms and weep with relief.

Which was almost exactly the way I felt.

He was a tower of strong muscle, carrying himself with undeniable grace, as did all those gifted with combat. No movement wasted, no attack he couldn't anticipate. His black hair fell to the right, grazing a mole on his cheek. His square jaw, in need of a shave, was set in determination, and his eyes glittered with anger. He carried a gun in his right hand, and the sword emerging from a back sheath announced that he'd come prepared to find Emporium Unbounded. Wet-looking patches spotted his black jeans and jacket. Definitely blood.

Ritter was back. After two months with no word, he was back.

"Gaven and I took care of their friends." He spoke in a clipped voice, one he might have used in his former life as a policeman a quarter of a century ago. I wondered if he was thinking of his family—and the woman he hadn't been able to save.

"Who are you?" Desperation laced Mari's voice.

Ignoring her, Ritter crossed the space between us. I felt burning inside him when he was still feet away. I'd always been able to catch glimpses of him like this, even from the first before I knew about my ability or how to use it. Desire swept through me, and I couldn't tell if it was his or mine—or if it mattered. I had a brief vision of going into his arms, of our mouths clinging together, our bodies melding. Everything in my body screamed that he was mine.

Yet he'd broken his promise, and in a world where almost

everyone I knew lied to survive, I valued truth more than just about anything. At least that's what I told myself.

He reached for me, but I held myself stiff.

"Erin," he began.

"Later." I pulled my arm from his grip, jerking my chin at the Hunters. "They'll be able to identify me, and we still don't know how they found Mari. Are you sure you got the rest of them?" The emotions swirling around him cut off when I pulled away, as though they'd never existed. I knew differently.

"I'm sure." His eyes glittered so darkly that the only color for them was black. He was nothing but empty space to my sensing now, and it wasn't likely he'd relax enough to let anything more slip. We all learned how to block or suffer the consequences. The Emporium had at least two sensing Unbounded, one more powerful than I dreamed of becoming. She'd almost controlled me once, and I knew she'd eventually come for me again. I might be young in Unbounded terms, but I was valuable—or so everyone told me. I hoped when the time came that I'd be ready for her.

For a brief moment I thought with envy of my former life as a law-school dropout working a dead-end job as an insurance claims agent. Nothing more exciting than talking to distressed people and pushing buttons on a keyboard.

No one trying to carve me or my family into pieces.

Except I didn't really want to go back. If it meant saving the lives that had been lost, I'd agree in a heartbeat, but that could never happen.

Being Unbounded changes everything.

CHAPTER 2

GAVEN MATERIALIZED FROM THE DARK AND BEGAN TALKING quietly with Mari. His face, the color of rich coffee, was sharp and dangerous-looking and his wiry body was pure corded muscle, but he had an easy way of speaking and I hoped he could calm her. There were other things I needed to do.

Kneeling next to the old Hunter, I reached out and touched his face, while Ritter stood over me, a silent brooding shadow. I wanted to ask him where he'd been, what had been more important than being at the hospital after the operation, but now wasn't the time. Maybe a part of me didn't want to know the answer.

I closed my eyes and pushed my awareness inside the Hunter's mind. I still trusted Ritter to watch over me. Didn't that say something?

Down. The Hunter's unconsciousness made this part easier—perhaps made it possible at all. Of course I wouldn't be able to learn much about the kind of person he was while he was out, just observe some of his memories. Down further. Until at last I dived into a lake of memories that appeared below me, my entry rippling the placid liquid, though I couldn't feel any wetness.

Images floated around me, muted by the Hunter's unconsciousness. I moved aside to let an image of a truck go by, and yet another of a laughing woman. The woman was older than me, and I couldn't help wondering about her. Was she his wife? His sister? If he were conscious, I might be able to tell.

I'd practiced unconscious memory manipulation with Ava, my ancestor, but this was the first time I'd done it on my own. I had to be sure to find the right memory. He'd lose anything I took with me, and the less I took, the more seamless it would be. Extracting larger memories would leave black spots, and even Hunters would begin to connect that to us—eventually.

There. An image of me entering the clearing. Exactly the one I needed. I snatched it in my hands and it vanished. But there were more thought bubbles of Mari, and the deeper I went the more there were of them. If I removed them all, his memory would have too many holes, and besides, others knew about her. She'd already been written up in their computer database, and I couldn't erase that.

Sighing, I sidestepped a scene of the Hunter spitting tobacco with some buddies and stroked upward in a single motion to the surface of the memory reservoir, separating myself from the old man.

I nodded at Ritter before moving to crouch next to the younger Hunter. "Impossible to remove the memories of Mari," I said in an undertone. "They've been watching her for years."

"Figured as much." Ritter picked up the fallen knife. "This one's bleeding."

"He shouldn't play with knives." I wasn't feeling as flippant as I sounded. I didn't want to go into this rapist's mind, even unconscious.

Down I went again, this time into black oil. Ava had said it wasn't always a lake, and I wondered if this was my representation of him or his own. His memory felt less crowded and I easily located the bubble I needed, the one that would keep me out of the Hunter's database for yet a while longer. The other memory of his attempted rape floated by, radiating sickness. Disgust rolled through me as I stepped out of the way.

I opened my eyes, still feeling slick with dirt and grease, wondering belatedly how the Hunters' minds would cope without the memories of me. Would they believe they'd been jumped from behind as they attacked Mari? It'd be the only reasonable explanation for the memory gap—if Unbounded abilities were anything near reasonable. In theory, a sensing Unbounded should also be able to input false memories into the unconscious mind that were as seamless as the real ones, but Ava said the knowledge to do so had been lost a thousand years ago, or the ability had been. She wasn't really sure which.

"You're bleeding." Ritter's mouth clenched tightly as he stared at my stomach and the rip in my shirt, the edges of the green material crimson with blood.

"I'm okay." I spoke quickly because Ritter was volatile, and while I had no love for this Hunter, I didn't want his blood on my hands. "They may know too much about Mari," I added, coming to my feet, "but it was only last week that she Changed, so maybe we can at least remove that."

"Then we'd better keep them unconscious until we talk to Ava." Ritter glanced at Gaven, who was still with Mari. "Gaven, we'll need to put them with the others."

Gaven strode toward us, and Mari glanced behind her as though preparing to run. Time to get back to work. Breathing in, I began absorbing nutrients from the air. I caught a hint of leaves and something fruity, not so much a taste on the tongue but a smell or a feeling. Strength tingled through my limbs, and the wound in my stomach no longer ached.

"I'm taking her to the palace," I told the men. The palace. The name my brother Jace had mockingly given to the sprawling rundown hotel where we'd been living for the past two months. At least it had enough room for all of us. "I'll leave these guys to you."

Without waiting for a response, I hurried to Mari's side. I could feel Ritter's gaze on me, but not a hint of his emotions came through. Once I would have been discouraged at the backward step, but for now I was relieved. I hadn't yet decided how I was going to play this.

Ava had warned me that Ritter didn't stick around, and I'd replied that at least he kept coming back. We were both right, but I didn't know if I could share a man with whatever else held so much fascination for him. I also didn't know if there was room enough inside him for both his obsessive hatred of the Emporium and his feelings for me. In the end, maybe I was better off without him. He was scarcely more than a killing machine. That was what the Emporium had made of him—what they'd made of us all.

Mari's gaze fixed on my bloodied shirt before going to my face. "I don't understand any of this. It's like a nightmare. Look, I'm getting out of here. I need to talk to Trevor."

It had to be shock that made her even consider going after him. "You can't. You're not safe with him."

"He loves me!" Tears started down her cheeks.

I shook my head. "He's a Hunter. Or at least connected with them. He was paid to watch you—you heard that yourself. Hunters kill people like you and me."

"What do you mean? Who are you?"

The men passed us with the unconscious Hunters. Ritter had tossed the older, heavier man over his shoulder, while Gaven dragged the younger man by the collar of his coat. Mari stared at them, her face nearly colorless.

"Look, Mari, do you know a woman named Stella Davies?"

She blinked, her attention coming back to me. "She used to come around when I was young. She was good friends with my mother. They wrote letters and talked on the phone all the time. She still sends me presents for my birthday and Christmas, but I haven't seen her in years."

Stella had stopped visiting because unlike Mari's mother, Stella hadn't aged. There were numerous advantages to aging only two years for every hundred that passed, but there were also huge drawbacks. The worst was that eventually you'd see most of your family age and die.

I was one of the lucky few who had a sibling with the Unbounded gene. I had Jace.

I tried not to think about our parents who weren't Unbounded. Or our older brother Chris and his children. That hurt too much.

"Well, I know Stella, too." Now the hard part, telling Mari I'd been sent to watch her, that in the past few weeks she'd Changed. I put my hand on her arm and propelled her gently after the men. To my relief, she didn't pull away—I really didn't want to force her. "Look, have you ever wondered about your father?"

"What do you mean? I told you before that my mother went to a sperm bank. I never received any information about him, except his general stats—you know, height, weight, race. That sort of thing." Her voice lowered. "But of course I wondered. I mean, what kind of man gives away part of himself like that? Isn't he even curious how his children might turn out?" She frowned, her eyes narrowing. "Why do you ask?"

"Because I know who he is. Or was." He'd been one of the Unbounded caught in the New York raid, cut into three precise pieces, all focus points severed. No chance of revival. I didn't add that we still hadn't discovered where the Emporium was keeping the few Renegades who were missing after the gruesome attack.

Maybe searching for them is what kept Ritter away.

"How do you know? Tell me," Mari said with a hint of demand that signaled an onset of the Unbounded confidence she would eventually possess.

I explained it all—about Stella being her ancestor and becoming friends with her mother and arranging things at the sperm bank so an Unbounded became her father. How we'd come to Oregon to watch her for signs of the Change and how she might live for two thousand years. I didn't mention the protecting part or how we could be killed. Time enough for that later. "So Stella is actually your fifth great-aunt or something like that. But she's only lived a couple of centuries—that's rather young in Unbounded terms."

"She's here in Portland?" Mari's voice shook and her face still resembled the color of paste. In all, I thought she'd taken it rather well. Better than I had.

"She's with a cousin of yours now—a fourth cousin. Oliver Parkin. He also Changed." His missing finger had miraculously regrown last month, and Stella had stepped in to prevent him from announcing it to the world.

Mari blinked and mumbled, "I have a cousin?"

"Several, in fact. But only one Unbounded." I certainly wasn't as good at this as Stella had promised I'd be. I wished I could reach out and soothe Mari's mind—it would be easy enough since I knew her so well and was still touching her arm—but I respected Mari too much to try to control her reaction. Instead, I erected a partial block in my own mind. Not thick enough to cause a total blackout, but enough to protect me from her confusion. Besides, I needed to focus my awareness on the darkness, in case any more surprises lurked there unseen.

The men headed toward a clump of trees where a jumble of other figures lay heaped on the frosted grass. I could tell from the position of one man that he was dead, but life forces still radiated from the others. Gaven released the younger Hunter and took a syringe with a needle from Ritter. Making sure their captives stayed unconscious and quiet. A man dressed suspiciously like Trevor lay with the men, but I caught Mari's attention before she saw him.

"We were relatively certain you'd be Unbounded with your parentage," I continued. "Well actually, not all that certain, but very hopeful. Your cousin has two siblings who didn't Change, and a younger brother who may or may not. It's too soon to tell. But we're sure now about both of you, and we'd like you to join us."

Mari stopped walking. "Join you?"

I held out my hand, palm up. "Trust me, okay? I know this is like nothing you've ever heard, but it's all true."

She put her hand on top of mine, her head tipping forward slightly. "I—I want to see Stella."

I smiled. "Ask her to show you her ring." I turned her hand over to show the ring's intertwining yellow-gold leaves. "She has one exactly like it." I hoped the connection would help Mari realize where she belonged. A proof of sorts.

Mari let her hand fall from mine. "If I'm going to live for two thousand years, what about Trevor?"

Even though I disliked him, I understood her pain. It was a lump that sat on your chest, invisible until from one moment to the next, it threatened to suffocate you. "Let's talk about that later, okay?"

She nodded, releasing a puff of air. "So that's why you're never winded when we go jogging. Because you're Unbounded? Your body is always healing itself?"

The grueling daily training in the wee hours of the morning had something to do with my physical condition, but mostly it *was* because of the gene. "You haven't been out of breath, either—at least not compared to last month."

I put an arm around her and led her in the direction of the parking lot, taking a wide circuit around the sprawled bodies and keeping up a steady conversation so she'd look in my direction instead of at the men. There was no way to hide all of them, but there was only one she really cared about and so far luck was on my side.

"Are your friends going to kill those men?" Mari asked.

"No. They'll just wake up with a bit of a headache. We don't kill people." Unless we had to, of course. I'd once killed a man I'd loved—or thought I had at the time. His belated Change meant I hadn't killed him after all, though death might have been better for him than his final fate, seeing as he now worked for the Emporium.

Silence fell between us, but it wasn't full of tension this time, and I relaxed slightly. The night seemed to be growing colder, which should keep people away from this remote area of the park, but I hoped Ritter and Gaven could finish up before some guy came to walk his dog.

When we reached my new Jeep Compass, I beeped the door

unlocked, but she hesitated before opening it, staring down at the shiny red surface. True darkness had fallen now, and her face was illuminated only by the lights in the parking area. I hoped she wasn't thinking about retrieving the car she shared with Trevor, which they'd left on the other side of the lot.

Her eyes lifted to me—large and brown. Tears made them shine in the reflected light. "Even though it all went really bad, I stood up to Trevor tonight. I wasn't even afraid. For a moment I thought he might start yelling or even hit me. I saw the stick—you know, that stick we've seen by the bench all week when we go jogging and keep wondering if someone's going to throw away. I pictured myself grabbing it and whacking him right back. But he didn't yell or try to hurt me. He just stared and pretended to listen until those men came, and then he left like he didn't care." Her face crumpled. "How can I still love him?"

I knew only too well. It had been like that for me with Tom. Almost worse was the dying of hope—which she'd realize soon enough.

Mari hiccuped. "I don't know who I am anymore."

Becoming Unbounded means you really do Change—not only physically but also mentally. Everything is different, including your dreams and all your relationships. Sometimes the new dreams were better than the old. I thought of Ritter and frowned. At least they should be.

"It'll be okay," I told her. "I promise."

I drove as quickly as I dared to the palace on the bank of the Willamette River, through traffic that was busy for a Thursday night. Pain flared beneath my temples. I was tired after my mental delve into the Hunters' minds, and I wanted nothing more than to get home and close my eyes until my body recovered. It was supposed to get easier, but my sensing ability wasn't increasing as quickly as I'd hoped. Or at all, if the truth be told. Ava had warned patience, but after showing so much initial promise in New York, where I'd reached down a long hallway to ask a Renegade for help, I'd expected more.

I guess once you become accustomed to being different—special—you crave even more. *Purely a mortal reaction,* I assured myself. Maybe after a few hundred years, I'd get over myself.

The palace had been used as a warehouse at one point, and huge metal storage containers, layered with a mess of peeling paint, loomed near the dilapidated dock. A single rowboat floated there, awaiting attention from my niece and nephew. I would be glad to leave Oregon just so I didn't have to worry about them drowning. They were so fragile, and though all of us kept an eye on them, it wasn't the same as when their mother had been alive.

Maybe I was more like Ritter than I realized, because Lorrie's death was one of the things I craved to avenge.

I parked my Compass in front of the ugliest container next to the other half dozen cars already there, all of which faced forward so the vehicles were ready in case of emergency. When everyone was home, we looked like a small auto dealership—a fancy new dealership. The neighbors probably thought we were running drugs.

Which, if you thought about Dimitri's experiments, maybe we were.

"Welcome to the palace," I said, flipping off the engine.

"This is where you live?" Mari studied the two-story structure doubtfully.

Seeing it through her eyes, I could understand the reservation. It was exactly what it seemed—a small, fifty-year-old hotel that hadn't undergone major repairs or upgrades for several decades, except for the gleaming bars over the windows and the new steel-reinforced doors. There was no yard to speak of, only dirt packed under a load of gravel Ava had ordered to prevent our vehicles from sinking into the mud during the wet season. A single pathetic street lamp illuminated the area with a weak, grungy light. The exterior clapboards had been patched, and were currently three different colors of green. A sagging porch ran across the front length of the house, but at some point part of it had been walled in to make a small office, which we used now for storing anything we didn't currently need. Most of Ritter's belongings were there, stacked in boxes up to the ceiling. The rest was in the room we'd saved for him, and I'd made sure the room was the draftiest one at the far end of the hotel. The only welcoming thing about the palace was the front door, which my niece had insisted on painting a bright yellow.

"Yep. Home, sweet home. Looks even better inside."

Mari laughed, a short staccato burst, and then bit her lip guiltily. She'd get over it.

As we started across the gravel to the door, a man with deeply bronzed skin ran out from behind the metal storage container to our right. "Geeve me your purses!" he demanded in heavily accented English. He waved a pistol. A small one. Not nearly as big as my nine mil.

For half a second, I thought he was another piece-of-garbage Hunter, who must have followed us, though I'd been careful to double back several times during our drive from the park. But a Hunter wouldn't care about our purses, unless he wanted to verify ID, and this man certainly wasn't an Emporium agent. His dark hair was lank and shaggy, his swarthy face unshaven. The jeans sticking out from under his ripped down jacket looked as if they hadn't been washed in a year.

My fear vanished. One common mortal thief was no match for any trained Unbounded—or even a partially trained one like me.

I arched a brow. "Uh, we don't have purses." Mari must have left hers in her car, and I didn't carry one.

"Your wallets then."

I shook my head. "Sorry." I couldn't help sounding amused. If he wanted my wallet, he'd have to take it from my coat pocket.

Mari clutched my arm, her body shaking. Her fear screamed in my mind. Apparently, she hadn't understood my brief explanation about our near immortality in the park. I wanted to remind her it was okay, that if he shot us, we wouldn't die. You even grew somewhat used to the pain. But she might not believe me until she experienced it for herself. Maybe that should be a requirement for all new Unbounded—to be shot through the heart so they realized what they had become.

"Geeve me the rings. Both rings." The man jabbed the gun in the direction of Mari's hand where it clamped my arm. The cheap wedding band wouldn't be missed, I suspected, but the other ring was the family heirloom that had belonged to Stella's little sister, who had died at least a hundred and forty years ago.

Pulling away from me, Mari began fumbling at the rings.

"Stop," I told her. No way was I going to let this jerk take them. Mari hesitated, her hands retightening on my arm like a vise.

The man waved the gun, his other hand going to the side of his head, as if to hold it steady so he could aim. "I'll shoot. I swear!"

With Hunters and possibly the Emporium on our tails, and whatever was going on in Mexico, we didn't have time for this, but I wasn't close enough to lunge at him without some kind of distraction, even if I could disentangle myself from Mari. Too bad my Sig was out of convenient reach in my holster. The knife in my boot could be a good option, if I pretended to reach for some money hidden there, but truthfully, I wasn't that good at knife-throwing, and I might kill the man.

The only thing left was my ability. As a sensing Unbounded, I should theoretically be able to influence the actions of a single man. In fact, I'd done it before—just barely and with great effort. That this man was alone and anxious worked in my favor, but the fact that he was a complete stranger and I wasn't touching him were definite drawbacks. A gift in combat or speed at this moment would have come in a lot handier.

I pushed out my thoughts, my head aching as it had in school after staying up all night cramming for a law exam. He'd been drinking, and I could feel his unbalance. The drunkenness would help since he'd be less likely to fight me. I pushed a little more. My head screamed.

Looking through the memories of a conscious person was far more chaotic than with someone who was unaware. There was no placid lake or thought bubbles. There were only images from the current world around us, and ideas that felt like sand running through my hands. Glimpses that I couldn't hold and study, but only peer at as they rushed by at lightning speed. Finding the right place to jump into the stream to observe was the challenge.

"Does your family know where you are?" I prompted.

Yes, that did the trick. As he considered my question, disjointed scenes rushed at me in the sand, like cars on a freeway. "What about your mother?" I asked. "When you call her in Dallas from the pay phone tonight, what are you going to tell her? And your grandpa? Your abuelo? He's a hero, isn't he? What would he say if he knew you were doing this? He gave up his life to save his town from being overrun by a Mexican drug cartel. You know he wouldn't approve."

The bum's eyes widened and his face paled. His gun lowered slightly. "How did you know?" Was it just me or had his accent suddenly diminished?

Something else in the sands of his memory, caught my attention: the bum lying under a sink, a wrench in hand, stopping to grin up at a raven-haired girl whose face radiated happiness. Then later, sitting on a paint can in a garage, drinking from a beer bottle and watching the same girl, tears streaming down her face, stalk to a small white car and drive away.

Fixing a sink? Garage full of paint cans and tools? It was embarrassing that those things were every bit as compelling to me as the story of his grandfather. I was sick of dripping water from my bathroom sink keeping me awake at night.

"Look, I can give you a job," I said. "Your girlfriend might change her mind about calling it quits if you find work, but drinking isn't going to get you there."

"I rob you, and you wanna hire me?" His voice was guttural.

"Well, we could use a handyman. I know that might not be your regular job, but you can fix things, right?" Hiring the bum likely meant no immediate personal connections to worry about—except the girlfriend who wasn't in the picture right now and the mother who lived far away in Dallas. We'd have to vet him to make sure he wasn't a true felon, of course, but having the courage to hold up two women while you were drunk wasn't necessarily a drawback in our business, especially when I could tell he didn't really want to hurt us.

A sound escaped his throat, signaling that he was close to breaking. Not good. I sent a wave of soothing emotions, but he shook his head as if trying to toss off an invisible net. Nausea curled my stomach, a direct result of my mental exertion. I definitely needed to refine my technique. At least my efforts had offered a distraction. I pulled from Mari's grasp and sprinted forward, diving at his gun and twisting it from his hand. Muttering a curse, he turned and ran.

I thought about giving chase, but Ava was waiting for me. "If you change your mind," I called after him, "we might be here a few more days!" With Mari and Stella's great-nephew hopefully onboard, we'd be able to leave Portland soon—preferably for a warmer climate.

I felt bad watching him run away. The man's grandfather had given his life for a cause he believed in, and I would have liked to give him the opportunity to fight for an equally important cause. Plus his handyman skills were more than attractive, since we hadn't yet found anyone suitably isolated to employ in that role on a permanent basis. That he could handle a gun was an added benefit. The others might have eventually thanked me; one thing I'd learned about Unbounded was that they loved their comfort.

He's probably a terrible repairman. The thought made me feel better. Good genes sometimes skipped generations.

I turned back to Mari. "Where were we?"

She shook her head, glancing in the direction the man had already disappeared. "Weren't you scared?"

"He wasn't going to shoot." Except by accident; he was drunk enough for that.

"How'd you know about his mom and his grandfather?"

"It's my gift. Every Unbounded has one. Very similar to talents that mortals have, though rather more unusual."

"You read minds?" She sounded horrified.

I shook my head. "Not exactly. Mostly I see scenes and sense feelings. I can pick up thoughts from some people, though." Ava and I could hold entire conversations without voicing a word. I could also tell an Unbounded from a mortal by simply looking at them—and detect the life force of everyone in a room, even if I couldn't see their physical body. There had only been one exception, that of another sensing Unbounded. "But don't worry. Most Unbounded can block me, and even mortals can if they're taught how."

"How?"

"Basically, you envision holding your thoughts in a tight ball, while pushing outward with white noise or blank thoughts. Or even a black wall. Whatever feels best. You'll know it's working when you hear a kind of rushing in your ears. After a bit of practice, you eventually won't need to tighten hard enough to hear the noise." It was something she'd need to learn fast because right now her emotions radiated from her like tangible jabs. Easy for someone like me to pick up and easier still for a sensing Unbounded from the Emporium to manipulate.

Mari looked like she was going to be sick. I put an arm around her, hurried her to the house, and punched in the code that would open the door and disconnect the alarm long enough for us to go inside. I could smell the roast our cook was making for a dinner most of us would eat but not really need or crave. I could no longer even remember what it was like to be hungry. My body never let me reach that point. Sometimes I actually missed the feeling.

We were met in a spacious foyer by a joyful bark and the click-clack of toenails on the worn wooden surface as Max, our loyal and quite useless mascot, came bounding down the stairs at the sound of the door. He was a beautiful mix of Collie and Chow, and though I didn't consider myself a dog person, I tolerated him because once he'd nearly died to save me. You couldn't fault dedication like that.

My ten-year-old nephew Spencer hurtled down the stairs in

Max's wake. He had blond hair and a bunch of freckles that had recently surfaced on his baby face, making him look rather spotted.

"You're home!" Spencer bounded into my arms as Max pushed into my legs, begging to be touched. "Can we go now?"

Go see his grandparents, he meant. I'd promised to take him and Kathy tonight. My mother and father—or the man I'd thought was my father—used to live with us here, but I'd convinced them they'd be more comfortable in their own place. What I really meant was safer. I'd hoped the kids would go stay with them, but my brother Chris wouldn't leave the Renegades and he wanted his kids with him. I didn't blame him for that, though I hoped his thirst for revenge didn't affect his children. Truth was, I wanted to save up every precious moment with them. They were eighth generation—which meant next to no chance of being Unbounded. I'd bury first Chris and then the kids before I'd age another two years.

But there was Jace. I had to remember that.

"We can't go see them right now, but maybe in a bit." I grabbed Max to prevent him from attacking Mari with wet kisses. He loved pretty much everyone, except people trying to kill me. "Where's Ava?" Although the door had been locked, I didn't like the idea of Spencer being alone. Obviously our hideout wasn't in the best neighborhood.

"In chambers." He rolled his eyes. "There's an emergency. They wouldn't let me in."

"Stella's here?"

"Yeah, and the new guy. Kathy's listening from the bathroom upstairs." His guilty expression told me that's where he'd been as well before Max alerted him to my arrival. His brow furrowed and his blue eyes became troubled. "Everyone's really freaking out. The Emporium did something again—in Mexico, I think. Cort and Dimitri left for there before I even got out of bed, and Dad's down at the airport getting Ava's plane ready in case she needs him to fly her there." He paused before adding. "Hey, did you know Ritter's coming back? Ava called him this morning. He was supposed to be here already, but he hasn't shown up yet."

I hadn't even thought about how Ritter had gotten to me so quickly. He must have been on his way here, and when I'd pushed the alert button, he'd have been notified just like everyone else in range. I wondered if Ava had ordered him to help me, or if he'd taken the responsibility on his own.

Maybe it didn't make a difference.

CHAPTER 3

I LOOKED AT MARI, TEMPTED TO LEAVE HER WITH SPENCER, BUT UNTIL I handed her off to Stella, she was really my business. Besides, unwatched she'd probably run off to find Trevor. Better that I keep an eye on her. She'd have a good long time to get over him—if she didn't get herself killed first.

"Hold Max," I told Spencer. He obliged, the dog straining at the collar and dragging the child's thin frame a few feet.

Taking Mari's arm, I led her past the front desk to the large back room we dubbed chambers. It held nothing more than a huge oblong table with enough chairs to spare, and today with Cort, Dimitri, and apparently most of our mortal security employees missing, only a third were full. Ava and my brother Jace looked up as we entered. Stella didn't. She had her neural headset on, her face directed toward a set of three flat screens on the desk, one of her brown eyes peering through an eyepiece connected to the headset.

As a technopath, Stella could interface directly with multiple computers at once, efficiently organizing, directing, and interpreting data through electrical impulses and eye movements. With the programs she created, she could monitor not only most of the communications in the world, but also when the next sale at the local grocery would begin. She was that good. When I thought about the amount of information available in the world, I was astounded that she or her programs could find anything useful to us, much less help us prevent the Emporium from whatever machinations they were planning.

Next to her sat Oliver, our other new Unbounded, Mari's fourth cousin. He also wore a blinking headset and was staring at the same monitors, but the frustration and disgust on his face told me he wasn't having success. Oliver was a few inches above average height, lean with impressive muscles, though nowhere near Ritter's broad-shouldered bulk. His brown face was a mixture of African American, Asian, and white, with the African American dominating his coloring and the tight curls in his short-cropped hair. He was decidedly attractive, but his self-centered personality annoyed me.

Jace popped up from his seat and took two strides in my direction. "How'd it go?" Eagerness laced his voice and danced in his blue eyes. My brother was twenty-eight, younger than me by three years, though we'd Changed within months of each other. The Change usually happens between the thirty-first and thirty-third birthdays, though sometimes it came as early as twenty-eight and as late as thirty-four. It can occur a few years earlier or later, but there were only a few documented cases.

One was my ex-boyfriend, Tom Carver.

"Well?" Jace pressed, one hand flipping back his white blond hair, now a tad too long. "Gaven called to say it was Hunters and to ask Ava what to do with them. Was there a fight?"

Poor Jace. He was young, full of testosterone, newly Unbounded, and already a better fighter than any of us except Ritter, yet no one dared let him off his chain quite yet. I loved my brother with a full-hearted devotion, but I was glad Ava hadn't sent him as my backup. Although he probably would have dispatched the Hunters with ease, he'd never been proven in a fight and it was hard to know exactly how he'd react. Even during his time in the army, he'd never encountered live combat, and if I'd been facing Emporium Unbounded, his eagerness and lack of experience might have endangered us both. Losing him to the Emporium wasn't a risk I ever wanted to take, especially when I still hadn't discovered the identity of his birth father. I had my suspicions, of course, rooted in the Emporium itself. Every time he smiled at me like he was doing now, it brought another face to mind—the face of a man who would have snuffed either of us out without a second thought.

I smiled at Jace. "Yes, there was a fight, but a bitty one. Hardly worth the effort."

"What?" Mari said next to me where she stood searching the new faces. "It was horrible! There were two guys, and they tried to . . . and then Erin starting punching and kicking . . ." Her voice trailed off.

Jace's eyes went past me to Mari. "Rats, I missed all the fun!"

His grin seemed to put Mari off-balance and she stared at the ground in silence.

"Mari," I said, "this is my brother, Jace Radkey. And that's Ava O'Hare. She's what we call the boss."

"Or mother," Jace added.

Ava was standing now. "Welcome, Mari. It's good to meet you."

Mari seemed helpless to answer, but everyone pretended she had.

"And you know Stella," I continued, "but she's rather busy right now. She's processing too much information at the moment to notice us, but she'll come around in a minute. Next to her is your cousin, Oliver Parkin."

As I spoke, Oliver tossed down his headset with a grunt of disgust. *So, not a technopath.* Whatever his ability finally turned out to be, I hoped it was something useful. He certainly hadn't shown much skill during our training sessions since Stella had brought him in. His confession about his Change to his girlfriend hadn't helped matters, and she'd gone screaming from his apartment, threatening to call the police. Ava and I'd been forced to masquerade as policewomen to get into her apartment so we could drug her and remove the memory from her unconscious mind.

"Hey, cuz," Oliver said. "Glad you're here."

Mari gave a nearly imperceptible smile. A good sign, I hoped.

I looked at Ava, my thoughts turning to Mexico. "Was it the compound?"

Located in the Mexican rainforest, the compound was where we kept Emporium prisoners, trying to rehabilitate them, if possible, or making them stand trial for their atrocities. Neither the location nor the process was ideal, but we Renegades were forced to do whatever it took to ensure the safety of the mortal population were trying to protect.

Ava's gray eyes, so like my own, stared back at me somberly. "Not the compound. They hit the research facility. Two days ago, actually. We only got word this morning."

Ice dripped into my veins. No wonder Stella was absorbed by her computers and monitors, in so deep that she couldn't break away—not even to say hello to her great-niece. She'd pinned all her hopes on the research facility. I glanced at her again and noticed that under the headpiece, her olive skin was more pale than usual, and there was an enhanced tightness around her mouth.

I shifted my gaze back at Ava. "How bad is it?"

Ava shook her head, and her golden hair swung slightly at the longest tips near her chin. She had smooth, clear, wrinkle-free skin, high cheekbones, and a nose that spread a tiny bit more than necessary. Ava was the epitome of a beautiful, successful leader. Though she appeared only a few years older than me, she'd already lived three hundred years. "We don't know yet. We haven't been able to contact them since the initial distress call. But Cort and Dimitri will land soon and should be able to discover more even before they drive out to the facility. If the worst has happened, Dimitri hopes to salvage what he can."

"It's the Emporium. It has to be."

Ava inclined her head, her eyes meeting mine impassively. "Most likely."

For Stella's sake, I hoped it was a false alarm, or that our physicians and lab personnel had escaped with their research. The life of Stella's husband depended on it. Bronson was mortal and at seventy much older than she was physically, but it was an autoimmune disease, not age, that was killing him. Stella had once been more at peace with his impending death, but her recent pregnancy had caused her to cling with hope to groundbreaking medical advances involving nanoparticles. Last week the information coming from the Mexican lab had indicated that curing him was a real possibility. We'd been expecting one of the doctors to arrive with the new formula.

Dimitri had originally arranged for several doctors in the U.S. to work on the problem of Bronson's illness, but one by one, the doctors' grants had been withdrawn and their jobs threatened. The Emporium, who invested deeply in health care, wasn't interested in cures, only in continued treatment. More suffering made money, not cures. They'd successfully blocked cures for cancers, muscular dystrophy, and paralysis due to spinal problems. Renegade Unbounded who were gifted in healing like Dimitri kept organizing research facilities, but the Emporium was just as good at ferreting them out and bribing government officials to impose prohibitive sanctions and restrictions—or threatening grants. With their genetic experiments and forced breeding, Emporium Unbounded agents were everywhere now, from the FDA to the senate. The facility in Mexico was one of the few unhindered research labs left to us—the only one with the promise of obliterating autoimmune diseases. Dimitri spent a couple weeks every month working there alongside his research scientists, and Cort double-checked all their data.

Stella removed her headset and stood gracefully, the multicolored greens of her dress briefly flowing before settling over her full breasts, narrow hips, and the slightly mounded belly where her child grew. Delicately boned, she had the same confident bearing as all Unbounded, but while most Unbounded were simply arresting, Stella was beautiful. Every feature on her face was absolutely perfect, from her wide brown eyes to her sculptured eyebrows and flawless golden skin. These were complemented by thick, shoulder-length dark hair and a heart-shaped face. Born of an Italian father and Japanese mother, her Asian heritage was prominent and exotic. I'd grown accustomed to her utter perfection, the effect not dimmed by the knowledge of the nanites she, as a technopath, used to achieve such results. Given another option, why live forever with plainness? Though I'd once felt a world of inadequacies around Stella, over the past months she'd become the sister I'd never had, and I no longer let her perfection intimidate me.

Mari caught her breath. "Stella! It really is you! I can't believe it!"

Stella smiled and hurried around the table to enfold Mari in her arms. "Oh, darling girl. I'm so sorry about the Hunters. I would have brought you in last week, but I wanted to give you more time to adjust."

"You look exactly the same as when I was a child." Mari hesitated before adding in a rush, "Then it's all true, isn't it?" The last words were garbled by sobs.

I looked away. So much emotion blasting the airwaves was an assault on my senses.

Jace caught my eyes and grinned. "You're bleeding."

"Was." My stomach felt fine now. In another hour, I wouldn't even have a scar. I looked down at Ava, who was sitting again in her chair, her body emanating coiled energy. "So, are we going to Mexico?" With Cort already there, Chris would have to fly the rest of us, and while worrying about Jace was hard enough, having my mortal brother in the midst of yet another crisis was not good for my peace of mind. I still blamed myself for his wife's death.

Ava's brow creased. "It depends on what Dimitri and Cort find there." She glanced at Stella. "There's no chatter about it anywhere, so I really can't plan anything right now. The lab's not exactly a secret, so it might be an Emporium ruse to flush us out. They don't like that we came out on top during our last struggle. I do wish Ritter had been here to go with them just in case."

"You could have sent me," Jace said. "Cort says I'm probably faster than Ritter now."

Somehow I doubted it, though I admired my brother's enthusiasm and I couldn't wait to see him spar with Ritter. Someone needed to remind him that being Unbounded didn't mean complete immortality—and that he still had a long way to go in training.

I waited for Ava to tell Jace he'd have been in the way, but her gravestone eyes observed him without expression. "You may still have your chance. Meanwhile, we have another problem to take care of. Two, actually."

"The Hunters, I suppose." I frowned. "There's no way to erase their knowledge of Mari altogether. She's already in their database. But we might be able to erase the fact that she actually Changed."

Ava jotted something on a paper in front of her. "I hope so, though that's not what I'm referring to. However, I did talk to Ritter after you left the park, and I sent George with the trailer. We'll bring the Hunters here to study the situation. If we can erase Mari's Change, I'll need your help."

I nodded. Delving inside people was exhausting, and though taking the Hunters' memories hadn't been too difficult, my run-in with the armed bum had left me depleted. Concentrating now, I increased my body's rate of absorption from the air. More nutrients should help me recover.

"The real concern with what happened tonight," Ava continued, "is how many other descendant lines might be compromised. Is this a one-time thing, or do the Hunters have a way to track our relatives who carry the Unbounded gene?"

My stomach tensed. If they did, it could devastate the entire Renegade movement unless we all acted fast. New Unbounded were the only way we'd survive the ongoing battle. "We'll have to contact the other groups."

"Stella already sent out a message," Ava said with a sigh. "But more pressing than all this is the problem of Cort's brother. He contacted us on our emergency line less than an hour ago, right before I called you. He wants to meet with Cort tonight. In person. Says it's urgent."

I blinked. "Keene? That brother?" Cort Bagley's Unbounded father was a member of the Emporium Triad, and Cort had many siblings, both mortal and Unbounded. Cort had defected years ago from the Emporium to Ava's group of Renegades, but his half brother Keene had remained embroiled in his father's cause, a mortal in the midst of Emporium Unbounded who considered themselves superior—almost gods—compared to the lowly mortals. Two months ago Keene had captured and taken me to the Emporium, but he'd eventually helped me escape. My life wasn't the only one he'd saved, and I owed him. "I thought Cort had lost all contact with Keene."

Stella, her arm still around Mari, turned her head in our direction. "He had for a while, but there's a chat group online where they sometimes talked in the past. Cort told me he's been keeping an eye out there, and Keene posted there last week."

I glanced at Ava to see if she'd known about this. Though each of us had our private lives, anything that might endanger the group had to be cleared through her.

She nodded. "I knew about it. They've been exchanging emails and talking on the phone. Cort's been trying to get him to work with us."

I was going to kill Cort for not telling me. "What does Keene want?"

"He wants to meet Cort—here in Portland. Tonight. With Cort in Mexico, that's impossible, but with everything that's going on, we feel we should meet him."

"Keene knows we're in Portland?" My eyes went from Ava to Stella and back.

Again Ava nodded, her lips tight with disapproval. "Apparently."

Not good. Our location was the one thing we and other groups of Renegades guarded with our lives. Not doing so always ended in a blood bath.

"We don't know *how* he knows," Stella said, always ready to give each of us a fair chance. "But the fact that he requested a meeting here is significant."

"Exactly." Ava's eyes still rested on my face. "We have to meet him. Or rather, you do, since Stella and I feel that you're the only one he'd talk to in Cort's absence. But keep in mind, it could be a trap."

"I'll go with her," Jace said.

I rolled my eyes. "No. I'll be fine." My brother had embraced near immortality with a passion that often overruled good sense, and I didn't want to have to worry about him.

"He should go," Ava countered. When I didn't reply, she added, "It's either him or Ritter. We have no idea if Keene's still working for his father and the Emporium. I expect you to be careful, but you can't go in without backup."

Unlike Ava, I trusted Keene—at least as much as you could trust anyone who knew about the Unbounded. He'd always told me the truth as he'd known it—even if it wasn't the entire truth, which was more than I could say about most men in my life, especially Ritter.

Who should be here any moment.

My traitorous body began to grow warm just thinking about him. Not good at all, especially in light of the Unbounded fertility rate and high probability of non-Unbounded offspring. Maybe after I'd lived a century or two, I'd learn to control my impulses. Besides, like many other Renegade Unbounded, Ritter had old-fashioned ideas about morality and family. It was all or nothing, and I didn't know if I was ready for two thousand years of commitment.

"Okay, Jace can come," I said. "Where does Keene want to meet? And when?"

Stella frowned, and even that didn't mar her beauty. "Eight o'clock. At a Chinese restaurant. I looked it up. It's reputable and in a good part of town. In fact, it's not too far from my apartment." Her apartment meant where Bronson lay dying, tended by either Stella or her live-in nurse twenty-four hours a day.

"Bronson's your husband, isn't he?" Mari asked hesitantly, her face pale and drawn.

Stella's frown disappeared, and I knew she was reminding herself that she had Mari and Oliver now, her beloved younger sister's Unbounded progeny to focus on—even if one day her own child didn't develop the active gene.

"He is, and you'll meet him soon." Stella looked over her shoulder where Oliver still sat at the table, leaning back, his long fingers tented over his stomach. "Meanwhile, Oliver can show you where you'll be sleeping. You'll be staying in my room here. I'm not usually there anyway. There's clothing in the closet. Feel free to use whatever you need. We'll get you more as soon as we can."

Mari's eyes widened. "But . . . I . . . all my things are at home . . . and I need to talk to Trevor."

Had I been this dense? "Listen, Mari," I said, stifling a sigh. "I told you at the park. You can't go home. Not ever again. Those people will hunt you now. Trevor sold you out. He's not there waiting for you. He never will be." I wanted to tell her she was one of the lucky women who got away, but she started crying again, crumpling in Stella's arms.

Stella glared at me. "Sorry," I mouthed with a shrug. So I wasn't the most empathetic person. I should be. After all, I was the one who could feel her emotions bouncing around like a bullet in my brain. I strengthened my mental barriers and immediately the desperation left me. *Ah.* I needed to remember to do that without having to concentrate so hard.

We all stood there a bit helplessly, not knowing what to do. I didn't think telling Mari that Trevor was unconscious would improve matters. *Maybe I should tell her how my old boyfriend helped the Emporium kidnap me.* Then again, it wasn't something I was willing to discuss with so many listening ears.

Oliver stood and came around the table. "Hey," he said to Mari, "it's really not that bad. They give you a bank account, and you don't have to worry about food anymore, or paying the rent.

Plus, you can jump off a building, splat on the ground, and come back to life as good as new."

The idiot. Exactly what we're looking for in new Unbounded. Oliver looked great—until he opened his mouth. We were trying to save the world and all Oliver worried about was the rent and interesting ways to off himself. I'd heard that a few of the younger Unbounded—meaning those who hadn't reached their first century—got high on dying and coming back to life, but in my experience, it wasn't all that pleasant. Of course I'd been in a hospital and pretty thoroughly drugged at the time.

"Better yet, they give you guns," Jace added, excitement lacing his voice. "Any kind you want. Bigger ones than I had in the army."

Mari stared at him in horror.

Okay. So Jace isn't much better.

Ava watched us all with an expression I couldn't exactly interpret, but it reminded me of a mother I'd seen on the news whose teens had been caught setting fire to a school. I didn't bother to try pulling any more from her thoughts; as a sensing Unbounded she could block me better than most without even trying.

"What about the second thing?" I asked her. "You said we had two problems to take care of besides the break-in at the lab." As if Keene's mysterious appearance wasn't complication enough.

Ava sighed. "It's that dog of yours."

Mine? I wouldn't exactly call Max that, though he'd belonged to my family. When we'd fled from Kansas, we'd had to take him with us. Where else would he go? "What's he done now?"

"He's suddenly forgotten that he's potty-trained, and he's left a surprise for you upstairs in the hall. If you'll remember, the housekeeper told us she'd vacuum up his hair, but she absolutely drew the line at messes."

Right. And in a fit of misguided loyalty, I'd promised to keep him in line.

"There's plenty of time to take care of it before you head out for your meeting," Ava added.

Snorting a laugh, Jace turned quickly on his heel to escape.

"Oh, no you don't." I grabbed his arm. "If you want to come with me to see Keene, you're helping me clean up after that mutt. Besides, you actually like him."

Jace groaned, but he didn't pull away.

"Just remember," Ava's voice floated after us. "The restaurant might be a trap."

Though my mind rejected the thought that Keene would try to hurt his brother, or me, I knew she was right. Trust was something that couldn't be earned with a single action. Or even several actions. In whatever agenda he was pushing, Keene could very well want us all dead.

CHAPTER 4

ALTHOUGH WE WERE EARLY FOR OUR APPOINTMENT, WE LEFT the palace in a hurry. I wanted to be gone before Ritter arrived with the trailer of unconscious Hunters and insisted on coming with us. Truth was, I didn't trust myself alone with him, and I was determined not to easily forget what he'd done. I hadn't asked for undying devotion or anything so awkward as that. I'd simply believed his promise to be there when I awoke from the heart transplant that saved my father's life—and took mine, however briefly.

I was sure Ritter could figure out something to do with himself tonight. By the time I returned from the restaurant with any information I could squeeze from Keene, I bet he'd have Oliver, Mari, Chris, and even Stella in the sprawling dining room turned gym, working on combat techniques.

"Okay, you stay out of sight," I told Jace, as I drove slowly past the restaurant. "Just because you've never officially met Keene doesn't mean he won't recognize you. He's probably seen your picture dozens of times."

"You think I don't know that?" Jace's normal good humor

vanished. "I have a bone to pick with that man. He almost killed me."

"Not him. Justine." His execution wasn't the only one my once best friend had ordered. "Keene just had instructions to bring you in. He didn't know she was taking orders directly from the Triad."

Jace grinned. "If I didn't know you better, I'd say you were sweet on this guy."

I *had* kissed Keene, but Jace didn't know that. Neither did Ritter.

I looped around the block and drove past the restaurant a second time. Whenever the Emporium might be involved, it paid to be careful. Many of their mortal children worked for the Emporium as little more than expendable slaves whose blind obedience made them dangerous. Keene was more than that, his intelligence and skill at fighting landing him a higher position than most mortals in the organization. It helped, of course, that his father was a member of their governing Triad. Keene had left the Emporium during my first run-in with the group, but he could have changed his mind. He'd do what he needed to survive.

"We'll park on the next block and walk back separately," I said.

"I'll follow you." Jace checked his .45 to make sure a bullet was in the chamber, though he'd already done that two times since we'd left the palace. Like me, he had a backup weapon and at least one knife, but his real strength was his hand-to-hand combat skills. Not only did he move with lightning speed, but his ability gave him a sort of precognition that told him where his opponent would strike next. Watching him these past months, I understood how Ritter had been able to tell from only one workout that combat wasn't my inborn ability. Jace was stronger, faster, and better than everyone else—except Ritter, who shared the combat ability. During our training together, I did manage to get in a rare surprise hit, which was better than most non-combat Unbounded. I wondered if the precognition meant that on some level Jace also had a bit of the sensing ability that ran through our mother's family line, but everyone assured me there wasn't a connection, and that no Unbounded ever possessed more than one family ability.

Which meant, since my ability was sensing and not combat, that I had to learn to fight the old-fashioned way instead of coming to it instinctively like Jace. Sometimes I felt all I did was train. Well, train and watch Mari. Now that I'd have more free time, I'd spend it tightening my moves. Because not honing my fighting skills meant endangering my friends.

I was definitely *not* trying to impress Ritter. We'd only worked out together a few times before he'd vanished, and he didn't really know me or my abilities. Attraction didn't count for anything.

"I'll find a table nearby," Jace said as I pulled into a parking place. "After I make sure he came alone. If he didn't, I'll take care of them."

"No, you give me the signal first. You know the drill. We don't attack unless we're in danger. We can't bring attention to ourselves."

"Yes, ma'am." Jace gave me an exaggerated salute.

Cold bit into me as I started walking. I pulled my long leather coat tighter, my eyes scanning the darkness and the few passersby. No Unbounded registered in my mind. There was nothing out of place, and nothing unusual on the rooftops that I could see. No suddenly extinguished light, no suspicious shapes. I turned my head every now and then to see if I could catch a glimpse of Jace tailing me, but his speed made him near invisible when he wanted to be. He was there, though, behind me. Or someone was. I could pinpoint a mental blip of light that signaled a life force.

All at once the light toned down a notch, and I told myself it was because Jace had finally remembered to protect his mind and not because he'd been attacked. If it had been an attack, I would have known. Or at least I hoped so.

Pushing out a breath, I rounded the corner of the block and strode onto the main street. There were more lights now, and more people, but no one looked threatening. Was Keene observing the restaurant from somewhere in the dark, or did he trust his brother? In his position, I wouldn't trust anyone.

Tasty aromas wafted through the streets, reminding me that I still hadn't eaten, and might not, though the meeting was at a restaurant. No matter—absorbing had brought my mental strength back to normal. I'd be more than ready to help Ava with the Hunters later. I reached out my mind for Jace, but with so many life forces gleaming from the people around me, I'd completely lost him.

A few whistled notes of a nameless song escaped my lips, a sure sign that I was anticipating this meeting. Keene and I had sparred both physically and with words, and though I'd been a prisoner, it hadn't been all bad. Except now the anticipation meant I needed to be more careful. I clamped my lips shut and the tune cut off abruptly. For all I knew, Keene was planning a press conference where he'd out both the Emporium and the Renegades. I hoped not. We weren't ready for that—yet. First we had to track down and remove Emporium agents who were embedded in high places.

The restaurant bustled with life, but there wasn't a waiting list. The hostess, a young Chinese girl with acne covering her rounded cheeks didn't recognize Keene's name when I asked, so I let her take me to a small table in the middle of the room. I felt exposed and uncomfortable under the bright lights without a wall to my back and a clean view of the entry, but this was Keene's show and I had to be available. I still couldn't see or sense Jace, and I was starting to worry. Before the Change my brother had been a fun-loving, capable man. Since the Change, he was still fun-loving and capable, but his reckless streak seemed to be growing. Funny how now that we could live two thousand years, I worried about him more than ever.

Minutes ticked by and Keene still hadn't shown. Only the waitress appeared, wanting my order. Looked like I was going to have that chance to eat whether I wanted it or not—and I wasn't that fond of Chinese food, though I loved the smell. I ordered something with chicken and leaned back, my arms folded. At least I could sense no Unbounded nearby; each of the diners around me were decidedly mortal.

A man in a black overcoat and gray knit cap came into view

from another aisle and slid into the seat opposite me, bringing a taste of chill and danger. His face was tan and lean to the point of gauntness, the lines hard. My hand went to my weapon, this time equipped with a silencer. "Easy," he said. His own hands were in his coat pockets, no doubt holding a pistol pointed in my direction.

"Keene." I recognized the voice if nothing else. Slowly, I placed my hands on the table where he could see them. He'd changed, or maybe I simply hadn't remembered him correctly. Most of our time together had been filled with terror, at least on my part.

"Where's my brother?" Keene's green eyes glittered, but his voice was casual.

Ah, the eyes were the same. And though he wasn't Unbounded, his body exuded a readiness. He was the best mortal fighter I'd ever seen, better than many Unbounded. "Actually, he left the country this morning."

"So they sent you." Not a hint of emotion escaped the mental shields he'd erected. I should have anticipated as much, since he'd been raised all his life to protect his thoughts. But a part of me was disappointed. I shrugged. "Guess they thought since you didn't kill me before, maybe you wouldn't again."

A smile broke through his reserve. "I'm glad you came. It's good to see you."

I was rather surprised at the warmth I felt for him myself. Perhaps because I'd spent the past two months angry at Ritter and romanticizing my time with Keene. There was probably a syndrome named after it.

"I ordered something," I said, allowing my hands to slip into my lap. "Are you hungry?"

He shook his head. "There isn't time. Look, I might as well just get down to it. The Triad is planning something, and I need help stopping it."

"You mean your father?" I arched one brow, aware that the way I said it was a challenge.

His mouth tightened. "My father's the genius behind Emporium success, but while he may be a lot of things, he's not a monster. You know as well as I do that it's the other two pulling the strings."

He meant Delia Vesey and Stefan Carrington. Stefan was ruthless and amoral, but it was the ancient Delia I feared most. She was able to control people with her strong sensing ability, to bend them to her will. I'd barely escaped her grasp with my mind intact.

"What are they planning?" As I spoke, I caught a glimpse of Jace at a table behind Keene, and the knot I hadn't been aware of in my stomach relaxed marginally.

"Who's there?" Keene asked.

"No one. I'm sure you watched me arrive."

"They wouldn't have sent you alone, and you were looking at something behind me just now. You relaxed." He turned to briefly study the diners, as though searching for something out of place.

His perception was uncanny. I guess living in a world of people who considered themselves gods encouraged you to learn a few tricks to carry your weight. "What makes you think I take orders?" I asked. "I heard you called and I wanted to see you, so here I am."

His turn to raise his brows. "You *wanted* to see me?"

"Of course." My smile was genuine. "I never got to thank you for what you did for Chris and Stella."

"You're welcome." He pulled off the knit cap, briefly revealing the ugly scar that ran the length of his right cheek near the jawline before his brown hair settled down to cover it. He was still arresting, despite the obvious weight loss. "I guess it was too much to hope you'd want a repeat of what happened in that elevator."

I held back my smile. "What, when you looked at me like I was a freak?"

"That was only after you tried to get into my mind."

"You were the one who'd kidnapped me, remember?"

He waved a hand. "Details, details."

The waitress arrived with my food, and I was grateful for the interruption. "Would you like anything, sir?" she asked.

He shook his head. "Just coffee. Thanks."

"Right away." The woman took several quick steps to a nearby alcove and returned almost immediately with a steaming cup of coffee.

"So what's going on?" I asked when she'd disappeared.

He glanced once more over his shoulder in my brother's direction, though I'd been trying hard not to look that way. Thankfully, Jace had moved and was no longer in plain sight.

Keene's eyes riveted on my chicken, which was swimming in some kind of unappetizing red sauce. "First you should know that I've been working with the Hunters."

"What?" My hands curled into fists, and the knot was back in my stomach, every bit as large.

"I've been able to keep tabs on what's going on in the Emporium that way. You know they infiltrate the Hunters. I told you that before."

"Yes, but isn't that kind of dangerous? Aren't they looking for you?"

He barked a laugh that sounded bitter. "You'd think. But apparently, I'm not important enough to worry too much about. I guess they figure in forty or fifty years it won't matter. I'll be dead."

I dropped my gaze. His bitterness toward his family was more than I could fix with a few words. When I looked up again, he'd grabbed my fork, pulled my plate closer, and was shoveling food down his throat.

Better him than me.

"Sorry," he mumbled after a few gulps. "It was a long flight."

"Be my guest. I wasn't hungry anyway. Now are you going to tell me what's going on?"

He swallowed. "The Hunters have started tracking known descendants of Renegade Unbounded."

Great. But at least it was verification that what happened today with Mari wasn't an isolated incident. Two days ago I would have kissed him for the information, and even now it was useful, but maybe I didn't have to let him know that. "Tell me something I haven't already figured out the hard way. I suppose the Emporium is behind this new little development?"

"Yes, though only by suggestion. The Hunters' files on Unbounded lineage are guarded very closely by those at the top of the Hunter hierarchy, presumably to protect their members who may be descended from Unbounded. The Emporium operatives don't have access—I've been trying to peek at them for years."

I relaxed slightly. That was good news for us. If the Emporium had gained access to those records, any descendant linked to us would soon be dead or prisoners to their breeding program.

"Unfortunately for the Emporium," Keene added, "the idea backfired. Apparently, the Hunters have records that involve them as well. Not surprising when you think about it. I mean, Hunters formed in the first place because they were upset at being abandoned by the Emporium when they failed to Change. It's only natural they would have kept track of everyone they knew before their abandonment, as well as their own descendants. Regardless, there have been half a dozen attacks on Emporium descendants in the past few months, occurring shortly after each victim's Change."

I couldn't find it in me to be unhappy about that. "I thought most mortal descendants of the Emporium were failed genetic experiments whose likelihood of having Unbounded offspring is virtually nil. So how did keeping track of the Emporium's mortal descendants lead to finding their Unbounded?" The experiments were a double-edged sword, causing more Unbounded in the first generation, but eliminating the possibility of the active gene occurring in the failed lines.

"The genetic experiments didn't used to be so intensive, and in the old days not everyone participated. Even now there are still unplanned pregnancies. Several of my mortal siblings have Unbounded children and grandchildren."

Something in his voice made me look at him more closely. Was he hoping his children would be Unbounded? Or the opposite?

"So there are Changes still happening in some of those initial family lines," he continued, "just as many as you'd see without interference. The Emporium has lost at least four new Unbounded to the Hunters."

Again, I didn't understand why he wanted me to care. On one level, I might mourn the loss of a life, but if it meant fewer mortals would be abused or one Renegade wasn't sliced apart, I was all for it. What was bad for the Emporium was good for just about everyone else in the world. "Poor babies."

He looked at me sharply. "You're different now."

So are you, I wanted to retort, but he'd always been dark and bitter, so it wasn't really true. "A lot has happened in the past two months."

"Right," he conceded.

I watched him take a couple more bites. "We've had our own run-in with the Hunters under similar conditions."

He swallowed. "Any casualties?"

"Not this time." Unless you counted a woman's broken heart. "In the future we'll keep a closer watch on potential Unbounded." At least the Hunters waited until Unbounded actually Changed. Unlike the Emporium. I was glad we didn't have anyone coming of age right away, but then again, Ava didn't tell me everything.

"That's not the only reason I came," Keene stopped chewing long enough to say. "There's something more the Triad is working on, and I didn't dare talk about it even over the supposedly secure channels. There's going to be an assassination." He leaned forward, the edges of his overcoat hanging perilously near the plate. "They're gunning for Greggory Bellers."

"Who's that?" The name sounded awfully familiar, but I couldn't place it.

"A senator from Arizona. Very respected and active in the field of medicine—plus his sister is the deputy commissioner over medical products at the FDA. Bellers is one of the good guys who's trying to do the right thing, red tape be damned. He's been a thorn in the Emporium's side for many years."

"I like him already."

Keene rolled his eyes. "I knew you would. Anyway, he's been responsible for bringing lifesaving research from overseas to the FDA for testing and trial. He's saved a lot of lives, and his connection to the FDA makes him a formidable opponent to whoever the Emporium has inside the organization."

Now he was making sense. "So he's costing the Emporium money."

"Well, yeah, though it hasn't been enough for them to worry about—at least not until now. The Emporium has enough overseas personnel that they're beginning to control drug development in Europe every bit as much as they do here. But Bellars is personally connected with promising research in Mexico where they aren't as active, research that will apparently revolutionize autoimmune diseases."

"Nanotechnology," I said, half under my breath.

"How did you know?" He permitted himself a tiny, slightly crooked grin. "Well, I guess everything's about nanotech these days, isn't it?"

I shook my head. "I knew I'd heard his name before." I waited a few seconds before adding. "We fund a research facility in Mexico. This morning we got word of some kind of attack. We haven't been able to get through to anyone there since. That's where your brother's headed now. He's probably already landed, or will soon."

Keene's brow furrowed. "It can't be coincidence."

"No. Not when I'm pretty sure this Bellers is our stateside contact with the FDA." That would teach me to be more involved in what the others were working on.

"Then he's more important than I suspected." Keene set down his fork, though his green eyes lingered hungrily on the food. From his pocket he drew out a plain white envelope and tossed it onto the table. "Look who the senator has for a new aide—as of two weeks ago." His tone told me I wasn't going to like it.

I pulled out two photographs. The first was a face I recognized all too well, evoking a lump of regret and anger so large I couldn't swallow: Tom Carver.

Tom, my ex-almost-fiancé had been a stockbroker before my Change, and he'd had to follow politics to read trends, but the Tom I knew wouldn't enjoy being the go-to boy for anyone, even an important senator. His feelings of inferiority already ran too deep, though I guess abandonment did that to a child. Whatever his profession, he wasn't a murderer, or at least he hadn't been before his Unbounded mother had gotten him involved with the Emporium. He looked good—better than when I'd known him. His brown hair had more highlights, he looked more fit, and his stance signaled self-assurance. He appeared ready to rule the world—and would if his newly returned mother had her way.

Keene was pretending to scan the restaurant, looking everywhere but at me. When I didn't speak, he risked a glance. "It gets worse," he said quietly.

I bit the inside of my lip and looked at the next picture. Tom at an airport, kissing the cheek of a gorgeous brunette wearing a short, red mini skirt and a tight tank top that accentuated her bust line. She was obviously wearing one of her favorite push-up bras—probably padded. Being Unbounded didn't necessarily mean well-endowed. Her tall heels made her only a few inches shorter than Tom, but she seemed dainty and fragile all the same. Even from the side, Tom looked happy.

I'd known that wherever Tom was, Justine wouldn't be far behind. Did he still believe she was the loyal sister who'd come to rescue him when he'd aged out of foster care seventeen years ago? Maybe she'd finally confessed the truth about being his mother. Whatever their real relationship, she probably controlled him as absolutely as before.

Wherever Justine was, death and destruction were never far behind, however masked it would be in the pheromones that aided in her seductions. Last I'd known, she'd been sleeping with Stefan Carrington in her attempt to influence the Triad, but it hadn't gotten her far.

I took a slow breath before saying, "When was this taken?"

"Three days ago. I did some research, and she was on her way to Mexico. I thought it odd for her to be leaving at the time, since I was investigating a possible threat to the senator, but now it makes sense."

I stood. "I'd better pass this along to Ava. Is there a place I can reach you in case we have questions?"

"Tell Cort to post on that group we use and I'll set up a time to talk. It's as anonymous as anything."

"Okay. Thanks for the information."

He leaned back, peering up at me. "Thank *you* for the food."

He'd finished only half of it. I forced a smile, "Maybe next time we'll have a whole dinner."

A grin spread across his face. "There's going to be a next time? I'd like that—a lot. But maybe then you'll introduce me to your brother instead of having him spy on us."

I laughed. I should have known he'd figure it out. "I don't know. Jace has a bone to pick with you. The last time you two met, he ended up almost dying."

"That wasn't my fault."

"Well, he might feel he has something to prove, especially after missing all the excitement earlier this evening."

"Excitement?" Keene's brow furrowed.

What would it hurt to tell him? "Run-in with Hunters. They'd been tracking one of our potentials, just like you said. But they were easy enough to deal with—this time."

Keene stood up so abruptly that his chair tipped backwards, clanking loudly on the travertine floor. In two steps he was by my side, one hand gripping my arm. "This evening?"

"Yes. Why does that matter?"

"Because the Emporium is monitoring the Hunters closely."

Before he'd finished the sentence, Jace materialized behind Keene, his rapid movement more astonishing to our neighboring diners than the fallen chair and Keene's urgency.

Keene stiffened but didn't turn around. "If the Hunters called it in before the pickup, the Emporium will know and come to make sure it's not one of ours—theirs." The slip of words made me wonder just how separated he really was from the Emporium.

Jace met my eyes. "He means they could have followed you from the park."

My gut wrenched at the idea. I'd been careful on the return trip to the palace, but if they'd planned it beforehand, they might have used a tracking device on my Jeep—on all the vehicles at the park—and though the disrupters we had in place at the palace would prevent any transmitting from that location, they could have followed the Jeep far enough to make the point moot.

"The children," I said.

Though Chris's children were eighth generation and not likely to carry the active Unbounded gene, their sensing lineage made them targets for the Emporium breeding experiments. Emporium agents might try to keep Spencer and Kathy alive during an attack, but the children were small and untrained and could be easily hurt in a direct confrontation. As new Unbounded, Mari and Oliver would also need protection, placing Ava, Stella, and Ritter at a severe disadvantage if they had to defend the palace.

"They should be okay. The palace has alarms, and our people have weapons," Jace said, though the worry emanating from him screamed the opposite.

"Let's go." Keene tossed a few bills onto the table as I reached for my phone. "There's no time to waste. I'll help if I can." Pulling on his knit cap, he strode toward the door, with Jace and me close behind.

I dialed Ava, but she didn't pick up. *Hurry.* I pushed myself to run faster, the outside cold piercing my lungs with icy needles.

We were halfway down the street before I began to question Keene's intentions. What if he had returned to the Emporium and this whole scenario was a setup? If we took him to the palace, we could be leading the Emporium Unbounded straight to the heart of our operation.

As if coming to the same conclusion, Jace choked out, "Our phones didn't signal an emergency."

"Maybe they don't know yet. No one's answering." I wanted to believe Keene, but before I did, he'd have to drop the barrier on his mind so I could make sure.

We rounded the corner, ignoring the stares of a couple we

passed. Two more steps and the phone in my hand let out three sharp beeps and began vibrating. Jace's did the same.

The emergency signal. We were too late. Keene had been right.

I put in my password—the real one, not the one that would erase the information on the phone—and pulled up our GPS app that would locate any of our Renegades within range. No one registered on the map, which meant all our people in Portland were at the palace where the disrupters were still in place.

All our people, including Ritter. His combat ability would even the odds considerably, but my worry cranked up a notch. We hadn't even talked. He hadn't explained where he'd been and why he'd left me.

We were about to cross a small intersecting street when the emotion hit. Tingling. An almost imperceptible change in the air. Excitement. Hate.

Just as quickly, the sensation vanished.

But I knew someone was out there. I could feel the life force high on a roof where no life force would normally be.

"Cover!" I barked, throwing myself against the nearest building, my eyes scanning the darkness. I unholstered my trusty Sig.

Jace dived into the shadows next to me, and Keene, with only a second's hesitation did the same. "Don't tell me," Keene said, drawing his own weapon, "you came here in the same vehicle you used at that park."

I nodded. The things you overlook when you're worried about those you love.

"Your shield," I reminded Jace. I didn't want any sensing Unbounded who might be out there tracking us by his fear—or picking up any plan we might formulate.

Something small and deadly slammed into the building not a foot from where I crouched.

"Sniper," Jace grunted. He aimed his pistol at the roof of the building opposite us, but could see nothing to fire at.

"Let's make a break that way," Keene motioned down a side street. "It rounds back on the main. My car's there."

I nodded. We really didn't have a choice. The one who'd be taking the most risk was Keene, since a bullet would hurt Jace and me but wouldn't be fatal.

Maybe that was worse, knowing what the Emporium planned for us.

"Now," I muttered, launching myself into the open. Another silenced shot crashed into the building.

The men ran after me, Jace soon far ahead, though I could tell he was holding back for my sake. I wanted to yell at him to forget me and get to the palace, but I couldn't find breath.

Ahead of me, Jace suddenly stopped.

"What—" My protest silenced as three figures stepped from the shadows in front of us. Two carried pistols and the third an assault rifle. Each of them had a sword strapped to their backs which showed they meant business. Swords were perfect for severing all three focus points from one another: the brain, the heart, and reproductive organs. Without at least two points connected the rest of the body could no longer regenerate.

An Emporium hit team.

CHAPTER 5

I SHOULD HAVE SENSED THE MEN BEFORE THEY APPEARED; EVEN THOUGH their life forces were darkened by their blocked minds, they had been within my range. That I hadn't instinctively found them showed I wasn't as ready as I hoped to use my gift in battle. I couldn't blame everything on my worry for Jace.

Holding my Sig on the three men, I glanced behind me, relieved to see we'd come far enough that we were probably out of the sniper's line of fire. At least until he moved or came to help his comrades. I shifted my attention back to the men. Unbounded confidence radiated from two of them. The other was mortal. I could feel all three life forces clearly now, which told me they probably weren't sensing Unbounded. That was good news, though it might not make much difference if both Unbounded were gifted in combat.

"Ah, crap!" Keene muttered.

"There's only three." Jace's gun wavered slightly.

"Two Unbounded," I told them in a low voice. "Guy on the right's a mortal."

"Well, well, look what we have here," said the Unbounded in

the middle. He was a Nordic-looking man, tall and extremely pale, apparently their leader. "You're surrounded. Come with us, and we won't hurt you."

"Yet," muttered the Hispanic Unbounded next to him. They both laughed.

"Put your guns down slowly now," the leader ordered. "Toss 'em on the ground."

None of us obeyed.

His grin was pure evil. "So that's the way you're going to play it, huh?"

"Three of us, three of you," I said. "Why don't you just walk away?" Even as I said it, I felt them coming fast. Running. Two more sparks that signaled life forces, their thoughts also dark.

The Nordic Unbounded laughed. "Because there's not just three of us."

The two new men stepped from the shadows behind us, armed with rifles. Knit caps, black coats, jeans, nose rings. Average American thugs, only meaner. *Hello sniper and friend.*

"Mortals," I whispered to Jace and Keene, lowering my gun, but not tossing it to the street. Not yet.

Keene took a step forward, ignoring the Hispanic who moved his assault rifle in his direction. "It's me, Keene McIntyre. My father's in the Triad. I'm Tihalt's son. I know you recognize me. At least I've seen you."

The Hispanic and the mortal shook their heads, but the leader laughed. "I know who you are—and I'm guessing with what happened two months ago, I'll get a bonus for you." He gestured toward me with his chin. "Unlike her, there's not even a standing order to bring you in alive."

Alive? No way. Letting them take us wasn't an option.

I looked at Jace, a signal, and he dropped the barrier over his mind so I could send him direction or at least sense what he planned to do. If I was wrong and one of these men could also sense, we'd be in trouble, but if I was right, it would give us the advantage of working as one. There was no way to get Keene to drop his shield so I could do the same with him, and I hoped his training would take over once the fight began.

Jace's emotions told me he was frightened and exhilarated all at once for his first real battle. My feelings leaned more toward worry. Though Ava and Dimitri were excellent fighters, they weren't gifted in combat and that meant Jace had learned all he could from them weeks ago and wasn't as prepared as he should have been. He should have trained with the best, but the best had disappeared for two months.

All Ritter's fault. If I survived the next few minutes, I would make Ritter's life miserable.

"My father will not be pleased if I'm hurt," Keene said. "I have information about the Hunters and the Renegades. It involves Mexico. Stuff he'll want to know."

"Mexico?" asked the blond leader. "Don't know what you're talking about."

"Of course not. It's on a need to know only." Keene's voice was practically a sneer. He was brave, I'd give him that.

Now would be the perfect time to act, with their attention on Keene. But doing so would almost invariably get him killed since that assault rifle was now only a foot away from his chest and the added guns behind us almost as close. Jace was fast, but not that fast. I had to act carefully—and soon. Every moment that ticked by meant one more that we weren't helping Ava and the children and the rest of our Renegade family.

"Shut up, mortal," I told Keene. "No use groveling. It is what it is."

Keene turned on me. "Oh? Why don't you make me, *Princess?*"

Jace snorted, and I felt his fear lessen. Good. He'd be more effective that way.

I leapt at Keene. It was a classic distraction move, one I believed the mortals would buy, but if the Unbounded had lived long enough the ruse might not work. Still, at the rate the Emporium were multiplying, the odds were good that neither of these Unbounded was more than a half century old.

Behind. Now, I thought at Jace, as I hit into Keene. Pushing off immediately, I rammed into the Hispanic's rifle. A dangerous move, but necessary since I seemed to be the only one they weren't interested in killing. I grabbed the barrel of the rifle and yanked it downward. The weapon began spitting bullets, peppering the space where I'd been, sounding like ten trucks backfiring all at once.

The noise of the gunshot worked both for and against us. Someone would call the police and that might cause a distraction, but it also meant we needed to dispatch these guys quickly before anyone else was endangered. Emporium Unbounded wouldn't hesitate to take out as many local authorities as necessary to achieve their goal of capturing or killing us. Besides, with the increasing number of Emporium agents in high places, being detained by the police might eventually mean ending up as Emporium prisoners anyway.

As I fell, I kept hold of the rifle, which jerked wildly in my hand as the Hispanic tried to pull it from my grasp, his finger still on the trigger. Twisting, I threw my weight into his arm, bringing the rifle up and around until the spray of bullets hit the mortal on the right. One down.

The Hispanic stopped firing. I kicked at his knee and felt it buckle. Too close now to use the rifle on me, he dropped it and went for another weapon. I pulled the trigger on my Sig. He jerked, but I hadn't hit him accurately enough to stop him. He pulled out a knife as I fired again. This time he went down, swiping at my right ankle with the knife. Deep. Too deep. Pain made my vision turn black. I pulled the trigger twice more. Then again.

The wail of a police siren cut into the night.

I pushed back the pain and the darkness receded. The Hispanic Unbounded lay still beside me, but he wouldn't be out for long. Where was my brother? Ah, there he was, standing over two unconscious mortals, without a scratch on him. The little brother whose shoes I used to help tie. I wasn't surprised. Even trained, they couldn't possibly be a match for him, unless they were as good as Keene.

The thought chopped off as I searched for Keene. He and the Nordic Unbounded were still exchanging blows, their weapons having fallen to the ground. Though the Unbounded appeared to be gifted in combat, Keene was as good as I remembered. He'd spent a lifetime trying to prove to a father who didn't care that he was good enough.

The sirens were coming closer.

Jace leapt toward Keene and the Unbounded. He landed two blows and a kick that made the Unbounded stagger. Another powerful jab from Keene and the man went down.

"We have to go," I gritted, staggering to my feet. My sliced ankle refused to hold me, and I crumpled to one knee.

Sweeping up his pistol, Keene ran toward me. "I got you." He shoved his arms, gun and all, under me and cradled me against his chest. A wave of agony burst through my ankle as he lurched forward.

Behind us, the blond Unbounded rolled, stretching for his gun. Jace fired a shot, without aiming. He didn't need to, his combat instinct finding exactly the right place. The man stopped moving. Normally, we'd take the Unbounded with us, but there was no chance of that now. The people in the morgue were due a nasty surprise when they returned to life as their bodies healed.

A crowd had begun to form at the end of the street, but they scattered to each side as we approached. "Better wait for the police," someone said.

Jace grinned like a maniac. "I don't think so." He waved his gun and the crowd retreated further. Only a few men held their ground, and I hoped none of them would try to be heroes.

We made it to Keene's sleek off-white sedan and sped into the night as the first police vehicles arrived. I turned to see a man pointing after us, and one of the cars began to give chase.

Great.

Keene squealed around a corner. "Where?" he barked.

"Three streets up. Turn left." The pain in my ankle was receding as my body rushed natural painkillers to the wound.

In the back, Jace fumbled in his pack, coming up with a clear gel in a syringe. He handed it to me. Excitement still radiated from him in waves that helped me endure the pain.

I accepted the curequick, though I normally avoided the stuff like the plague. It was addictive, even for Unbounded, but it sped up our already accelerated healing rate by as much as five times. I'd need that before the night was out. I pulled up my pant leg. Blood still poured from the wound, which would explain my dizziness, and through the flesh and sliced ligaments, I could see bone. I eased the needle into my leg as close to the wound as possible and pressed down the stopper. Immediately, I felt my body consuming the curequick, using its energy to make repairs.

"The police car's still behind us," Keene said. "Are we leading it to your hideout then?"

"No, turn here. On the third street take a left. But you have to go faster or we won't lose him."

Keene stomped on the gas.

We were prepared for this. The first thing Ava did when we moved to a new city was to set up alternate hideouts, emergency stores, and extra vehicles. Part of our training was memorizing all of the locations. I hoped my memory wasn't rusty. No use asking Jace. For all his combat ability, he'd never been able to fix places in his mind.

Jace was staring at his phone. "Still no answer at the palace, but you've got the right place for the safe house. It's coming up quick."

Right. The information was also on our phones. Must be the pain that made me forget.

"You guys jump out," Keene said. "I'll keep going. Lead them away." Determination radiated from him—and worry. Why wasn't he blocking his emotions? He'd been in enough tough situations that it couldn't simply be because he was distracted. Which meant he was allowing me to sense them. Was it so I'd trust him?

He glanced over at me, his hair curling out at the ends beneath his knit cap and his green eyes intense. Something warm ran between us. It felt a lot like trust.

"No, I'll do it." Jace said. "I'll dump the car and get away on foot. I'm familiar with this area—you're not." His eyes switched to me. "I'll meet you five blocks south at that tobacco shop. You know the one."

Keene's eyes asked a question, and I nodded. "He'll easily outrun them on foot."

Without waiting for more, Jace climbed between the two front seats, shoving Keene against the door. "Now," he said, grabbing the wheel. "I'll brake just around that turn. I won't be stopping, though."

There was nothing for it but to open the doors and wait for the brakes to screech. I caught a glimpse of Keene clinging to the driver's side door, just as I clung to mine. My ankle wasn't healed yet, though the bleeding had slowed to almost nothing. I had to plan my fall well, or I wouldn't get out of the way before the police car arrived. Any more delays could mean the difference between life and death at the palace.

The car slowed and I launched from the vehicle with my good ankle, tucking and rolling as I hit the pavement. Bruises healed a lot faster than broken bones, and rolling helped limit breakage. For an instant, I caught sight of Jace's worried face turned in my direction, but thoughts of him fled as pain from my ankle forced me to bite back a scream. Jace hurtled ahead, the engine roaring. I was up and hopping the few remaining steps to the row of parked cars before Keene recovered from his own fall and joined me. We dived behind a battered black truck half a second before the police car screeched around the corner.

Pressed together on the freezing ground beside the truck, we waited, tensing for the sound of brakes. But the police car passed and the siren began fading.

Keene watched me, our faces inches apart. His emotions had suddenly gone dark. My heart thumped crazily, but I told myself it was the danger and our success. There was no time for anything else.

"Come on." I used the truck to help me rise.

"Can you walk?"

"I think so, but it's still not ready." Ready for a fight, I meant.

He nodded and put an arm around me. "Where to?"

"It's that green car over there."

"That piece of junk?"

"Hey, everyone leaves it alone. Key is somewhere near the back passenger side wheel in a magnet box. I'll need the first aid kit in the back of the trunk. You drive. I'll give you directions to the tobacco shop."

I limped over to the car, leaning heavily on Keene. The vehicle might look like a rattletrap, but it had a new, powerful engine and a full tank of gas. After opening my door, Keene went to the trunk for the first aid kit. He handed it to me before sliding into his seat and pulling from the curb.

I guided Keene through the streets, my thoughts colliding wildly in my head. Were Ava and the others okay? I hadn't even seen Kathy today. The slight twelve-year-old looked more and more like her mother every day, and sometimes that hurt more than I believed possible.

"There. Straight ahead."

Keene squinted at the night. "I don't see him."

"Give him a moment."

The brightness of my brother's mind told me he was close. Even so, when Jace stepped from the shadows, I gave an internal sigh of relief.

Keene opened his door. "You drive," he told Jace, sliding over on the long seat. He grabbed a roll of gauze from my hand. "Let me do that."

My brother drove wildly through the streets of Portland. I knew I should tell him to go slower so we wouldn't attract more police, but I wanted to get there every bit as fast as he did.

With sure and surprisingly gentle hands, Keene bandaged my ankle in the now-crowded front seat, using a splint on the outside for additional support. He knew as well as I did that any show of weakness during a battle with the Emporium Unbounded could mean death. "That won't be comfortable," he said, tapping the splint. "But it'll give you extra stability until the ligaments heal the rest of the way."

Already I felt much better. I reached out, absorbing, gaining strength. I would need it. We all would. I shoved an energy bar from the first aid kit at Keene. "Eat this."

He tore off the wrapper. "How far?"

Jace was the one who replied. "Almost there."

Minutes later, Jace turned onto the road leading to the palace. "I'll dump the car at the bread factory."

I nodded. Not close enough to alert any lookouts the Emporium might have, but it would take less than two minutes to steal across the space between the two buildings.

Seconds later, Jace jumped out and opened the back door, dislodging the seat cushion to reveal two assault rifles, several handguns and various magazines.

"Nice," Keene took a rifle for himself.

"Just don't shoot any of ours," I told him. I'd never trained on the rifles myself. Neither had Jace, but that didn't stop him from taking the other one. I popped a fresh magazine into my Sig and took a couple extra.

I held my own as we slunk through the darkness toward the old hotel, though I favored my ankle instinctively. Were we in time? I didn't fool myself that we'd been the only target. The Emporium had perfected their attack methods over millennia.

Lights burned inside the palace, but there was no sound or movement. A Land Cruiser that hadn't been there before sat in the gravel lot—probably Ritter's—and the trailer that Ava had sent for the Hunters. Keene motioned to it, and we followed him there.

"No sign of them," Keene said, his back against the trailer.

Tentatively, I reached out my mind. Doing so might alert the Emporium to our presence if they had a strong sensing Unbounded with them, but it was a risk I had to take, even though I wasn't strong enough this far away to reach any of them except Ava.

All at once I felt her. Faintly and distorted. Like looking down the wrong end of a pair of binoculars. Red filled my vision. Blood. *We're here,* I told her. The connection broke, and I sagged against the trailer, my head throbbing.

"You okay?" Jace grabbed my shoulder.

"It's bad in there." Fighting weakness in my knees, I breathed in deeply, absorbing from the air, rich with moisture from the nearby river. "Be careful. There's at least one person standing guard on the right side of the palace. Must be watching the door."

Jace edged around the back of the trailer. "Why is this unlocked? Cover me while I check it out." He darted around the back, pulled open one of the trailer's doors, and jumped inside. Less than thirty seconds later, he jumped down. "Ah, crap." Leaning over, he vomited on the ground.

Keene and I hurried to peer inside. Dimly lit by the single streetlight, the limp bodies of the Hunters sprawled inside, each with a gaping cut across their throats. Mari's dead husband stared back at us, his eyes wide with horror. My stomach churned, but I didn't follow Jace's example.

"The Emporium's here, all right," Keene said grimly, gazing at the palace. "Bars on the windows. How do we get in? If your people are holed up in one of those rooms, they don't have long."

Jace wiped his mouth on his sleeve. "The doors." His eyes when they met mine were troubled, but there was no shielding my little brother from this. He was Unbounded and both blood and death were a part of our future.

I nodded. "That's right. I vote for a direct assault." Ritter might have been able to come up with something else, but he wasn't here and Jace was too inexperienced. We had only Keene, once our enemy, to guide us.

"Let's go, then." Keene started across the gravel, ducking behind the next car.

"You go," Jace told me. "I'll cover you."

I followed Keene, not even limping now. A silenced bullet whizzed past me, and less than a heartbeat later, Jace fired two shots. A man staggered from the shadows at the far end of the house. “Mortal,” I called as he fell. That meant he was probably down to stay.

The front door was ajar and Keene kicked it opened.

From the back of the house we heard a crash and the piercing scream of a child.

CHAPTER 6

SPENCER! THOUGH IT COULD JUST AS EASILY BE KATHY'S SCREAM.

Two men emerged from corners of the lobby. *Unbounded.* I didn't have time to shout a warning before Keene began firing, diving for the cover of the front desk. Everything exploded into sound and movement. Jace at the door, running so fast he was a blur. A window shattering, the chandelier swinging wildly. Two more men and a woman leaping down the stairs. Two mortals, one Unbounded. There had to be more in the hotel or Ava and the others would have appeared by now.

With so many of them, we didn't stand much of a chance. Leaving Jace and Keene to deal with the newcomers, I headed toward the conference room where I thought I'd heard the scream. It was empty, but huge holes in the conference table and Stella's wrecked computers showed I was on the right trail. A small potted plant that normally sat in the middle of the table, lay tipped on its side, dirt scattered everywhere. For two months I'd watered the stupid thing—only to have it end up like this. It seemed to embody everything the Emporium stood for.

I sprinted to the other side of the room, fear choking me. The plant could be saved or replaced, but not the children. I had to hurry. Out the far door and down another hall I went, checking doors along the way—closets, office, weapons pantry. I found nothing but bullet holes, blood, and the occasional body. Not ours. At least not yet.

A subdued life force signaled the presence of someone behind me, someone who was shielding. I turned, pulling the trigger on my Sig, but the man was already diving to the side, anticipating my move. The bullet dug into the wall. "Stop! It's me."

I hesitated. "Ritter?"

"Yep. Try not to shoot at me again, okay? At least not tonight." His voice was casual but his emotions flared, breaking through his control: relief at seeing me, anger, desire for revenge. A cut marred the brow above his left eye and the skin of his cheek below it, as though someone had sliced him with a knife. Red stained his blue T-shirt and a blood-saturated rag circled one of his biceps. It was all I could do not to throw myself at him to make sure he was really okay.

Another scream shattered my relief at seeing him alive. This time I was sure it came from Spencer.

"Where are the kids?" I barked.

"They were with Stella and Oliver in the gym." He motioned in the direction I'd been heading. "Ava and I were in the upstairs sitting room. We had a dozen Emporium agents break in there. I just now got free. Ava's gone to help Jace."

I started forward, with Ritter following close behind. Had Stella and the kids been able to hide? No. Something had made Spencer scream. I looked back at Ritter. "What about Mari?"

"She was with us, but she—" He broke off, his brow gathering. "She . . . disappeared."

Disappeared? There was no time to pursue that further. We'd reached the double doors of the gym. One was shut, but the other lay askew on its hinges. We could hear fighting inside.

Without hesitation, Ritter slipped through the door first, his black eyes glittering dangerously, although he carried no weapons that I could see. I hurried after him. In the middle of the gym Stella battled two Unbounded women with a bo staff. Guns littered the floor and all the women bled from various wounds. A short distance behind Stella, two Unbounded men sprawled on the ground, riddled with bullets. One moved slightly even as I caught sight of him. Oliver lay between the two men, his face deathly pale. He pushed to a seated position, his blood-drenched chest convulsing with the effort.

But where were the children?

A bark directed my attention to a table next to the small fridge we'd installed in the corner. The kids huddled under this, Kathy with her arms around Spencer, shielding him with her body. Max stood in front of them, growling deep in his throat, his feet apart and eyes blazing.

A mortal near them was shoving a new magazine into his pistol. *Kill the damn mutt.* The thought came to me as clearly as if he'd spoken.

I launched toward the man as Stella fell with a cry. One of her opponents jumped on her, pushing a staff against her throat, the small mound of Stella's baby between them. *No!* While Stella wouldn't die from being choked, she would lose consciousness and any extended lack of air would kill her child, if the fight already hadn't done irrevocable damage.

Ritter was already halfway to her. No chance for me to fire now without hitting one of them. The other Unbounded woman raced toward Oliver, who'd regained his feet. He brought up an escrima stick to defend himself, but his apparent weakness and her solid bulk promised a short fight. I'd help him—after I saved the children.

The mortal saw me coming and shifted his pistol in my direction. I was faster. Two shots and he was down.

"Behind you!" Kathy shouted.

I turned to see one of the wounded Unbounded men coming toward me, moving with a speed and agility that signaled his talent was combat. I pulled the trigger, but he was too fast and the shot went wide. A left hook sent me to the ground. I twisted as I fell, kicking out at him. He staggered, giving me enough time to get to my feet. I punched; he blocked. He punched; I ducked. Veins bulged in his neck, and his dark eyes were murderous. No matter how much I'd trained, this wasn't a fight I could win.

Behind the man, I glimpsed Ritter now fighting both female Unbounded. He moved with incredible speed, blocking before a punch was thrown, stepping out of reach at the last moment. At least one of the women was also gifted in combat. Probably both. It was a miracle Stella had been able to protect the others as long as she had. She wasn't moving now.

"Stop or I'll kill her!" The mortal I'd shot had come to one elbow, his gun pointed toward Kathy. Max growled, but that was no defense against a bullet.

Pain exploded in my head and in my ribs as my Unbounded opponent rewarded my distraction with the mortal. I fell, gasping for breath. The room spun around me. I struggled to my feet, half blinded. What should I do? I felt paralyzed. If we gave up, most of us were as good as dead anyway. My brother had forgiven me for the death of his wife, but losing his children—I didn't know if either of us could recover from that.

A sudden, strange pulse waved through the room, stealing what breath I had left with its intensity.

"Police!" came a shout near the door.

What? I jerked my head toward the door where a dozen armed men had appeared in SWAT clothing. They looked competent, dangerous, and willing to kill. Two near the front also looked familiar, but I couldn't place them. Relief swept through me for an instant before I realized that something didn't fit.

There were no sparks of life forces, no *feeling* that marked one real person, much less a dozen determined men. If they were blocking, I'd still be able to at least sense their presence this close. So either they were all sensing Unbounded who could hide their presence from me, or they didn't exist at all. Yet I caught a whiff of tobacco and gun oil. They even smelled real. It had to be some kind of a trick. An illusion meant to confuse. But whose? The Emporium Unbounded were every bit as surprised as I was, their shields wavering enough that I could sense their shock quite clearly. How could I use that to my advantage?

I couldn't. Not with that gun aimed at Kathy.

Wait. It wasn't quite aimed at her. The man, gaping at the police, had lowered it so the barrel pointed downward.

Ritter's mind was still dark, so there was no way for me to warn him that the policemen weren't really there without also alerting the Emporium agents. Diving for my Sig, I rolled and came up shooting. First the mortal and then my Unbounded opponent. I emptied the rest of the magazine. If that didn't do it, I had nothing left.

Ritter was only a heartbeat behind me. One powerful blow took out the larger Unbounded woman. The other, seeing the change in the battle, backed away from him, glancing toward the officers near the door, who still looked tough and ready but unmoving. Even as we watched, they vanished, taking the smell of tobacco with them.

The Emporium woman fled the room.

Ritter glanced at me. "I'm okay," I shouted. "Go."

Actually, my eyesight was still half dark, and I almost couldn't breathe. A couple ribs were busted at the least. But I wanted revenge every bit as much as he did.

He dipped his head once and sprang after her, the taut lines of his body screaming in anticipation.

I breathed in deeply, absorbing consciously. I needed energy.

"Are you okay?" Kathy's voice, stronger than I expected. She scuttled over to me, with Spencer still clinging to her waist.

I forced myself to a seated position and tried not to wince as I put my arms around them. "I'm fine. Are you guys hurt?" Max licked my hand.

"We're okay," Kathy said. "Stella was great. She wouldn't let them get to us."

My eyes went to Stella. She was breathing but unconscious. I wished Dimitri were here and not in Mexico. He'd be able to tell in an instant if the baby was okay, and with his ability, he could often prolong life simply with the touch of his hands.

"Oliver helped," Kathy added. "He was shooting like crazy."

Oliver. He was sitting on the floor, staring vacantly at the door, his confusion pounding at my senses. I caught a glimpse of the SWAT team in his mind, exactly as it had appeared. But there was also a TV, and now I recognized characters from a popular weekly show.

All at once, I understood what Ava and Oliver himself hadn't yet realized. He could create illusions. I'd read documentation about the ability, but it had been lost among Unbounded for centuries, along with some of the other mental gifts. The theory was that both mathematics and sensing had to be in the Unbounded's heritage in order to develop the ability.

Oliver. Useless, full-of-himself Oliver had a gift that might prove vital to the Renegade movement. It was almost too much to believe.

"I'd better see to Stella. Kathy, stay here with Spencer. It's going to be okay. Uncle Jace and Ritter will make sure." I extracted myself from them, told Max to stay, and climbed awkwardly to my feet, gritting my teeth against the pain in my ribs that was echoed by a renewed throbbing in my ankle. It felt a lot like broken glass inside the skin.

I took my gun with me, slapping in a new magazine, and double-checking on the unconscious Unbounded. The two men weren't even breathing, but that could change at any minute as their bodies made repairs.

Kneeling beside Stella, I shook her head gently. No response. She was cut, scraped, and bruised over much of her exposed body. No telling what internal injuries she may have suffered. My hands went to the tiny mound of her growing baby. Two months ago I'd been able to tell that she was pregnant before she was sure that her missed cycle meant anything important. She was scarcely more than three months along now. Had she been heavier and a bit taller, her baby bulge might not be noticeable at all.

Looking one last time at the fallen Unbounded to make sure they weren't moving, I closed my eyes and reached out. All I felt was a pounding in my head and an urge to vomit. Some talent I had.

Wait. There it was, a tiny, almost imperceptible spark of life, a minuscule pumping, so subtle compared to the ache in my head. My relief turned to worry as I contemplated the faint heartbeat. Every so often, the beat missed, as though it struggled to continue.

Stella had lost so much, and without Dimitri here, I feared she would lose this final piece of her husband.

Live, I told the baby, knowing the effort was useless. I wasn't a healer. The outcome would be whatever was destined.

"Is she all right?" Oliver had lost his fascination with the door and pulled himself over to where I sat. Blood stained the entire front of his shirt and the way he held himself, I knew it was his own.

"She'll be fine. Don't know about the baby."

Oliver frowned. "I was no good to her. All I could do was fire the gun. She was like a maniac, trying to save us all."

I swallowed hard. "But you did help. You saved all of us with that illusion."

"What are you . . ." He stopped. "That was real? I thought I was hallucinating."

"You didn't think it was strange they looked like those actors in that show you watch every week?"

He gave me a weak smile. "Does this mean I'm part of the group?"

"You always were."

"No. I was useless."

I sighed. "We all felt that way in the beginning." Who was I kidding? I still felt that way most days. It only meant I had to work harder.

Clattering down the hall diverted my attention. Lifting my gun,

I aimed at the door, releasing a sharp breath as Jace's head came into view. He nodded at me and began checking the Unbounded.

Ava appeared moments later, several syringes in her hand. She tossed one to Jace. "Give ten mils to each. That should hold them at least twenty-four hours."

"That one's human," I said, knowing ten milligrams of Ava's cocktail would kill a mortal.

Jace checked his pulse. "Won't matter. He's dead."

Dead.

My eyes burned as I stared at the inert form, knowing his death represented how far I was willing to go to protect my family and friends. Saving them should make seeing his lifeless body easier, but somehow it didn't. "All of ours okay?" I asked.

Ava knelt next to me, uncapping a syringe. Curequick gel by the thickness of the needle. "Everyone's fine except Gaven. I'm sorry, but he's dead."

I lifted eyes that wouldn't focus properly. Gaven? Only hours ago he'd been calming Mari in the park. He'd survived government black ops and years with the Renegades, but now he was gone. "What about Mari?" I choked.

Ava began injecting Stella near the worst of her wounds. "I'm not sure. She disappeared during the fighting."

"Do you think they have her?" Mari was an innocent. There was no way she could protect herself.

"I don't think so, but it is a possibility. It all happened so fast. We were defending ourselves when we heard you come in downstairs, and when I looked around, she wasn't there." Ava sighed. "Ritter's searching for her now. Look, I need you to get Stella and Oliver and the kids out of here. Go to Stella's. I can't send anyone with you since I need the others to clean up here, but you can call Chris and tell him to meet you there. He should be finished fueling the plane by now. I'd planned for him to stay there in case we decided to fly out tonight, but Cort and Dimitri are going to have to be on their own for a while. We're not leaving any of these bastards to fight again."

There was no venom in her voice, only a determined calmness, but her choice of words chilled me. Ava never swore. Few of the older Renegade Unbounded did. They'd been raised in a time where gutter words signaled poor education, children respected their elders, and marriage meant a lifetime commitment.

That was one of the reasons I'd trusted Ritter's promise.

"Okay," I said, taking a syringe from her. I should use it on myself, but Oliver needed it worse than I did. He'd collapsed again and seemed to be struggling for breath. One of the bullets must have clipped his lung. Besides, there should still be enough curequick in my system from earlier to help me recover now.

"I may need to call someone to look at them." I told Ava, as I inserted the needle into Oliver's chest. He flinched but didn't open his eyes. Both he and Stella would eventually heal without help, though getting out bullets and stopping the bleeding would speed up matters. Besides, I was worried about the baby.

"What about that doctor you have working with your dad?" Ava put her arms under Stella and lifted the shorter woman.

I nodded. Dimitri would be better, but Wade Crampton would do in a pinch. The doctor worked at the local university teaching and conducting research on transplants with government grants. I'd hired him on the side to piggyback a study on his research that might reduce my father's dependence on anti-rejection drugs for his heart. Or my heart, actually. The one that now beat in his chest. I'd grown a new one since the hospital and didn't miss it.

"Come on, kids," I said to Kathy and Spencer. "Help me walk. Let's get out of here." My body was healing, but I was still having trouble seeing. I hoped Ritter could find Mari because I wasn't confident in my ability to drive us safely to Stella's, and Oliver wasn't going to be much help.

Ava carried Stella, while Jace staggered under Oliver's weight. Pain filled my steps, but after the first few minutes, my ankle became completely numb. In the lobby, we passed Marco, George, and Charles, our three remaining mortal employees, who were busy moving the unconscious Unbounded out to Dimitri's truck.

"At least two got away," Marco told Ava as he went to help Jace carry Oliver. Marco was short and stocky with olive skin and dark hair and rolling eyes that missed nothing. He and Gaven had been best friends.

Ava nodded. "I know. They'll alert others or whoever they have on the police payroll. We'll have to torch the place. I'll get what we need from the rooms. You guys grab the electronics and weapons. We don't have much time."

Part of the training for each Renegade was to keep vital documents and important items in one place in case abandoning the safe house became necessary. Copies were kept in a bank safe deposit box for much of it, including stacks of fake IDs and irreplaceable keepsakes. We'd moved before, but this was the first time I'd experienced a complete abandonment.

I thought of the new pair of jeans in my closet that fit like a comfortable glove and had taken a week of horrendous shopping to find, and the black outfit Stella had especially made for me with numerous pockets for hidden weapons. I called it my catwoman suit. I wondered if there would be time to retrieve them. Silly and human of me. It could all be replaced. Though we couldn't begin to compete with the Emporium for funds, individual Renegades had amassed large amounts of money, and Ava had allotted me a monthly share of her funds by right of my Change. There had been no strings attached, but I felt indebted to her, and now that I was finished with watching Mari, I hoped to earn my own way.

If people stopped trying to kill me long enough.

As we loaded the kids, Stella, Oliver, and the dog into our brown van, I belatedly remembered Keene. Where was he? I'd asked Ava if everyone was okay, and I'd meant him as well, but I hadn't seen him around and it was possible she hadn't included him in her count. Breath catching in my throat, I turned to Ava. "Cort's brother. Is he—?" I couldn't finish.

"He's helping Ritter search for Mari."

I let out a sigh of relief that I told myself was only because

I felt responsible for bringing him here. I still had to tell Ava what he'd said about why we'd been attacked tonight and about Justine going to Mexico.

"Later." Ava touched my cheek. Until that moment, I hadn't realized that not only had I dropped my mental shield, but I was projecting my thoughts. "I'll be there as soon I can." Love came through both her touch and thoughts, in complete contrast with the gruesome blood covering her clothing.

"Okay, but we have to go to Mexico."

She nodded. "I figured as much."

I took the keys and started around to the driver's side, stopping as Ritter strode from the darkness carrying Mari in his arms. Her blouse was splattered with blood. I took two steps toward him, but the pain in my ribs at the sudden movement made me stop again.

"What's wrong with her?" I asked. Mari's eyes were open, but they were unfocused and staring.

"Found her in the trailer. She was holding one of the Hunter's hands."

"Her husband," I guessed. "How did she get in there? Or even know where he was?"

"I don't know, but she may need a doctor." Ritter's voice was gruff, but there was an underlying softness that reminded me that he'd experienced something much worse with his own family.

I put my face close to Mari's. "I'm sorry, Mari. So sorry. But it's going to be okay. You're safe. I'm going to help you."

No response.

"Let's get her into the van," Ava said.

Leaving them to put Mari in with the others, I hobbled around to the driver's door and yanked it open. Painfully, I climbed onto the seat. In an hour, I'd feel a hundred times better, but for now, I'd been distinctly reminded that I wasn't actually immortal. Reaching over to pull the door shut, it rammed into something solid.

Ritter. He stood there looking terrible and fierce, his mind closed to me. His face was streaked with blood, though his lips were remarkably untouched. The cut over his left eye was healing and the bleeding had stopped, but there was a new cut on his jaw that gaped. He looked me over as I did him, his black eyes probing. Apparently satisfied, he reached for my hand, and at his touch, my flesh burned.

He must have seen something in my eyes because for a brief second, I caught a glimpse of the maelstrom of emotions in his mind. *Mine,* his thoughts said.

Before I could refute his claim on me, he was closed again. Or had it been my thought, not his? I needed a shrink when a man covered in blood was so attractive to me that I wanted to melt into him.

"Double back three times to make sure you're not followed," he said. "Go straight to Stella's. Don't stop anywhere. Leave the keys in the van. We'll dispose of it as soon as we get there. I've checked for tracking devices and changed the plates, but once you're at Stella's, turn on the alarms and keep your gun loaded."

"You're wasting breath," I spat. "I've been training for months, even if you haven't been here to teach me."

"Good. Don't go anywhere."

The stupid idiot. "I'll take care of them. Just clean up here." Actually, I had no idea how I'd get them into Stella's apartment. I couldn't exactly ask Bronson's nurse for help. The woman had worked for Stella in Kansas, and had moved here with them when it was clear Bronson needed around-the-clock care, but Stella had always been careful not to overlap her separate lives.

I tugged on the door, but Ritter didn't move. "So do you promise not to go anywhere?" The demand had left his voice, and I caught a hint of the man inside who'd once needed someone.

I swallowed hard and muttered, "Yes." I'd promise with the same level of commitment he'd given me when he made his promise two months ago.

He nodded and stepped back, leaving me with a disappointment I couldn't place. Now who was the idiot?

I put the van into gear and stepped on the gas. Before I'd left the parking lot, Ava and Ritter had already disappeared. Without warning, a man rose up in my headlights, and I slammed on the brakes with my good left foot to avoid hitting him. *What now?*

"Who is it?" Kathy sounded close to breaking.

I glanced at the seat next to me where the kids huddled together. "A friend. Cort's brother. You remember him, don't you? He helped us escape the Emporium."

"Not really."

I unrolled the window, one hand on the gun in my lap. "Where've you been?" I asked Keene.

"I ran into another Unbounded." He rubbed his jaw and winced. "Where are you going?"

"Can't tell you."

"Fair enough. Look, I've been thinking about sticking around a bit. See if Cort needs my help in Mexico."

I shrugged. "You'll have to talk to Ava."

"Yeah, but first I'm talking to you."

"I'm fine with it." Provided she could verify that he wasn't still working for the Emporium. Too much had happened today to allow me to trust him without question. Justine had used far more elaborate schemes to earn my trust.

He grinned and slapped the side of the van as I revved the engine and drove away.

CHAPTER 7

BY THE TIME I'D MADE SURE I WASN'T BEING FOLLOWED AND HAD arrived at the gated community where Stella lived, I felt substantially better. I no longer had trouble focusing, and the pain in my chest had lessened. I still couldn't feel my ankle, but that was probably a good thing. Oliver had also recovered somewhat, though Stella hadn't regained consciousness and Mari was still staring, unseeing.

All the buildings looked almost exactly alike, with six apartments, two to each floor, and outside stairs and balconies. Stella's apartment was located on the top.

"I can walk. I think," Oliver said.

"Okay, this is what we're going to do," I told the kids. "Spencer, you need to guide Mari. I think I can get her to walk. Kathy, you help Oliver, and I'll carry Stella. Let's see if we can do it in one trip. I don't want to leave anyone here."

"We can do it," Kathy said. She had regained a little color in her cheeks, and even Spencer had released his hold on his sister.

"Let's go."

"Wait," Kathy said. "Grandma Ava gave us blankets. She said

we should wrap it around them to hide the . . . the blood."

Right. If any of the neighbors saw us before we got inside they might call the police. Even then the nurse could still call them, but hopefully the large paycheck Stella gave her would guarantee at least temporary silence. I put my Sig in my coat pocket and prayed I wouldn't have to drop Stella to get access to it.

Everything went well until we reached the stairs where Mari balked. Kathy had to leave Oliver to help Spencer lift Mari up the first flight, and Oliver almost tumbled back down. Thankfully, he caught the railing at the last moment and Spencer pulled him to safety. Max docilely followed along behind us, for once not even barking.

Although Stella's door looked like all the others in the community, I knew it had been built to withstand a lot more than an ordinary steel door. The inside walls had been reinforced as well, the decorating over the top so expert that no one would ever know. For all her nerdy computer skills, Stella was also a master at design. In addition to this apartment, she also owned the one next door. That apartment was for emergencies, the outside entrance nailed shut so it was accessible only from inside the first apartment through a hidden panel at the back of a closet. I'd put the children there now.

Kathy opened the door, which was good because the code changed weekly, and I couldn't remember what it was now, though Stella had sent it to my phone like always. She never took chances with Bronson. He might be dying, but her greatest hope was that he would live to see their child born.

We were all inside and Kathy was resetting the alarm when Bronson's nurse hurried into the room, pulling on her robe. Martha Cox was a short, broad lady with gray hair, large hands, and a no-nonsense attitude that amused Bronson on his good days. Or used to when he'd had good days. She also possessed the kindest blue eyes in the history of eyes.

Now those eyes riveted on Stella. "What happened? Is the baby okay?"

The two questions I couldn't answer. "I don't know about the baby, and Stella will have to explain later. Right now we need to get her into bed."

"She might need a doctor."

"I have one coming." I'd called on the way, and it would take Wade an hour to get here from the university lab where he was probably pulling one of his all-nighters.

Martha directed me to the guest bedroom where together we removed Stella's dress, patched up the wounds we could see, cleaned off most of the blood, and tucked her inside warm blankets. Already her wounds were healing, but Stella didn't wake.

"Poor thing," Martha said, smoothing Stella's forehead.

"She's going to be okay. It's the baby I'm worried about." I might not know exactly what the baby meant to Stella—no one did except maybe Ava, who'd lost every bit as much—but I knew enough. The loss would devastate her.

Losing the baby now will save her the pain of watching her child grow old and die later. I pushed the thought away. We couldn't start thinking that way because there was always a chance our children would carry the gene. Unbounded children meant carrying on the battle against the Emporium, especially when we'd lost so many of our experienced Unbounded recently. There were fewer than a hundred Renegades now, and from the intel we could gather, Emporium Unbounded outnumbered us at least four to one.

"You stay with her," I told Martha. "I'll settle the others."

"I don't know where we're going to put them. There's a couch bed, and the little ones can go down in my room."

"I'll take care of it."

She nodded. "I'll have to peek in on Bronson, but besides that I'll sleep in this chair in case she needs anything." She pointed to the off-white easy chair near the dresser that looked more comfortable than any chair had a right to look. Stella's decorating magic once again.

"Ava will be here soon. She can take over for you then."

Back in the sitting room, the kids sprawled on the floor with Max, Oliver lay on the leather sofa wrapped in his blanket, and Mari sat on the edge of a love seat, still staring straight ahead.

"Come on," I told the kids.

"Oliver's asleep," Kathy said. "He sounds funny."

Actually, his breathing was a lot better than back at the palace. Maybe he wouldn't need the doctor after all. "Let him sleep. Let's get you to bed."

"Where are we going to sleep?" Kathy asked. "Stella only has three rooms."

"Actually, there's another one. It's secret." I forced a smile. "Come on. I'll show you."

"I want my daddy." Spencer looked up at me, his eyes full of tears.

"He's coming," I told him. "But we'll wait in the secret room for him. No one knows it's there so we'll be super safe."

He blinked. "Not even the Emporium?"

"Nope." I picked him up and he clung to my neck so tightly I felt choked and my ribs screamed in protest. No matter. "You were so brave and helpful tonight," I added.

"Like a real Renegade?" he asked.

"Yes."

He seemed satisfied with that, so I took them down the hall to the linen closet, showing them the panel that unlatched and revealed the entry to the adjoining apartment. Just in case, I sent out my thoughts, but I could sense no one there. No emotions or life forces. Even so, I kept one hand near my gun until I checked out the rooms, one by one.

"It really is secret," Spencer said, the tenseness seeping from his little body.

The apartment was slightly smaller than the other, with only two bedrooms and bathroom, but Stella had cleaned it recently and the aroma of flowers wafted up from the plug-in air freshener. Two queen-sized mattresses sitting directly on the floor in each room made up the entirety of the furniture. That's all

I needed. Within minutes, I had the kids nestled together in one of the beds under a couple blankets I swiped from Stella's linen closet.

Spencer dropped off almost immediately, his arms around Max, but Kathy stared at the ceiling. "Gaven always used to play cards with me," she whispered. "I'm going to miss him."

"We all will."

She nodded and snuggled up to her brother, shutting her eyes. I lay down next to her, cradling her body with my own. "It's going to be okay, Kathy."

Her hand found mine. "I know."

I felt like a liar because I didn't really know anything. Anything except that I wasn't going to let my brother put these children in danger again.

Where else would they be safe? I couldn't think of anywhere unless it was completely unconnected to any Unbounded. Could I give them up if it came to that?

What choice was there really?

Leaving the kids sleeping, I double-checked the bars on the shuttered windows before going back to the other apartment. The doctor would be arriving any minute, and I'd have to go down to the gate to let him in. Out in the living room, Oliver was still on the couch, his breathing raspy but steady. Mari had slumped onto one arm of the chair and her eyes were closed. She didn't move when I called her name. The blood splattered on her peach blouse had dried nearly black. I'd find her something new to wear in the morning.

Gun in hand, I punched in the codes to the alarm, setting it again behind me. Hopping into the van, I drove to the gate and waited. Finally, a battered blue car of indeterminate make drove up, and I watched Wade Crampton, his rotund figure still clad in a white smock, squeeze from the car. He glanced behind him worriedly as I jumped from the van and opened the gate.

"Expecting someone?"

"No." He hesitated, swallowing hard as his eyes wandered

over my jeans and coat. Belatedly, I realized that like the other Unbounded, copious amounts of blood stained my clothing.

"Well, maybe," he said finally. "Look, I know you said you need a doctor to look at your friend, but I only agreed to come because I need to talk to you."

I didn't like the sound of that. I wanted to ask him if he was being followed, but why would I even suspect such a thing? I'd made sure there was no connection between us, and every time he'd taken samples from my father, it had been at his lab. No way could the Emporium have connected anything he did with the Renegades.

"We'll talk later," I said. "Right now I need you to look at my friend. She's about three months along and she's had some severe trauma tonight. I want to know if there's anything we can do for the baby."

He ran a hand through his sparse brown hair. "Why don't you take her to the emergency?"

"I can't. That's all."

He shook his head. "I'll look at her—not that I know anything about obstetrics—but after this, I'm out."

"Out? What are you talking about?"

"I'm talking about the fact that my government grant has been threatened because of the work I was doing for you. And the dean of the university has told me if I lose the grant, then I lose my job."

"How would they even know you were doing anything for me? I thought we agreed you'd keep it a secret and work on it only after hours." My hand clenched the Sig in my coat pocket.

He took a step back. "Well, it was an article I wrote for a journal. It was just hypothesizing about the possibility of doing away with immune-suppression drugs, citing that fourth experiment with your father that induced nausea. I mean, it did work somewhat, despite that side effect, and it was only a matter of time before someone else made the connection and I—"

"You wanted credit," I growled. "That was *not* our agreement. We said no publicity until after a solution was found." Because then no matter what the Emporium chose to do with the discovery, my father would at least benefit.

The doctor looked miserable, the sagging flesh on his cheeks reminding me of a hound dog. "That's not the worst—well, it is for me. But someone's also been following me to work and back. Not the same car every day, but enough repeats that I noticed." Which, given his absorption in his work, must have been a lot.

So how much money does the Emporium have invested in transplant drugs? I hadn't thought it would be enough to interest them even if they had caught wind of the doctor's experiments, but apparently I'd been wrong. Or maybe his research had wider applications that I hadn't anticipated. Whatever the reason, there was a very real possibility that the Emporium or their agents had followed him here. They might even have put a tracking device on his car.

"We *are* through," I said. "Get in your car and drive away now. Fast. You rip up this address, and if anyone asks, you don't remember it. If you're ever asked, say you had a flat and had to stop here—whatever. But you don't know me, and I had nothing to do with that research."

He stared at me, his round eyes large. "What about your friend?"

"What friend?" I drew my gun.

He stumbled back several feet. "Okay, okay. I really don't know anything about obstetrics. You can check hormone levels to see if they're normal, but if she's going to miscarry, you probably won't be able to prevent it. Nothing you can do but make her rest and hope the baby makes it."

"Go." If my gun hadn't already been racked, I'd rack it again for the scare factor.

The doctor yanked open his door and pressed himself inside. The engine flared to life and for an instant, I was blinded by his headlights. Then he was gone. I crossed to one of the gate columns and leaned against it. Waiting. If there was going to be trouble, a car would come soon and I'd press the emergency button on my cell phone. The night air was turning colder and already my hand holding the Sig was going numb.

A car came ten minutes later, but it was Ava's sedan, followed by two others. I breathed a sigh of relief and stepped into view. Ava killed her engine and met me at the gate. "Something wrong?"

I shook my head. "Just a minor complication, I hope." I explained about the doctor.

My guilt at not letting him see Stella must have come through because Ava put her hand on my arm. "You did the right thing. I can take care of her. I'll call Dimitri or one of our friends in New York, and they can walk me through what needs to be done. I've had enough practice over the years. But I suspect the doctor is right. Only time will tell about Stella's child."

I wondered if she was thinking about the babies her first husband had murdered before she became Unbounded. Or the children she had later, who'd grown up and become old and died while she still looked young enough to be their granddaughter. It was a sobering thought.

"Where are Jace and Ritter?" I asked.

"Securing the Unbounded at the airport. They'll go with you to Mexico in the morning."

"You've heard from Dimitri and Cort then?"

She nodded. "The lab's been ruined by fire, completely demolished, and several people were killed. But we believe the scientists got away with the records. They're trying to find them now." She paused and then added, "Dimitri and Cort are not the only ones looking for the men."

"It's Justine," I said, my throat tight. "She flew down there days ago."

"I know. I talked with Cort's brother."

"Cort and Dimitri will need help. We should leave tonight."

"Morning's soon enough. We'll need to pack some survival gear. Apparently, they're going deeper into the jungle."

I nodded. "I'll dump the van, then." For a moment I thought she'd protest, but at last she gave a sharp nod. "The kids are in

Stella's second apartment," I said, turning back to the van. "Just follow the smell of the dog."

Ava laughed. "I'll take care of them."

I knew she would. They were her posterity every bit as much as I was.

I drove, glancing behind me every so often to make sure no one followed. Crossing the Hawthorne Bridge heading west, I traded the van for one of our stashed emergency vehicles. I knew I should go to Stella's to rest before the next adventure.

Instead, I found myself driving to my parents' apartment where I let myself in the lobby with my key. Chris, Jace, and I all had one, despite the potential danger if we were caught by the Emporium. I thought of the home my parents had left behind in Kansas not too far from where my mortal grandmother still lived. She had refused to come with us when we'd fled after the Emporium had tried to kill the family, and I didn't blame her. Her whole life was there, and she was beyond the age of dodging bullets. So far she had remained safe.

My parents had left behind their house, their friends, and my dad's job. They were in limbo, and I felt guilty for the disruption of their lives, but I didn't know how to fix it. A part of me hoped that when we moved on, they'd remain in Portland under their assumed names. I told them they would be like any parents whose children lived out-of-town, that we'd just have to be more careful when we visited.

I knew it was a lie and so did they.

I took the elevator, but I didn't stop on their floor. They'd be asleep now, my father still recovering from his heart surgery. At least I'd given him that. Our relationship had changed since the operation, though I didn't know if that resulted more from his uneasiness with the knowledge that I'd died for him, or from my own emotions after discovering he wasn't my biological father. Not that I would ever tell him or my mother the truth of what had happened at the fertility clinic where I was conceived.

Up I continued, until the last floor where I made my way to

the rooftop. The building only had six floors, so it wasn't very tall, but the moment I stepped outside, my heart started pounding, my knees grew weak, and my stomach heaved. It was all I could do not to drop to my knees and crawl. In determination, I walked steadily past several plastic crates and a row of dead potted plants to the edge where a short wall prevented an accidental fall. The corner had a cement post that was wide enough to sit on—if you had the stomach for it. I eased on top of it and let out a cloud of breath into the cold night air.

It had taken two months until I'd been able to get from the door to the edge without crawling, and even now I had to cling to the cement post as I sat on it, pushing mentally at the weight of the black sky that threatened to crush me. One false move and I risked plummeting—not to my death, but to a very painful, if short, recovery.

That I, an Unbounded destined to live two thousand years, should be chained to acute acrophobia was a terrible, ironic joke. An absurdity I intended to put to rest. So far, I'd had no luck. My fear, dizziness, and nausea had not abated one iota. But I had been able to force myself to the edge, and that was progress. The next time I was caught on a roof in an Unbounded struggle, I wouldn't be at such a disadvantage.

I hoped.

After a moment, I forced myself to open my eyes and look down. My stomach tightened but I didn't lose my dinner as I had in the past. The fact that I hadn't eaten real food probably helped. What I absorbed in the course of a day went directly to my blood, not to my stomach.

When my queasiness settled marginally, I began sending out my thoughts, focusing first on the pedestrians below. Except that it was nearing midnight, and there was only one couple, who quickly vanished into a nearby building. Then I pushed further outward, into the surrounding buildings. My head ached horribly, but I could "see" the pinpoints of light that signaled living beings. But this far away, I didn't get the slightest hint of their emotions.

Despite Ava's tutelage and assertions that I was making progress, I was nowhere near where I wanted to be. Delia Vesey of the Emporium Triad had been able to force her way into my mind long enough to plant ideas, and she'd accomplished it so smoothly, that at first I hadn't known she was in my mind. While I had been able to insert messages into *willing* conscious minds, I'd had no luck figuring out how to subtly plant an idea in a conscious mind. She'd also been able to exert enough mental control that she'd prevented me from leaving her quarters at the Emporium. I'd succeeded in making it to the door, but it hadn't been easy. Each limb had felt as if it weighed a hundred pounds. I had no idea how she'd managed that, but I hadn't been able to control anyone physically for any length of time.

Of course, she had perfected her methods over seventeen hundred years, and I didn't have the luxury of time to learn. Our battle with the Emporium was ramping up. They owned several seats in congress already, and there were rumors about the vice president's son—rumors Stella hadn't been able to disprove. It was only a matter of time before the Emporium wasn't satisfied with simply assassinating senators they didn't like.

On the other hand, if what history recounted was true, even Delia's abilities were weak compared to the old days. Legend told of Unbounded with telekinesis, true precognition, psychometry, astral projection, and numerous other abilities. Now the gifts were much fewer, and some variations almost nil. I didn't know if my own lack of progress was due to a dilution of the gene or lack of practice. I had to find out. I had to be ready.

Perhaps in this millennia-long battle, when both sides had focused heavily on the combat and scientific abilities, only the knowledge to unlock my particular ability had been lost. After all, Oliver was three generations from his closest Unbounded progenitor, and his illusion had been lifelike with no training at all. The knowledge had been in his genes all along, his terror the key. So sitting in this place where I feared falling, maybe I could not only defeat my acrophobia but access my own key.

A long shot, yes. Irrational, maybe. But I was running out of options.

Frowning, I let go of my death grip on the edge of the freezing cement and rubbed my right ankle, itching now beneath Keene's bandage. There was no pain. Slowly, I unraveled the gauze and removed the splint, followed by more gauze, saturated with dark blood. Underneath the last layer, the skin had knitted together, leaving no scar or sign of damage. Okay, so there were perks to being Unbounded that I sometimes took for granted.

The night was cold, too cold, and I wouldn't be able to last out here much longer. While it technically wouldn't cause my death, I could freeze.

I had one more thing to try tonight. I kept thinking that if I could *stand* on this cement post, maybe I'd finally conquer my fear. Besides, my backside was so numb with cold I could no longer feel it, despite the warm interior padding of my leather coat. I took a searing breath and held it, inching one knee onto the cement.

I made it to both knees before dizziness forced me back down. I slid into a quivering heap, not on the post, but onto the roof next to it. Drawing my knees to my chest, I curled in on myself for a long moment. Maybe it was time to go home. Well, I had no place to call home now, but I should get to Stella's. Ava might have news for me.

Except that I was no longer alone on the roof. Someone had breached the door. I could feel the pulsating of a life force, though a barrier over the mind prevented me from receiving any emotion.

Unbounded, I thought.

CHAPTER 8

UNBOUNDED OR SOMEONE WHO KNEW ABOUT US, OR ABOUT ME in particular or he wouldn't be here on this roof. But no one had followed me.

I eased toward a long plastic crate with a greasy exterior. The lid came off easily, and from underneath an old blanket, I withdrew two of the four-foot pieces of especially hardened wood I kept inside. One of these I placed on the rooftop in easy reach—a backup in case I lost the first in battle. I had my gun, of course, but depending on who my visitor was, I'd try to get rid of him the old-fashioned way. It was a lot easier taking a prisoner who could walk than hauling out a limp body. Besides, I'd already killed a man tonight, and I hadn't even examined my feelings about that. I felt changed somehow—and not in a good way.

My body tingled with alertness. With the curequick and the time that had passed since the fighting, I felt remarkably better. My ribs didn't even ache. Part of my sudden well-being was the spurt of adrenalin that accompanied me during each confrontation since my Change. As if my body longed for the battle.

I didn't fight it. Whoever tracked me here was going to seriously wish they hadn't found me.

A figure came into sight and the urge to fight increased. I knew that shape only too well, despite our time apart. I also recognized the mind barrier now, hard and unyielding. Determined. Yet if I got close enough, it was one of the few I had managed to breach momentarily.

Maybe I wasn't such a failure after all.

He was going to pay. I jumped up from my crouched position. "So you're following me now? Guess that means your GPS locator is working." I meant to sound strong and flippant, but I'd forgotten I was on the roof and my sudden change in height sent my head spinning. I had to get away from the edge. Gripping my stick and picking up the second as well, I took several large steps forward.

"You said we'd talk later," Ritter said. "It's later."

"Well, that's kind of stupid. Later could mean next year or next decade." I could see him now, barely illuminated by the light coming from several taller buildings. Unlike me, he'd taken the opportunity to change clothes; though his jeans looked the same, they were no longer stained with blood. The darkness worked in my favor up here because away from the edge I could pretend we were in the workout room instead of on a roof where I might fall. I tossed him one of the sticks. They weren't quite bo staff size, being shorter and thicker, but close enough, and they did a lot less damage than a handgun. We needed to save some energy for the Emporium agents in Mexico.

I swung a test blow, and he brought his stick up forcefully, knocking me back. He arched a brow. "That's how you've been training?"

The stupid, self-satisfied jerk. "I guess without you around we're all helpless." I slammed the stick at him again, whirling and whipping it to gain more power. He barely brought up his weapon in time. *Ha, take that!* He countered with an attack of his own that my eyes could scarcely follow, but I was ready with a series of moves Jace and I'd worked on for weeks. I feinted, stepped to the side, feinted again, launched into a fancy form that was meant for show, not battle, stopping short to whirl and slam the stick into my opponent. Ritter let out a grunt of pain.

Score!

"Maybe you *have* learned a thing or two." His voice told me I was in trouble now. Well, let him do his worst. I might not be able to beat him or even touch him again with the stick, but I wouldn't give up either.

I barely blocked his next blow and the next. I stepped backwards, scrambling for purchase. I feinted before my next strike and we met solidly, my arms vibrating with the shock. *Ouch.*

On and on we went, thrusting and parrying. Sweat trickled down my neck and into my shirt. Ritter was poetry in motion. How could he be so fierce and beautiful at the same time?

"Be careful," he said, holding back on a jab that I wouldn't have been able to block. "You're near the edge."

I glanced behind me, saw the drop, the apartment lights running down the next building. The black sky seemed to crash over me with a weight of a thousand gravities. "Oh, crap!" I dropped my stick and sat down inelegantly. *Breathe. You are not on a roof. Breathe.*

Ritter sat beside me, and he didn't speak, for which I was grateful. Otherwise, I might throw up on him, making a bad situation worse. I should have known better than to spar with him here.

What was I trying to prove anyway? It wasn't like I'd ever be able to beat him.

We sat in silence while our sweat cooled and our body heat became numbness. "We should go back," I said when I could no longer feel my toes or fingers. "Ava will worry."

Actually, Ava would know where we were if she checked her GPS locator, so she wouldn't be concerned. At first being trackable had worried me, but we weren't in danger of being traced by anyone from outside because each chip emitted a constantly changing pattern programmed and regularly changed by Stella. I sometimes resented the intrusiveness, but I knew where the locator was in my arm—and how to remove it if I really wanted to.

Ritter's jaw tightened briefly before he spoke, emphasizing the shadow of a beard that was beginning to show on his face. "Why are you so angry? What's changed?" The cut on his eye was gone, though there was a slight droop below his left eye, not a defect that his Unbounded genes would have fixed, but part of his genetic makeup.

"Angry?" I clenched my fists. "You know what, figure it out for yourself." I jumped to my feet—well, at least I got to my feet, which given the circumstances was a tremendous accomplishment. Grabbing my stick, I swung, not holding back. His stick went up, blocking.

I retreated toward the door, away from the edge, until I no longer felt the huge pressure of the sky overhead. I still felt like throwing up, but I'd grown accustomed to that feeling and it wouldn't hamper me too much. It was the main reason I came up here.

He lunged, and I blocked. I lunged, and he blocked.

"Not bad," Ritter said. "You've been practicing."

No thanks to you. I smirked. "Ava and Dimitri are good teachers."

"Of course they are. I trained them."

Leave it to him to take credit, though he'd abandoned all of us.

Our sticks met in a solid *clack!* I stumbled backward, falling to the cement that lined the rooftop, one elbow in a gutter that ran to the edge. He was on me in an instant, his weight pinning me. I was no match for him. Not even in two hundred years would I be.

Unless I could figure out how to use my own ability against him.

I reached out, thrusting my mind at the blackness of his barriers, my arms pushing against his chest. The mind shield seemed every bit as strong and unyielding as the hard body on mine, a blackness with only one tiny ray of light. I dove for the light, slithering inside.

All at once, the barrier was gone. My mind flared with need, desire, and frustration. Not my feelings but his, mirroring mine. Together doubled in intensity. He froze, his hands pinning mine, his body holding me down. Our hearts beat out a single rhythm.

In the next instant we were kissing. Urgency filled my mind. Pleasure at his touch. No, his pleasure. Did it make a difference? His lips parted and mine opened to him. The world turned now for quite another reason. He kissed my lips, my face, my neck, and I kissed him back greedily, wanting more.

"I can feel your emotions," he murmured against my cheek.

He was wrong. He could only feel the surface ones, the ones I sent him—the need, the want, the anger—not the hurt, the part of me that wanted to beg for an explanation.

I could hurt him, I realized, now that his mind was open and unguarded. I could dig in. Twist and damage. Ava had warned me repeatedly to be careful when we practiced, saying I could hurt an unshielded mind, but until this moment, I hadn't understood the concept fully. No wonder one of the first things taught new Unbounded was to shield their minds. I was a weapon—the trick was getting inside. My determination and proximity to Ritter had aided me, but if I could learn to do it from a distance, I might be of more use to the Renegades.

If I probed a bit, I might also learn where he'd been these past two months. What he valued more than us. Than me.

His mouth lowered again, angling toward mine.

I lashed out, sending a hot sphere of anger into his mind, pushing at him physically as well. He sucked in a breath, and his barrier clamped back into place. "You really have been practicing."

"Get. Off. Me." Let him wonder that my body arched toward his even while I was pushing him away.

He rolled off, but his hand grabbed mine. "Why?"

He meant my anger. I shook my hand free. "Look, it's not going to work. Stay away from me."

His lips hardened. It was the right thing to say. Or rather the wrong thing if I wanted an explanation. But I was finished wanting anything from him.

At least that's what I told myself.

I headed for the door, going inside with a sharp sensation of relief. The nausea would take time to abate, I knew from experience, but the pressure and the immediate fear of falling was gone.

Ritter came after me, his face a mask of impassivity. For a moment, I felt a sharp, stabbing disappointment. What did I really know about this man? I knew he'd lost his family and his dark-haired fiancée two hundred and forty years ago. I knew that he wore her engagement band on a necklace, along with his mother's and one that had belonged to his little sister. I knew he still had vivid nightmares about that night, that he'd dedicated his life to revenge, and that his loyalty to the Renegades was unquestionable. I knew he liked plants and dogs. I knew that I was more attracted to him than I'd ever been to Tom, a man I'd almost married. I knew he'd broken his own rule of getting involved when he'd met me. Loving anyone meant losing, in his book.

In all, it wasn't much. I'd only caught a few glimpses of the real man. We couldn't possibly know each other well enough to handle the attraction between us. Maybe Stella was right that he was too filled with anger to make any sort of relationship work. I'd be better off with Cort, or a mortal like Keene.

Then again, maybe if Ritter finally had a real focus for his anger, he'd be able to work out his pain and plan for a future that didn't involve maiming or death. I could give him that release. I'd learned two months ago who'd been directly responsible for the death of his family and the attempt on his life. There had been time to tell him before he'd taken off, but I hadn't told him or anyone. I was still protecting her, my once best friend, Justine.

Or maybe I was worried that taking ultimate revenge would sever him from any connection with humanity—and with me.

Maybe I'd chosen wrong.

Sometimes life really sucked. Because if I had told him, Justine might not be in Mexico now causing us trouble. That meant it was my fault. Whatever happened, I couldn't let myself forget that she was the reason my niece and nephew were motherless.

Maybe I was the one who wanted to keep the revenge for myself.

Down in the lobby, Ritter reached for the door but didn't step through. He turned his glittering eyes toward me.

"This is *not* over. You and I both know that. But go ahead and pretend for now."

Ignoring him, I stalked out into the night.

CHAPTER 9

I EXPECTED TO FIND EVERYONE SLEEPING WHEN I ARRIVED AT STELLA'S, but instead there was a bustle of activity. Only the kids, Stella, Mari, and Oliver slept, while everyone else sorted through the equipment that had been salvaged from the palace. Ritter, who'd followed me home, began hauling bags out to the vehicles.

Ava smiled when she handed me a duffel bag of clothing, complete with my favorite jeans and catwoman outfit. "I figured it'd save time grabbing some clothing for everyone since you're taking off in a few hours."

The emphasis on "you're" drew my attention. "You're not coming?"

"For now I'm staying with Stella and Oliver. And Mari, of course. With Dimitri gone, there's no one else."

"How is Stella?"

Ava frowned. "I don't know how she held off so many, but her body certainly paid the price. If she'd been mortal, she'd have died a dozen times. She will live, of course."

She didn't mention the baby, and I didn't ask. I already knew. I could tell in the sadness emanating from the thoughts she'd let me glimpse. Instead she said, "You'd better clean up. We've almost finished packing for the trip."

Jace came in from outside. "Where've you been? I was worried."

"At Mom and Dad's."

"On the roof? Again? 'Cause I know you didn't wake them up to tell them about our wonderful evening." He shook his head. "Sometimes I think you have an addiction to fear. That can't be good for you."

"Shut up." He was the only one who knew my secret about the roof. Well, him and now Ritter. I knew it was a little crazy, but in all my research it seemed the only way to permanently cure myself.

Jace grinned. "Did Ritter find you? He was looking for you earlier."

Without replying, I turned and went to find a shower. The hot water felt good on my skin, and I stood under it taking inventory. My ribs were good, my ankle fine, I still had a bruise the size of a fist between my breasts, but it was fading fast. The only real problem was the headache that always plagued me after I used my ability. Ava told me the pain wouldn't come as often as time went on, and my head did hurt less now when I was doing ordinary kinds of mental drills. But today had been so far from ordinary that my brain had every right to protest.

The hot water made me sleepy, and it took great effort to turn it off and step out into the comparatively frigid air. I grabbed a blue towel from the rack and began drying myself before dressing in my black stretch uniform. This one had short sleeves, though there was a matching jacket if I needed more coverage. Two pistols, three knives of various sizes, and a two-way radio went into the hidden pockets. Over this I dragged a larger pair of jeans and a camouflage jacket. I was as ready as I'd ever get.

I'd started down the hall when a gravelly voice called out. I hesitated at a partially open door, pushing it open. It was the master bedroom, the one Stella shared with Bronson—or had before his illness made the nurse's constant presence necessary. Bronson was struggling to sit up in the huge bed. Martha lay on a little cot tucked into a corner of the room, sound asleep.

I approached the bed, and Bronson stopped struggling as he recognized me. "Do you need something?" I asked, wondering if he'd awakened because of all the commotion.

He nodded and lifted a pale hand in the direction of the nightstand. "Water, please. If you would. Don't want to wake Martha, but I can't quite . . ." He trailed off, and it was easy to sense his frustration. Unlike the others, he didn't try to block his mind. Not anymore.

I helped him drink, one hand on the tall glass, the other behind his head. Bronson was one of those rare men whose aging made him more elegant and, well, beautiful. Once he'd been an electrician, his hands sure and steady, his body unfailing. When I'd first met him, his smile, his bearing, his zest for life, and especially his adoration of Stella had made me aware of how lucky she was to have shared the past twenty-four years of her life with such a partner. That had been on a good day, during the time when he still got around on his own.

Now, only months later, the illness had robbed him of his strength, aging him and deepening the divide between them. His skin stretched tight over his skull, his eyes were sunken, and his pain required medication for large parts of the day that dulled his mind and stole his wit. Yet, there was still something shining and refined about him.

He drank slowly, one determined swallow after the next. At last he began to draw away, and I laid his head back on the pillow, replacing the water on the nightstand. "Thank you," he whispered.

"You're welcome." How did he endure this half life? His mind was still active but his body had completely failed him. No wonder he was frustrated.

I looked up from the glass to find Bronson watching me, more alert than I'd seen him in weeks—which probably meant he was in a lot of pain and needed more medication. "Is she working?" he asked, giving me a little smile. "She works too hard, but I'm glad.

It's difficult having her see me this way. Hard to believe I once carried her over the threshold."

I laughed because I knew he was trying to be amusing. "You still will."

He sobered immediately. "I'm not sure about that. Look, I know you two have become close, and I know I don't have to ask you to take care of her because all you Renegades take care of each other, but my Stella, my star, is made for loving, despite her obsession with her computers. She will love our baby and that's going to help when I'm gone, but it's not enough. Or someday if she learns the child isn't Unbounded . . ." He trailed off.

"I'll take care of her."

"I want her to love and be loved. By a man. She deserves that. I wish I could spend the next thousand years with her but I don't . . ." A tear escaped the corner of his eye. "What a cruel life this is. Sometimes, I'm glad to be leaving."

He didn't really mean it, but I understood. I wanted to reach out and touch his hand, but that would bring his emotions even more clearly into focus for me, and I couldn't risk that. Not now when my own emotions were so volatile.

"I'll take care of her," I repeated. "Sleep now. She'll be in to see you tomorrow." I hoped.

Meanwhile, I'd go to Mexico and find that cure and give Stella back Bronson, for however many years he'd have left. Maybe they would have a child after all.

I checked on Stella next and found my older brother standing over her. Chris was blond like Jace and me, only darker, and he shared my gray eyes. "Hey," I said.

"Hey." He glanced down at the sleeping woman. She looked a lot better now than when I'd put her into bed, though her face still showed several large bruises and quickly sealing cuts. She looked fragile and beautiful.

"She protected my kids." Chris shook his head. "I should have been there."

"You probably would have been killed."

His head jerked toward me. "Why? Because I'm not Unbounded? I've been training as hard as the rest of you."

"If she'd been mortal, she'd be dead," I retorted, "and so would Oliver and most of the rest of us. Gaven *is* dead, and you know how good he was. Chris, can't you see that this is no life for children? They should be as far away from us as you can take them."

Tears filled his eyes and for a moment he couldn't speak. I couldn't tell what he was feeling, though, because I had slammed my own barriers over my mind the minute I'd seen him in the room. I knew how he was beginning to feel about Stella, even if he didn't admit to it himself.

"No," he said at last, his voice so soft I had to strain to hear. "No." His voice grew stronger. "Do we need a better stronghold? Yes. Do we need more protection? Backups? Yes. Yes, to all of it. But the kids need the knowledge and truth. They need to understand what we work for so they can be a part of fixing what's wrong with the world. But that's not all, Erin. Renegades *need* the kids. We need the kids to remind us we aren't like the Emporium. We don't abandon our children, taking them back only if it turns out they have the active gene. We don't treat mortals like second-class citizens when they work with us. We don't prolong human suffering for profit. We keep the kids with us so we can remember why we fight. We keep them so you Unbounded will remain human."

I closed my burning eyes for a long minute. Struggling. Struggling because I wanted what he said to be true. "Okay. Okay. But never again like this. They stay with Mom and Dad until we build this place of yours—or ten of them if that's what it takes to keep them safe. If you don't want to leave them with Mom and Dad, then you take them somewhere until it's built. They deserve some kind of childhood. They don't deserve nightmares like tonight."

He hugged me tightly. "Okay."

I felt like a cheat. As if I gave in because of my need to be with the children, to drink in their innocence and believe that someday everything would be right with the world. Because maybe if having them with us was right, bringing my own child into existence one day wouldn't be such a selfish and terrible thing.

Chris left and I was alone with the unconscious Stella. "I'll bring back what they have for Bronson," I told her. "I'm so sorry about your baby."

Was it terrible of me to be the tiniest bit glad that I had to leave so I wouldn't be around when she learned what had happened? She'd given her baby's life for Chris's children and for Oliver. How can you repay something like that?

Out in the living room, the preparations were winding down. Crates, boxes, and mounds of loose items rescued from the palace filled every available spot, but we'd had to leave so much more behind. Tears choked my throat until I spied the small potted plant from the conference room. *Really? The plant?* Yet I somehow felt much better. I knew who'd rescued it.

I started for the door, but to my surprise, Mari had awakened and arose from the couch to follow me. "No, you stay here," I told her.

She stopped moving, her small face averted, but when I opened the door, she followed me outside and down the stairs. The others were gathered near the vehicles, talking so quietly I was sure the neighbors hadn't been disturbed. It was dark enough that it was hard to see, but the sky to the east was marginally lighter, signaling the approach of morning.

Ava turned from the others, meeting me at the bottom of the stairs. "Where's Chris?"

"Inside. I think he's saying goodbye to the kids." From the corner of my eye, I saw Mari sit on the bottom step, still staring into nothingness.

"I'm dropping them at your parents' tomorrow and sending them all on a trip to Disneyland," Ava said. "They've been studying hard and need a break."

The children's home schooling regime was varied and odd, though advanced, with each Unbounded tutoring them in their specialty and Chris taking whatever subjects were left. Since most of us would be gone, a vacation was exactly what they needed. Maybe it would help them forget. And heal.

I took a step in the direction of the vehicles, but my step faltered as I turned back to face Ava. "Before I leave, there's something I want to know." My voice was scarcely a whisper.

"Oh?" Ava cocked her head, waiting.

"Who is my father?" A lousy time to bring it up, but after the night we'd had I didn't want to wake up and realize one day that I'd waited one day too long. If there was one thing I'd learned about life as Unbounded it was that everything frequently changed in an instant. Stella was a prime example.

A swift intake of air told me my question had taken her by surprise. "I thought you knew."

I glanced at the cars, making sure the others were still busy and far enough away not to overhear. "You mean Stefan Carrington? I know he's not my father." I let anger show in the words. Even after two months, neither she nor Dimitri had hinted at the truth of my own conception. Instead, they'd continued to allow me to believe that I was the biological daughter of an Emporium Triad leader. What I wanted now was the truth. A woman deserved to know who her father was. "When I was held at the Emporium headquarters, Laurence said you didn't use Stefan's genetically enhanced sperm that you stole from the Emporium. It arrived too late when my mother was at the fertility clinic. Stefan can't be my father."

I also knew the man I grew up believing to be my father no longer had viable sperm, so they hadn't used his that day as my mother believed. Laurence had lied about a lot of things and had betrayed us all, an act that even his final sacrifice hadn't erased, but he hadn't lied about this. I'd seen the truth in his mind. When he'd told me who my real father was, I'd been violently glad I wasn't the biological daughter of one of the Emporium's Triad, although lately I'd begun to worry on an entirely new level about what had actually become of Stefan's genetic material.

Ava sighed, the weight of all her three hundred years in the sound. "Stefan isn't your father. But if you know that, you must already know who your real father is, and you should be talking to him, not to me."

"Why hasn't Dimitri told me himself?"

The fatigue in her face vanished. "Oh, Erin, he's wanted to. But he's been concerned with how you'd take it. He worries that you'll think he considered it a duty."

"Wasn't it?" I felt like exploding.

"Talk to him."

I held Ava's gaze for a long minute, but hers didn't waver and in the end it was me who looked away first. Defeat notwithstanding, I wasn't finished yet. "So what did you do with Stefan's sperm?"

She didn't respond for the space of several heartbeats. "We kept it until it was needed."

Exactly what I'd feared. "For Jace," I said. My brother, in his euphoria at his Change, hadn't thought to question where he'd gotten his ability—or his blue eyes. We had an ancestor who'd been gifted in combat, but the genes were twelve generations removed, and though that didn't bother Jace, it didn't seem likely to me. Maybe because I knew his birth had been engineered like mine.

Jace's parentage also explained why Stefan Carrington had looked familiar to me when I'd met him. The recognition hadn't been on a primitive level, or because of some Unbounded link. It was because in him I'd seen my little brother's features. "Oh, Ava, what have you done?" They'd be looking for him once they knew.

Her lips tightened. "I did what we had to in order to survive. They were further ahead in their genetics. It was simple mathematics."

"We have to tell him."

"Does it really matter? Wasn't it better when you didn't know?"

"Yes." Heaven help me, she was right. I told myself that not telling Jace meant I was protecting him, but keeping the secret probably meant I was a liar like everyone else. What I didn't want was his relationship with the man we called our father to change . . . like mine had. Even so, I wouldn't relinquish the knowledge of my own parentage. It added to who I was and what I was becoming.

Pushing these thoughts away for later, I indicated Mari, who still sat on the steps. “She seems to think she’s going with me.”

Ava went to Mari, helped her rise, and put an arm around her. “Come back to the apartment with me, dear. Stella’s going to need you when she wakes. You’ll need each other. We should also change your clothes. How does that sound?” Mari said nothing but didn’t resist as Ava guided her up the stairs.

“Oh, and Erin,” Ava said from the second stair. “Ritter will be in charge once Dimitri fills you all in there, but . . .” She hesitated, glancing beyond me at the others, now climbing into two different vehicles. “But speak up if you sense something that doesn’t feel quite right. Genuine threats aren’t always obvious, and neither is the way we sense them.”

I knew she regretted not being able to go, but as our leader, she had to take care of all of us. Leaving behind our two newest Unbounded with an unconscious Stella wasn’t an option, and she was the only one skilled enough in medicine to care for them properly.

I nodded and headed for the front passenger door of the blue van, glad to find Jace and not Ritter behind the wheel. But he wasn’t alone. A man I didn’t recognize sat in the backseat. He had long, greasy black hair that looked in desperate need of a wash, but his face was clean-shaven. I couldn’t see what he was wearing in the darkness, but something didn’t smell quite fresh. Before I could ask about him, Chris came sprinting down the stairs and over to the van, jumping into the backseat near the stranger.

“Cutting it kind of short.” Jace started the van and followed the Land Cruiser ahead of us.

“We almost left you.”

Chris laughed. “Unless you’ve learned to fly a plane in the past couple of hours, you aren’t going to Mexico without me.”

Jace and I exchanged a private glance. No, we couldn’t leave without Chris, but we could make sure he stayed with the plane.

Strange to think Chris used to be the one to take care of us as kids, and now he was the most vulnerable.

"Who's our friend?" I whispered to Jace in a low voice as we cleared the community gate.

Jace frowned and leaned toward me. "You don't know? Found him hanging around outside the palace after we started the fire. He saw us start it. I didn't want to leave him there to tip off the police when they arrived. He said you offered him a job, so we took him to Stella's."

What? I turned and stared at the man. Wait, I did know him. He was the bum who'd tried to rob Mari and me earlier outside the palace. He'd shaven, but it was the same Hispanic guy. Only he appeared to be a bit more sober now.

I stretched closer to Jace. "Are you crazy? He tried to hold me up."

"You didn't offer him a job?"

"I guess. But I didn't mean today." I paused before adding, "He knows how to fix sinks."

"Really?" A smiled tugged at his lips. "Then you did the right thing. Don't worry. I made sure he didn't have a gun."

"Does Ava know?"

"Of course. Marco called his contact at the government and they vetted him while you were playing on the roof. No police record or hint of involvement with the Emporium. Got laid off a few years back, though, and never recovered financially. But Ritter didn't want to leave him with Ava. She has enough on her plate without having to keep an eye on him. Besides, he told me his mother lived in Mexico City and he'd love to visit. We'll give him money for a taxi when we land there to pass customs. Pick him up on the way back. That's far enough away not to cause Ava—or us—trouble."

"He lied," I growled. "His mother lives in Dallas, Texas. I saw it in his mind."

"Oh." Jace glanced back. "Should have known it was too good to be true. Should we dump him at the next street?"

"You can't. He still knows about that fire—and where Stella lives. If he leads the police there, the Emporium will know their location. They have too many eyes in law enforcement—and the fire won't cover up the death of the mortals we left there."

"Well, since Cort is the only one who knows Spanish, maybe he'll actually come in handy."

I rolled my eyes. "Just so long as you're the one who explains that to Ritter."

"We'll find some place to stash him. Don't worry. He's been cleared, remember? Marco even had him sign a non-disclosure doc."

I knew what dire threats and consequences the disclosure document held—none of which would hold up in any mortal courtroom but were worded strongly enough to make an employee think hard about exposing our nature. However, I doubted any of it would make a difference to the bum the next time he was drunk.

"What are you two whispering about?" Chris called from the back.

"Nothing," Jace and I said at the same time.

"Okay, but Benito and I are hungry. Can we stop for something?"

I looked back at him, exasperated. "There'll be food on the plane."

"Are you sure? Because I didn't see any earlier and no one packed more than a few energy bars. You guys seem to forget that some of us still need real food."

Mortals were sometimes a big pain. "I'll take care of it." Actually, now that he'd brought it up, I felt like sinking my teeth into a bit of old-fashioned comfort myself—preferably in the form of some kind of chocolate. I spent the next fifteen minutes on the phone, working out the details of a food order with a restaurant at the airport. Both Chris and I would soon have our appetites fulfilled.

At the airport, we had to pass through a special security, but someone had planned for our arrival and the inspection was only cursory. I wondered how much that cost because unlike the Emporium, we didn't have many agents in high positions. Still, Ava and Dimitri had been around long enough to form numerous alliances.

Cort and Dimitri had taken Cort's smaller plane, so we were stuck with Ava's corporate jet. Light now filled the horizon and washed over the tarmac where the others were already loading gear from the Land Cruiser into the cargo hold. Ritter glanced in our direction, his eyes going from my face to our new tagalong and shaking his head, a sure indication of his irritation at having to drag the man along. Ignoring him, I hefted my duffel and another box and started for the hold. But I stopped short as a car roared toward us, parking near the other vehicles.

Keene jumped from the car. "Sorry I'm late," he called. "I have news, though. Not good."

"You're coming with us?" I hadn't been sure Ava would allow it, but I considered him a useful addition. Unlike Chris, Keene could hold his own in a fight, and he'd been at this a good while longer than either me or my brothers.

"You'd know that if you weren't spending all your time on rooftops," Jace said under his breath. I gave him a withering glare, which he returned with a smirk. Why I'd ever thought he was my favorite sibling was beyond me.

"Of course I'm coming," Keene said. "About time I had a reunion with my brother." He flashed me a smile that didn't reach his worried eyes.

"You said you had bad news?" Ritter didn't look pleased to see Keene.

"I checked with my people in Arizona, and Senator Bellars left for Mexico yesterday afternoon. The official word is that he's working with some corporations there to import their products. However, the real reason is because he heard about whatever happened to your lab in Mexico."

"Oh, no," I said.

Keene nodded. "No better place than Mexico for him to

disappear, especially if he decides to head into the Lacandon Jungle by himself. He's made it easy for them. Though I suppose that was the point of the setup. Get rid of both him and the lab in the same week."

"How'd you know where our lab is?" Ritter growled.

I wondered the same thing. I'd told Keene at the restaurant that we had a lab in Mexico, but I hadn't said where.

"Ava told me." Keene met Ritter's stare. "I'm not your enemy. Not any longer. We're working for the same thing here. With Justine in Mexico neither Senator Bellars nor my brother is safe."

Ritter kept his eyes locked on Keene for several tense seconds, but he finally nodded. "You'd better be able to follow orders. I give them only once."

Keene nodded. "I'll get my bag."

Ritter watched him stride away. As I turned to put away my own duffel, I caught a glimpse of Ritter's head turning toward me, his dark eyes full of pain.

I stopped mid-step. "What?" I asked.

He arched a brow. "Nothing." Turning, he stalked back to the Land Cruiser, leaving me wondering. There had been something. Maybe.

Sighing, I continued to the plane. I hadn't gone three steps before Benito came rushing after me. Guess for now he belonged to me, or at least I was responsible for him. "So you're Benito," I said, wishing I'd worn gloves to protect my hands from the biting cold.

He dipped his head. "Yes. Benito Hernández. Thank you for giving me a job."

Sure enough, though he had an accent, it was nowhere near as heavy as when he'd held me up. "You lied about your mother living in Mexico."

He nodded.

"Don't lie again. I'll know." I wouldn't unless I searched his mind and right now I was so tired I probably couldn't see anything if I tried, but he didn't know that.

His dark eyes went wide—with fear, I suspected, rather than innocence. But his next words surprised me. "I really 'preciate you giving me a job. No one has wanted to take a risk on me for a long time. I won't let you down. That's a promise." He sounded sincere, but maybe he was accustomed to saying whatever he needed to get by. Regardless, if he stuck around, he might get enough of the whole picture that his professed loyalty would become real.

"We'll see," I said.

"I can take that." He tugged at my bag.

Not until he took a bath. And probably not even then. I wanted to keep what little I still owned, at least until I got a chance to go shopping. "No, thanks. I got it. Uh," I added, "you do actually speak Spanish, right?" For all I knew, his accent wasn't even Hispanic, even though his grandfather was from Mexico.

He nodded. "Sí. I speak it much better than English."

"Hey, look, the food's already here." Chris called to us, his mouth already full. "Come and eat, Benito. Then you can help me get the rest of the food onto the plane."

Leave it to my big brother to find the food. Well, I guess we didn't want our pilot fainting from lack of nourishment. Benito joined Chris at the metal cart, filled not only with steaming dishes meant for now, but ones we could microwave later. As they ate, the rest of us piled everything into the cargo hold.

"That's it, then," Marco said. He saluted Ritter. "George and I are off."

"You two aren't going with us?" I asked.

It was Ritter who answered. "Ava wants them to, but that would leave her with only Charles. I convinced her to let them stay."

I nodded. It would make me feel better knowing Ava had help. "It's not like we're going to confront the Emporium head on," I said. "It's just finding our scientists and the research, right? In and out."

"Something like that." Ritter's growl was hardly convincing. Whatever he planned, he wanted to make the Emporium pay.

This worried me because it might make him sloppy, though the idea of Ritter being sloppy seemed ludicrous.

"Don't forget we're also warning the senator and doing something about his fake aide." Keene thrust his hands deep into the pockets of his jeans. He hadn't worn them at the restaurant, so he'd apparently cleaned up like the rest of us.

"Let's go." I hurried up the stairs into the plane behind Chris and Benito, their arms loaded with food trays.

"Very nice," Benito said as his eyes wandered over the interior.

It wasn't a luxury liner by most standards, but it did seem spacious compared to commercial flights. One side of the plane held four sets of double seats, arranged so two sets faced each other around a table. On the other side of the aisle there were two single facing seats, also with a table. Ten seats altogether, wide enough to be comfortable, and the two single seats actually swiveled. A small bar with a refrigerator and microwave took up the remaining space behind the single seats, with storage space for food supplies. Beyond this were two bathrooms.

Another section at the rear of the plane after the bathrooms had three triple bunks on one side and a storage area on the other. The last time we'd used the plane, I'd thought it strange to have bunks so tightly packed, and even stranger that metal grates locked in place over each opening. Who could sleep in such a closed space? Even sailors on a submarine had more room. Now I knew they were used regularly to transport unconscious Emporium Unbounded to the rehabilitation compound in Mexico. We'd captured eleven Unbounded and mortal Emporium agents last night, so those nine spots were overfilled on this trip. I was glad curtains covered the bunks.

After indicating one of the single seats to Benito, I settled in one of the four seats across the aisle, far enough away not to feel smothered, but close enough to keep an eye on him. I folded up the arm rest between the seats and turned sideways, lifting my feet onto the spare seat, staking out my space. With any luck, Ritter would be up in the cockpit with Chris, and Keene and Jace would take the other seats behind me so I could get some sleep. My nerves were jumpy, and since my acrophobia was never activated by flying, I guessed the jumpiness was from lack of rest. Unbounded didn't need a lot of sleep, but we did need some.

The nerves might also have a tiny bit to do with the fact that this was the first operation I'd been on since New York—and that day still haunted me.

"Uh, can I use the bathroom?" Benito asked with a grimace.

I sighed. "Not until the plane is in the air."

I already regretted allowing him to come along. But what other choice did we have? There was nowhere we could leave him to make sure he didn't go to the police, which would put Ava and Stella in danger. We'd have to do as Jace suggested and stash him someplace out of the way in Mexico until we finished whatever we needed to do. Because even though he'd been cleared by Marco, his reappearance at the palace on the night of the Emporium attack was too much of a coincidence for me. In my experience, coincidences were almost never a good sign.

CHAPTER 10

I SLEPT THE ENTIRE TEN-PLUS HOURS TO OUR DESTINATION, ROUSING only briefly when we stopped to pay respects to officials in Mexico City. Since our destination was a private airport south of Villahermosa, we had no choice but to land and pass through customs at the larger airport first, or risk being shot down.

Passing customs in our case basically meant an exchange of money. Though foreigners weren't officially allowed to bring arms into the country without a special permit, we had a proven, albeit expensive, system to secretly transport whatever we wanted into Mexico. Unfortunately, the stop meant more than a two-hour delay in our trip. Afterward, we would have been able to fly closer to our final destination outside Palenque, but the size of our aircraft limited our landing choices. Cort's smaller plane was far more versatile.

Upon first waking, I was dismayed that I'd forgotten to watch Benito, but then I caught sight of Ritter across from him playing cards.

Cards? I didn't know Ritter even played cards.

There was a lot I didn't know about him. Maybe I wouldn't

even like the real him. Maybe what was between us was simple physical attraction.

Though if it was simple, I'd like to know what complicated meant.

Someone chuckling nearby made me aware that I was not alone in my four-seat section. I looked over at Keene where he sprawled on the two seats facing me. "Don't worry," he said. "Ritter hasn't let him out of his sight. Either him or the woman."

"Woman? What woman?"

He grinned. "You snore, you know that?"

My hands clenched. "What woman?"

"That woman."

I sat up and looked behind me where he was pointing, craning my neck to see over the high-backed seats. My jaw dropped when I saw Mari lying on the two seats immediately behind me, curled in a fetal position. Someone had put a blanket over her. "How'd she get here?"

"That's what I'd like to know." Ritter rose and crossed the space between us. "After takeoff, she was just there. No one saw her get on."

Had she been there all along? I didn't think so. Chris and Benito had passed her location when they'd stored the food. And how had she been able to get here from Ava's? It didn't make sense. Unless the whole catatonic bit was an act and she was actually working with her husband and the Hunters. I rejected that immediately because her fear at the park had been real. However, she could have been hired by someone else.

Maybe even the Emporium.

I met Ritter's eyes and he nodded, obviously interpreting my expression and agreeing. No wonder he'd kept an eye on her.

I went to Mari, automatically doing an inventory of the weight my different weapons added to my body: pistol at my back, two knives on one thigh, extra knife at my calf, extra pistol on the other. Everything intact. I sat on the edge of the table opposite her two seats and leaned over, reaching for her shoulder. "Uh, Mari."

She jerked, her eyes flying open. "Trevor," she moaned.

Pain flew from her in waves, unfiltered. *Crap!* I slammed my mental shield shut. Apparently, my mind was back in top form, and touching her had opened an unexpected link. I saw nothing about Hunters or secret agendas, though she could be hiding that behind the more immediate emotion of loss. For a moment I felt dizzy.

"Mari," I said again, moving to the edge of her seat, helping her sit up. "How did you get here?"

Her gaze went past me to Ritter. "Thank you for the blanket." Then her eyes slid back to mine. "I don't remember." At least she was responding, which was more than she'd been doing before. She was wearing the same pants she'd worn to work yesterday, but someone had given her a clean yellow T-shirt.

"Does Ava know?" I said to Ritter.

"We radioed when she first—"

A terrified scream covered whatever else he'd been about to say. I jumped to my feet, turning to see Benito at the back of the plane past the bathrooms, one corner of the curtain over the metal bunks clutched in his hand.

"Damn it, Benito! What are you doing back there?" Ritter strode toward him.

"I need to use the bathroom."

Ritter snorted. "We said you couldn't unless we're in the air. Besides, you've already gone six times."

"But . . . they're all bloody! This one no has face!" Only it came out "Thees one," his accent deepening under distress. Benito stared at us in horror. "What kind of people are you? I change my mind. I no want to be involved."

"Shut up." Ritter yanked the curtain down. "You have no choice. Now go sit in your seat and stay there until we tell you, or you'll join them." He shoved Benito down the aisle. "Keene, don't let him move an inch."

Keene nodded, his eyes glittering in amusement.

"They no stink. Why they no stink?" Benito's voice rose to

a yelp as Keene's hand gripped his shoulder, pushing him into a chair.

Of course they didn't stink. Besides severing the three focus points of an Unbounded, the only other way to kill them is to lock them in a sealed container where they can't absorb nutrients until the tissue between focus points rotted completely, which could take years, given the Unbounded protective system. A miserable, painful way to die. Incineration didn't even work in most cases because the Unbounded body would burn to a hard, impenetrable shell on the outside, preserving the inner focus points for later regeneration.

Pushing the thoughts back into a remote corner of my mind that I reserved for nightmares, I said, "They aren't dead, or we wouldn't have brought them. Not all of them are even wounded that badly." The mortals, I meant, and someone had bandaged them.

Benito opened his mouth, but a glare from Ritter stopped him from saying anything more.

I turned back to Mari, who was staring vacantly again. *Great, just great.* I glanced over to see Ritter watching me, the mocking smile on his face telling me he knew exactly how Benito came to be our problem.

I flashed him a confident smile and sat beside Mari. "It's okay," I told her. "Everything is going to be okay."

Chris emerged from the cockpit. "We're about to have visitors," he announced.

"No worries. They're expecting us." Us with our strange cargo and weapons, Ritter meant.

We headed toward the door, which Chris was already opening. I checked my phone. Four o'clock local time, which gave us several hours before sunset. I went down the stairs after Ritter and Chris, followed closely by Jace. Sunlight met our gazes and the outside air felt warm compared to the controlled air inside the plane. Shielding my eyes as they adjusted to the brightness, I breathed in the aroma of lush vegetation, and for the first time in a month I felt warm. Maybe I'd make a habit of coming here during the winter. Or some other warm place. No way did I want to waste even another year enduring freezing temperatures. For now, I could definitely lose my camouflage jacket and the bodysuit under my jeans.

The area was deserted except for a small wooden building at the edge of the clearing next to the runway. Two vehicles thundered toward us across the dirt expanse that separated us from the building, kicking up dust behind them. One of the vehicles was a battered car, the second looked like an army surplus all-terrain vehicle with a raised green body, four large tires, and a green tarp that laced over the back half. Our ride, I assumed.

Jace's eyes lit up. "Now that's what I'm talking about."

"Is that an army Humvee?" Chris appeared equally fascinated.

"No. Similar, though," Jace said. "It's a Pinzgauer. An old one, but reliable from what I've read. Several European armies use them. The Swiss, for one. Brits, too. A lot of people call them Pinz for short."

"Cool," Chris said.

Even Ritter couldn't keep his eyes from the Pinz. "The cab and the bottom half of the back are armored," he told them. "I keep it stashed nearby for when we need it."

Men and their toys. "I thought we were going low profile," I muttered.

At the top of the stairs, Keene laughed. "Good point. It'll be great off-road, but we'll be rather conspicuous in town."

"The scientists we're looking for don't live in town." Ritter flicked a glance toward the men who'd parked several yards away and were climbing from the vehicles.

"No, but if my information is correct the senator should be in Palenque by now," Keene said. "We need to get to him before the Emporium does. There are far too many ways he could be hurt or disappear in the jungle."

"Senator eaten by a croc." Jace pretended to read newspaper headlines. "Are there even crocs here?"

Ritter nodded. "Big crocs. Scorpions, too."

"And lots of men with big guns," Benito said, poking his nose out the plane door. When Ritter scowled at him, he lifted his hands to chest level. "I'm jest sayin'. They should leave *you* alone, but if an ordinary person showed up with all that stuff you brought, one of the drug cartels would make sure they didn't have it long." He cast a backward glance. "Can I come out? Because it's creepy in here with all those d—"

Before he could finish, Ritter made a motion with his finger and Keene grabbed Benito, practically hauling him down the stairs.

"You can stay out," Ritter said, "but don't say a word. Now start unloading."

"Wait. I can translate." Benito stumbled toward the hold.

Keene looked at Ritter, who shook his head. "We don't need him for that yet. We can get by here."

"I really think I should come with you guys." Chris stepped closer to Ritter, his voice an undertone. "What use will I be hanging out here?"

"You're going to make sure we have a plane to come back to." Ritter sounded weary, and I knew it was a conversation they'd revisited several times. If I'd been awake during the flight, I would have told Chris to save his breath. Ritter was as immovable as the mountains and twice as hard as any stone. "You're also going to make sure those men don't see our, uh, interesting cargo while we unload it. When we come back, we may need to get out fast. So stay alert and keep your phone on."

I felt Chris's disappointment, but at the same time I was infinitely grateful to Ritter. One less mortal to worry about. One less family member to protect or to mourn.

The short, swarthy driver of the Pinz approached hesitantly, going directly to Ritter and handing him the keys. Ritter nodded his thanks.

"You leeve it like usual?" the man asked in barely understandable English.

"Yes," Ritter said.

"Muy bien." He bowed and backed away.

The other Mexican driver was younger and taller, his smile ready. The darkness of his skin made Benito look pale in comparison. "You want I should help unload?" His eyes wandered to where Keene and Benito had opened the hold.

"No." Ritter's answer was terse, and I had to agree. We could afford to pay a tip, but there was the little matter of eleven apparently dead or unconscious men to deal with.

The young man's face fell, but he flashed us a white smile. "Who ees dee pilot?"

Ritter thumbed at Chris. "Him."

"Come, señor. We have a beery nice siesta for you."

Chris hesitated, his eyes falling to Jace and me. I knew it was still hard for him, who had always been the elder, the protector, to leave us to go into danger without him, but he'd have to get over it.

"Keep an eye out." Jace stepped forward and clasped his hand. Chris nodded at me over Jace's shoulder, and I dipped my head in unspoken agreement to watch over him. Without another word, Chris turned and followed the Mexicans back to their sedan. I knew he was armed, and with the money we'd paid to land here, he should be perfectly safe. Not like the rest of us.

"What about her?" Jace pointed at Mari, who'd followed us outside but stood vacantly at the bottom of the stairs.

Ritter glanced after the receding sedan. "No," I said. "She comes with us. We need to get her to Dimitri. He'll be able to help her."

Ritter met my eyes. "And until then?"

I didn't really know. We knew Dimitri and Cort were tracking the scientists, but until they contacted us, we had no idea where they were. "Have you tried to call Cort?"

Ritter nodded. "No response. There aren't any phone towers around, though, and he could be too deep in the jungle for the satellites to work. Let's get going and then we'll try again."

"Come on, Mari." I put an arm around her and began walking toward the Pinz.

"I don't know how we're going to fit all those unconscious Unbounded inside with all our gear," Jace said behind me. "That thing only holds eight in the back comfortably. And that's conscious people."

Ritter took out his phone. "We've done it before, but today we won't have to. By the time we get the Pinz loaded, our people will be here and we can hand off the prisoners." He didn't sound happy about leaving them to others, and I could understand why. If our Unbounded captives escaped or were rescued before they arrived at the prison compound we shared with the other Renegades, it'd make the attack in Portland—and especially Gaven's death—that much worse.

"Good." Unlike Ritter, Jace sounded relieved not to have to cram in with the bloodied Emporium agents.

Ritter hesitated a second and then said, "Erin?"

"What?" I glanced at him, barely catching the keys he lobbed in my direction.

"Turn it around, would you? It'll be easier loading if you back up. Make sure you do it at an angle to block the view from that building, but far enough away that a van can squeeze near the stairs." His grin was a challenge, one that my Unbounded genes took to immediately. *I bet you can't do it,* it said.

I'll take that bet and raise you five. "Sure thing."

After settling Mari in the roomy passenger seat, I brought the Pinzgauer to life and turned it around, revving the engine to make a point. To my surprise, its maneuverability belied its size. Okay, I liked it—a lot. I put it into place with a cloud of dirt and a flare I didn't know I possessed.

It helped that I could also see the vehicle from the back through Jace's eyes, the link between us comfortable and familiar. *That kid has to learn to protect his mind.* Remembering my fight with Ritter, I sent a warning pulse—*shield!*—and smirked when I glanced in the mirror and saw Jace jerk and trip over his own feet.

As we finish loading our supplies, a large gray van appeared and sped toward us on the runway. Ritter stood at attention between the plane and the Pinz, his favorite SA58 FAL assault rifle strapped across his chest, his eyes moving back and forth between the van and the jungle surrounding the airstrip.

Recognizing our vulnerability, I sent my thoughts out to the trees, probing for but not finding the bright pinpoints that signaled life. There were only smaller pinpoints, so many that at first I didn't realize what they were. They weren't as vivid as I expected, though their dullness appeared to result from their oneness with nature, rather than their smaller size. *Animals.* Yes, that was it. Not insects that didn't register but warm-blooded creatures with some degree of intelligence.

Keene took cover on the side of the Pinz, his hands also gripping a rifle. Taking his cue from the others, Jace stepped behind the plane's stairway, motioning to Benito. I eased next to them, my mind now going toward the van, which screeched to a stop several feet away.

"Two people," I told the others.

A slender, dark-skinned woman dressed in camouflage pants and a green tank top emerged from the passenger door, her long black hair twisted into countless small braids. I knew her at once: Tenika Vasco, Unbounded, originally from Angola. Two months ago, she had taken lead over the Renegades in New York after the death of their former leader. I'd only met her a few times, but I liked and respected her. Ritter and I stepped forward to meet her wide smile.

"Tenika." Ritter nodded and extended his closed fist in the traditional greeting.

"Ritter."

"They didn't tell me you'd be here."

"I wanted it to be a surprise." Her words held the merest hint of a Portuguese accent. Ignoring his fist, she moved closer and planted a kiss directly on his mouth. I knew this was how she teased him, and that she was one of the few people Ritter had ever let inside his emotional barriers, however momentarily, but that didn't stop the ridiculous surge of jealousy inside my chest. Part of me wanted to pull out a gun and growl at her.

Ritter chuckled. "So what *are* you doing here? Any news on the missing Renegades?"

"Afraid not. We had a run in with Emporium agents last week, and I'm here making a drop, same as you. I needed to get away, so I left Yuan-Xin in charge and came myself. I haven't had a break in months."

I had to stop myself from grimacing. Since when was transporting prisoners a break?

"When I heard what happened at your lab," Tenika continued, "I offered to help transport your prisoners to save you time. I know Stella was really counting on that research, and we were here anyway."

"Thanks for staying."

"Can't have them getting away. And the compound really doesn't have enough personnel for pickups, though they did spare someone to help me find you." Tenika jerked her head toward the van, indicating her companion. "Told him to stay inside until I checked you all out. He's got a cannon in there that makes your rifle look like a child's toy. He's covering me." She winked and turned in my direction, extending her fist, and I hit my knuckles into hers with a tad more force than I'd intended.

"The Emporium's using the Hunters to track us," I said.

She nodded. "Ava filled me in, and I've spread the word. I'm pretty sure that's what happened to us last week, though we didn't realize it at the time. Everyone will be on the lookout." Everyone meant our ninety or so Renegades scattered in different cities across the world.

"Hey, Jace." Tenika offered him her fist.

"What, I don't get a kiss?"

She laughed. "Naw. You're still wet behind the ears." Her gaze went beyond him to Keene. "Who's your friend?"

I made the introductions, but Keene apparently was in her files and she scowled at his name. "I thought I knew you. Why are you here?" Her voice held command, and I felt the urge to answer, though she hadn't addressed me.

Keene laughed. "Your hypnosuggestion won't work with me. Not if I don't listen long enough. You might say I've developed an immunity. However, rest assured that I've left the Emporium."

She regarded him with narrowed eyes for several long seconds, as if weighing his words. Then she turned and motioned to the van. The driver's door burst open and a broad man with unruly blond hair and a ready smile emerged. Definitely Unbounded. He wore a pistol at his hip, but he must have decided to leave his "cannon" inside the van.

"Hello. I'm Irwin Stafford," he said to me after he greeted Ritter. "I help run the facility here." Though he was obviously Australian by his accent, his ruddy skin was tanned even darker, making it almost impossible to tell his age. If I had to guess, I'd say late thirties, which for Unbounded meant three or four hundred years old.

"Nice to meet you." I extended my fist.

Irwin smiled again. "The pleasure's all mine. We don't see a lot of new faces around here. At least not those on our side."

"Wait, wait, wait!" Benito inched forward from where he'd been crouching out of Tenika's sight next to the airplane stairs. "I know you. You're that crocodile hunter guy. Aren't you? You look just like him. Well, maybe a bit younger. But . . . aren't you supposed to be dead?"

Irwin sighed. "Now you know why I'm hanging out at the prison facility. Everyone recognizes me everywhere else. I hope it's not too much longer until people forget. Good thing there's a lot of interesting wildlife down here, or I'd be totally bored."

He wasn't the only famous Unbounded whose death had to be faked when the lack of aging could no longer be hidden. President Kennedy, his son, and Tenika's second in command Yuan-Xin—once known as Bruce Lee—were only a few of the others I'd heard about. Some had been rushed out of sight only to die for real in battles against the Emporium. Irwin's exile was his own fault for allowing himself to become a celebrity.

"A new name might help." I wondered if he still craved the limelight.

He grinned. "Yeah. Guess I kind of got attached."

"So can I see you wrestle a croc?" Benito asked.

"Uh, I don't think so." A hardness filled Irwin's face as he refocused on the task at hand. "So where are your passengers?"

"Inside the plane." I wanted to ask him the reform rate of his prisoners versus how many Emporium Unbounded they had to try and execute for their crimes, but I found I didn't really want to know. Not yet.

Ritter and the others were already heading up the stairs, and I followed quickly. The faster we got this over with, the faster we'd warn the senator and get on with the search for the scientists and their research. I wanted to bring Stella good news for a change.

Ritter's step faltered near the second set of four seats, but he recovered quickly and continued on to the back. No one else appeared to notice. I was almost afraid of what I might find inside, yet nothing prepared me to see Mari curled across two seats, once more asleep.

Jace stopped and stared, his eyes going to me. "Wasn't she in the Pinz? How did she get in here?"

There was only one answer that made sense in my mind. Mari might be a shifter, a teleporter who could travel through space. She was talented in math, and it was logical that tough equations would be needed to shift, but to actually suspect it was happening under my nose was nothing short of miraculous. If I was right, her existence might signal a new era for Unbounded. Shifting hadn't been seen for a thousand years.

"Better help them," I said to Jace. He nodded and hurried down the aisle.

Belatedly, I remembered Benito and went outside to check on him, but he'd settled in the back of the Pinz on one of the bench seats that lined each side of the vehicle. When he spied me staring down at him from the plane, he shook his head and crossed himself. "I don't touch dead people."

"I told you they're not dead."

He snorted. "They look dead."

"Stay right there."

"Where else would I go?" He gave me a bland smile. "I have no money."

I'd have to see that he remained without funds for as long as we were here. At least that way he'd be close where I could watch him—until we dumped him someplace safe.

With two extra hands, the transfer of the captives went quickly, though Irwin insisted on giving them all an additional dose of sedatives.

"That's going to knock them out for another few days," Keene mumbled.

Tenika shot him a glance. "What's that to you?"

"Nothing." But his scowl didn't vanish.

"Things sometimes go wrong," Irwin said, as though commenting on the weather. "Occasionally, we have to stash them and retrieve later. With only two of us to transport this many, we'd be fools to leave anything to chance."

The idea of hiding the captives under a bush was ludicrous, but not as much as it would be in, say, downtown Portland. It was Irwin's turf and he seemed to know his business.

"Just make sure you keep track of which ones are mortal," I said. "Don't give them too much."

"Uh, I'm guessing those would be the ones with mortal written on their foreheads," Irwin said. "In permanent marker, no less."

Who on earth did that?

"We know you don't have a sensing Unbounded to help you tell them apart," Ritter said, avoiding my eyes. That man never ceased to surprise me.

Irwin grinned. "We usually just wait to see which ones heal fast."

"Works for us." Tenika slapped Ritter firmly on the back with a familiarity I envied. I wondered what stories she might tell of him if we had more time. "Luck."

"You, too." There was real warmth in Ritter's voice.

"Call if you need help. Like Irwin said, we could stash these guys in a swamp somewhere. The crocs might do us a favor."

We all laughed, though ultimately I knew our attempt to reform the Unbounded we captured was one more thing setting us apart from the Emporium. I watched with relief as the van sped away.

"Don't know what they want with dead people anyway," Benito complained from the back of the Pinz.

Ritter pretended not to hear. "Erin, better get Mari out of the plane so we can close the doors. Try to keep an eye on her until we can find someone to watch her. Jace, you'll ride shotgun. Stay alert. Keene, you're in the back with the others."

Keene smiled lazily. "Aye, aye, captain." He winked at me. "Any time."

Ritter scowled and headed for the Pinz. "Can I drive?" Jace asked, running along beside him. "Please?"

Within a few minutes we were speeding down the dirt road. Well, not speeding, exactly, because the Pinz could go no more than just under seventy miles an hour, but with the vegetation whipping by, it felt faster than that. Every now and then Jace had to slow the vehicle as he drove over rocks, rotted logs, and brush, or skirted the deeper potholes and puddles of mud.

Mari slept on one of the bench seats, and I sat next to her, making sure one of the sudden lurches didn't throw her to the floor. Keene and Benito sat opposite me making a late lunch of food they'd raided from the plane.

The interior was open to the front cab, and I raised my voice to address Ritter. "Any word from Cort and Dimitri?" I'd seen him talking on his phone a few moments earlier, half leaning out the window to find a clear connection with the overhead satellite, but he hadn't shared any information. I was tempted to try to contact Cort myself but even if I could get a satellite signal through the thick canvass, on ops like this we weren't supposed to bypass our leader.

Ritter turned in the passenger side seat, where the FAL rifle in his hands looked a part of him. He stared at me blankly for a few seconds as he digested my words, as though having difficulty pulling his thoughts back from wherever they had been.

I thought of our fight on the rooftop, the feel of his body pressed against mine. *Stop,* I told myself.

"No word yet," Ritter said finally. "Every time I've tried, there hasn't been an answer. I'll call again now."

So he hadn't been talking to Cort. Then who? Not Ava because he'd called her from the plane. Maybe it had something to do with where he'd been for the past two months. Until that moment, I'd told myself he'd been following leads to find the missing Renegades, but now I wasn't so sure. Ava told me he took off regularly, returning only to train our group or to participate in missions. He could have an entire life that no one knew about. He certainly had one that didn't include me. That meant I needed him like I needed to get hooked on curequick.

Holding the phone out the window to connect better, Ritter dialed. I edged closer to eavesdrop, nearly losing my balance as Jace drove over some washboards. I glanced back at Mari, but she appeared undisturbed. It wasn't a natural sleep, though, and I worried for her state of mind. Anyone could break under so much trauma. The sooner we could get her to Dimitri and his healing hands, the better.

"Good, you answered," Ritter leaned out the window to talk, his voice rising to carry over the sound of the engine. "I was beginning to worry. Say again? Oh, we're traveling toward Palenque. We hoped you'd be nearby. Where are you?" A long pause. "Any news?" Ritter's neck tensed. "They after you now? Okay, send me the coordinates. We'll get there as soon as we can."

Ritter turned back to me, suddenly moving into my space—or his space rather, since I was leaning so far over his seat. I pulled back as Keene stepped up beside me, stooping as I was so our heads didn't hit the tarp overhead. "Well?" I asked.

Ritter frowned. "Cort and Dimitri have one of the scientists, but the Emporium beat them to the other, and he's the one who had the thumb drive with the research. Cort and Dimitri aren't far behind the Emporium, but their Jeep died on them."

"What else?" I didn't need my sensing ability to know there was more.

"I'm not exactly sure because he kept cutting out. But he's worried." Ritter looked past me to Keene. "We're going to have to meet them instead of heading directly to Palenque."

Keene shook his head. "I have to disagree. The senator's more important. If he's killed, his death could affect thousands."

"The one versus the many." Ritter's voice was hard. "That might mean something if the one wasn't family." His words chilled me because they so closely resembled my own feelings. I wanted to help the senator, but saving Bronson for Stella, even if only for the twenty or so years he had left of his regular life span, was more important to me at the moment. It was an emotional decision, but if we lost that emotion, didn't we lose the very thing that kept us human?

I placed a hand on Keene's arm. "If the Emporium has the scientist, we may all be heading to the same place anyway."

Keene nodded and moved back to his seat, picking up his discarded plate and tossing me a brownie wrapped in standard airline plastic wrap.

I slumped onto the seat next to Mari. "Thanks." It was the first food I'd had all day, and it felt comforting to bite into.

The interior of the Pinz was sweltering, and I was glad I'd ditched my extra clothing earlier. The brown tank was perfect, but the loose jeans chafed my waist. I should have worn my favorite jeans instead. For now, I pulled the jeans a bit lower on my hips.

I looked up to see Keene watching me, an unreadable expression in his eyes. He glanced at Benito on the other side of his bench, but the man had propped his feet up on one of our tent bags, his head back and eyes closed, his hands folded over his stomach.

Keene leaned forward, his eyes holding mine. "I've missed you."

"That's funny. I seem to remember annoying you more than anything."

"That, too." His grin sent warmth to my belly.

He didn't say more, or ask me if I'd missed him. That's the way Keene was. He didn't ask for anything, and he didn't make me feel as if I was losing myself. I leaned forward until our heads were inches apart. "I'm sure we'll have ample opportunity to annoy each other on this trip, don't you think?"

"I'm looking forward to it." Keene laughed, the sound coming a little too loud with my proximity, and I glanced at the front to see if they'd noticed. Ritter's gaze flicked toward us and back to the window again. A muscle twitched in his jaw.

"Holy crap!" Jace slammed on the brakes, throwing me into the supplies. "I don't like the look of this."

CHAPTER 11

JUMPING TO MY FEET, I PEERED THROUGH THE FRONT WINDOW. THREE huge trees had fallen over the dirt road, one lying on the other two.

"No way we're getting over that," Jace said. "And it'd take the rest of the day to get through even with our chainsaw. We'll have to go around. Hopefully we can find another road. I saw a break in the trees a quarter mile back, I think."

"Might be a trap." Ritter looked at me. "Erin, what do you sense?"

I'd been checking as we sped along, but now I climbed outside and did a deeper search. The vegetation framing the road had thickened and I suspected we were close to our original destination of Palenque, which seemed to be a gateway to the Lacandon Jungle, but nothing alerted my senses. There were numerous tiny life forces, but nothing large enough to be human. I was almost sure we were alone, but it was the "almost" that worried me. If Ava were here, she'd be able to tell for certain. Besides, my range didn't extend that far. What if Emporium agents or some worse danger lurked just beyond the trees?

I didn't realize how exposed I was until I noticed Ritter and Keene flanking me, both gripping their weapons and scanning the greenery. "There's no one out there," I said. "Not close anyway."

Ritter nodded. "We go back, then." The tenseness in his voice reminded me that every passing moment meant more space between us and the kidnapped scientist who held Bronson's possible cure.

Night came early in November, and even earlier in the jungle, but despite the increasing darkness, we found the break in the trees easily, and it turned out to be a rather passable, if narrow, road. Ritter wasn't happy about the foliage overhead, though, which made it difficult to follow the GPS coordinates on his sat phone. Fortunately, he was also equipped with a compass and there were enough breaks in the foliage to occasionally verify our position with the GPS.

"This might actually get us to Cort and Dimitri faster than that main road," Ritter called back to us at one point.

I might have been happy at the news, but something was bothering me. I couldn't put a name to it, but something *felt* wrong. "Stop!" I jumped to my feet and lurched to stand near my brother's shoulder. "I mean, don't stop, just slow down."

"But we're not going very fast now." Jace pointed to the speedometer. "Impossible in the darkness with all this brush."

"Do as she says." Ritter's voice was calm but firm. "Now."

Color leaked from Jace's face, but he nodded and did as commanded.

"There are people ahead," I said after a moment of searching. "They're really close." Their life forces were clearer with every passing foot. "They're not together, though. Scattered, unmoving. It's almost as if—"

"Ambush." Ritter didn't sound surprised. "How many?"

"Eight. That I can see." I hesitated before adding. "But my range isn't very far. There could be more."

Ritter's hand went to his door. "Erin, take over driving for Jace.

Keene and Jace, you're with me." He pushed the door open and jumped into the darkness.

That's right, leave the woman to face an ambush in the dark with only two helpless people for backup. But I trusted Ritter. Whatever was or was not between us, I knew he'd give his life to protect me.

Awkwardly, I slipped into the driver's seat as Jace opened the door and dropped from the Pinz. I glanced around, but Keene was already gone. He'd wakened Benito, who now scrambled toward the front.

"Where did they go?"

I explained the situation as clearly as I could. "Just roll up that window over there and lock the door. Then get in the back and cinch up that tarp covering the opening. Tie it down tight and stay still. Don't try anything. We're trained for this. We'll take care of you." I hoped I was telling the truth.

Blood rushed through my veins in anticipation. I drew my Sig and set it in my lap, needing both hands to keep the Pinz creeping through the rough terrain. I wasn't going even five miles an hour now. We approached the first hidden assailant, and belatedly I wondered how the men would find them. Worse, what if these were the Emporium agents and they had a sensing Unbounded with them who might be masking the presence of even more people hiding close by?

No. I pushed this thought aside. The Emporium had an agenda with the lab and the scientists. They wouldn't waste time creating traps unless they were certain they were being pursued, and Cort hadn't given us any indication of that. Besides, these life forces were bright, signaling unshielded minds, though I was too far away to decipher their emotions.

I drove slowly onward, passing three more people, once again hidden in the dark brush. When would they act? And where was Ritter? Wait. I could sense someone moving fast through the foliage, toward one of the people I'd passed. It was Jace, still having a problem masking himself. Concentrating harder, I also sensed Ritter and Keene, though the mental light emitting from their minds was considerably dimmer than Jace's signature, and at this range I couldn't tell one from the other.

I passed two more hidden watchers and was coming up on the last two when a stack of fallen trees blocked my path, resolving my curiosity about how they planned on stopping the Pinz. These weren't huge trees like those stretched across the larger road, but big enough that we'd have to get out to move them before continuing on.

I wished one of the others could communicate by sensing so I could tell them, but I'd have to trust that they knew their jobs. If I pushed hard, I could probably send a thought to Jace's mind—he might be within my range—but I needed to stay sharp and ready to use my ability against our attackers.

Taking my foot from the gas, I let the Pinz lurch to a stop before the log barrier. I left the engine running, hesitating to leave the safety of the cab because the second I did, I'd be a target. I didn't know if they intended to murder as well as rob us. It might not make a difference in the end. Better to wait.

A swarthy, dark-haired man carrying a huge assault rifle rushed the Pinz from the side, aiming his weapon at my closed window. He was short and wide, with muscles as large as Ritter's, his face brown and wrinkled by the sun. Definite mortal.

He blurted something in Spanish, and motioned with his gun. "He wants you to get out," Benito said from the back.

"No, he wants to dance," I retorted. To the man outside I shook my head.

Grinding out what I assumed were threats and curses, he let fly a few bullets into the air before pointing the gun back at me. Leaving my Sig in my lap, I brought my hands to my face, feigning fear.

He growled and reached for the door.

"Just a little closer," I murmured. "Benito, lock the door after me. Keep out of sight." Some distance away, I sensed Jace had reached his target, and I had to assume the others were equally in place. No way I'd let them have all the fun.

Thrusting my weight into the door, I slammed it into the man, feeling a satisfying *clunk!* He staggered backward, bringing up his rifle. Leaping from the cab, I fired as I rolled. One, two, three, bullets from my Sig before he went down.

Another figure emerged partially from the foliage, the bright life force signaling that he wasn't one of ours. I fired, and he dodged behind a tree. Hard to see what I was shooting at in the dark. Before I could move to find a better shot, bullets sprayed the brush behind me, drawing my attention back to the broad man, who apparently wasn't out of the game after all. I dodged, tossing one of my knives. He cried out and went still. More bullets, this time from the guy behind the tree. A shot ricocheted off a boulder near me, sending a shard deep into my hand. My gun dropped to the ground. I threw another knife with my left hand, but it slammed uselessly into the tree. My third knife followed.

Crap! I'd never been very good at throwing knives. I needed my backup .380 Ruger, but it was on my right calf, which made it awkward to grab with my undamaged left hand. More bullets plastered the ground. I scuttled backward, falling to my seat. Crab walking with one hand, past the fallen man toward the pile of logs. Finally, I managed to get out my spare gun. Only six shots. Without coming fully to my feet, I dived behind the logs and began shooting. More shots alerted me that similar battles were taking place out of my sight. I hoped we were winning.

My opponent abruptly ceased firing, though I doubted it was because of anything I'd done. I started to climb to my feet, but the crunch of brush from behind sounded as loud as a shout. I froze and looked around to see a man looming over me, his gun pointed at my face.

Great.

His gaze flicked to the large man sprawled on the other side of the logs and then back to me. His thoughts came to me jumbled and angry, images that spanned our different languages. As his stream of thoughts moved rapidly past me, I realized the fallen man was his brother. I saw flashes of the people they'd killed, women they'd raped, one only a child whom they'd later sold to militants. One thing for certain, he was going to pull the trigger. It wouldn't kill me, but it would hurt, and it'd stop me from helping Stella.

I lashed out. White fire to his mind. At the same time I lunged toward him, grabbing at the knife on his waist. No, not a knife. Longer and thicker. A machete. I fumbled getting it out. Wasted precious seconds. His mind recovered, and his finger started to press the trigger. I jabbed out with the machete.

Warm blood spurted over my hand as he curled toward me. I pushed him away, pulling the machete from his stomach in case I needed to use it again. The gun in his hand jerked but the shot went wide. Another shot rang out from somewhere behind me. My opponent stiffened, his gun falling to the brush. He breathed in wetly, his eyes wide and staring as he stood there, not understanding yet that he was dead. At last he fell, not gracefully or silently, but like a stiff log thumping onto rocky ground. I stood there for what seemed an eternal moment watching him, feeling the uselessness of a wasted life.

Ritter appeared at my side so silently that I hadn't heard him approach. "Don't ever, ever hesitate," he growled. "You're lucky he missed, and I didn't." He didn't ask if I was okay, for which I was grateful, but his eyes ran over my body, searching for wounds. He took my injured hand, but already the throbbing had diminished.

"It'll heal faster with stitches," Ritter said. "I can do it."

"Jace?"

"He's fine. Keene, too. He's good, even for a mortal." The grudging admiration in his voice might have had me mocking him in another setting. His eyes fell to the machete, which he took from my hand and cleaned first on a plant and then on the pant leg of the fallen man. "I've never seen anything quite like this. It's very old." He untied the leather scabbard from its previous owner and handed it to me. "You earned it."

I took it numbly and secured it around my waist, the decorative grass strands on the scabbard splaying over my jeans. Maybe

I wouldn't keep the machete, but it felt wrong to leave the weapon behind. I never wanted any man to use it against innocents again.

Jace strode into the clearing. "Any idea who these guys are?"

Time to go back to work. I strode to the big man I'd shot earlier. He was still alive, as I would have explained to his brother, given the chance. Kneeling beside him, I placed my good hand on his temple. Jace knelt beside me.

I found the lake of the man's unconsciousness and dived deep, searching his memories. Bypassing the ugly memories, especially the ones containing women or children. There it was. The young Mexican from the airport. I swam to the top and opened my eyes.

"It was the young guy from the airport. He told them our direction and that we were carrying valuable cargo. From what I could tell, they often pay him for information with the agreement that they won't approach his airport or attack the people who land there while they're nearby."

"What about Chris?" Jace clenched his fists.

Ritter somehow held the first aid kit in his hands. "He'll be fine. We haven't paid the guy the second half of our fee." He took out a needle and injected curequick into the back of my hand. It must have also contained anesthesia because I didn't feel the four stitches he threaded through my skin. "There, good as new," he said when he'd finished.

Keene came from the other side of the path, where he and Jace had tied up two of the attackers who'd survived the ambush. "I don't know who has jurisdiction here, but I'm sure these guys are wanted for a lot of crimes."

"We'll have Ava call in a few favors to get officials to pick them up," Ritter said. "Meanwhile, we'd better move these logs. Get that lazy Benito out here, would you? He has to pull his weight somehow."

I went to retrieve my knives, easily finding two of the three, but I gave the last one up for lost. I'd have to restock from the supplies. As I strode toward the others to lend a hand, a soft whisper penetrated my thoughts. Stopping, I scanned the trees around us.

Nothing.

I pushed my mind out to the jungle, searching for the whisper. Still nothing. At least nothing within range. Maybe if I pushed harder, though my head already pounded.

Hello, what's this? I'd found something—a whole lot of something. Whatever it was resembled the darker, one-with-nature life forces of the animals but was substantially larger. Human size.

"Erin, where're you going?"

I ignored Jace's call and continued past the blocked path and down the narrow dirt road. The jungle encroached on all sides, teeming with life and vegetation. I hadn't gone far when I reached a Jeep hooked up to a trailer. On top of the trailer sat a large bamboo cage, and crammed inside were at least a dozen people, including a wizened man and a young woman with a babe in her arms. They looked beaten and starved. Only the ancient man stood as I came into view.

"Come quick!" I yelled, turning to see that Benito had already followed me, apparently his curiosity getting the best of him. He'd found a brown fedora somewhere, and I suspected he'd taken it from one of the bandits. It rode low over his eyes, making him look rather mysterious.

Pulling off several duffel bags, I jumped up on the back of the trailer. "It's locked." I thought about searching the bandits for the keys or maybe shooting the lock off, but I didn't want to wait or risk hurting these people.

I pulled out the machete. The woman holding the baby gasped, her frightened eyes pleading. "I'm not going to hurt you," I said. "Benito, tell them I'm going to free them."

Benito rattled off something in Spanish, and one of the men replied. Benito shook his head. "Sorry. They don't speak Spanish exactly. I think I might have understood a word or two, but maybe not."

I began working on the leather ties that held the door in place. The leather was tough, but the machete cut through with little effort. By the time I'd finished, Ritter, Jace, and Keene had arrived.

I swung the door open and jumped down. For a moment, no one inside the cage moved. I reached out my thoughts, and received images of mistrust and fear.

After several silent moments, the old man hobbled to the door hesitantly, as if waiting for a trap. He spoke, and this time Ritter answered in the same musical speech. I turned and stared at Ritter. The old man shook his head and said something else now, and Ritter nodded.

"What's he saying?" I asked. "What language is that?"

Ritter glanced at me. "It's a Mayan dialect."

"You don't know Spanish but you know Mayan?"

"This dialect is commonly used in the villages near the prison compound. They were there long before the Spaniards came to the New World."

That's right. He'd been alive during the early years of American colonization. After his Change, he must have spent time in Mexico at the compound. That fit with his thirst for revenge. "So they're Mayans?"

"Actually, Maya," Ritter said. "Most scholars use Mayan only in referring to their language."

The more I learned about the world, the less I felt I knew.

Ritter's eyes fell to the machete at my waist. "He also says the machete you freed them with has been in his family for hundreds of years. Those bandits took it from him."

Naturally. The bandits wouldn't want them cutting their way out of the cage. As I started to unloose the leather ties to return it to the wizened Maya, the man extended his hand and barked three words, ordering me to stop. I understood his intent, if not the words. This close, I could feel his thoughts swirling, easily discernible, yet not in the same way as a regular mortal—though mortal he definitely was. The difference was intangible, nothing I could explain. A definite signature. Like the animals, these people were close to the earth that gave them life.

"Really, I don't want it," I said, pushing out an image of me giving it back.

A darkness fell over the man's mind, as if he'd erected a wall of granite between us. He spoke again, but I had no inkling of what he was saying. Before I could calculate the odds of a primitive native in a jungle being able to block me, Ritter spoke.

"He says it's yours now, as payment for freeing them. He insists upon settling the debt. He says the metal is special, no longer forged, and that it will protect you in your long journey."

So now I was supposed to believe in magic? Then again, why not? Magic could explain Unbounded abilities every bit as much as parapsychology and genetics. Besides, these primitive people believed a host of things that weren't true. Come to think of it, so did a lot of modern people.

"Well, he got the long journey part right." I inclined my head toward the old man. "Thank you." Odd that I felt better about keeping the machete already. He returned my nod solemnly.

The other prisoners had left the cage and stood at the edge of the clearing. They looked tired and hungry, and I wondered if we had enough supplies to feed them. But already, they were easing into the jungle, disappearing before my eyes, as though becoming part of the growth around us.

Jace opened his mouth to protest, but I shook my head. "Let them go. They know the land. They'll be fine now."

"The bandits sell them to the militants as slaves," Ritter said. "You probably saved their lives."

Jace took a step toward me. "Hey, can I see that machete?"

"Later," Ritter said. "We need to get going."

"I'll follow in their Jeep," Keene said. "That way maybe once we hook up with your friends, I can head out to Palenque to warn the senator." Keene looked at Ritter as he spoke, the words not quite a question.

"Good idea." Ritter turned on his heel as Keene began unhitching the trailer from the Jeep.

Deciding I'd better check on Mari, I hurried back to the Pinz. To my relief, she was still inside, though no longer asleep. She sat on the bench gazing into nothingness.

"It's okay," I told her. "We're almost there."

No answer.

Ritter grabbed a sledge hammer from the tools we'd brought and started off again.

"Where are you going?" I asked. While I'd been freeing the prisoners, the men had cleared the logs enough that we should already be able to pass.

"To take care of that cage." His eyes met mine, leaking emotion I couldn't sense from his blocked mind. "You and Jace bring the Pinz and meet me there."

Taking care of the cage. He was right, of course, which meant that maybe I didn't have to worry about him being so focused on revenge that he would endanger the mission. If he could think about destroying the cage in an effort to prevent more slave-runners from taking advantage of it, his head was on straight.

So what did that say about us?

Probably nothing. Trust had to go both ways, and I still wanted to know about those missing months. But right now I had to focus on Stella and finding that research.

"Come on, Jace," I said. "Hurry up, or I'll drive."

CHAPTER 12

THE NIGHT GRADUALLY THICKENED UNTIL I FELT I HAD NEVER experienced darkness before. The rumble of the engine drowned out the mysterious calls and growls emanating from the jungle, but I knew the wild animals were out there watching us. Something followed us for several miles. Probably a jaguar, according to Ritter.

Mari sat at the end of our bench, wedged in behind Ritter's seat, with her knees up to her chest and her arms around them. She looked forlorn. Every time I tried to touch her, I experienced a range of emotions that left me wanting to vomit. There were so many things I wanted to ask her, especially about her ability, but she was in no condition to respond, much less make any sense.

When Benito had seen how quickly the wound in my hand was healing with the curequick, he'd crossed himself several times, and when Jace had slowed down over some thick brush encroaching upon the road, he'd leapt out of the Pinz to ride with Keene. I wasn't offended. Much.

Less than thirty minutes later, Cort and Dimitri appeared abruptly in front of the Pinz, and Jace nearly ran them over before

Ritter ordered him to stop. It was near six o'clock, a mere two hours after our initial landing and less than eighty-five minutes since we'd left the plane. It seemed much longer.

Cort Bagley stepped forward as I jumped out the back to meet them, his piercing blue eyes locking onto my face. He cleared his throat before speaking. "Glad you made it in one piece," he said, enveloping me in a hug. "There are some nasty bandits in these parts." He had short, muddy brown hair and was of average height for a man, slightly taller than Dimitri. His face was ordinary, almost nerdy, but like all Unbounded, the self-assurance he exuded made him attractive, although I considered him another brother. I hadn't realized how I'd missed him.

"Yeah," I said. "Bandits. Who knew?" I left him to greet the others and turned to Dimitri.

Dimitri Sidorov had lived over a thousand years and was by far the oldest of the Unbounded in our immediate group. A short, broad man with longish dark brown hair, a mustache, and intense brown eyes, he exuded an animal attractiveness. Like Cort, he dressed in dark canvas pants and a T-shirt, but his clothing looked somewhat more attractive on him, as if the style had been designed for his breadth. Lately it had been other, less noticeable things about him that fascinated me: the wide oval shape of his eyes, his narrow nose, the way his jaw twitched when he was forced to confront something he wanted to reject. These were traits I shared with my birth father.

He hugged me like he meant it. Though he'd never been a real father to me, he was one of the most thoughtful and considerate Renegades I'd met. Perhaps it was the bedside manner he'd cultivated over his years as a physician. Perhaps it was all the women he'd loved and buried. Perhaps it was because he was in love with Ava and didn't yet seem to know it.

"How's Ava doing?" he asked. With the attack and everything that was going on, he meant.

I shrugged. "She's Ava."

He chuckled. "Right."

Beyond him, Cort was talking to Keene. There was a strong familial resemblance, and I wondered how their father felt, being a member of the Emporium Triad, to have two sons defect—especially Cort, an Unbounded who shared his ability in science. Maybe he had so many children it didn't matter.

"Look, we've brought Mari," I told Dimitri. "There's something wrong with her. She was there at the attack, and she saw her husband after he'd been killed."

"He can look at her as we go," Ritter said. "We need to catch up to those Emporium agents."

"I'm afraid we won't be able to track them in the dark." Cort detached himself from his brother and walked toward us. "The good news is they won't be able to go far, either. They had a Jeep, same as us. Even with headlights, there's no way they can continue safely on this terrain, unless they're heading to a main road, and that's not the direction they were going. My guess is they'll make camp. They can't have more than forty-five minutes on us. Unfortunately, we have more to worry about than just the research and the man they took."

Ritter's brow furrowed. "What do you mean?"

"It's better you hear it from the research scientist, the one we found. I'm still not sure how the whole thing works." It was an admission many Unbounded might not make, but Cort didn't need any false confidence.

"Bring the scientist," Dimitri told him. "The rest of you can begin setting up the tents. I want to look at Mari."

Though a part of me was as anxious to get going as Ritter, I was relieved that he'd examine Mari now. The image of her vacant face never left me.

As we approached the back of the Pinz, my brother's voice carried to us, softer than I'd ever heard it. "It's going to be all right, you know. All of this is a shock, but you're special, and you'll be doing things many people only wish they could do." A pause. "I'm really sorry about your husband, that you found him that way. And I'm sorry for what he did to you. Not all men are like him.

There's a lot you can trust. Dimitri, for one. He's the doctor. And Cort, and Chris, and . . . and me."

I lifted up the tarp opening to find Jace sitting next to Mari, a flashlight in his hand. "You left her in the dark," he told me.

In my rush to bring Dimitri to Mari, I hadn't even considered the dark or how being alone might affect her. That Jace had been sensitive enough to remember Mari told me he was finally growing up a little.

"The dark might actually be soothing." Dimitri swung himself up. "As long as she feels safe here." He stepped over several bags as Jace relinquished his seat next to Mari.

Ritter appeared at the back of the Pinz as I climbed inside, reaching for the duffels holding the tents and tossing one to Keene. With a pitying glance at Mari, they both disappeared.

Dimitri took Mari's hands. "Hello, Mari, I'm Dimitri Sidorov, one of Stella's friends. You look a little like her. You know, she's been waiting a long time for you to join us. We all have. I'm very pleased to make your acquaintance."

Mari stared at him, her brown eyes reflecting the glare from Jace's flashlight. She didn't speak, but she seemed aware, which was more than she'd been for the past few hours.

"I'm just going to touch your head now." He brought up his hands, laying the palms on her cheeks, sliding up to her temples and back into her hairline. She didn't flinch, but after a moment her eyes closed. "There now," Dimitri said softly. "The pain is going away. Relax. You poor child."

Dimitri remained in that position for much longer than I expected. After a few moments more, Mari let go of her knees and slumped to the side. Dimitri helped her lie down on the bench seat. "Sleep, child. Things will be much better in the morning." He replaced his hands on her head, his face intent.

I looked at Jace, who shrugged.

At last Dimitri withdrew his hands. "I can't see her thoughts as you and Ava can, but I can feel the wound in her mind."

"Can you heal her?"

"If I had my drugs, it would be easier, but I can still do it. I've induced a sleep already. Now I will help her back onto the path." He reached out and took my hand. "Place your hand on her forehead. Tell me what you see."

I scooted closer, closing my eyes and reaching out with my thoughts. Mari's unconscious mind wasn't a lake, but a colorful meadow of grasses. I smelled flowers and earth and rain, though the sky was clear. Instead of bubbles, there were floating flowers, each one holding a memory. The more luscious the flower, the more enjoyable the memory. In the middle of the meadow, a deep, ugly gouge marred the beauty, emitting a dark haze that blotted out the brightness. Mari stood there on the edge, nearly falling inside the dark pit. Wilted, foul-smelling memory flowers pushed at her from behind, forcing her ever closer to her doom.

The ugly gouge had to be a representation that either she or I was creating, a visual representation of her pain and the terror of these past few days. "Should I take the memories?" I asked, telling Dimitri what I saw. I pushed at the memory in the park where she'd almost been raped, and sidestepped the one where she'd watched Ritter cut a man in two during the fight at the palace. Blood red tinged the hazy darkness around us.

"No," Dimitri's voice came to me from far away. "She must deal with them herself. She'll face worse yet in her life. She needs to grow stronger." His hands closed over mine, and I felt his strength, both mentally and physically. The gash in the land in front of Mari began to seal. Surprised, I sent the thoughts to Dimitri's mind.

"That is my ability," he said. "I can feel any wound and can lend my strength, healing part of it so that the patient will recover enough to take over healing completely and go forward, leaving either the physical illness or damaging memories in the past. But what an interesting representation." He didn't sound surprised, and I guessed that he and Ava had worked together to heal others like Mari. No wonder it was so easy for me to send the images to him.

Or maybe it was because we shared the same blood.

"How long until she's healed?" I asked.

"I can never be sure. But not long, I suspect. She feels determined to me."

Even as I watched, the representation of Mari pushed at one of the foulest memories. Not the one of her husband's death, but of the one where he betrayed her. She took a step forward, and the meadow in that spot healed even as I watched.

That's it, Mari. Be strong.

She didn't look my way, which was probably for the best. I walked away from the gloom into the light, the meadow vanishing as I released my touch and opened my eyes. Jace stared at me worriedly. "She's going to be okay," I told him.

He nodded. "I'd better help with the tents. You can stay with her."

"I'll stay with her," Dimitri said. "I shouldn't leave her for at least another ten minutes." Sweat beaded on his forehead, a sure sign of the toll his healing exacted from him.

There's always a price. I thought of the exhaustion my own mind had gone through the past few hours. At the same time, my headache wasn't as bad as I expected. A good sign that I was inching further along in my progress.

We left Dimitri sitting there with the flashlight in case he needed it. Outside, Cort waited for us, holding a glowing lantern. Next to him stood a lanky, distinguished-looking man with dark graying hair, who looked more like a tennis player than a scientist, except for the slightly hunched shoulders that told of hours peering into a microscope.

Cort cleared his throat as Ritter and Keene joined us. "This is Dr. Sven Hertenstein," he said. "He's a research scientist from Sweden, an expert on autoimmune diseases." He introduced each of us quickly and then addressed Hertenstein. "Tell them what you told me about your research."

"You mean the failed research?" Hertenstein asked in perfect British English. "The side effect?" Even the name sounded ominous. At Cort's nod, he continued, "As we reported last week, we have created a promising formula. At the very least it will extend your patient's life, but it may even be the beginning of a cure. However, during the testing several weeks ago, we found something very disturbing. So disturbing that while we made notations about the effect the drug had on our subjects, we didn't report it to you. My colleague and I felt it better to keep quiet and destroy what we'd made. Since it bore no relation to what we'd been hired to do, we felt it was in everyone's best interest."

I had the feeling he was trying to justify his action rather than get to the point, and I waved my hand impatiently. "What did this drug do exactly?"

He rubbed his long fingers together nervously, his light-colored eyes glancing from me to Ritter and back again. It was natural that he'd pinpointed Ritter as someone in charge, but I found it interesting that he seemed equally concerned with pleasing me. "It did suppress the immune system as we hoped, but it also suppressed the emotional and physical reactions our body makes when confronted with a moral choice. It causes psychosis. Basically, when given the drug, the patient has no sense of wrong and no ability to tell reality from a dream or, say, a computer game. The result is someone who will take a suggestion and follow it through simply because it sounds interesting. There's nothing left in the subject's brain to tell him it might not be a good idea. No stops."

His lips thinned as he paused and took a breath. "Let's put it this way. It would work well for an invading army—if you didn't mind that your soldiers killed just as many of each other as they did the enemy. It's untraceable because it imitates the body's natural immune system. Within hours the patient returns to normal, feeling as if he's been dreaming."

Ritter's eyes narrowed. "So what you're saying is if someone got a hold of this drug, they could use a person—any person—as a weapon. An uncontrollable weapon."

"But you destroyed it," I said. It made sense to me why they weren't excited to report their findings. Destroying the drug was the only moral option.

The doctor's face looked gray in the light of the lantern. "Our mistake"—he fumbled on the word—"was that we kept the notes. When the lab was attacked and began burning, we managed to save all our research on that special drive your programmer gave us, including those notes. We also took a large quantity of the base formula we use in our tests. It saves days of preparation and we knew how eager you were to have our new formula. My colleague kept it all with him when we split up because we were afraid I'd be captured when I went to make the call to your people. We planned to meet up later where we live in the forest. It's a remote enough place that we believed the research would be safe. However, when I got there, he was being forced at gunpoint to leave with those men."

"That's when we showed up," Cort took over as the scientist lapsed into silence. "We tracked them until our Jeep busted its axle."

I frowned. "I hate the idea of the Emporium having access to that drug as much as anyone, but they won't have time to analyze the data before we catch up to them."

Hertenstein shook his head. "You don't understand. At the lab, they killed our assistants. We only got away because we were at the other end of the building and someone turned on the intercom so we heard much of what was happening. The men who came wanted only to destroy our research. That much was clear. But something changed. I believe the only reason they kept my colleague alive was because he told them about the drug with the side effects." His head drooped. "I can't blame him really. The lab . . . the screaming . . . the threats . . . it was horrible."

Beside me, Keene shifted, speaking for the first time. "If Justine has that drug, her plan to assassinate the senator would be that much easier. She could grab anyone off the street, a kid or a police officer, and give him the senator's picture and an assault rifle. No covering up needed on her part. It'd be just another misguided youth who stole a gun and went berserk, or an underpaid cop with a grudge."

"That's right." Cort met his gaze solemnly. "Even more important, they could use it again and again—in schools, in government buildings, in subways, in meetings between government heads. The Emporium has been trying to create something like this, something untraceable for years. I know for a fact they've conducted tests in relation to anti-depression drugs—with some very gruesome results that get politicians across the country arguing about gun control, when in actuality the real culprit is their drug. If they get hold of this formula, it's the beginning of the end. With mass killings on the table, every government in the world would be forced to make concessions in order to protect their people. I believe the Emporium would take the leverage this drug would give them and announce their existence to the world."

That meant they would no longer work from the shadows. They would control everything and everyone.

CHAPTER 13

"THEN WHAT ARE WE DOING STANDING HERE?" I ASKED. "DARKNESS or no, we have to find them now. Maybe I can help—if we get close enough." I'd already cast my mind as far as I could into the jungle and had found nothing except animals.

Cort shook his head. "Uh," he said, pausing to clear his throat, "we've discussed it thoroughly and we're reasonably certain the Emporium will test the drug here in Mexico—and probably on Senator Bellars, since they seem to want so badly to kill him. But there is a bit of good news. The drug has an incubation period. Even with the base they stole from the lab, they'll need eight hours to prepare it. They'll also have to find supplies and a place to set up a lab. That means only a handful of villages within driving distance, or maybe even Palenque itself. If we wait until light, we can be sure we're on their trail, especially now that Ritter's here to track them. What we can't risk is going past them or the wrong way because then we would find them too late. As far as we can determine, we don't think they know we're here."

Ritter nodded. "We leave at first light then. I want everyone ready a half hour before."

"No." Keene shook his head. "I understand that we can't risk losing them, but we have two vehicles. Barring the possibility that they have a secret headquarters, which I admit they might have in some remote village, Palenque is the closest and likeliest place. It's also where Senator Bellars is. We need to warn him. He's done too much good to leave his safety to chance. Whether they try out this new drug or go with their original assassination plan, Senator Bellars is still at risk."

Ritter's black eyes glistened and the coiled strength in his body gave the impression he was about to pounce. Silence ticked by, and then he nodded. "You start now for Palenque. We'll give you enough ammo to protect yourself. Even with how slow you'll have to drive in the dark, you should make it there in a few hours. It's pretty much southeast of our current position. You'll probably need to do some backtracking until you find a good road."

Keene nodded, his gaze now going to his brother. "You could come with me."

Cort tilted his head as if seriously considering the offer. Finally, he spoke. "They have a large contingent of Unbounded. When we run into them, it's not going to be pretty. I'd better stay to help. But you're right that you shouldn't go alone. You may need backup." He looked at Ritter, his arched brow a question.

"We need Dimitri." Ritter's gaze hesitated on Jace for the merest instant before passing to me. "Erin, you go. And take Hertenstein and Mari. Stash them in a hotel somewhere before you check on the senator."

"What? No way," I said at the same time Benito whined, "What about me? I want to go."

"I'd like to stay," Hertenstein said. "I can handle a gun."

"No, you aren't trained for combat and we can't risk losing you." The way Ritter said it made me think he'd planned a separation all along, though perhaps he wouldn't have acted until morning, if Keene hadn't pushed the matter.

"I'm not going," I said. I could handle myself in a fight, and I could also tell when we were getting close to the Emporium agents and how many mortals there were versus Unbounded. No way was I going to allow Ritter's overprotectiveness to endanger the mission.

He grabbed my arm. "Excuse us a moment. Erin and I are going to have a chat."

"Fine." I pulled from his grasp and stalked toward the trees.

"Meanwhile," Ritter called over his shoulder, "one of you better get on the phone and try to reach Ava and see if she can aim the satellites away from this area. The Emporium will have satellite phones, just like us, and it's only a matter of time until they think of sending an electronic copy of the research back to Emporium headquarters."

"Already did that," Cort said, "except for the one satellite that you were using to find us, and that's directed away now. We also had a technopath watching for information to come through. He's still watching. We're pretty sure they haven't gotten it out, though there were several calls made from this area, so we have to assume they've been in contact with someone here—perhaps to whoever is watching the senator. That means they'll have a plan. But keep in mind that once they're closer to town and in range of a cell phone tower, all our eavesdropping and satellite adjusting won't do any good. We have to catch up to them before then."

"We will." Ritter's voice was a growl of suppressed anger that sent a shiver crawling across my shoulders.

I waited for him at the edge of the dirt road. Apparently, that wasn't far enough, and he passed me, going deeper into the darkness of the jungle.

"I can help," I said to his back. "You know that. I don't care about the senator." Not exactly true, but he'd get the point.

Ritter whirled on me, silent and deadly. "You *do* care about Keene."

It wasn't a question, but I felt compelled to answer. "Of course I do. We're friends."

His nostrils flared and his jaw clenched, as though struggling not to respond. Silence reigned for a moment, except for the croaking call of something in the trees. Ritter glanced back at the faded glow of the lantern. "Your *friend* Keene will need you to make sure he's not attacked by more bandits tonight. Or, worse, the Emporium. We have no idea where they are and if Keene should stumble across their camp in the middle of the night, he'll be dead—no matter how good a fighter he is. Truthfully, I'd rather send Jace, but he's a little rash. Plus, I'm still not convinced Keene is everything he pretends to be. You, I can trust to keep an eye on him. You're also familiar with Justine. If she's behind the attack on the senator, my bet is that she's not out traipsing through the jungle. Cort said they haven't seen her, and the sooner we know where she is the better."

I hated that he made sense. Justine always made her underlings do the dirty work. Well, anything dirty that required actual work. She stepped in only when she wouldn't break a fingernail. Regardless, she always seemed to delight in causing the suffering of others.

"You know," I said, scrambling for another excuse to stay, "it could be that Justine's presence here has nothing to do with the lab or the senator. Maybe she's here for another reason. Maybe she has something more to hide."

"Our missing people you mean? From the New York raid?"

I felt guilty at the slight hope in his voice. "Well, you didn't find any other sign of them these past months, did you?" Okay, so I was fishing just a bit.

"Not a trace. But I had some other—" Breaking off, he looked past me into the night. His expression showed nothing, but this hesitancy wasn't like him and I was tempted to try to push past his mental shields—not that I'd succeed. His eyes came back to me. "Either way, Keene needs someone to keep an eye on him. He used to work closely with Justine and that makes him suspect."

I didn't want to go with Keene. I wanted to find the research so I could take it back to Stella. I wanted to give her and Bronson another chance. "Maybe you're just trying to get rid of me so you can have your revenge," I said. "Kill as many of the Emporium as you can."

He was next to me so fast that I didn't see him move. He looked mean and angry, but his dark eyes also showed something more. Something I might translate as hurt if I didn't know better. "This isn't about revenge. It's about getting those files. I know how important your ability can be, but for a fight, I need the others more." He paused for several seconds before adding. "Besides, you are also too important to lose. You and Ava are the only sensing Unbounded the Renegades have left."

"I don't need your protection." I had half a mind to pull my new machete and try it out on him, though I knew it wouldn't do any good. He'd know it was coming and counter the move.

He'd know it was coming. So would Jace. And while Dimitri and Cort weren't gifted in combat, their many years of practice made them more valuable in a fight than I could hope to be for years. I had to believe that for Ritter the mission was everything, even above his thirst for revenge or his desire to protect me. Unfortunately, that meant sending me with Keene really was his best plan. Maybe he wasn't trying to protect me or make me pay for being angry at him.

"Erin." He was still next to me, closer than I wanted him to be. I started to step back, but his hand clamped onto my upper arm. "Why are you so angry at me? What happened when I was gone?"

"What happened? *What happened?*" Was I supposed to be grateful he'd asked? "Nothing really. Let's see. I learned how to fight, I helped set up a new headquarters, I spent eight hours every day at a mindless job so I could keep an eye on Mari. Oh, and yeah, I donated my heart to my father so he wouldn't die. Everyone was in the room when I woke up, except for the person who promised to be there." Was he really so stupid that he didn't know? I didn't want to be the weepy female pining for her mate, but a promise was a promise. How trust was built.

"So? You're awake and I'm here now."

Did he really just say that? No apology, no explanation, nothing? "You could have been dead for all I knew."

His grip tightened. "You're still thinking like a mortal. A hiccup lasts longer for a mortal than two months for us."

His words were a slap in the face. Was that all this was, a misinterpretation?

He sighed and this time his grip eased. "Anyway, something came up. A responsibility."

Was he going to tell me what? Because I was through asking. I met his stare impassively.

"I have a son."

"You what?" My perception of him careened in yet another direction. According to Stella, there'd never been any other romantic attachment since his fiancée had been slaughtered and his own life saved. Then again, two hundred and forty years was a long time to be celibate. Maybe revenge wasn't always enough. Was the mother Unbounded? Jealousy stabbed through me.

"A foster son, actually. The great-grandson of a friend who was as close as a brother to me. I took care of the boy when he was a teen." Weariness settled over Ritter's face, weighing down his shoulders. "He was in trouble."

"Where?"

"London."

"I see." Pulling information from him was like learning how to throw knives—a ton of effort for not much result. I was debating whether or not to press further when Keene spoke from behind us.

"You about finished here? Because I'm leaving." I turned to see him, a dark shadow framed by the dim light of the lantern coming from the road behind him. "What's the final verdict? You going or staying, Erin?"

"Going," Ritter and I said together.

I started toward Keene, but Ritter, still facing me, stepped closer and grabbed my hand. We stood, arms touching, me facing Keene and the light while Ritter faced the darkness of the jungle. "Be careful," Ritter said. He hesitated before adding, "Please."

I looked up at him. His eyes were holes of darkness but in his mind was a slice of light, a door to his soul. I reached out mentally and was swept up in emotions and experiences. Rushing to the park in response to my emergency call, kissing on the rooftop, drowning in touch, despair at the distance between us. And hope. Hope as new and burning and bright as ever revenge had been. I'd never felt so much in a glance, not even with my sensing working at full thrust. Impossible to tell where his emotions left off and mine began. I wanted him. Not just him, but all of his past, his failures, his pains. Heat pulsed through me, enveloping me with sensation.

In less than an instant it was over. The door slammed shut, the light extinguished. Tension stretched, meeting at our hands like a bomb about to explode.

He released me. I moved forward at the same moment he stepped toward the trees. "Going to make the rounds," he said. "Tell Jace to finish the tents."

I was grateful he wouldn't be there to see us off. After what had happened in that moment, I didn't know if I'd be able to drive away or that he'd be able to let me go. Later we would talk. Later I'd learn about this foster son. Later, I'd forgive him, and he'd forgive me.

Keene was already heading back to the vehicles, and I had to jog to keep up. "So what was that?" he said in an undertone. "It's not like you to give in."

"I'm the only one who can keep track of you," I retorted. "So watch yourself."

He stopped abruptly, and I banged into his arm. "Do you love him, Erin? Because centuries is a lot of commitment. I know how most of the older Renegade Unbounded are. Old-fashioned to a fault. Like my brother."

"Not you?"

"What does it matter? In sixty years I'll be dead. I'm not even in the running."

I wondered what that was supposed to mean. Emotions emanated from him, ripe for the taking, but my senses were so shaken and raw already that I didn't dare reach out to determine his real meaning, even though he was apparently extending an invitation.

We both started walking again. "I'll need my duffel," I said.

"Already in the Jeep."

Apparently, I'd been the only one certain I'd be staying.

"Hope you don't mind sitting with Mari in the back," Keene added. "She's still out and she'll need to lay her head on your lap. It'll be tight with you two and Benito in the back."

Given a choice, I would have preferred sitting with the Swiss doctor, but Benito was still my duty. I hoped he began pulling his weight soon, or I'd never live it down. "That's fine."

"Oh, and Cort wants a peek at that machete. I told him none of us recognized the metal." He gave a short, mirthless laugh. "That's my brother for you. Always the scientist."

The others were standing around the Jeep, except for Mari, who I surmised was still inside the Pinz. I pulled the machete from its scabbard and handed it to Cort. "You wanted to see this? The native who gave it to me said it was very old." I turned to Dimitri. "Anything special I need to do for Mari?"

"No. She should be a lot better when she wakes up. She's a strong young woman."

"Good." She'd have to be, or we'd lose her sooner rather than later. "Look, there's something I need to ask you before you go." I took a few steps away from the others, and he followed me.

"Is it about Ritter?" Dimitri asked, his voice teasing. "Don't judge the boy too harshly. I assure you he'll mellow in a hundred years or so—if he lives that long."

Boy? Only Dimitri could call him that. "It's not Ritter." Actually, I'd love to hear more, but there wasn't time. Besides, though Dimitri had never been anything to me but kind, I wasn't ready to expose my inner feelings to a man who hadn't even told me he was my biological father.

"It's Mari actually. She keeps appearing in places that she simply couldn't be. I leave her at Stella's with Ava and then suddenly she's with us in the plane. Or one minute she's in the Pinz and the next she's back in the plane. She doesn't seem to know how she got there. I thought the shifting ability disappeared."

"It did." Dimitri glanced back toward the Pinz. "If she has the gift, it will be a huge boon to the Renegades."

"But how do I keep her where she's supposed to be?" The fact that he was ready to consider it told me more than anything that I was probably right. "If she's doing it without awareness, how can I stop her from getting herself killed?" I felt ill when I thought about her suddenly appearing in the midst of a fight like the one we'd had with the bandits.

Dimitri's brow furrowed. "Well, typically shifters are limited to places they've visited. Or occasionally they can find certain people."

"She'd never been to the plane before."

"No, but she spent a lot of time with you. It's possible you've forged a link."

"So she was searching for me subconsciously."

"Perhaps. Or it might be kind of similar to what happens when you're sparring with Jace, the way you can sometimes tell what he's going to do, as if you also have the combat ability. Cort and I were talking on the flight here, and we think you're doing that because of your close connection with your brother, borrowing his gift, so to speak. We want to do some tests because if it's true, it may be possible for you to use that in battle, and not just from your brother, but from anyone with the ability, especially if they let you into their minds willingly."

"Which would be hard to do if there are sensing Emporium Unbounded around."

Dimitri nodded. "There are drawbacks. But all our abilities stem from our brains, even the ones that seem purely physical, so theoretically, a sensing Unbounded should be able to access the abilities of others. If only partially."

"You think I used Mari's ability to bring her to me?" I only wished I could be so strong. "I think I'd know if I did something like that."

He shrugged. "Or it could have been all her."

Had I been thinking of Mari when we'd boarded the plane? It didn't really matter because no way was my range that far. She must have acted on her own.

"Now that Mari's on her way to recovery," Dimitri continued, "I think the way to keep her safe is to explain it to her and warn her to be careful. We have no idea what distance or other limitations apply, but it will likely hold to the rules of physics." He chuckled and added, "Or physics as people like Cort understand it. Once we get home, he'll be able to set up some short experiments to teach her the basics. He'll be in heaven with so much new information to record."

I stifled a laugh. "That's an understatement. Just wait until he learns about Oliver."

"What about Oliver?"

I shook my head. "Later." There was much we'd have to leave for later, including the most important conversation Dimitri and I would ever have. "I'd better go before Keene takes off without me and gets himself killed."

Dimitri nodded. "Go."

I was both glad and sad that he didn't warn me to be careful. Did it mean he trusted me, or that I was just one more Renegade to him, equal in importance to all the rest?

Why did I need more?

I went back to the Jeep to find everyone who was going with us inside except Mari. I was glad the vehicle didn't have a top or I might get claustrophobic. Pulling on a lightweight jacket from my bag, I zipped it all the way up. Though the night wasn't chilly, it was definitely colder now without the sun, and the wind hitting us in the Jeep was bound to lower the temperature further.

Jace appeared at my elbow. "Take care." My brother's voice sounded excited, as though anticipating the fighting that would come.

I knew it was in his nature, that his ability ached to be used, but I also remembered how he'd thrown up after seeing the dead

Hunters, and that worried me. Yet he'd more than held his own in last night's violent battle with the Emporium and also during our encounter with the bandits.

"You, too." It was difficult to leave him. For the first time I wished, however briefly, that he hadn't Changed, that he was still living an ordinary life away from so much danger.

We left it at that. Jace and I had always been close; we didn't need more. Definitely no last minute pleas to be careful—we both knew that neither of us was likely to be overly cautious, so there was no point.

Cort put away a magnifying glass he was using to study the machete and handed it to me. "It's been several hundred years since I've seen one of these. The last time was in Jerusalem. It's very rare. I'm not sure how one would appear here, though, or what the connection might be."

"What's it made of?"

He shook his head. "I couldn't tell then when I tested it, and I still don't know. Not even the pattern in the metal is familiar." That was part of his scientific ability, to see and understand how things acted on an atomic level. "With the equipment we have today, I might be able to learn more."

I grinned. "Maybe you'll prove Ava's theory of aliens being responsible for the Unbounded gene."

"I doubt it. What I can tell you is that there's a legend that goes along with these blades. They can only freely be given to a new owner. If one is stolen or taken by force, it will eventually turn on its holder."

I shuddered, thinking of the man I'd sliced. In his case it had been true.

"Good thing that old man gave it to you," Keene said from the Jeep. "Now would you get in so we can go?"

Cort rolled his eyes. "I wouldn't put too much stock in legends. They often have origin in a bottle of cheap wine." Always the gentleman, he helped me into the Jeep.

Dimitri arrived carrying a blanket-wrapped Mari and settled

her between me and Benito. Mari stirred only slightly as her head sank onto my lap. "Let her sleep as long as possible."

Cort held his fist out to Keene in farewell. Keene met it solemnly before starting the engine. I waved goodbye.

We didn't see Ritter as we left, though I sensed a life force hidden among the trees less than half a mile later. The thoughts were tight and dark, with no readable emotions, but I knew it was him.

CHAPTER 14

WITHOUT THE SATELLITES, WE HAD TO RELY ON A COMPASS AND the Jeep headlights to find our way, backtracking several times when the road petered out or became impassable. Dr. Hertenstein turned out to be a great help, especially as the rainforest thinned and he recognized his surroundings.

"We'll meet the main road soon," he said. "But there's a fork up ahead, if we're on the path I think we are."

"Good." Keene sounded tense, and I couldn't blame him.

His tenseness was why I hadn't told him we were being followed by an animal, who came closer every time we slowed to a crawl. Whether out of curiosity or because we looked like prey, I couldn't say, but I kept my reloaded Sig close.

As we navigated the crater-sized potholes near the fork, I sensed the creature again and reached out my mind, probing—finding an awareness driven by instinct, a consciousness so foreign that it seemed more alien to my experience than the jungle around us. More alien but somehow regal. I didn't want to have to kill it. I wished there were a way to communicate with the animal. One more thing to research.

Shortly later, we found the main road. "I hope it's not too far," Keene said. "We filled up partway from the gas containers in the Pinz, but all that backtracking cost us."

"We're not too far away now," Hertenstein answered. "Maybe forty-five minutes."

Keene sped up. "We should have enough gas then."

Mari was stirring finally, and I switched my attention to her. Now that we were going faster, it was unlikely we could be attacked by some large animal, or even by bandits. I hadn't sensed any human life forces since we'd left the others, not even the darker signals put out by the natives we'd met.

Mari lifted her head and gazed around, slowly taking in her surroundings. Her long hair twirled in the wind, though the silky strands didn't seem to tangle. "Where's Dimitri?" There was a touch of panic to her tone.

"He stayed back with the others. They're following the people who kidnapped one of our scientists. But you don't need Dimitri now. You're strong enough on your own."

She couldn't remember much of anything, so I filled her in on what had happened since the attack at the palace. Benito watched us with one eye, his head resting on the side of the Jeep, his stolen fedora clutched in one hand. I lowered my voice. I didn't really trust him yet, and the way he kept looking at my hand, nearly healed now, unsettled me. I'd have to get Keene to remove the stitches when we stopped.

"Look," I told Mari, "you seem to have a very unusual ability. Do you remember how you found yourself in—" I broke off. I had been going to say "the trailer," but maybe bringing up her husband's death wasn't exactly the best idea right now. "In the plane?" I finished.

She shook her head. "Not really. Well, sort of. I was looking for you, and there you were. It's kind of like remembering a dream. How did I get there?"

"You're what's called a shifter. I think it has something to do with the way you can calculate all those numbers without a machine.

Somehow you're moving through space. Teleporting. But try not to do it again until we experiment with your ability. That way you can make sure you don't end up somewhere dangerous." I didn't add that there was no one who could really teach her, that Cort would be using ancient documents and logic to make calculations. Then again, logic and numbers were things Mari understood.

Wonder filled her eyes. "That's so cool." She sounded like her old self again—no, more self-possessed. Her Unbounded genes were taking over, remaking her.

The wind pushed my hair forward and I pulled it back from my mouth with a smile. "Yeah. It is cool." I fumbled for the knife I'd restored to the sheath on my calf. "Do you think you can cut these stitches?"

WE REACHED PALENQUE SHORTLY BEFORE NINE O'CLOCK. THE CITY OF approximately forty thousand was busy this Friday night, especially the closer we got to the hotel district near the interior.

"There are about seventy or so hotels in the city," Hertenstein said. "They even have a small airport, though where you landed is much closer to our lab."

"So all these people are what, tourists?" Mari gestured to the groups walking along the sidewalk.

He nodded. "We're not far from the Palenque ruins. Same name as this city, different place. So a lot of people visit the area. Tourism is a big part of the economy."

"I had no idea," I said.

"Not many do." Hertenstein frowned. "Unfortunately, tourism has added to the deforestation that's been going on in the rainforests, though it's certainly not the biggest cause. Nowadays, it's not uncommon to see black howler monkeys sneaking into Palenque to find food."

No monkey in sight at the moment, only a bunch of people walking around with cameras hanging from their necks.

"So where will we find the senator?" I asked.

Keene pulled over and took out his phone. "He's at a hotel called Misión Palenque. I have the address somewhere. We'll stop for gas and ask for directions."

After filling up the tank at a remarkably modern gas station, we drove to Misión Palenque. According to the guidebook we'd purchased, the hotel featured a main building with several wings branching off like the spokes on a wagon wheel. Luscious trees and dense vegetation filled the space between the spokes, and I found myself searching the darkness for signs of Hertenstein's black howler monkeys.

"So what's the plan?" I looked down at my jeans, spotted with dirt and blood and smeared with green stains from the jungle. I didn't want to think about what was on my top and was glad to have it covered by my black jacket. "We'll have to clean up a bit. If we go searching for the senator looking like this, his security will tackle us and throw us in a Mexican jail. Especially this late."

Keene's gaze wandered down my body a bit slowly for my comfort, and then passed to his own clothes. "The night has barely begun for the tourists, and my bet is the senator is still at dinner. But you get a room while I go visit his room to make sure."

"No way," I said. "You're not going alone."

He contemplated me for a few seconds. "Keeping an eye on me?"

"I'm your backup. Remember, he's got at least one Unbounded with him. And knowing who that is, there are probably more." I hoped my voice didn't portray my own nervousness at seeing Tom again. I didn't love him anymore, but two months didn't erase all the memories.

"Okay, we'll get a room first. The others can wait there for us."

Mari was my biggest concern, but while I didn't want to leave her alone, I certainly didn't want to drag her on our visit to the senator either. My eyes went to Hertenstein. He seemed responsible enough to keep an eye on both her and Benito. He'd said he knew how to use a gun.

"Benito can get the room," I said. "He'll be less noticeable."

Benito nodded. "I will need a credit card."

"Of course," Keene said dryly.

I fished in my bag for a card, choosing one with a generic business name. "Just one room," I said. "We won't be here long and anything else will raise suspicion." Finally the man was doing something to contribute. I wondered if we could get some new clothes for him, or at least send his out to be washed. He still reeked, though the smell had been slightly better since the plane, where he'd removed his old coat. "I'll go with you into the lobby."

"Better let Hertenstein go," Keene said. "In case the senator's aide happens to be there."

I drew out my backup Ruger and handed it to the doctor. "Just aim and fire. It's racked and there's no safety. Stay near the door. Try not to look like you're with Benito."

He nodded and slid the gun into his pocket.

Within fifteen minutes, Benito was back, grinning. "All finished. Vámanos. Let's go."

The small room held two double beds with white bedspreads and cherry frames. A huge mirror, a dresser, and a TV graced one wall, while a table and matching chairs filled the small area next to the beds. Keene was already pulling off his T-shirt, replacing it with a dark green button-up shirt with short sleeves. Mari averted her gaze and Hertenstein headed for the bathroom, but I stared in fascination at the long scar that curved from Keene's left kidney to the middle of his chest. Faded and old now, but it was a wonder that he'd survived.

He quirked a brow when he saw me staring, yanking his shirt closed and buttoning it. "A present from your Renegades."

"That'll teach you to be on the wrong side of the fight."

"Oh? You sure they're telling you the whole truth now?" From his bag he removed a green blazer, so dark it looked almost black.

I took several steps toward him. "We all keep secrets. All of us. But don't tell me you still think the Renegades are anything like the Emporium."

He held my gaze. "Fine. That's why I'm here, but ultimately I fight for mortals not Unbounded."

"So do I." Yet I wondered if that was really true. I also wanted Unbounded to live freely and openly instead of hiding in the darkness of false identities and faked deaths.

"Mortals?" Benito whispered. "You two are vampires, aren't you?"

"Shut up," Keene and I said at the same time. Mari laughed.

Hertenstein was out of the bathroom, and I hurried toward it, hefting my bag. "Seven minutes," I said. "That's all I need."

I used three minutes to shower, two to dry off, and the remaining two to dry and change into my cat suit, loading the special pockets up with weapons. There was even a side pocket that held the machete and its sheath, though I'd need to wear the longer fitted jacket to cover the hilt, and I'd have to leave behind the soft leather piece that had originally tied the sheath around my hips. The jacket added a flare of dressiness, which would compete easily with Keene's jeans and blazer, while the stretch material didn't hinder my movement.

I emerged, my blond hair still wet and curling slightly where it brushed my shoulders. Keene handed me back my Ruger. "I gave him one of the spares."

"What about Mari?"

We both looked at her. "Do you know how to shoot?" Keene asked.

She shook her head, a scowl on her face. "No."

"Time to learn." I chose a Smith and Wesson nine mil from the weapons bag. It was easy to shoot and had a laser on the top to make targeting easier. A useful gadget, the laser, though I noticed the more experienced Unbounded never used them, except on the sniper rifles.

"I, but, what, uh." Mari stumbled to a stop and reached for the gun, a glint of excitement on her face.

I held it away from her and popped out the magazine. "The magazine has ten rounds. Rounds means bullets. To fire, you first have to rack it by pulling the top part back like this." I demonstrated. "With the magazine in, that will put a bullet in the chamber so you can fire." I pulled the trigger, gun pointed at the carpet, and was rewarded with a soft click. "Now you try."

She racked it hesitantly and then dry-fired.

"Perfect. Only do it faster if someone comes." Taking the gun, I reinserted the magazine and handed it back to her. "Most of us wear our guns ready, but I want you to rack it only if you think you're in danger, okay? We don't use guns with safeties. They're mostly a liability." I was worried more about her shooting an innocent bystander than herself.

"What about me?" Benito asked.

"Oh yeah, if Benito tries to leave, shoot him," I said.

"What you talkin' about?" Benito slathered on the accent again. "I work for you."

"You have to prove yourself like everyone else. And so far, all you've been doing is a lot of complaining."

"Okay, okay." He held up his hands to ward me off. "Just don't drink my blood."

I managed to stop myself from strangling him. "You'd have to bathe first anyway."

Mari let out an amused snort. She looked better, and I hoped she'd stay that way. She probably would if I could keep her out of the line of fire in the immediate future.

I looked at Hertenstein. "Keep a low profile. You're in charge. Lock up behind us."

Before he could reply, a knock at the door threw Keene and me into action. Pulling his gun, he pressed himself next to the entertainment center, while I chose the closet. "Benito, get the door," Keene growled. "Ask who it is first. You others get in the bathroom and shut the door until we call you."

"Why can't I go to the bathroom?" Benito darted a frightened glance toward the door.

"Go!" I barked.

He jumped into movement. "¿Quién es?" I didn't recognize the

Spanish words, but the meaning was bright in his mind: "Who is it?"

"Servicio."

Benito relaxed. "Oh, yes. I did order food. That was very fast."

Keene and I held our positions, but the waiter who came inside and left a cart seemed innocent enough. After he left, Keene checked out the cart's contents. "Hamburgers," he said with disgust. "Couldn't you order anything better?"

Benito shrugged and dug in.

"You can come out," I called, tapping on the bathroom door.

Mari emerged first. "Oh, good. Food. I'm hungry. Well, not exactly hungry, but I should be. I haven't eaten in forever." I didn't have time to explain absorbing, and from what I could tell, Hertenstein wasn't aware of our true natures, so it would have to wait.

"Come on," I started for the door, and Keene followed. "What's the plan anyway? How are we going to find out what room the senator's in?"

"I have the number, of course."

"And how are we going to convince him that he's in danger? Won't he think we're wackos?"

"Not if we're from the FBI."

"You have a fake ID?"

"I have the ID. Not fake."

We'd reached the end of the hall, and I stopped and looked at him. "That's what you've been doing these past months, joining the FBI?"

He shook his head. "I've been working with them for years now. One of the IDs the Emporium set up for me."

The idea of the Emporium infiltrating the FBI was disturbing, though not a real surprise. "So the senator's going to accept that the FBI sent someone to warn him about an assassination attempt? I'm not sure he'll buy it, especially since his cover story is that he's here to negotiate a simple import deal. Nothing the FBI or anyone else should care about."

"His commercial flight landed early this morning, and he's had plenty of time to send someone to check out the lab by now. He'll know something serious is up and that will work in our favor. Besides, I've met him before. He doesn't know I'm with the FBI, but a familiar face shouldn't hurt."

I searched Keene's face. "Don't tell me. You were the one keeping an eye on him for the Emporium."

"He's been a thorn in their side for a long time."

"You would have killed him?"

"I don't know. If I thought he was a danger, then yes, I would." He stared at me without expression. "Maybe that's why I'm trying so hard to save him now."

He had killed for the Emporium and their idea of utopia. Of course he had. And when it came right down to it, I was no better. I'd also killed, though in my defense, I'd been attacked first. Either way, killing changes a person. It forced you make a judgment about the value of a single human life as compared to whoever—or whatever—you were trying to protect.

Keene started walking again, and I followed. "What if Tom answers the door?" I asked. "Wouldn't an aide typically do stuff like that?"

"We'll break in. Subdue Tom if we can't find the senator alone." Keene gave me a smile that made me feel warm inside, and I grinned back. Nothing for bonding like breaking and entering.

The senator's room was on the ground floor, and breaking in became a simple matter of cutting out the window with a handy tool Keene kept in a pocket of his jeans. No alarms sounded and no one challenged us from inside or out, though we could hear people talking nearby at the outdoor pool. A light was on inside the senator's room, but it was deserted, as was the rest of the suite.

I whistled. "Quite a bit better accommodations than we have. I was wondering why a senator would want to stay here."

"The senator is actually one of the few who is conscious of spending the taxpayers' dollar," Keene said dryly.

"Which is why he's here and we're squeezed into economy."

"We're trying to keep a low profile."

I sighed. "Okay, so what now?" I sat on the silky red bedspread.

"I was positive he'd have finished eating by now since you took so long in the shower, but maybe not."

I rolled my eyes. "The restaurant then." Where we were sure to run into Tom, and maybe Justine. My stomach roiled at the thought.

We used the door this time, and thankfully no one was in the hallway. Pulling out the brochure of the hotel that I'd snagged from the room, we tracked our way to the dining room. We stood by the entrance, and Keene peered in. "He's there. By that fern."

Following his direction, my eyes landed not on the Senator, but on one of his two companions: Tom Carver. He had brown hair a shade lighter than Keene, tanned skin, blue eyes that changed shade with his clothing color. Tonight he wore a gray tailored suit that cost more than he'd ever make as a senator's aide. He was good looking in a casual sort of way that didn't scream attention. Except now he did call my attention because unlike before, he exuded the confidence of an Unbounded. Hard to believe that if he hadn't Changed, he would have been dead at my hand. Tom laughed at something the senator said. I couldn't hear him, but I knew what he'd sound like, and that left an odd feeling in my chest. I reached out mentally to him, but like a good little Unbounded, his mind was dark.

My eyes shifted to Senator Greggory Bellars seated across from Tom. My first impression was a poof of wavy, sand-colored hair and large eyebrows. He appeared to be in his late fifties, a tall, pale man with an aura of presence. He wasn't fat, but neither did he appear to spend a lot of time in the gym, his fitness due more to good genes than care.

"The third man is the body guard," Keene said, as I pulled back out of sight.

A couple approached us in the hallway, and Keene reached for me, as though to tell me a secret or kiss my ear. I snuck a glance, but the couple wasn't anyone we knew. Definitely not Unbounded.

The woman had to be cold in the nighty she was wearing for a dress, even on this mild evening.

"You see Justine in there?" I asked.

Keene shook his head. "What about Unbounded? Any more besides Tom?"

I scanned the restaurant. "I don't think so. Quite a few people here, though, and Justine could have a sensing Unbounded to block me."

"She doesn't know you're involved."

Something in the words made me uneasy, though he was right and there was no way she could know I'd come here, not unless Keene had reported it to her, and I'd already decided to trust him. "I guess we wait," I said. "They'll have to finish sometime. At least we know he's safe for the moment."

"If they haven't poisoned the food."

I rolled my eyes. "Right." The aromas were delicious and I took the opportunity to consciously absorb from the air, enjoying the hint of something exotic that seeped in through my pores.

Another couple passed, and Keene stepped even closer. We were only inches apart. I could smell the slight aroma of mint on his breath. One brow rose, emphasizing the glittering green of his eyes. "Do you think we're too conspicuous?" he asked.

"Only because you're standing so close." My heart had launched into high gear with the emotions I sensed radiating from him. He wasn't exactly leaving his mind open, but he wasn't blocking everything, and I felt myself reacting. Keene was a smart, sexy, normal male. Well, as normal as you could get living with the knowledge of Unbounded. He never lied, and I always knew where I stood with him. He was clearly interested in me, and we had a lot in common. His only drawback was that he'd die before I aged another year.

A memory of Bronson lying on his sickbed flashed into mind, and I backed away from Keene. "The host is coming over," I said. "Probably to stop us from scaring off his clientele. Let's take a little walk."

Keene nodded. "Right. Keep an eye out for Unbounded."

We went back three times before the senator finished his meal and started to leave the dining room. I worried about how to get rid of Tom, but he checked his cell phone, showing something to the senator, who nodded like a king giving permission. I knew Tom would hate that, and nearly laughed when he simply smiled and walked away, heading to another exit.

"I should follow Tom while you talk to the senator."

"Too late. Here he comes." Keene stepped in front of Senator Bellars in the hallway, holding out his badge. "Hello, Senator Bellars."

Senator Bellars looked hard at Keene's ID, his blond eyebrows rising like lazy caterpillars. "FBI? Wait, I remember you. But you never said anything about being FBI. I guess this isn't a chance meeting."

"No, it's not. Is there somewhere we can talk?" Keene glanced at the bodyguard. "It's urgent."

"Aren't you going to introduce your companion?"

"This is Agent Morse." Keene stumbled only slightly on the fake name. I hoped Bellars didn't ask to see my badge.

"Nice to meet you." Bellars offered me his hand, all smiles and friendliness. I took it, reaching out also with my mind. The face people showed the world was almost never their true one, and I wanted to see what kind of a man he was.

His mind was open, refreshing after being with Ritter and Keene, and even the natives in the jungle. I sensed only worry and determination to make things right. My smile widened. But he clearly didn't trust Keene and was thinking about asking for my badge, so I needed a distraction. "Nice to meet you, Senator Bellars. We have a mutual friend, I believe. Stella Davis? She funds a lab down here."

He nodded. "Yes, I do know her, though we've met only once. Beautiful and smart." He said it with an admiration I'd grown accustomed to hearing in regards to Stella. "We're both contributors to the lab, although she and her partners have donated far more than I have. The lab is part of why I'm here. It burned to the ground a few days ago. I booked a plane the minute I heard something was wrong. I asked my people to contact Stella, but they haven't been able to get her on the phone."

"We know about the lab." Keene opened a door in the hallway and turned on the lights. "This room's empty. We can talk in here."

Senator Bellars nodded at his bodyguard, who entered before him, checking out the room. After assuring himself it was empty, the man stood at attention by the door, his hand near a weapon I couldn't see under his blazer but knew was there.

Bellars smiled without mockery. "You can speak in front of him. He's been with me ten years."

"Don't let anyone in," I told the bodyguard. "Especially his aide."

The man blinked in surprise and looked at the senator, who nodded.

Despite the senator's reassurance, we moved farther into the room, away from the bodyguard. The large space was set up for a presentation, with rows of chairs facing a podium and a white screen.

"What's this all about?" the senator asked.

"It's your aide," I said. "He's going to try to kill you."

CHAPTER 15

"TOM?" SENATOR BELLARS LAUGHED, STARING AT ME AS THOUGH awaiting the punch line.

"It's true." Keene drew out the white envelope from his blazer pocket. "We believe he's working with a woman and that they are also connected to the attack on the lab. Have you ever seen this woman before?" He handed Bellars the photograph of Tom kissing Justine's cheek at the airport.

Senator Bellars shook his head. "No. Who is it?"

"An operative." Keene took back the photo. "She could be wearing a wig or have short hair. Are you sure you haven't seen her—or noticed your aide talking to her?"

Bellars glanced again at the photograph Keene still held out. "No, I haven't. Believe me, I'd notice a woman like that." He glanced at me and added as though feeling the need to excuse himself for the comment, "At least since the death of my wife last year." He looked back at Keene. "Look, you say this woman's an operative, but for whom? And why would anyone want me dead? I may have access to some sensitive information, but no more than hundreds of others."

"It's the drug companies," I said. "The autoimmune cure the lab was working on has a very real chance of getting to market with your help."

Understanding dawned on his pale features. "They can't keep making money if people are cured." His lips tightened in anger. "My wife died from an autoimmune disease, you know, that's why I agreed to be involved. I will *never* back down. Unfortunately, I've been out to the lab, and there's nothing but ashes. I can't find any of the scientists or a trace of their research. I had a whole team of locals searching with me."

"We believe at least one scientist has been captured by the group in question—and that they have access to the research."

"Which should mean I'm no longer a target." The senator folded his arms across his chest. "Without the research, I can't help get it to market."

Keene shook his head. "According to our intelligence, you're still in danger. You said yourself you wouldn't stop, and with what the scientists have learned over the years, there's a good chance they can get to this point again a lot quicker. Unless they take you out, stealing the research isn't going to make much difference. Your presence in Palenque puts you in grave danger. A lot of suspicious accidents happen here. We need to get you out."

"No, no." Bellars waved Keene's words away. "You're reading a lot more into my importance than is merited. Stella and the others who are funding the project would be better targets."

"Not if they're well protected," Keene said.

"Even if what you say is true, I can't leave now. Tomorrow afternoon at four there's going to be a celebration, and I'm the guest of honor." Bellars gave a self-deprecatory laugh. "I helped raise money to build a school here, and we've been able to put in quite a few wells in nearby villages to give children fresh water. When they heard I was in town, they threw together this event. People will be traveling from all over the municipality to attend. I can't disappoint them."

I groaned inwardly, meeting Keene's troubled gaze. "That's

when she'll do it." I felt sick. Tom had probably already reported the impending celebration, and wherever Justine was, she'd take full advantage to try out the new drug. The mistake drug. There could be hundreds of casualties—and no way to connect it to Justine, the Emporium, or the drug companies they supported.

"You'll have to disappoint them or a lot of people will die," Keene said.

Senator Bellars' furry eyebrows rose. "A lot of people? Aren't you exaggerating? If I'm the target, my opponents have no reason to hurt anyone else. I'll be careful, but I'm not going to let these people win."

"You don't know this woman," I said. "She has a way of convincing almost anyone to help her." How to explain an Unbounded talent, especially one as elusive as pheromone manipulation? "Keene can get you out of town safely."

Bellars' face flushed red. "I'm not going anywhere. You know what I think? Something rings fishy about all this. Your partner flashed me his badge, but I certainly noticed that you didn't show me yours." His gaze swung to Keene. "Without calling the FBI and verifying for myself that you are with the agency *and* that you are here on their command, I have no reason to trust either of you. I've had numerous death threats over the years, and I'm not about to turn chicken now. If you're really concerned, you guys find the woman and get it taken care of, but I'm staying here and doing my job."

"What about Tom?" Did Bellars believe at least that part of our story? I couldn't tell, though he was sincere in his determination. Near the door, the bodyguard's hand had inched closer to his gun. He wasn't close enough to overhear much, but perhaps he was reacting to the senator's irritated tone and stiff body language.

"Tom's the most efficient aide I've ever had. Only two weeks and he's made everything in my schedule run smoothly, not to mention my personal life. I admit that I'm hoping you're wrong about him." Senator Bellars sighed. "I'll have my bodyguard watch him. I know a few good men here I can also hire, and I am friends with the local police. I'll be careful. Tomorrow at the celebration, we'll have everyone checked before they can get close to the podium."

I knew it wouldn't be enough. The Emporium didn't play fair in any kind of fight, and that meant we'd have to take matters into our own hands—starting with Tom because he could help us find Justine and the scientist.

"Where's the celebration going to be held?" Keene asked.

"At the ruins. Couple miles out of town." A grin cut the senator's face. "Maya kids are going to sing and do a dance. Nice little show for the tourists."

Keene and I traded another hard look. Tourists and children. We had to stop Justine from hurting any of them, but the site of the ruins would be impossible to secure on such short notice, especially with only two of us.

Senator Bellars walked to the door. "Should I send Tom home?"

I stifled the urge to tell him Tom was likely to kill him if he realized anyone was onto him. "Better to find some legitimate business you can use to keep him occupied," I said. "I wouldn't sleep in the same hotel room, though, and I certainly wouldn't go anywhere alone with him."

Bellars stopped at the door. "How can I reach you?"

Keene exchanged numbers with him while I impatiently waited for them to finish. I was sure Justine, with her flare for the dramatic, would choose the celebration to act, so he might be safe enough for the time being. If he wouldn't let Keene get him out of town, I'd forget him and go back to helping Stella.

"He can't hold that meeting tomorrow," Keene said as the door shut behind the senator. "If I have to shoot him myself, I'm not going to let those children and their parents pay for his arrogance."

"Not arrogance," I told him. "Disbelief coupled with a strong desire to do what he thinks is right. He's already come this far without letting anyone push him around."

Keene snorted. "He's going to get people killed."

"Not if we can help it. But if it gets to that, try to aim for his arm, okay?" I gave him a flat stare. "Once we get the research, we'll still need help getting the drug to market."

"I'll keep that in mind." He scowled.

"What?"

"Something the senator said about why they'd still be gunning for him since they have the research. He's right, you know. If the Emporium has the research, they really don't need to kill him now. Why not let things go on as they are for a while longer?"

"Because they want to test the drug, right? Isn't that what Cort and the others believe?"

"Wouldn't the States be a better place for a test? I mean, let's be honest. Who's really going to care more than a few minutes about some dead Maya children?"

He was probably right. "There will be outrage for the tourists, at least. Or maybe that's the point. They could want to test on an insignificant population that won't make big headlines. That allows for more surprise at home when they hit something big."

"I still think there's more to it," Keene said. "My informant at the Emporium was adamant that they were going to get rid of the senator. It didn't seem based on whether or not they stole any research."

"Well, whatever the Emporium plan is now, Justine came here to assassinate the senator, and if I know anything about her, it's that she hates to leave things undone."

"You got that right." He reached for the door. "Anyway, I'll do some more digging. See if anything new pops up."

"What about Bellars? You think he'll call the FBI about us?"

"He might. But I suspect he won't because he wants to do his own thing. If he does call them, he'll be told the FBI has no official business here." Keene gave me a half grin. "The FBI denies a lot things, though, and he knows that. So he'd really be right back where he started. Guess I'm camping outside the senator's rooms while I do a little calling. What about you?"

"I'm going to look for Tom."

"Have fun with that." He cracked a smile that didn't match the hardness in his voice. "But keep in mind that if he sees you, it's over. You'll have to take him out of the game." His voice became marginally softer. "Or at least make sure he's out of commission for the duration."

Did he think I couldn't do it? If I did, would Tom end up at the compound with our other prisoners? He hadn't been with the Emporium long. Maybe he'd be one of our success stories.

"I'll do what I have to do." I moved down the hall, my soft leather shoes making no sound on the carpet. I glanced over my shoulder as I turned the corner, but Keene was already striding in the opposite direction.

Torn between checking on Mari and finding Tom, I finally decided that Mari was safe enough with the Swiss doctor, though maybe I'd move them after I saw what Tom was up to. Benito was still an unproven factor in all this, and regardless of what I decided to do with Mari, he could stay where he was until we finished our mission. Free room service would probably keep him satisfied for days.

Slipping through the hotel, I checked all the common areas, even standing outside the men's restroom and reaching out my thoughts to see if anyone was inside. Tom wasn't in the building, so I stepped out into the night, breathing in the rich scent of foliage and earth. The air was so much warmer than in Portland that for a moment I let myself revel in the difference—until my position under the lights near the building made me feel exposed. I headed out over a path through a garden, moving into the tree line. Crickets chirped, something chittered, and a rustle sounded as something scurried away from my feet. Once I felt secure from prying eyes, I began examining the grounds. People were gathered on patios and around the pool, though no one was in the water. Lively music came from a large group on a patio, where a dozen or more couples were dancing. No Tom.

After circling the entire hotel, I still hadn't found any sign of Tom. Had he left the hotel altogether? I didn't know if that was a good sign or a bad one. I debated if I should hang out in the parking lot or head back to the senator's room. Maybe Keene had spotted Tom.

Or maybe I should keep trying. I slipped deeper into the trees, reaching out mentally, probing. Life forces were ahead. I soon caught sight of a large hot tub built into the earth in a secluded clearing, jungle trees all around. Three couples cuddled in the warm water, while another couple kissed on a lounge chair.

No Tom, so I continued searching.

In theory, I should be able to reach out and find him. Delia from the Triad had been able to span floors in the old Emporium headquarters in Los Angeles. She had years of practice, but I was young, strong . . . and apparently not very good at what I did.

Running water from a fountain alerted my attention, but with my senses in high gear, I knew no one was nearby. I sat on the rock wall border and closed my eyes. Tom. I pictured him as I liked to remember him best—standing with me on the top of a cliff with our bicycles in Kansas, far enough from the edge that my fear of heights wasn't triggered. We'd made it up the difficult trail, sweat dripping from our bodies, chests heaving. The sunset was glorious, though it meant we still had to set up a tent so we'd have somewhere to spend the night.

Tom's eyes often changed shades of blue, but that day they were like an inviting lake on a summer day. My favorite.

"Erin, I want to do this every day of my life."

"What? You're insane." It had been fun, but the four-hour assent and three-hour return was far too taxing for every day. "Maybe every month. Except in winter."

He grinned, smoothing back his brown hair from his tanned face. "I mean you and me. We should get married."

"Married. Wow."

He took my hand, spreading heat through my body. "Just think about it."

All at once I found him. His mind was still dark, though not as dark as in the restaurant. Perhaps he wasn't expecting someone like me. Or maybe like Jace he was too new to be consistent at blocking. Regardless, he was close by, if I could sense even this much of him.

Rising, I followed the hint of his mind, hoping the link would grow stronger with proximity. Up ahead was another small clearing where a foursome played cards under a weak lantern hanging from a pole. Skirting the light, I continued on.

Someone was with Tom, but that person's mind was shut tight. Unbounded, probably, or someone like Keene who'd grown up with them. I walked more slowly and carefully. From my previous circuit, I knew the parking lot was up ahead. Maybe he'd just returned from wherever he'd gone. Was he with Justine? My stomach churned, but whether with anticipation or dread, I couldn't say. If I could follow Justine, I might discover where they planned to take the kidnapped scientist.

Tom stood talking with someone who was hidden from my view behind a blue SUV. I hugged a bush leading into the parking lot, pushing my thoughts out harder. It was definitely Tom, and though I couldn't sense all his thoughts, I knew he was with Justine. I could see the picture of her foremost in his mind. He thought she was beautiful, this "sister" of his. He still didn't know she was really his mother.

This surface glimpse was all I could see of his mind, but their meeting in the open like this concerned me. It was almost as if they expected someone to come calling. Not just someone but a sensing Unbounded. Maybe even me in particular. I pulled my mind from Tom and sent it searching again, beginning at my current location and expanding in ever-widening arcs.

I found the dark presence seconds before it hurtled in my direction.

Throwing myself sideways, I tucked into a roll and was up and running before my attacker reached me. He registered on my senses as Unbounded, and he was fast, which likely meant gifted in combat. Justine had always been able to surround herself with useful people. I reached for my gun, but he knocked it from my hand. I whirled to face him.

He stood there, a grin stretching under his large, flat nose. I knew him, at least by first name: Edgel. He looked angrier and more determined than during our last encounter when he'd been under Keene's command. Everything about him was dark, from his boots and canvas pants to his ebony skin and close-cropped black hair. A black knife jutted wickedly from his hand.

I pulled the machete. In retrospect, it was a dumb thing to do because I hadn't trained with the weapon. Still, it seemed to fit the occasion. I lunged. He was faster, dancing out of reach and back in, nearly slicing my arm in the process.

I swung again, and this time I hit his knife. It shattered.

Before I had a chance to marvel at my accomplishment or at the craftsmanship of the machete's blade, Edgel was in motion again, his foot crashing into my arm like a sledge hammer. The machete went flying.

"Edgel, stop!" I commanded.

He blinked, as though surprised I remembered his name. "Why? I owe you for shooting Justine's brother. Thinking he was dead almost destroyed her. I can't kill you because Stefan won't let me, but no one said anything about not hurting you."

Stefan? This was the second time Emporium agents had indicated that the Triad member had a vested interest in my well-being. Looked like they still wanted me for their breeding program. Whatever the motive, there was probably no use in reminding Edgel that Justine had tried to murder my family.

Edgel lunged, a huge fist coming toward me. I dodged easily but didn't anticipate his other hand, which caught me on the side of my face. Pain exploded in my head.

Stupid, I thought. I pushed my hand through a slit in my bodysuit and whipped out one of my knives from my thigh sheath. For the first time in my life, I managed to sink it deep into my target, though farther above Edgel's heart than where I'd intended. He grunted and pulled it out, dripping blood and grinning.

Now he had the knife. Not exactly the way I'd take someone's weapon from them but effective. I wouldn't be able to outrun it, and he wouldn't miss.

Unless there was something more I could do mentally. Maybe shock his mind into missing. Desperately, I battered at the dark wall of his mind. If Ritter had sometimes had a hole in his barrier when he was distracted, maybe Edgel did, too. He grinned in anticipation. His arm went back.

There it was. I dived into the hole, at the same time releasing a mental scream. The knife flew past me. Edgel's face contorted, but he was already in motion, one hand coming toward me in a blow that would knock me off my feet. I ducked and was about to step to the side, when I sensed his foot coming up. No, it wasn't there yet, but it would be. I knew it. I stepped the other way and lashed out with my own kick. Solid flesh met my blow. Exactly as I expected.

Pivoting, I sent a jab to the wound in his chest. He grunted in pain, but his fists were already coming at me again. No, they *would* come at me. I knew how to avoid them. I also knew it wasn't my ability that warned me of the coming blow, but Edgel's own combat gift.

Dimitri was right. Maybe it was his suggestion that made me aware of what I was doing. Because I'd felt this before when sparring with Jace.

Edgel's next two punches missed me, but there was no way to avoid the third. I landed two myself. My shoulder ached where he'd hit, and I suspected something had cracked or broken. Even borrowing his ability, I wasn't going to win. Edgel had too much training—not to mention six inches and forty pounds on me. But I could distract him enough to reach for the Ruger at my ankle.

I threw another knife from the sheath at my thigh, knowing he would dodge. I reached for the gun.

Too late.

A soft sound whizzed toward me and my right arm burst into fire.

CHAPTER 16

"THAT'S QUITE ENOUGH," CAME A SILKY FEMALE VOICE.

I wanted to curl up and cry at the pain, but I wouldn't give her the satisfaction. Clenching my jaw, I turned to meet her. "Justine."

She stood pointing a gleaming silver pistol at my chest, her face mocking. Blue eyes, small nose, high, prominent cheekbones. She looked exactly the same as when we'd been best friends, before I'd heard about Unbounded or the war between the Emporium and Renegades. When I'd thought she cared about me. When I'd thought Tom's love was real and not engineered by his so-called sister. Only her hair was different. Instead of the dyed blond, it was a rich brown—her natural color, which she'd once hated. Like me, she wore all black, but her jeans ended with pointed, high heeled boots.

Behind her, Tom stood, his face impassive. His eyes appeared dark, so unlike those belonging to the man that day on the cliff that it was like looking at a stranger. The Unbounded certainty made him far more compelling and attractive than when he'd been mortal, average. If he had already Changed when we first met,

I guessed I wouldn't have hesitated to accept his proposal as I did after our bike ride to the cliff.

"What a nice surprise running into you." Justine gave me a smile that didn't reach her eyes. She tossed her head, making the long locks glisten under the lamplight. "No, Edgel," she said, her eyes going past me. "You had your chance. Don't feel too bad for losing. Remember her heritage."

My heritage? Coupled with what Edgel had said, that could only mean she still thought Stefan Carrington was my biological father and that I was gifted in combat. Which in turn meant Tom hadn't told Justine the truth about my ability or my parentage—and yet he'd known about both.

"You're looking good. I like the hair," I told Justine. My arm throbbed and it was all I could do to make my voice sound bored. "How did you know I was here?"

Justine scowled. "We were actually expecting that traitor Keene, but it was very kind of you to show up, too. Once I realized you'd come with him, I knew it was only a matter of time until you tried to follow Tom. So we waited until you did."

I hated being predictable, especially to Justine. I pushed at her mind, but it was tightly locked. Still, if I could find a hole, maybe I could inflict a little damage that would help me escape. Unfortunately, my head pounded from my previous effort, the customary dull aching, interspersed with searing flashes of lightning that threatened to bring tears to my eyes. Well, I needed to learn what they knew anyway, and it wasn't like Tom would let me go easily. I could also sense Edgel behind me, ready to use any excuse to make me pay for his humiliation in front of Justine.

"Sorry to disappoint you," I said, pretending to scan the area. "Keene doesn't seem to be here. I could give him a message, if you like, the next time I see him."

Justine chuckled, and this time her eyes showed genuine amusement. "Ah, Erin, I've missed you."

Something caught in my chest, a feeling I didn't want to experience. I missed Justine, too. Finding her and Tom at that low point in my life after leaving law school had saved me. Or so I'd thought at the time. That was before I knew I was being manipulated.

Justine's eyes roamed over my outfit. "Edgel, get her weapons and check her for more. Hand them to Tom." She spied the machete as Edgel retrieved it from the ground. "Wait, what's that?" She laughed. "Why, Erin, how native of you."

"It was a gift. I'll take it back if you don't mind."

"Funny." She handed it to Tom.

Edgel relieved me of the machete's sheath and found my extra gun and the knife I wore at my ankle. He glared at me the entire time, his hands rough during the search. I ignored him.

"She's bleeding," Tom said unnecessarily.

The flow of blood from the bullet hole halfway between my elbow and shoulder was actually slowing a bit, which was good because I was feeling rather dizzy and nauseated, though whether from blood loss or overusing my ability, I couldn't say. It was hard to think between those flashes of agony in my brain.

"Yes, I can see that." Justine stepped toward me, carefully avoiding the blood pooling on the ground beside me. "We have something to ease the pain. We call it tonic. Would you like some?"

Similar to our curequick, I was betting, and much more aptly named. Cort and I had an ongoing argument about how stupid curequick sounded. "I'm good," I said. "That stuff's addictive, you know." Another searing pain made me wince, which ruined my show of strength.

Justine studied me for a full thirty seconds without comment. When she spoke, her voice was silky and compelling. "Who else are you here with? Where are they?"

The words held the promise of untold sexual pleasure and the fulfillment of every wild dream. Well, not the words exactly, but the pheromones accompanying them. She wasn't a hypnopath like Tenika, compelling people with speech, rather her ability to emit pheromones attracted others and made them want to please her. Pheromones worked on everyone regardless of gender or sexual orientation, but it was a weak ability because once you were aware of the manipulation, you could resist it—if you wanted. Justine hated that aspect, though I'd observed enough people around her to know that many never became immune. Take Edgel, for instance. He was old enough to know better, yet he hung on her every word like a teenage boy with his first crush.

"I'm here alone," I said, shifting my position so that the pain in my arm increased. Something to focus on instead of the desire to please her. I wouldn't let her pheromones fool me into thinking I mattered to her as anything other than an incubator for her Unbounded grandchildren. Pheromones might be undetectable to the conscious mind, but I recognized their presence by my reaction to them.

"You're lying." Her voice became hard and the pheromones thicker. "We know Keene has an informant at the Emporium. Sweet little mortal receptionist. We fed her information about our intentions toward the senator, knowing Keene wouldn't be able to resist getting involved. He's been fouling up quite a few of our operations these past few months. How convenient to bring you along, though. Couldn't have planned it better myself. Two birds with one stone and all that." She stepped around me, close enough that our shoulders brushed. I could smell her spicy signature perfume. With her boots, we were about the same height, and she leaned and whispered in my ear. "Tell me where Keene is, Erin. You can trust me. Tom and I care about you."

My gaze went to Tom, whose eyes hadn't left my face. I wondered how he really felt about me. Not that it mattered. "Then let me go."

Justine laughed softly, her breath warm on my ear. "Don't be ridiculous. You and Tom need some time alone. I know you have a lot to talk about. But first, we need to see who might be looking for you. Did you and Keene bring any more of Ava's motley clan? That might upset things a tad. Why don't you make it easy for everyone and tell me right now?"

Cort had said the Emporium agents didn't seem aware they were being followed in the jungle, but surely they'd known we'd come once we heard of the fire. Maybe they hoped we'd think it was an accident. With only a few survivors, which they were doing their best to mop up, how would we ever know?

Wait. Had she said "any *more* of Ava's motley clan?" Because that sounded like she was aware of at least some of them.

"She's not going to tell you," Tom said.

My eyes flicked back to him. "Oh, so you *can* speak."

"I'll get her back to the room," he continued, ignoring me. "You go grab those supplies. That clerk should have them here by now. Hurry, I'll need to check in with the senator before he goes to sleep."

"What senator exactly?" I asked. "How does he work into all this?" I really wanted to ask about the agents who'd stolen the research, but mentioning them would warn Justine that we were onto them.

"Don't play stupid," Tom growled. "You know what our plans are, or you wouldn't be here with Keene."

"The senator has nothing to do with me," I retorted. Was it even remotely possible that he and Justine were here only for Senator Bellars and weren't connected with the lab? I didn't think so.

Tom arched a brow. "Then why are you here?"

"Vacation. I hear they have some wonderful ruins around here."

Justine snorted impatiently. "Watch her. I'll meet you back at the room."

I waited for her to hand over the gun, but Tom pulled out one of his own. The way he handled it told me he'd been practicing.

"Edgel will go with you." Justine's trust in Tom apparently did not extend far.

Tom didn't protest. "There's more than we're seeing here. A lot more. There's a pattern I can't quite make out."

A pattern? That had to be something related to his ability.

Justine smiled at him as though he'd said something brilliant. "Great. Try to figure it out, would you?"

Tom shrugged off his suit jacket and tossed it to Justine. "Drape it over her shoulder."

"That's right, can't have her bleeding all over the place in front of the other guests." Justine positioned the jacket and then kissed the air near my cheek mockingly before striding away. All of us watched her swaying back and forth until she was out of sight and the pheromones began to dissipate.

Tom put his hand with the pistol in his pocket to hide it. "Let's go, Erin."

I considered running, but Edgel loomed nearby, his stoic face belying the anger that exuded from the taut lines of his body. Every place he'd hit me ached—my cheek especially—and my head was growing fuzzy. The worst was the gunshot; I was pretty sure the bullet was still deep inside my flesh.

Holding my right arm with my left to minimize the pain, I preceded Tom back inside the hotel. "So, what's your plan?" I probed. "Are you going to kill someone?" I tried to make it sound ludicrous, but the attempt fell flat. I glanced over my shoulder.

Tom frowned. "I have a duty to protect the Emporium's interests."

"Don't you mean the Triad's interests?"

"Same thing."

"I don't think so." I stopped walking and waited until a foursome passed us in the otherwise deserted hallway. "Do you really believe in their vision of utopia? Because it sounds to me an awful lot like Unbounded ruling the world."

Tom laughed. "What's wrong with that? Look, Erin, I spent years investing money for rich people who were ahead in this world only because they're rich. I have a chance now to be one of those people, and I'm not passing it up. The mortals don't really matter to me. Their lives are too short to make any impact. Now get going."

He propelled me ahead with a gentle shove that felt like a baseball bat to my shoulder. "Sorry," he muttered when I winced, but he didn't sound repentant.

We marched toward the senator's wing. When I realized the direction we were heading, I began hoping we'd run into Keene.

I even sent my mind searching for him, but my thoughts didn't seem to get past the pounding in my head. I was having problems seeing now, and the urge to vomit was growing.

I stumbled on the stairs to the second floor, but when Tom reached out to me, I hurried ahead blindly—only to run into a wide man in a white linen shirt and a thick gold necklace. Both of which I saw very close up, since my nose hit his chest. Agony from my shoulder made the rest of him a blur.

"Too much to drink," Tom apologized, scooping me into his arms. Blackness ate at the edges of my consciousness. The arms around me felt familiar but far from safe, unlike when I was with Ritter, though as far as I knew, Tom had never killed anyone and Ritter had killed many times.

Where was Ritter now? And Keene? The worst was not knowing if Justine and Tom had discovered Mari and Hertenstein. If we didn't recover the research, the doctor was Stella's only hope at recreating the formula for Bronson, and Mari's ability made her invaluable to the Renegades. If Justine found them, I'd never forgive myself.

My sight was clearing a bit, and I could see Edgel reaching to unlock a door. *Now,* I thought. Twisting, I slammed the palm of my hand into Tom's chin. With enough force, apparently, to make him drop me. Liquid fire erupted from my wound. I heaved twice, but nothing came up except the sour taste of bile.

A sound behind me. I lashed out a foot, felt it connect and heard a satisfying grunt. I scrambled to my feet and half stumbled, half fell down the stairs.

"Get her!" Tom's voice.

That I made it to the bottom of the stairs was small comfort. I turned to see a fist coming straight at my eyes. I crumpled from the impact.

"Guess I made it here just in time." Justine stared down at where I'd fallen. For someone who looked so feminine, she had a fantastic right hook.

By the time Edgel scraped me off the floor, Tom had the door to the room open. Inside, Mari sat on a chair, her hands tied and her eyes wide. She'd been crying, and there was a fresh cut on her bottom lip.

I glared at Tom as Edgel set me inside the door and shut it behind me. "She has nothing to do with this!"

Tom arched a brow. "Uh, you're the one who brought her."

Ignoring him, I went to Mari, anger fueling my strength. "Did they hurt you?" Something about her expression wasn't right, though she hadn't retreated into herself as she had before.

She shook her head, a sob coming from her throat. "They broke in. We hadn't even eaten yet. And the doctor . . . they . . . they—oh, God, help us! They shot him!" Her voice rose hysterically, and I could barely understand her through her convulsive sobs. "There was bl-blood everywhere. All o-over the bed and . . . the wall. It was horr-horrible!"

I hugged her with my good arm. "It's going to be okay," I whispered in her ear. "Just don't tell them anything. Nothing at all, got it?" What if she'd already told them about Ritter and the others? If she had, it might become impossible for them to retrieve the research.

I was yanked from Mari before she gave any response, pain bursting through my body at the sudden movement. I twisted to see Edgel grinning at me.

Justine watched us with a half smile on her face. "It was the Mexican."

I blinked. "Benito's yours?" Though I'd suspected the coincidence of his appearance, I didn't want to believe it.

"Of course he's not ours," Tom answered with a little shudder.

Justine laughed. "No, but he was the reason we found you. Half the staff here is on our payroll, and they've looked closely at every single new guest since our arrival. Benito did fool us for a bit, but there aren't many lowlifes dressed like him at a place like this, much less ones using business credit cards. The clerk checked him out like all the others and reported it when our automated checks showed the credit card came from a dummy corporation.

It was easy enough to verify everything with a listening device on the room service cart."

Justine smiled and added, "Of course, we wouldn't have been watching at all if we hadn't baited Keene in the first place. You are all just icing on the cake."

She walked over to the mound on one of the two beds, ripping off a blanket to reveal Benito, whose unnatural position for a moment made me suspect he was dead. "Wake up, you." Justine jabbed at his shoulder. "Get into that bathroom and clean up. You stink, and I won't endure another minute of your presence."

Benito struggled to a sitting position as she shoved a plastic bag of clothing at his stomach, nearly toppling him again. He groaned but pushed doggedly to his feet. His face was mottled black on the left cheekbone, his right eye black and puffy, and he limped as he passed. He hesitated near me. Was that relief in his eyes? *Poor thing.* There was nothing I could do to help either him or Mari.

"And use soap," Justine shot after him. She nodded at Edgel. "Keep an eye on him." Taking a few steps toward Mari, she squatted down beside her. "Judging by her healing face, I'd say she's Unbounded." Glancing over at me, she reached out and stroked Mari's hand. "Tell me, dear, what is your ability? Who are your ancestors?"

Pheromones swirled around us, making me feel dizzy and wanting. Was it my imagination or could I actually smell the faint scent of musk? Justine might have been too busy earlier laying a trap for me to get much information from Mari, but she wasn't holding back now. With everything Mari had been through the past few days, she wouldn't be strong enough to resist Justine. She wouldn't even know what pheromone manipulation was.

Mari's gaze shifted to me and just as quickly back to Justine. "I don't know what you're talking about."

"Yes, you do." Justine's voice crooned. "You can trust me. I'm your friend. Who else is here? Did you come with others?"

Mari's nostrils flared. "Go to hell."

I had never been more proud of anyone than of Mari at that moment.

Justine's slapped her hard across the face. I lunged to stop another blow, but someone moved behind me. Pain exploded in my brain and blackness filled the world.

CHAPTER 17

FINGERS OF LIGHT STREAMED IN FROM CURTAINS NEXT TO THE BED, the pale rays falling over my face. I snapped open my eyes and looked around. I lay on a silky coverlet in the middle of a big bed, probably still at the Misión Palenque. My hands and feet were tied to the bedframe. I was wearing my stretch suit, minus the jacket, and my shoulder was wrapped in a thick bandage.

The lack of pain and light told me I'd been out a long time. Not a natural sleep, either, if the drug paraphernalia on the nightstand was any indication. An enjoyable buzz hummed in my veins, telling me they'd also given me their curequick equivalent. Despite this, I felt cold, as if someone had left the air conditioning on and hadn't remembered to cover me with a blanket.

Voices floated to me from what I thought might be the door to the room. "You should have done it." Justine's brittle voice. "Why do you think I got the second room?"

The ropes holding me seemed to have significant give, so I reached a hand toward the closest syringe on the nightstand. A needle would make a sort of weapon, even if a poor one. But my hand stopped short of the syringe.

"Maybe you like them helpless and unwilling, but I don't." The second voice was Tom's. "There was a time Erin *wanted* to be in my arms."

I strained harder. One finger touched the syringe, and I flicked it off the nightstand onto the bed—only to discover that it didn't have a needle. I pushed it off the bed so it wouldn't be found.

"Those days are over," Justine was saying now. "What's important now is that you have this opportunity. You owe it to the Emporium and to me."

I felt sick at the meaning of her words, and what she planned for me. I reached for another syringe but came up several inches short.

"I don't *owe* anyone," Tom said. "I'm not your useless mortal brother anymore. I have my own agenda."

"It's *our* agenda, and you were never useless, not as long as you were with her. That's why you shouldn't have passed it up. Think—a grandchild to not one but *two* of the Emporium's Triad. If that child were Unbounded, we could control the very future of the Emporium. Of the world." Her tone was vicious and excited.

Grandchild of two Emporium Triad members? Since she believed me to be Stefan's offspring, that could only mean that Tihalt McIntyre, Cort and Keene's father, was Tom's biological father. He was a scientist like Cort and the real genius behind the Emporium's genetic success, though less driven politically than his partners. I'd only met the man once, but he didn't seem Justine's type.

Justine's next words made me forget about Tihalt completely. "Sensing is in our family line as well as Erin's, and with those drugs you've been taking, the chance of having a sensing offspring is higher than it has ever been."

"You mean so you'll have someone to go up against Delia."

"Of course." She paused. "It's time I take my rightful place in the Triad. But even if the child only has the combat ability like Erin—or your ability to see patterns in events—it will still be important because of the lineage. Unfortunately, once we get to the Emporium, the point will be moot. You know they have other plans for her, and those don't include you fathering her baby. We can delay our arrival there a few days, but next time don't hesitate."

"I'll do what I need to do. I should check on her, though. She should be waking."

"Hurry, the others are ready. I'll send Edgel to help you after I get them in the car. We can't waste any more time looking for Keene." She laughed. "Maybe we'll get lucky and he'll be with the senator later."

Straining my entire body, my fingers touched the edge of a syringe. Again I flicked and was rewarded when it landed on the bed, flashing a glimpse of silver.

"Oh, and remember to keep your mental shields up," Justine added. "We still don't know who else might be here from her group. We may have captured them all, but I'm reluctant to believe that Ava sent Erin here without more support, even if she can fight like a demon."

That explained why Justine's mental shield was so tight that I couldn't even get surface emotions from her.

"Maybe she came on her own," Tom said. "Without Ava's knowledge."

"Maybe. Just be careful."

I pulled the syringe closer, palming it as Tom's footsteps approached. Rapidly, I calculated my chances. He was heavier than I was, but he couldn't be better trained. Despite the drugged sleep, I felt rested, which meant my headache was gone and I could use my ability again—provided I could find an opening in his barrier. I slipped the syringe under my thigh as he came into view.

"Good morning," he said.

I stared at him without speaking.

My silence didn't faze him. "I'm going to untie you now. Please don't try to get away, or I can't guarantee what Justine will do to your friends." He couldn't have said anything else that would have as effectively ended my escape plan. I couldn't leave Mari and Benito to Justine's revenge. Any plan I came up with needed to include them.

"Your wound healed nicely, thanks to Edgel's skill at taking out bullets," Tom continued, freeing my hands. "Sorry about the ropes, but I couldn't be in here every second. We had to track down some supplies."

I bit back a retort only because he hadn't raped me, at least not yet. With the high Unbounded fertility rate, I might have already been expecting his child, so I was more grateful than I probably should be. "What kind of supplies?" I sat up, careful to keep the syringe hidden.

He considered me for several seconds before shaking his head. "You'll see soon enough."

I pushed at his mind, finding nothing but an impenetrable barrier, stronger even than Justine's. Odd. Something about it seemed familiar, but I couldn't place it. "This is a mistake, Tom."

"Stop talking. Edgel's waiting."

He was different now. Before, I could always get him talking, could get him to bend to what I wanted, but he'd Changed as surely as I had. I'd once worried that he was too weak a man for me to respect, though part of that was Justine's interference. She'd always been so strong by comparison. Regardless, the Change in him was far too late. I felt nothing but anger toward Tom, so either what I'd felt for him had emerged only from Justine's pheromone-filled suggestions, or my Change had ruined me for him. I couldn't even hate him. Not really. Not when I knew Justine was pulling his strings.

He unwound the large bandage from my arm to reveal only a slight wound where the bullet had struck me. He covered this with a smaller bandage. "Practically as good as new. And the bruise on your cheek is almost gone."

I rolled my eyes. "Lucky me."

He began gathering the medical supplies, tucking them into the black bag on the nightstand. I took the opportunity to shift my position on the bed, slipping the syringe into the pocket that had contained my machete.

"I need to use the bathroom," I said. I really did, though the syringe was my real reason. He might overlook the bulge, but Justine and Edgel wouldn't.

"Hurry then."

I hesitated at the bathroom door. "So, what happened with your senator last night?"

"He was asleep by the time I finally got back. His bodyguard said he'd call me this morning. In a couple hours. I'll be back before then. Big day for us."

"Are you really going to kill him?"

"So you *do* know."

"Are you?"

"Not me. Or Justine. But he is going to die. We have to protect the Emporium."

"Don't you mean their money?"

He gave me a flat grin. "Money is life. That's the one important thing I learned as a stockbroker. Money creates power and that is the only thing in the end that matters."

"What about friendship? Love? Family?"

In a few steps he was across the room. "What are you asking?" He reached out to touch my arm. All at once he was a little boy seeking approval—an unbalanced little boy with a big gun in his pocket. A boy who'd been tossed into the foster care system by a woman now pretending to be his sister. A man who'd been deeply wounded when he realized I was Unbounded while he hadn't yet Changed.

I shook my head, backing rapidly into the bathroom. "Nothing."

"You call them mortals every bit as much as I do, Erin. They don't really matter. We matter. We are the Unboundaried, remember? They told you where the term Unbounded came from, didn't they? Normal rules or boundaries do not apply to us."

I shut the door and leaned against it, my heart pounding. I knew that look in his eyes. He'd had it when he wanted a new bicycle or a car, a promotion at work, and even when looking for the house he bought with Justine. Not because he really needed or wanted these things, but for the prestige they lent to his life. How he was perceived by others. That was more important than all the stability and love in the world. He intended to use me to secure his position in the Emporium hierarchy every bit as much as Justine.

I knew then that I'd have to kill him—again. Really and finally. He was more dangerous than even Justine. Though they shared an obsession with power, his weakness made him unstable. At least I knew where Justine stood.

Dragging in a breath, I removed the syringe from my pocket, taking off the cap and checking the thickness of the needle. Several inches long and thick enough to do some real damage in a pinch, especially if I managed to get it into an eye or a vital organ, but the larger needle size meant the contents of the syringe was a curequick type of mixture and not a sedative. If I used the needle on someone, I'd have to be careful not to release the liquid, or whoever I stabbed wouldn't stay injured as long. But I'd keep the stuff inside for now in case I needed the curequick myself. Replacing the cap, I tucked the syringe into my bra, pushing it as far back under my arm as I could. It was more than uncomfortable, but for now it was the safest place.

I preceded Tom from the room, where we were joined by Edgel, dressed all in black, including a calf-length leather coat, which reminded me of my own back at home. He wouldn't be able to wear that in a few hours when the day's heat set in. His eyes skimmed over my face, catching in my hair, which I realized was probably bloody and matted. My appearance had been my last concern in the bathroom.

Edgel fell into step beside me, instead of behind with Tom.

"How did you do that last night?" he asked quietly. I'd never heard him speak except in anger or protest, so the mild tone surprised me.

"What?"

"Last night when we were fighting. You did something to my mind. I assume it was an extension of our combat ability. How did you do it? Who taught it to you?"

His position in Justine's group indicated that he wasn't overly concerned with being in charge, but apparently the good little soldier wanted to improve himself. Unfortunately, if Justine got wind of my little mental trick, she might put two and two together and figure out my real ability. Then she might decide to bypass grandchildren altogether and dedicate her life to using me against Delia.

I nearly stopped walking at the thought. Maybe that's why Tom hadn't told her about me. He'd be out of the picture as surely as his potential offspring. Keeping quiet was a nice move on his part—but it made him far more frightening.

"I didn't do anything to your mind," I said to Edgel. "Maybe you're sick or something."

He blinked twice and then nodded. "Okay, I can understand why you won't share the information. I'll figure it out myself."

We reached the outside door, where I saw that the light coming into the hotel room had been deceiving. The world was paused in the early hour before the sunrise proper, when light had begun to fill one half of the sky but didn't quite bend to shine into all the crevices of the earth. That meant I'd probably been unconscious less than five hours.

"Do you have family?" I asked Edgel.

He did the blinking thing again, which told me my question had succeeded in derailing his thoughts. Just when I thought he wasn't going to answer, he spoke. "I have contributed to the genetic research we conduct, of course, and I have three Unbounded sons. I don't know where the mortals are."

"Cast off, huh?"

"I don't have control over that." His eyes avoided mine. Something he wasn't willing to say? Or maybe felt guilty about? "Anyway, they're better off with their own kind."

We arrived at the parking lot and I could see the blue SUV

from last night. *They better have Mari inside.* If not, I'd use my needle here and now. I quickened my pace and the men did as well.

Justine climbed from the vehicle as we approached. Today she wore low-riding jeans, and a jean jacket over a maroon tank top that showed a slice of tanned stomach. Around her hips she wore my machete, complete with the sheath and the leather waist tie she must have taken from my hotel room. She looked carefree, sexy, and dangerous. I wondered if she'd cleaned up the doctor's corpse before or after collecting the leather tie.

I strained to see through the tinted glass of the SUV. Yes, Mari was inside, and Benito as well.

Tom unlocked the gray BMW in the next stall. Probably the senator's car. That reminded me of Keene. Was he still watching the senator? Hadn't he checked on Mari and the others? I pushed out my thoughts, but excepting Justine, Tom, and Edgel, there were no life forces nearby with the dark signature I attributed to those who could block their thoughts.

Edgel reached for the back door on the passenger side of the SUV and motioned for me to get in beside Mari. She wore my favorite jeans, and the red T-shirt I'd packed in my duffel, so apparently Justine had been thorough in raiding the hotel room. The jeans looked good on Mari, though a little big. She reached for my hand. "I thought they killed you."

Her thoughts were coming clearly to me, unlike the Unbounded around me. More clearly than I'd been able to achieve before with a simple touch: relief to see me, hope that I'd get us out of this mess, and vivid fear overshadowing all the rest. I threw up my barriers at the assault. "Not quite."

She squeezed my hand and whispered. "I didn't tell them anything. Neither did Benito, and they hit him again."

I looked past her to Benito on her other side. If anything, his face looked more bruised and battered than the night before, but that was due mostly to the changing color of his wounds. I couldn't see any new damage, but if he had kept his mouth shut, I was going to give the man a raise.

He nodded a greeting and mouthed, "What's the plan?"

I held up a hand for him to wait. The only plan I'd come up with so far actually didn't include him, and it involved more than a little luck. For the moment, I needed to see where we were going. I wished I had my phone and GPS, but anything I could learn might help me in the long run.

"No talking," Justine said. She nodded at Edgel, and he rested his gun casually on the side of his bucket seat, his finger on the trigger. The gun wasn't pointed at me or Mari, but at Benito. So much for any heroics I might concoct.

We drove southwest through town, the buildings and houses growing more sparse until they quit completely or were swallowed by rainforest. Soon we turned onto a narrow dirt and grass trail, canopied by lush trees and foliage. We were back in the jungle.

I put my arm around Mari and leaned in. "When they aren't looking, shift. *After* we stop." I couldn't remember much from my college physics class but I did recall something about objects in motion remaining in motion. I'd rather her not appear somewhere going the same speed we were driving now and ramming into a wall or a person.

Her eyes whipped to mine. She shook her head.

I nodded encouragingly.

"I don't know how." Her words were scarcely a breath.

That could be a problem. "You have to try." I couldn't help her. I knew less about the ability than she did, with her mathematic skills.

Her eyes narrowed in thought. Several more minutes passed before she looked at me and shook her head. "Can't."

Edgel adjusted his position in the front, meeting my gaze, and Mari and I fell silent. Her face was still drawn, and I knew she was trying to remember. Maybe there was a way I could help. I eased down my barriers, allowing her thoughts to tumble in, emphasized by our proximity and her stress.

The house . . . the plane . . . how? Don't remember . . . got to figure it out . . . impossible.

Part of the problem was that she didn't believe she could shift at all, and for that I couldn't blame her. Could I help without throwing her back to the catatonic state she'd suffered before Dimitri stepped in? Though I believed any damage I inflicted would heal, as with any other wound, having her regress right now meant she wouldn't get free. There was so much I didn't know.

In the sands of Mari's conscious memories, I saw the SUV, the hotel, Tom cracking the gun on my head last night. I paused at that. *Tom was the one who hit me?* Recovering from the surprise, I continued my search.

Remember the Pinz at the airport when we arrived. I pushed the thought into the stream of Mari's mind. She gasped and Edgel turned his pistol toward her.

Justine looked at the mirror. "What?" she barked.

Mari shook her head.

It's me, I told her, pushing the images gently at her. I'm trying to help you find the memory. *Think of the Pinz. I put you there, and you shifted back to the plane. Remember?*

Nothing but confusion from Mari, so this time I sent a picture. Me guiding her to the Pinz, and then finding her in the plane. She nodded her understanding, and my eyes went to the front to see if Justine or Edgel had noticed. *So far so good.*

Mari continued sifting through her memories. How odd that though she was going backward over the events of the past day, the sands of her memories still seemed to flow in the same direction, slightly elevated on one side and going down, past me, and out of sight. That I'd made a representation of myself in Mari's mind was an interesting thing. I'd never done that before.

I caught a glimpse of a woman with tiny braids in her black hair, coming onto the plane to help move the prisoners. Tenika. *What we're looking for is very close.* I stuck my imaginary hands into the sands, willing them to slow.

Mari gave a little groan, and I pulled away, sending her a silent apology. In the sands, the plane disappeared and Mari was in the Pinz. *There,* I told her. *That's when you shifted.*

At that moment the SUV lurched to a stop. I looked through the windshield to see a young boy leading a cow in front of us across the narrow dirt road. Half a dozen poor huts rose along the road behind them, scattered at long, irregular distances. The cow stopped to nibble a patch of grass springing from the dirt. Justine swore under her breath, but she smiled sweetly at the boy and the ancient man who accompanied him.

Maya, I thought, recognizing the earthiness of their thought signatures. We'd come suddenly upon this tiny village, and it was like walking into another world. No TV satellites, Internet, running water, bathrooms, or neighborhood store.

"The plan should have been for them to meet us in Palenque," Justine muttered.

Edgel shook his head. "We all agreed it'd be too easy for the Renegades to find us at a hotel. Besides, you're forgetting that the formula is unstable in the beginning. It's not like we could move it if we were discovered. Better not to risk ruining it."

Justine put the SUV back into motion, and I returned my attention to Mari.

"Where?" Mari formed the word with a breath.

"Dimitri?" Was it too much to hope that she could find him? Probably, although he'd been with her for some time last night. Since I had no idea how shifters focused on people or locations, I couldn't say what was or wasn't possible. Still, the hotel might be easier, since it wouldn't be moving about.

"Hotel?" I mouthed. I hoped my desperation didn't show in my face. "Find Keene." If she told him what happened, he'd somehow contact the others. The most important thing to me was that she got away. Wherever she hid, I'd find her later. Or one of the Renegades would. I hoped.

I wondered if she should try to take Benito with her, but Dimitri had said the ability relied somewhat on the laws of physics, and that might mean she couldn't take anyone she couldn't physically carry. Maybe. It was also possible that she could shift with an elephant. I didn't dare risk finding out—if she managed to shift at all.

Less than a minute later, we came to another stop outside a hut with a roof made of tin sheets, an upgrade from the thatch on the other huts we'd passed. Logs poked out from under the house at regular intervals, raising it off the ground a foot. Probably to keep out the rain.

"Home, sweet home," Justine trilled.

Beside me there was a brief suction of air and for a moment I struggled to catch my breath. But just that fast the sensation ended.

This time it was Benito's turn to cry out. We all turned in his direction.

The seat next to him was empty. Mari was gone.

CHAPTER 18

JUSTINE WAS OUT OF THE SUV AND AROUND TO MY DOOR IN AN instant, yanking it open. "Where is she?" She reached up and grabbed me, pulling me close, her hands locking on my throat. "Where did she go?"

I pushed her away, and she tripped backwards, scrambling for purchase on the ground. "What do you mean? You were right here, same as me. I don't know where she is."

Justine regained her footing and whipped out her gun, pointing it at my face. "Start talking." The hand holding the gun shook.

Edgel slid into his customary place next to her, alert and ready. No chance of doing anything without him stepping in, even if I could dodge the bullet she was planning on putting into me just to alleviate her fury.

"We didn't do nothin'!" Benito shouted around me. "She just disappeared. What kind of people are you? What did you do with her?"

I nearly laughed. Not a good thing to do when an angry woman was pointing a gun at your face, but Benito's idea was a good one, even if he didn't know it.

"Yeah, where is she, Justine? What kind of trick are you trying to pull?" I even managed to sound outraged.

Tom appeared beside Justine. His eyes ran over the inside of the SUV, stopping at the empty place where Mari had been. "Where is she?" The question was obviously meant for Justine.

At the panic in his voice, Justine's fury drained, starting at her face and moving down to her extremities. Her hands stopped shaking. "That's what I'm trying to determine, dear."

"She just disappeared," Benito insisted. "I swear. There was a pop." His accent was back, so strong I could barely understand him.

Justine's gun held steady. "You know what this means, don't you, Tom?" When he shook his head, she continued. "The girl is a shifter."

He looked at her blankly. "A what?"

"A teleporter." Her smile had returned, icy hard. "Get back to the hotel and find her. There's a distance limit for shifters so she can't be far. Take your black bag and make sure she doesn't get away again. With that ability, she's worth a hundred other Unbounded. There's only one known to have survived, and he's too old now to walk, much less shift more than a few feet."

The Emporium had a shifter? That was interesting news. He must be nearing the outside range of our longevity, if he couldn't shift. That meant the ability was related to health and strength, and I was glad I hadn't asked Mari to take Benito. She might not have made it past the bumper. As to where she ended up, I had no clue. Probably back at the hotel. If she didn't make it out of there soon, Tom would find her.

"What about the senator?" Tom asked.

Justine waved his words away. "Fake an illness, or a death threat. Hint that you might have found one of the scientists and need to follow up. Whatever it takes. She's more important than he is."

Tom nodded. "I'll help you get into the house first. They'll need to start the minute they arrive."

Her jaw tightened but she didn't snap as I expected, only

stepped away from the vehicle. At least she lowered her gun, which made my rapid heartbeat begin to slow.

Tom motioned me from the SUV, and I slid out, jumping into the vegetation that had been cut short in a half-hearted attempt to stop the encroaching jungle. Years from now when these huts were gone, the jungle would still be here, slowly absorbing the signs of humanity. Unless a company bought out the village, cut down the trees, and ruined the earth. Dr. Hertenstein had seemed to think the Mexican government was more interested in kickbacks than protecting the environment.

A pit formed in my gut at the thought of the doctor. He was dead. One more casualty in Justine's quest for power. The woman ruined everything she touched.

Tom and Edgel began unloading boxes from the back of the SUV. "You might as well make yourselves useful." Tom shoved a large box into my hands, and I took it, wishing I could see what it held. Benito was likewise burdened, and together we hefted our cargo up the dirt path.

Inside, the hut was empty except for several hammocks strung in an alcove—one on top of the other—a wood stove that stood lone sentinel on the other side of the alcove wall, and in front of this a mound of uneven logs were stacked in a neat pile. The alcove was the only relief in the otherwise oblong room. Tom lowered the plastic tables he carried, unfolding the squares to make rectangular tables.

Justine threw Edgel a length of rope. "Secure them. Hands and feet both. We have work to do and can't be distracted."

Edgel directed us to sit on the floor in the corner farthest from the door. The floor was wood, but rough and unvarnished, the grain filled with dirt that had probably been there a decade. Ignoring him, I strode to the alcove and sat on the lowest hammock.

With a glance at Justine, who hadn't noticed my rebellion, Edgel shoved Benito in my direction.

"Find your own hammock," I said when Benito tried to sit next to me. I was grateful he'd changed clothes, but that didn't mean we needed to get chummy. He nodded and pulled himself onto the hammock above me. The man's expression was stunned and beaten, and I felt sorry for him. At least he was no longer talking about vampires.

Edgel didn't hesitate in securing me first. He knew I was the danger, though I couldn't do anything until the odds were more even. At least he tied my hands in front instead of behind my back. It was a start. One way or the other, I was going to get Benito out of here.

"I have a daughter, too," Edgel said abruptly as he tied the last knot on my wrists. "A mortal. Her mother died in childbirth thirty-five years ago. I raised her. She's married now. Has a little girl and boy. Eight and ten. She thinks I'm dead, but I check up on them. She doesn't know anything about Unbounded." He stole a furtive glance at Justine, who was setting up a gas camp stove. Something in his voice had changed. Something important. I placed my hand on his arm, pushed at his mind . . . and saw a woman's face. Stately, her skin three shades lighter than her father's but strongly resembling him in the eyes.

He'd never told the Emporium about her or her children. Interesting.

There was nothing more. No sand or flashes of other memories. He'd relaxed his control only for a brief moment, perhaps because he believed he was a safe distance from anyone with the sensing ability.

Maybe if I delved deeper, I could change something in his mind. Perhaps convince him to loosen my knots or get himself lost in the forest. It couldn't hurt to try, especially if he'd relaxed this much.

Fingers closed over my tied hands and yanked them from Edgel. Tom. I glared at him as he pushed me back into the hammock. "Give us a moment," he said to Edgel.

Obviously Tom suspected I was trying to influence Edgel, though theoretically it was impossible for a sensing Unbounded to break through the mental shield of an experienced Unbounded.

Tom couldn't know that I'd been able to wiggle my way inside barriers when my target was distracted. But what worried me more was that Tom still hadn't told Justine or Edgel about my true ability. Why wouldn't he warn them, especially if he feared what I could do while touching Edgel?

I reached for Tom's hand, gripping it with both of mine, which were still firmly tied together. "Why?" I breathed out the word, faintly aware of Edgel retreating to the tables with Justine. I pushed hard at Tom's mind as I spoke, but I couldn't get through. No holes anywhere. Just impenetrable blackness. How could he be so strong in only two months? Especially when earlier I'd been able to sense and track him.

"Why, what?" Tom's warm smile chilled me. He'd fooled me once before with that same smile at the Emporium headquarters when Delia had messed with his mind.

I shuddered at the thought. Yet earlier I'd also sensed something familiar about him. Was that something Delia's mental signature? I'd never heard of such a thing or considered it possible. I'd have to ask Cort if there was any mention of it in his records. But the sinking feeling in my chest told me Delia had done something to Tom.

I pulled away from him, feeling ill. "If you find Mari," I said, leaning back in the hammock, "you'd be better off helping her escape."

He chuckled. "I don't think so. I could use a peek into the Triad's secret files, and with her ability, I may have that opportunity."

"Is that what you think? Then you don't know Delia Vesey very well."

His face paled. "That old woman has nothing to do with me."

I sat up again and hissed, "Then why is her mark all over you? And why haven't you told Justine about me?"

"What are you talking about?" His brow puckered, his face close to mine. "Tell Justine what about you? Delia's mark?"

The world tilted. Either Tom had become an excellent liar or he really didn't know. "What do you remember from that day at the Emporium?" I asked softly. "When the grenade went off."

His jaw jutted forward. "You mean how you shot me in the head?"

"She was using you. Delia was. Don't you remember?"

"It's kind of foggy, thanks to you. I'm told it's normal to have a tiny bit of memory loss with that much damage."

He was wrong. We aren't like ordinary humans. All our memories, everything that we are is held in each of the focus points. That is how we are still ourselves after regeneration from severe injury or even temporary death. Tom's systems should have recovered completely.

Unless Delia had prevented it. She hadn't told the rest of the Triad about my ability two months ago, and from the reaction of the Emporium agents I'd encountered this week, she still hadn't shared the information. Which meant she was coming for me . . . eventually. She'd offered me my heart's desire and made the idea of being a god who ruled over mortals sound logical. She scared me more than any Unbounded I'd ever met.

I glanced at Justine across the room, now examining a glass beaker. Did she know Tom might be a puppet for Delia, perhaps spying on everything she did? The woman hadn't been in control of the Triad for over a thousand years for nothing. Obviously, there was a lot I could learn from her—though I might not survive the lesson.

"Never mind," I told Tom. "We can talk about it later."

He smiled, his voice going soft. "I'd like that. And don't worry about Edgel. I'll tell Justine to keep him away from you."

Away from me? Understanding dawned. He hadn't been trying to keep Edgel safe from me, he'd been trying to keep *me* safe from Edgel. "Edgel?" I said with a smirk. "He has no interest in me. He's so smitten with Justine's pheromones that he can't see straight."

Tom laughed as though we were on a date instead of in the roles of kidnapper and kidnappee. "Well, I'd better go find your friend before she scares someone."

He'd flipped so fast between anger, jealousy, and love that I suspected Delia had damaged huge parts of his mind. How long would it take to heal? Was it possible mental wounds didn't heal? There simply wasn't enough information or sensing Unbounded to determine, but whether or not the damage might be permanent was something I had to know before I did any more tramping around in my friends' minds.

One thing I did know was that when a child in any Unbounded line was conceived, the egg was genetically predisposed to choose the healthiest sperm. That didn't guarantee that the gene would become active after the thirtieth birthday, or that the child would be born without flaws, but it did help create the best possible combination. Even the mortal offspring of Unbounded had a lot going for them physically and mentally. Tom hadn't been unbalanced when we were together, so something had changed. Justine and her pheromones? Delia mucking about in Tom's mind? No way to know.

Across the room, Tom paused to talk to Justine, who was filling a beaker with some kind of amber fluid. Edgel lit the first of several camp stoves sitting on one of the tables.

"Benito," I said softly. "Your hands aren't tied, are they?"

"Not yet. I think they forgot."

Overlooked. But not for long. "When they're distracted, come down here and untie me," I said. "Wait until Tom leaves. Then I'm going to make a distraction, and I want you to get out of here. Run into the jungle. Whatever. Just get away and hide. Later, when they're gone you can ask the villagers for help."

"What about you?" He shifted position nervously.

Even with Tom gone, there was no way I could take out both Justine and Edgel, but if I could tap into Edgel's talent, I might be able to distract them long enough to get Benito's pending death off my conscience. I could also destroy as many of their supplies as possible. Even a delay of a few hours might close the window for any action at the senator's celebration this afternoon.

Seconds passed in torturous agony. Tom finally turned toward the door, and Benito slid down next to me where I sat sideways in the hammock. I pulled my knees toward my chest, my feet inside the edges of the hammock, my hands in my lap out of sight. Benito did the same. His fingers were surprisingly steady and the rope quickly dropped away from my hands. I took a breath, my nerves tight and anxious to act.

"She's leaving, too," Benito whispered.

Better for me, but not so great for Benito to sneak out, since there was only one door and she'd be out there. "You'll have to get out the door and run around the hut. Fast. Got it?"

"Got it." He hesitated. "What if they kill you?"

"They won't. Just go. Don't make me sorry for bringing you along." This time he didn't reply.

I waited until Edgel bent over the third camp stove. "Now!" I pushed Benito hard, jumping from the hammock myself, reaching around the alcove wall for one of the logs near the wood stove. I hurled it across the room at Edgel, reaching for another before the first hit its target.

Dodging with a graceful move that ordinarily would have awed me, Edgel stepped to the side, deflecting the log with a metal container he swept up from the table. Before I could blink he leapt over the table and came at me, his fists up, an eager grin on his face. Oh, yeah, he was hoping to make up for last night.

I kicked out and he took the hit without flinching, using the added momentum of the blow to whirl himself around to deliver a powerful strike. I managed to block with the second piece of log I'd pulled from the stack, but his foot caught me in the ribs throwing me back into the wall.

Not going well. He had been ready for me, and I suspected he'd "overlooked" Benito's hands on purpose to have this chance to prove himself. To me? To Justine? To himself? It didn't matter. As long as he didn't go for his gun, I wouldn't complain.

Desperately, I banged at his mental block, but unlike the previous night, I had no weapons to throw at him for a distraction. There was only one way to make sure Benito got free. Pushing off from the wall, I launched myself at Edgel, reaching at the same time for the syringe in my bra.

True to his ability, Edgel had anticipated my move and was ready to meet me. But he hadn't anticipated the needle. It sank into his eye as deep as it could go. I kept pushing until the syringe disappeared partway into his socket. His mouth opened to scream, and I jabbed my fist into his throat to cut off the sound. I followed with another punch at the syringe, my hand erupting in pain. Edgel's good eye rolled upward as he collapsed to the floor.

I leaned over for a moment, sucking in a breath, fire burning in my newly broken ribs. "Aieee." I had at least a few minutes before he healed enough to be trouble—even in Unbounded, the brain was vulnerable—and those few minutes would be all I'd need to torch this place. I could see myself emerging from the jungle when Ritter and the others arrived, having single-handedly stopped Justine's assassination plan. No need for Ritter to lose himself in revenge. Jace would be disappointed, but he'd also be proud.

From the edge of my vision something moved by the door. I whipped upright to meet this new threat, barely blocking the oncoming blow. Justine laughed, her other fist coming at me before I could react. The blow caught me off balance and sent me sprawling.

"Getting slow, are we?" Justine pulled out her pistol and pointed it at me.

The next minute the grin slid from her face as she crumpled to the ground, a huge rock falling with her. I stared in amazement as Benito stood there, shock on his bruised face. "I found it right outside the door," he said. "Saw her going back inside. Thought it might be useful."

I shook my head. "You're crazy."

"Let's get out of here."

Fear radiated from him, bright and debilitating. I threw up my barriers and shook my head. "I have to get rid of these supplies so they can't make their drug. Burn it all, if I can. You go. I'll meet you behind this hut. Hide in the trees and wait for me."

He nodded once, his eyes sweeping uneasily over Justine and Edgel. I didn't wait to see him go but started toward the tables.

A lighter lay beside one of the camp stoves, and shredding a couple of the boxes that had held the supplies would help create a decent blaze. I began ripping the first one, piling it by the wall.

What could I do with Justine and Edgel? I'd like to examine their thoughts—since they were unconscious, their shields would be gone, or at least greatly diminished—but I couldn't take the time now. I had no idea when the men that Ritter and the others were following would end up here, but it had to be soon given the eight hours it took to prepare the drug. I didn't even dare waste time tying them up. At least the fire wouldn't kill them permanently, and as long as we retrieved them before the Emporium did, we'd be able to question them once they healed.

I'd begun stacking whole boxes in a bonfire pile when a sound at the door broke my concentration. "Benito, I said you should—"

Too late I noticed he was backing in, his hands above his head. Pushing out my thoughts, I felt them, two life forces, only one shielding his mind. The shielding life force was closer, probably the focus of Benito's terror, while the unshielded life force was several yards away in front of the hut, his unbridled fear choking the breath from my throat.

"Well, what have we here?" A man came into view through the door, his gun pointed at Benito. My jaw tensed as I recognized one of Stefan's sons, and thus my supposed half brother. He was slightly built, with wispy hair, his face small and crunched, as if his features hadn't time to fully develop, but his movements showed Unbounded assurance.

"Jonny," I said.

He laughed, his blue eyes crinkling at the sides. "Hello, Erin. Didn't expect to see you here." I started to get up, but he waved his gun. "Don't try anything. You know how fast I am. I'd hate to have to shoot you."

His speed was a variation of the combat ability, a poor one in his opinion, though I'd been impressed. Unfortunately for him, he was the result of a forced Changing at eighteen by the Emporium, a semi-successful experiment that ended in the death of at least one of Jonny's close friends. As a side effect of the experiment, he was now aging at five times the rate of a normal Unbounded. He already looked near thirty, when at his real age of a hundred and fifteen, he should still look nineteen. In my mind, he was a child in an adult body, which was silly, given that he was far older than I was, but it was a perception left over from our first meeting that I hadn't been able to shake.

"You don't sound all that sorry," I said.

He laughed again. "Not really, after the night I had. Look, tie up this fellow before I wake Justine." He blew out a short blast of air. "Don't know which of you did this to her, but it ain't going to be pretty when she wakes up."

Benito shot me a frightened look.

As if on cue, Justine stirred. Benito stumbled rapidly back from her, falling into the bottom hammock.

Justine pushed to a seated position, shaking her head as though to clear it. "Jonny," she purred, reaching for her gun. "You're a bit early."

He pulled out a thumb drive from his pocket. "We had a little trouble. Caught wind of some Renegades following us. The rest of the gang stayed and set a trap for them, while I grabbed the scientist and came here."

"Nice. Where is he?" She climbed to her feet. Behind her, Benito shrank into a miserable ball.

"The scientist? Outside on a horse. He's a little worse for wear. He couldn't keep up with me on foot, of course, and I couldn't carry him the whole way, so I hijacked the horse for us a while back. I don't think he's ever ridden before. He kept falling off, so I had to tie him on. He should still be there—along with the stuff we took from the lab."

"He ready to start cooking?"

"Sure. It's not like he ran for more than a few miles." Jonny snorted and rolled his eyes. "Actually staggered would be a more accurate term, despite all my pushing. He should have your drug all mixed before the others deal with those Renegades and catch up to us."

"Good." Justine glanced at Benito, who lowered his gaze. "You, I'll deal with later. In fact, I've just decided that you'll play a starring role in my plans this afternoon."

I didn't like the sound of that.

Her gaze switched to me. "Ready to give up yet, Erin? You can't beat me." She waved me over to the hammock.

I had no choice but to obey. Minutes later, Benito and I were securely tied in separate hammocks, and Justine was administering Emporium tonic to Edgel. I didn't bother telling her that he'd already received a full dose from my needle. Near the tables, a portly, red-haired scientist wearing broken eyeglasses mixed chemicals with shaking hands. The fear coming from his unshuttered mind was numbing, and I had to close myself off completely.

What sort of trap had Jonny and his friends set for Ritter and the others? Jonny had almost caused Ritter's death at our past encounter. He was both quick and intelligent, and any plan he'd helped concoct would be a good one. Though he was bitter about the experiments enacted upon him, he was fiercely loyal to Stefan and the Emporium.

"You're sure you can do this within eight hours?" Justine left Edgel and sauntered over to the scientist.

He nodded. "Seven and a half. That is, uh, if you have all the supplies." I pegged him as an American by his accent.

"We have them." Justine studied the doctor through half-closed eyelids. "There are enough pharmaceutical companies around that we were able to buy what we needed."

His head jerked. "Yes. Th-they're ruining the rainforest."

"Don't be so nervous." Justine's soothing voice paled in comparison with the huge amount of pheromones floating around her. I could feel them around me, promising me secret pleasure. "You don't have anything to worry about as long as you fix this up for us. We'll have you back home in no time."

The scientist's hands stopped shaking. "You're very beautiful."

"Thank you." Justine ran a finger down his cheek, her long nails painted purple like her shirt. Had she planned that in advance or had she found time to visit a nail salon here? Maybe Edgel had hidden talents I wasn't aware of.

"You'll do your very best for me, won't you?" Justine added.

The scientist nodded and reached for a beaker.

I tore my eyes away from the pathetic sight. First they frighten the poor doctor nearly to death and then they overdose him on Justine. He didn't stand a chance. "Why didn't you do what I told you to?" I asked Benito. "If you'd left the first time, it'd only be me stuck here."

He shrugged. "It's a jungle. I don't like snakes."

But I knew he'd stayed out of loyalty, and that meant I was once again responsible for whatever happened to him. Better that I'd given him my wallet and Mari's ring back in Portland.

If only there was a way to warn Ritter. I had to try. Dropping my mental shield, I reached out past the scientist's eager flurry, searching the surrounding area. Maybe if they were close enough, I could reach my brother, Jace. Searching . . . harder . . . reaching. A dull throb began in my temples and at the base of my head. Nothing, but the whisper of the native life, blending in with the jungle around us.

Frowning, I'd begun pulling in my thoughts when my mind stumbled on something. Mari. Her fear and eagerness burst through my mind. I stiffened. Had she shifted back here? That was the only explanation for why I felt her so close.

Jonny stretched and walked toward the door. "Going to look around," he called to Justine. "If those guys spring that trap right, it shouldn't be long before they're here." Without waiting for her agreement, he strode outside.

I waited for the shout of discovery or the sound of a bullet shattering the peace of the village, but nothing happened. I closed my eyes and concentrated on Mari, but she was gone—if she'd ever been here at all. Was I imagining things? Or had she popped in while trying to get away from Tom?

I hadn't felt so helpless in a long time, but there didn't seem to be any way to get free, so I let myself slip back into worrying about Jace and the others. Would Cort die without knowing Tom was his brother? Would I forever mourn the fact that I'd never be able to clear the air with Dimitri?

I felt most stupid about not working things out with Ritter. I'd been so busy trying to punish him for lost time that I may have squandered all the time we'd had left.

CHAPTER 19

Minutes ticked into one hour, and then two. After three hours my position on the hammock had become torture. Above me, Benito snored, apparently undisturbed by his tied hands. The scientist, his fear allayed by Justine's pheromones, worked feverishly, eager to please, looking every so often at a laptop screen where Jonny had plugged in his thumb drive.

Edgel had mostly recovered and now shot me black stares with his undamaged eye whenever I shifted position. When he wasn't glaring at me, he was walking to the door and peering out, seemingly as worried as I was when no one else appeared. I imagined Jace fighting in the jungle. I should never have left him. And Ritter. I couldn't even go there.

Finally, the scientist sighed. "Okay, now we just have to wait."

"That's it?" Justine asked. "It's not sensitive to movement anymore?"

He grinned. "We don't have to worry about that now. But these two mixtures must sit separately for three hours by themselves."

"Exactly three?"

"Doesn't really matter. But at least three before they're mixed.

Not more than ten. The real trick is that this frozen mixture"—he motioned to a test tube in a case of dry ice—"must stay frozen until it goes in with the others, and it must be in at least fifty-five minutes before it is injected into the subject."

"In with the mixture? Or after it's thawed and mixed?" She caressed the upper part of his arm, rubbing up and down.

He leaned into her hand. "Oh, you add it in frozen. Mix only after it dissolves. That takes about twenty minutes. Mix by swirling together in the test tube. No spoon or anything needed. The three mixtures stay together fifty-five minutes from the time it thaws. It'll stay good for about twenty-four hours, but after that it degrades. We never tested stabilizers or anything. It's all written in my notes."

"You're certain it will work?"

"We tried it out on our test subjects." He frowned when she took her hand away. "Fortunately, it was in a controlled environment, and we were able to sedate them until it wore off. The effect on their immune system was remarkable, though, and it pointed us in the right direction for our main objective. We had to remove all the negative aspects, of course."

"Negative meaning that your subjects will do anything suggested to them."

"Or any thought that crosses their mind." His brow furrowed. "Violent things, that is. To themselves, others, anyone. We didn't test exactly why. We thought it best not to . . ." He shook his head. "After a few hours there's no trace of the drug in their bodies—or at least nothing that doesn't look like it should already be there. You're not really going to use this, are you?"

Justine's eyes met mine. "Oh, yes. We are. But don't worry. It's for a very good cause, and you won't be blamed." She broke eye contact with me and waved at Edgel. "The doctor here needs to go for a walk. Take care of him would you? We don't need his services any longer."

"No!" I sat up, straining against my bonds.

Apart from the fact that he was an innocent here, I needed him for Stella and Bronson. If I didn't manage to get that thumb drive, he'd be their only hope.

"I do need to see a man about a dog," the scientist said, winking at me. "I'll be right back."

"Sure you will." Justine kissed her finger and placed it on the man's lips. "Goodbye, uh, Mr. Scientist." She didn't even know his name.

He laughed. "You'd better be here when I get back. I don't like these other guys so well."

"Come on." Edgel put a hand on his shoulder.

"No! Please, Justine," I said. "It's for a friend."

Justine sauntered in my direction. "What friend?"

Edgel paused at the door, and I was sensing something from him now. Something about his daughter. But it vanished as he pulled the door open.

"Don't do it!" I called after him, but already he was taking out his gun. My stomach churned.

"You know I can't let him live." Justine's voice came from so close it startled me. "We have too much invested in autoimmune medicines to allow a cure."

I searched her face. "I just need it for a friend."

She sat down in the hammock beside me. "I'm sorry. I really am." She sighed deeply. "You know sometimes I really hate all this. One of the best times of my life was when Tom and I met you and we were all just ordinary people. I loved all the things we did together."

"It was all a lie."

She gave a soft groan. "It still meant something. I miss those days."

I believed her. Not only because she wasn't emitting pheromones, but because of the emotions peeling off her. Not a glimpse into her mind exactly, but like Edgel earlier, a loosening of control. Even so, I would not be moved. She didn't deserve forgiveness, and I wouldn't give it to her.

"You've never told him you're his mother," I said.

She started at that, an involuntary jerk that told me she'd thought her secret safe. "I don't plan to. Yet."

"Does Tihalt know he has another son?"

"Oh." She waved that aside. "Everyone is required to participate in the genetic experiments, even Tihalt, and I simply used my ability to exchange a few tubes. He doesn't know—yet." She smiled. "But he will. I've been planning this a long time."

"This? You mean taking control of the Triad."

She shrugged. "Delia's ruled it for long enough."

"Stefan is no pansy."

Justine laughed. "Oh, no. That he is not. But him I can work with. He is a man after all."

"I think you've bitten off more than you can chew."

"Perhaps." She sighed. "See? Isn't this nice? All this exchange of information? If we worked together, there's no end to what we could do."

"Until I wanted to do something you didn't approve of." Why was I sitting here chatting with her when so many lives hung in the balance? But there didn't seem to be another option. Even if I attacked her now, and managed to knock her out somehow, my hands were still tied so tight they were numb, the two ends of the rope firmly knotted on the opposite sides of the hammock out of my reach.

"Something I don't approve of? You mean like that delicious Renegade you had with you in New York?" She licked her lips, and I caught a subtle shift in my emotions that told me she'd resorted to pheromones again. She should realize by now that though I wasn't immune, I was able to resist. "I don't blame you for the attraction," she added. "But Tom really is better for you."

"I don't love Tom."

"So you're with that Renegade now?" Justine's expression was calm, but her eyes glittered dangerously.

I stared right back. She didn't deserve an answer. "You helped murder his family."

"I was protecting the Emporium. *My* family. That we missed

him was unfortunate. Apparently more unfortunate than I knew at the time, if he's influencing you. Did you tell him it was me who was there that day when his family died? Tom said he told you. I bet him you wouldn't say anything." She laughed at my grimace. "I'll have to tell Tom I was right. That should tell you something, Erin. Think about it."

Edgel returned to the hut alone. He dug into a box and pulled out a couple of bullets, refilling those missing from his magazine. Pushing out with my mind, I searched for the life force that had been the scientist. It was gone.

I swallowed bile, feeling completely and utterly useless. "Go away, Justine," I told her. "Leave me alone. And quit it with the pheromones."

"Fine." Justine bounced from the hammock, but she didn't leave. Instead, she leaned over to whisper. "Do you know about his son?"

I froze. "What do you know about it?"

"There's a facility in London. A hospital for the very wealthy. Place is like Fort Knox. Not even we can penetrate it. We've tailed Ritter there several times there over the years."

"So?"

"The hospital deals only with addiction."

I considered for a moment. Her comments told me Ritter's foster son was Unbounded, something I hadn't realized during my discussion with him in the forest. I'd figured he was a mortal, probably still fairly young, but his being Unbounded changed my perception about what kind of worry Ritter had endured. Alcohol didn't stay in our systems long, and for recreational drugs—or any drug—to work for more than a few hours, an Unbounded had to ingest it in extremely concentrated quantities, like the drug we used to keep Emporium Unbounded unconscious during transport. The only exception was curequick. That also didn't stay in the system long, but it was potent enough in its regular form to cause addiction in even a short time, and it was easily available among Unbounded, so the dosage could be repeated often.

I'd heard enough horror stories about curequick addiction to make me shun it for everything but emergencies.

Justine laughed. "We all have our dirty little secrets."

I knew she'd kill Ritter as readily as he'd kill her, given the chance, and his foster son might be that chance. I'd have to warn Ritter.

"Was he one of the Renegades following my people in the jungle?" Justine asked, sympathy oozing from her voice. "Poor, Erin. For what it's worth, I'm very sorry. But believe me, you're better off without him."

Without waiting for an answer, she strode over to Edgel. "Let's get this ready to go. Jonny hasn't returned from his little scouting tour, and I don't like that we can't contact them and that someone's messing with the satellites. They should have arrived hours ago. Make sure we keep everything just as our dearly departed doctor set it up. Leave all the equipment. Like him, it's no longer necessary. There won't be time for a second batch."

If the drug didn't work, would they resort to their original plan, or take out the senator later? Or was there some added angle we weren't seeing, as Keene suspected? Justine's emotions had gone completely dark again, another indication of her worry.

Edgel got down to work. I'd heard of people cutting off their own limbs to escape a difficult situation, and if I had something sharp, I'd be tempted to cut off my hand to free it from the rope. At least my limb would regrow. Sitting there doing nothing was driving me insane. There wasn't much to pack. Justine and Edgel carried the necessary items out to her SUV and were back within minutes, but this time Jonny was with them, and he was breathing hard. "You're sure?" Justine was saying to him.

Jonny nodded. "I can only assume things didn't go exactly as planned."

Yes! Hope changed everything.

"Get them." Justine gestured toward Benito and me, pulling out my machete and handing it to Jonny. "We're leaving now. Hurry!"

"We aren't staying to help?" Edgel beat Jonny to the hammock and cut Benito's rope with his own knife, tossing the man over his shoulder.

"I can't risk them getting back the drug or the information." She hesitated, gauging Edgel's reaction before adding. "You can stick around, if you must, but stay out of sight until our guys arrive. Surround the Renegades. But make sure you don't get caught. I'll need you later."

Edgel gave her a hard look, apparently irritated at her attempt to school him in combat strategy. Justine must have forgotten to emit her pheromones to ease his annoyance. "Just keep that research safe," he said. "I'll take care of the rest."

Jonny cut the ends of my rope and handed the machete back to Justine. While she grabbed a few more items from a table, he drew his pistol, pulled me to my feet, and shoved me toward the door, holding my rope like a leash. I dragged my feet. "Don't make me shoot you." His smile didn't falter, but his tone didn't quite contain his usual youthful exuberance.

Shooting me was exactly what he would have to do to get me into Justine's SUV.

I waited to act until we cleared the door. By that time, Edgel had already dumped Benito into the SUV and was disappearing into the forest with an automatic rifle. Jonny's eyes followed him, a surge of jealousy breaking through his defenses. Accompanying the emotion was the desperate wish that his Change hadn't been forced early, and the belief that if it hadn't, he would have developed the full combat ability instead of only the speed. For the moment, his bitterness blotted out everything else. That he could just as well be wrong in his assumption didn't make a difference.

"Hurry it up, Jonny," Justine barked as she strode past us to the SUV.

Gathering up a bit of slack from the rope, I took a few steps away from Jonny and yanked as hard as I could, pulling it from his grasp. He stumbled but recovered faster than I could blink.

I ran.

A shot whizzed past me, and I belatedly remembered to dodge. Unfortunately, I was heading in the direction of the jungle where Edgel had disappeared. Half expecting him to materialize, I hurtled on.

Something large slammed into me from behind: Jonny. I tumbled to the ground, kicking out at him. Air whooshed from his lungs as he toppled backward. Had he dropped his gun? I jumped to my feet, ignoring the screaming in my ribs. The idiot had broken another of my ribs, and after I'd healed from Edgel's punch this morning.

Jonny was on his feet even before I was. The gun wasn't in his hand. I lashed out, finding flesh. Jonny's response was a terrific blow to my stomach. Agony erupted in my ribs.

"Hurry, hurry!" Justine shouted. "They're coming!"

Sure enough, farther down in the sparse village, the Pinz was moving as fast as it could toward us.

I slugged Jonny with my tied hands, catching him on the jaw, but not hard enough to do much good. He was even faster at dodging than Jace or Ritter. I had to give him that. If I could land even one solid blow, he'd be out. He wasn't much bigger than I was.

Justine revved the engine and zoomed past us. Jonny threw one last punch and took off after her on foot. My head reeled.

The Pinz roared toward me, the passenger door opening. Ritter held out an arm, and I reached for him. Again the agony exploding in my chest as he pulled me inside. To my relief, Jace was driving. He looked no worse for wear, except for a layer of dirty sweat on his face. There was no sign of Cort and Dimtri.

The Pinz had only one front passenger seat, so I stayed on Ritter's lap. It wasn't a bad place to be. His arms encircled me, the hard warmth of his chest giving me the ridiculous feeling of being safe. A knife had somehow materialized in his hands, and he began severing my bonds.

"Benito?" he asked.

"Justine's got him in that SUV."

Jace scowled. "We'll never catch them. Not unless she stays in the jungle."

"We can't go after them anyway. We need to get back to Cort and Dimitri." Ritter sounded worried.

"Where are they?"

"Back a couple miles. That's where the Emporium caught up to us."

I couldn't believe they'd leave the others.

As if sensing my disapproval, Ritter said shortly, "We all agreed we had to risk getting the research. We failed. Now we go back."

Jace was already guiding the Pinz around the hut, thundering over tall brush instead of wasting time backing up to turn around. "We got you, at least."

"How'd you even know I was here?" My body jolted to the side as Jace swung back to the shorter vegetation between the scattered huts. Ritter's grasp tightened, holding me in place. His touch felt right. I wanted to apologize, but now wasn't the time.

"We scouted around at first light this morning. Found their trail just like we planned. Like a sign inviting us to come along. Easy." Ritter's breath felt hot on the back of my neck. "Too easy, apparently. We were getting in the Pinz to follow when Mari showed up."

"Mari?"

Jace guffawed. "Yeah, Dimitri was behind a bush taking care of business, and he turned around and there she was. Her ability led her right to him. She told us they had taken you someplace, and we figured that's where they were going, so we followed a little faster. But like Ritter said, it was too easy. Like they wanted us to catch up. We began to suspect a trap. That's when Ritter had the great idea to send Mari back with a GPS and get a reading where you actually were."

So I *had* sensed Mari. "It was a risk. What if she'd been caught?"

"She wanted to do it," Ritter said. "And a good thing she did because they were leading us completely the wrong way. So, we turned around and came after you."

"They sent one man and the scientist," I explained. "They arrived hours ago. They've made that drug Hertenstein warned us about. It's not quite finished, but Justine apparently has everything they need. They're going to use it during the senator's celebration this afternoon. There's supposed to be a lot of people there. School children will be performing. Worse, they'll be in range of a cell tower soon. We won't be able to stop them from getting out copies of the research."

The men took a moment to absorb the information. "We still have to do what we can," Jace said. "To save those children, I mean."

Ritter nodded. "I agree. And there's always a possibility we'll get the research back, especially with how power-hungry Justine is. She may want to keep the new drug to herself for now." His words made me feel better, though not by much.

"She killed both scientists," I said, my stomach curling at the memory. "At this point, I'd be happy just to get a copy of the research for Stella, regardless of what Justine does with it."

"This could be the beginning of the end." The grimness in Ritter's voice reminded me of the high stakes. No longer was it just Bronson's life at stake. This was the future of the world—and who would run it.

It seemed we'd lost already. Yet not one of us would give up.

"Almost there." Ritter stared out the windshield.

I craned my neck and squinted, seeing only two abandoned jeeps in the overgrown path ahead. "Those belong to the Emporium, I'm guessing, but where are they?"

"Jungle. I guess."

"But Mari doesn't know how to fight."

"She's not there."

"What?"

Ritter shrugged. "She shifted when they caught up to us. She seems to have gotten the hang of popping in and out. We don't know where she went, but she'll be okay."

Unless she'd gone back to the hotel and Tom found her. But

surely she'd be expecting him to look for her there. Knowing her value, at least he wouldn't kill her right away.

"I need weapons." Twisting my body, I put my foot on the seat between Ritter's legs and hoisted myself into the back. A jolt of the Pinz landed me on top of a mound of supplies, and pain knifed through me again. I went for the large green duffel where we kept a variety of smaller weapons. I began stocking up, feeling an odd nostalgia for the machete. I hadn't given it to Justine, but nothing had happened to her, so maybe whatever ancient magic permeated the strange metal needed more time. Or it was nonsense.

Grabbing a clear bottle of curequick, I chugged it down. No time to worry about addiction. I needed to be in top form. I'd been absorbing, but my ribs needed some extra attention. Even with the curequick, I couldn't heal instantly, but in ten minutes I'd be feeling a lot better. By four o'clock, I'd be ready to face Justine again. I really needed to find her before then.

"Grab a vest, too," Ritter said.

I didn't like the extra weight, but it would be better not to risk a bullet to the heart. Even dying temporarily would mean less chance of helping Bronson.

The Pinz lurched to a stop, and I turned to say, "There's a group of people to the left. They're all running. We'd get there faster if you can drive through the trees."

Jace was only too happy to try. The Pinz rocked back and forth as we rolled through the jungle, crushing vegetation as we went. I staggered to the front of the back section, so I could cling to the edges of Ritter and Jace's seats and peer through the windshield. We were going up an incline, leaving a battered trail of jungle vegetation behind us. I hoped we weren't displacing any more black howler monkeys.

The blocked minds I'd felt before must have moved out of reach because they'd all vanished. When I tried to reach further, my mind sent a white flash of hot pain.

"Can't go on," Jace said, as we caught sight of a huge pile of rocks beneath a tall cliff. "Brush is too thick."

I pushed outward again, catching only the faintest pinpoints of several life forces. "I think they're behind those rocks." Not rocks, really, but boulders that years ago must have fallen from the cliff and rolled to their current position, now covered by abundant vines. I could hear the sound of running water in the distance.

Slinging on his FAL, Ritter opened his door and jumped out, landing at the same time as Jace. I climbed over the seat and joined them. We could hear rushing water but couldn't see its source.

"Anything?" Jace asked as we ran toward the rocks. "Look for two people by themselves."

I shook my head. "Sorry. Too far away."

A single gunshot marred nature's melody and cut short any discussion. We ran faster, jumping thick vines and old logs, skirting taller brush and trees. Within minutes we reached the rocks that now loomed over us. Ritter motioned for Jace to go one way and me the other, while he began climbing the rocks. Three more rapid gunshots cranked up our pace.

I was nearly around the rocks when an earthy consciousness appeared on my radar, moving fast. A sound escaped my lips. Ritter appeared far above me on the rocks. "What is it?" he called.

"Him." I tipped my head at a native who had emerged from the trees. His face was dark and leathery, but his bare arms were strong and supple. He wore brown pants, a loosely-woven top the color of mixed jungle greens, and a belt that tied at the waist and hung down with a fringed end. A worn but colorful cloth bag graced his shoulder, and a brown hat sat on graying hair that twisted into two long braids. It was impossible for me to guess his age, but his dark eyes were bottomless, as though they'd seen more than his share of both beauty and heartache. He held up a hand, blocking my passage.

"I don't think he wants me to go any further," I called to Ritter. "Better tell him we have to help our friends."

"Assuming he can communicate in any of the dialects I know." Ritter jumped the twenty-odd feet from his perch on the rocks, somehow landing without injuring himself. He began speaking in the flowing, musical language he'd used yesterday with the other Maya. When the man didn't respond, Ritter tried again. More music, but this time with a faint rush of the wind.

Still no response, though the man appeared to be listening. I reached out to him, pushing at the sand stream of his thoughts until images rushed toward me, flavored by a language I didn't understand. Fortunately, images didn't require language. "It's sacred ground," I said. "I'm seeing religious rites. And a burial site, a tomb behind the waterfall. He's upset."

Jace appeared behind us. "What's the holdup? I was almost around the rock when two natives just like this guy appeared out of nowhere, blocking my path. I was about to go through them when I thought I heard Erin calling."

"Must have been me projecting. Sorry." I shot him a frown. "You need to keep your shield up." So did I. "Anyway, we're not sure what's going on yet."

Ritter made still another attempt at communication, this time stumbling over the words.

The Maya nodded and replied briefly.

"Not the same dialect at all," Ritter said, "but I think he more or less understood me every time I tried. All the dialects have similarities. I have no idea what he said back, though."

I pushed an image of Cort and Dimitri toward the Maya. In my make-believe image they were running from men with guns and long swords, like Ritter and Jace wore in their back sheaths. Edgel hadn't been wearing a sword, but he'd been in public at the hotel. I was sure at least a few of the other Emporium agents would have them.

The Maya's gaze shifted to me, his head tilting to one side as if listening. "Our friends," I said, sending the image again. "We have to help them." Lacking another idea, I pushed out an image of Cort and Dimitri huddled together behind Ritter, who stood at attention with his sword raised in a protective stance—a gun seemed wrong for this place.

The Maya held up both hands and spoke. In his mind, I saw us climbing back into the Pinz.

"What's he saying?" Jace asked.

Ritter shook his head. "I think he wants us to leave. It's hard to tell." Three more gunshots pierced the forest calm. "We can't wait any longer. We'll have to go around him. Or through him." Ritter sounded as though he already regretted the decision and the damage we would cause.

Yet the picture in the Maya's mind showed Dimitri and Cort standing outside the Pinz beside the Maya himself. "Ask him if he'll bring them to us."

"What?" Ritter arched a brow.

"It's worth a shot. As satisfying as getting rid of those Emporium Unbounded would be, we've got planning to do if we're going to stop Justine. The important thing right now is getting Cort and Dimitri back safely." There was also the very big chance that one or more of us wouldn't make it out alive, and I didn't like the odds. The Emporium hadn't spent years breeding Unbounded with the combat ability for nothing.

Ritter hesitated, his jaw clenched. "Okay." He rambled off words in the less familiar dialect. The old man put his hands together and nodded, rattling more liquid words. Ritter looked back at me helplessly. "I asked him how he'd do it, but I didn't really get what he said."

"I don't like this." Jace dug at the ground with a boot. "This is the Emporium we're talking about. They're not giving up just because it's a burial ground. We have to go in and get them."

"Give them a few minutes." I looked up to address the Maya, but he'd disappeared.

"We could go for them now." Jace took a couple steps forward.

"No," Ritter and I said together. Grabbing Jace, we turned in the direction of the Pinz. The way back seemed much longer. We were only halfway when a flurry of rapid shots halted our progress.

"Machine gun," Jace said grimly. "Or something similar."

"Forget this!" Gritting his teeth, Ritter whirled, launching into a run. Jace hurtled after him. Ritter was nearly back to the mound of rocks when the vines covering them began moving. The vines pushed aside, revealing a cave—and the barrel of a gun.

Ritter raised his own rifle, leaping to the side to find cover.

CHAPTER 20

DIMITRI'S WIDE SHOULDERS EDGED FROM THE CAVE OPENING, his rifle ready. Cort was right behind him, followed by the Maya we'd just talked to—or someone who looked enough like him to be his brother. He wasn't wearing the colorful cloth bag, though, so maybe it wasn't the same man.

"Oh, it's you." Dimitri relaxed and lowered his gun as he saw Ritter. Jace and I skidded to a halt. "That's a relief."

"What happened?" Jace asked.

Cort pushed past Dimitri. "We were pinned down behind the waterfall. Fortunately, this fellow appeared and showed us an underground tunnel that came up on the other side of these rocks. There's a cave—or a tunnel, rather—that goes straight through this whole rock pile. Unfortunately, the Emporium caught sight of us going into the other side. But I guess you heard the shooting."

"We gonna take 'em?" Jace's face glowed.

"No!" everyone said.

Guttural shouts came from the tunnel.

"Get to the Pinz," Ritter barked. "Hurry!"

Dimitri led the way at a run. Cort spoke to the Maya, making an urgent motion with his hands. I ran after Dimitri. When I looked back again, the Maya had vanished. Jace hurtled past me, leapt into the cab of the Pinz, and brought the engine to life with a roar. He was turning the vehicle before I reached it, and I jumped into the back, rotating to see Cort coming fast. Ritter was a blur behind him.

"All in!" I shouted to Jace as the others vaulted into the back. Jace stepped on the gas and we left the rocks behind before anyone else had emerged from the cave. We clung to the benches to avoid being tossed around like our supplies. Something heavy crashed against my leg; I pushed it away. Only Ritter didn't secure himself. He crouched near the back, his rifle ready, shifting his weight with each lurch, somehow maintaining balance.

Jace continued in a mad race down the incline that had seemed so gradual on the way up. I was glad I hadn't eaten any real food since yesterday, or I might have lost it all over the supplies, and Ritter would request additional training for me.

When we neared the two deserted Jeeps we'd passed earlier, Ritter pulled a rocket launcher from one of the cases in the back, though how he managed when Jace wasn't slowing down was a mystery. "Let's make it harder for them to catch up to us."

Destroying their transportation was a great idea. We were far enough away from the Palenque ruins that they wouldn't get there in time to help Justine carry out the assassination.

Swiftly, Ritter lifted the weapon. "Ears!" He shouted as we roared past the Jeeps.

A flash of red made me grab his arm. "Wait!"

He hesitated, blinking as he spotted Mari standing near the Jeeps, her red T-shirt clearly visible under her blue bulletproof vest.

"Jace! Stop!" I screamed. Dimitri and Cort echoed my plea, and we all tumbled from our places as he slammed on the brakes. Ritter was back on his feet instantly, reaching for Mari as she ran toward the Pinz.

A spray of bullets from the far side of the clearing had us all ducking for cover. Mari suddenly disappeared from outside and reappeared next to me. "Go!" Dimitri shouted. Jace punched the Pinz into motion.

Ritter swept up the rocket launcher again and fired. One of the Jeeps erupted in an impressive explosion. Before Ritter could take another shot, Edgel appeared behind the Pinz, showering the back with more bullets. We hit the floor. Next time, I was going to request a complete hard body Pinz instead of one with a back tarp. Not as much protection as we needed.

Jace drove faster, and Edgel's figure receded. "Everyone okay?" Ritter asked.

"I'm going to need some bandages," Dimitri said. "And some curequick."

I turned to see Cort sprawled half on the bench and half on the supplies. Blood dripped from his neck and out the bottom of his bulletproof vest.

"Injectable," Dimitri added, checking Cort's pulse. "He's unconscious. I'll need a painkiller as well. Looks like one of the bullets hit him under the arm. Might have hit his heart because I can't find a pulse. Another got him in the neck. I won't be able to remove the bullets while we're moving."

I found the syringes with curequick while Ritter dug for the bandages. I began injecting Cort's chest and neck, and then sat next to Mari while Ritter assisted Dimitri in packing Cort's wounds. We didn't dare stop, but the less blood he lost now meant a faster recovery. It was strange seeing Cort like this. He seemed to be dead and he had no heartbeat, but before long, he'd heal enough to wake.

Mari frowned at Cort's inert body. "He really is going to be okay, right?"

"Yeah," I said. "Believe me, this isn't the first time for him. But what about you? How are you feeling?"

"I'm good." She gave me a lopsided smile. "In fact, I'm embarrassed to say that I'm *really* good. Oh, Erin, it's everything you said it was! I feel . . . I feel . . . incredible!"

I had to admit she was looking pretty incredible, and not all of it could be attributed to my favorite jeans. Her silky black hair lay around her—not tangled but definitely windblown—her face had a healthy color, and her eyes gleamed with excitement.

"Shifting . . . it's like I . . . was meant to do it." She lifted her hands, fingers splayed as though trying to capture something invisible. "I see the numbers and all I have to do is move them around until they fit where I want to go. Then I'm moving through space. It's like finding what I was meant to do, like I've been searching for something my whole life and it was there all along inside me. I feel alive for the first time!" She paused before adding, "I've hardly even thought of Trevor. Isn't that terrible?"

"No, it's not terrible at all."

"I'm different," she said fiercely, "and I like it. I like it a whole lot."

That was good because she really didn't have a choice. You couldn't cut out the Unbounded gene. It would do whatever it wanted in remaking us. I glanced over at the men. "They told me you gave them my location, but what happened after that?"

"Well, we went to find you. But the Emporium caught up to us somehow and they had some heavy guns, so Dimitri and Cort decided to create a distraction. There were so many bullets flying around that Dimitri told me to shift out. That's all I know. When I couldn't stand not knowing anymore, I shifted back, right to the same place I'd left. I hid in the trees until I saw you coming, and then I shifted right by the Jeeps so you'd see me."

"You almost got yourself blown up."

She shrugged. "Yeah, I guess that wasn't such a good idea. I was just so glad to find you guys."

"Where'd you go?"

Her eyes widened. "That's another reason I couldn't risk that you wouldn't see me. When I shifted back to the hotel, I found Keene. He's been trying to reach you all. When he couldn't at least get you on your phone, he figured something was wrong." She lowered her voice and whispered. "He wanted me to let him know once they found you."

The comment made me aware that Ritter had finished with Cort and was watching me, his dark eyes shuttered. I didn't look away for a long moment.

"Anyway, nothing's changed with the senator," Mari continued. "But Keene's got some feelers out about what's happening."

I shook my head. "We need to warn him to be more careful. Apparently, he's been causing a lot of headaches for the Emporium and they decided to plug the leak. His coming here was a setup. They know about his informant."

Dimitri looked up from Cort. "Mari, we can't stop for at least another few miles, but would you be able to find Keene again without putting yourself in danger?"

"Yeah. We set a place to meet." She felt the pocket of her jeans, frowning when she realized she didn't have a phone. Almost immediately, her frown vanished. "Wait, that's right. I don't need the time. I'm supposed to meet him in eighteen minutes." Scarcely concealed contentment laced her voice.

"How do you know that?" I asked.

"Easy—I've been counting in my mind. We agreed on forty minutes, but some of that time I was waiting in the trees."

"We should be able to stop before then," Ritter said. "I hope he doesn't get himself killed." He took a compass from a pocket. "Hopefully, we'll find an actual road soon. We need to get to those ruins. There should be a hotel nearby to stash Cort."

We moved along in silence for several minutes, jostling back and forth over the uneven jungle trail. Dimitri sat on a duffel that held one of the tents, a hand on Cort's exposed flesh above the bandage. This put Dimitri in the aisle, brushing up against my knee, but neither of us moved away. I didn't know what that meant.

"You don't think the Emporium will hurt those Maya back there, do you?" I asked no one in particular, wiping a trickle of sweat that skidded down my temple. The heat inside the Pinz was growing more intense by the moment, signaling the passage of the day.

Ritter took his gaze from the terrain behind us. "I doubt it. They're less than ants to the Emporium, and they know how to make themselves scarce."

"Yeah, they did that at that little village." I sighed. "Guess they'll think twice about renting one of their huts to someone in the future." I wondered what Justine had paid them, or if she'd simply turned on the pheromones. Somehow the Maya we'd seen in the jungle didn't seem the type to lust after her.

"Not sure how that Maya figured out we were the good guys," Dimitri said.

Ritter's hand ran down his weapon—still the rocket launcher. "Probably because you weren't shooting up their artifacts."

"How many more minutes?" Dimitri asked Mari, who lay on half of our shared bench, her head propped on a green army blanket behind Jace's seat.

She squinted at the ceiling in concentration. "Seven. But we both agreed to wait for ten or fifteen minutes, if we could, so I can be late."

"Erin?" Ritter looked at me.

I shook my head. "I can't sense anyone close. I think we lost them. At this point they might be more interested in meeting up with Justine than tracking us."

"We're all headed to the same place." Ritter handed me the rocket launcher. "Keep an eye out. I need to talk to Jace about where to stop."

I nodded as he squeezed past. "I don't even know how to shoot this," I told Dimitri.

"Nothing to it really. Aim and shoot."

"Ha. If I see something, you're taking it."

He laughed. "Okay."

I glanced at Cort. "There's something else I learned. Tom is Cort's brother. Half brother, I mean. Like Keene. But there's something wrong with him. His mind, I mean. I think that woman Delia did something to him. If I'm right, why hasn't he healed?"

Dimitri looked pensive. "Most damage I've seen does heal,

even mental damage. Unintentional damage, that is. But both the Emporium and the Renegades have been fighting for so long that we really have depended too much on the combat ability. Only in the last hundred years when things have become so regulated—when people dying or disappearing is noticeable and punishable—have we realized that brute force isn't going to win the war. So it doesn't surprise me to learn that the Emporium might be investigating intentional mental damage as an option. For the record, I've known Unbounded who were actually insane, and I couldn't heal them." He sighed, shaking his head. "Frankly, it's been a lot of years since I've heard of anything like that."

"You helped Mari." I glanced over to where she lay resting.

"Her mental state was shock, not a true psychosis or a manipulation by a sensing Unbounded. There's a huge difference."

"Well, she seems to be adjusting."

Dimitri smiled. "She does at that."

We fell silent, with nothing but the sound of the engine and the rocking of the Pinz between us. Emotions rose to choke me. This broad man who'd been born in Russia a thousand years ago was my biological father. I knew he cared about me as a Renegade. Why did I want anything more?

I chewed on my bottom lip. We were entering into battle, and we might never have another opportunity to settle what was between us. "I know what happened in the fertility clinic," I said quietly.

For a moment, I thought my voice was too soft for him to understand. Then his body shifted toward me, one hand still resting on Cort's chest. His dark eyes urged me on.

"Laurence told me before he died. Why didn't you tell me?"

He remained quiet for several more violent lurches of the Pinz, which seemed to last forever. Finally, the words came. "I didn't want to come between you and your father."

Anger flared in my chest—not a reaction I expected. "What about you? What about when I was growing up? You missed out on everything. Was it just a duty? Building one more Unbounded for the Renegades?"

He shook his head, his free hand going to my knee. "Oh, Erin, it's not like that."

"No? You've lived so long and had so many children. I guess one more really doesn't make a difference." It was still hard for me to understand. I hadn't missed him growing up. The man I'd believed to be my father had always been there, but it hurt now that Dimitri hadn't *wanted* to be at my milestones.

Dimitri drew his hand away from Cort. There wasn't room for him on the bench next to me because of Mari's feet, but he turned fully toward me, squatting on the floor, his back forming a barrier between us and the rest of the group, though none of them could possibly hear us over the engine, not even Mari.

"Of course I wanted to be a part of your life, but I knew it would only confuse you. Who would I have been? The odd man next door? A male teacher with a questionable attachment to a female student? Your parents didn't know me, and I couldn't be there in any real way for you. Your parents deserved to have you to themselves the way they planned without an uninvited sperm donor appearing on their doorstep. Remember, they still believe the clinic used your father's sperm, though he would never have been able to father another child. He was lucky to get Chris."

"So if I hadn't Changed, I would never have known the truth?"

"You would have been better off." He took my hand in his. "Still, I kept track of you, as did Ava. Of course I hoped that we'd have . . . more. Look, I may have been absent in your youth, but think of it this way. I'm the one who gets to spend my remaining thousand years at your side. I'm the one who will be here to put your pieces back together when you need me, and together we're going to make the world safer for mortals and Unbounded. Your mortal father won't have that chance. He'll never know the depths of the relationship we'll have. He'll never understand your true abilities. It was only fair to give him the first part of your life. Can you understand that?"

Strangely enough I could. Once again I felt slapped with the notion of our near immortality. Like Ritter had said, I was still thinking like a mortal. "I don't know if I could do it. Give up a child even if it was for their own good."

He nodded, his expression grave. "I was raised in an era where people took care of their children. They were faithful to their spouses and families. They believed in God and consequences. I've lived long enough to know that children who have two parents who live together and love each other are very lucky. I would never have taken that away from you, regardless of the cost to myself."

There was a slight hollowness in his voice that I hadn't noticed before. Tentatively, I reached out and felt for his emotions, surprised that he'd also dropped his barriers enough to reveal his surface emotions. I felt love, friendship, eagerness, and yes, duty, all rolled into one. But clearest of all was hope for a close relationship in the future.

Moments passed, while neither of us spoke or moved.

The Pinz rolled to a stop, and Ritter edged toward us through the piles of supplies, carrying one of the remaining containers of gasoline. If he thought it odd to see Dimitri crouching near me, he didn't mention it. He stepped around Dimitri, reaching for the rocket launcher.

Mari stretched on the bench. "I'm three minutes late."

"He'll wait," I said. "But you need to come right back. Tom's looking for you. He won't be above shooting and drugging you. He's good with drugs." The words came without bitterness, which surprised me. I felt sorry for Tom.

"See if Keene can follow Tom, or knows where he is," Ritter added. "If we can get to Justine before she finishes the drug, it will simplify things."

Mari nodded. "Okay. I'll shift from outside. I want to make sure I get my bearings, so I can get back."

"Wait." Ritter held up a hand. "Erin, is anyone nearby?"

"No." I jumped out to the ground, wincing at the jolt. Ritter swung himself down next to me, followed by Dimitri who reached up to help Mari from the Pinz.

Mari looked around. "It's so peaceful here." Jace had found

a wider road—or at least a path with less vegetation than the trail we'd been using before—and Mari was right. The area did feel peaceful, and not as if the jungle would take it back at any second.

The next second I felt that brief suction and she was gone. She didn't fade away or open any door. One moment she was there, and the next she wasn't. The memory of her exultant smile stayed with me, though.

"How are your ribs?" Ritter asked. "Do you need Dimitri to look at you?"

"I'm okay."

He nodded. "I'm going to put in the last two cans of gas. We'll have to find more soon."

Jace walked toward us, lifting and stretching first one leg and then the other. "How long do we give her?"

"Until she comes back." Ritter said.

Jace nodded and didn't ask what we'd do if she didn't return. He retraced his steps to the front of the Pinz, exuding disappointment and frustration. I hurried after him. "What's wrong?"

He turned to me, the emotions abruptly vanishing. "Maybe we should have fought them. I *hate* letting them go. We could have taken them." His hands clenched at his sides. "I don't know why Ritter wouldn't let us. Look what they did to you and Cort."

"Maybe we could have beaten them, but this isn't about revenge right now. And it's definitely not a game. There are more important things at stake. We need to think of those children. Living to fight another day is the Renegade motto."

"Well, maybe I'm sick of that motto!"

I laughed. "That's your genes talking. Your genes urge you to fight as though you really are immortal, but they don't know anything about the Emporium and their methods. You have to control your lust for revenge. "

"Oh, like Ritter does that? We all know he's a bloodthirsty bastard."

"Yeah, but he didn't risk the mission going after them, did he?"

Jace sighed. "I know it was the right thing to do. But it just . . . bites."

"Maybe. But you've battled enough already to know that it's not all glory. Remember the Hunters in the trailer? Don't think I didn't notice your reaction. Murder like that is common with the Emporium, and you'll have to get used to it or you might find throwing up gives someone the opportunity to cut you in three."

"That's different." His face paled. "Those men were unconscious, and they were killed in cold blood. It's not the same as fighting a man who's trying to kill you."

"All dead men look the same once they stop moving. Just don't be so anxious to fight, okay?"

"I can't. Like you said, it's in my genes. I *need* to fight and protect. And you have to stop looking at me like your kid brother. You have to trust my ability." His eyes challenged mine, and I knew he was right. I had to stop treating him like a boy who couldn't handle himself.

I nodded. "You're right."

Even as his expression relaxed, a shout called our attention. "She's back!"

We hurried over to where Mari stood in the same place she'd left. "That was fast," I said.

"He was waiting for me." Her bright tone was a little forced. "Look, he found out something. It's not just the senator who's going to be at that celebration this afternoon. Remember the senator's sister, the bigwig at the FDA? Well, she just arrived at the hotel. Apparently, she donated some money to a charity and won a trip to Cancun so she was close anyway, and since she was also involved in raising money for the school—and immunizations and medicines for the children—they're going to honor her, too."

"No," I groaned.

"It's a set up," Ritter said.

Dimitri nodded. "It's no coincidence, that's for sure. Looks like the Emporium has been planning this a long time."

"Hey, where do I sign up?" Jace snarled. "Donate money and get a trip? Wasn't she suspicious?"

"Happens all the time," Dimitri said. "A perk to encourage donations from the wealthy."

I put a hand on my brother's arm. His emotions were pinging around again, threatening to overwhelm me with eagerness and anger. An odd combination but understandable given the context. "Regardless of whether or not Justine finishes that drug, they won't be able to pass up a chance to take out both a problematic senator and a deputy commissioner at the FDA. As I understand it from Keene, she's one of the few at the FDA who are interested in approving real cures. With her dead, the Emporium won't have to worry about her lowering their drug profits."

"No doubt they have their own operative ready to step in and fill her shoes," Mari said. "Well, at least that's what Keene says. Anyway, he wants us to meet him at a hotel near the ruins. I have the name on this paper." She waved it with a grin. "This is positively the most thrilling thing that has happened to me in my entire life. Is it always like this?"

I thought of the months I'd spent going to Mari's work, keeping an eye on her, when only our daily workouts and reading kept me sane. Had I ever been so eager and naive? "Sure," I said. "But you get used to it." Dimitri laughed and even Ritter cracked a smile.

"Let's get going." Ritter motioned toward the Pinz.

"Wait a minute," Mari said. "Where's Benito? I thought he was in the front with Jace."

Everyone looked away, leaving me to answer. "They still have him." At her dismayed response, I added, "It gets worse. Justine said something about him being the star of her show. I believe she means to use him as the shooter."

Mari sucked in a breath. "But that means . . ."

I nodded. "We may have to kill him."

CHAPTER 21

We were all silent as Jace drove on, finally discovering a paved road lined not by jungle foliage but by fields. How could I live with myself if we had to kill Benito? He was my responsibility, and I'd failed him.

Stupid man should have escaped into the jungle when I gave him the chance. The thought only made me feel worse. I wondered about his mother in Dallas and if she had any other children.

I wasn't the only one agitated. Ritter kept pacing from one end of the Pinz to the other, searching for any sign of danger. It almost made me crazy, but I knew for him it was a necessary release. No wonder he took off between operations. No wonder that when he *was* around, he trained everyone until they hoped he'd leave.

Except for me. I'd never wanted him to leave.

On the bench, Cort gave a sudden gasp as he started breathing again. Dimitri checked his pulse. "Looks like he's back. Should be regaining consciousness soon."

As if on cue, Cort moaned. "Feels like those vampire hunters all over again."

Ritter laughed. "Welcome back, buddy."

We arrived near the hotel rendezvous in slightly over an hour, leaving the Pinz hidden in some trees half a mile away. Cort insisted on walking, though it was clear he labored with every step. No one mentioned his struggle, though Dimitri put an arm around him to lend support. Given the pain etched on Cort's face, Dimitri's healing touch was the only thing allowing him to continue.

The hotel was small and clean, and no one looked at us oddly when we entered. With the duffels of supplies we carried, maybe we looked just like tourists, despite our layer of grime. Keene met us inside the lobby and ushered us to a small room where Jace began pacing, as Keene, Ritter, Dimitri, and Mari crowded around the table to plan. I joined them after making Cort lie down on one of the queen beds.

"I've been searching all day, but I haven't found any sign of Justine or her crew," Keene said. "I had track of Tom for a while, but lost him in the excitement when the senator's sister arrived. I've been to most of the nearby hotels and bribed every employee I could find, but not one of them has contacted me. Bottom line is that we're running out of time. We have less than an hour and a half before the celebration."

"Justine used a hut at some village to mix the drug," Jace stopped pacing long enough to say. "Maybe she's got another place like that lined up. It'd have to be closer, though."

Ritter scowled. "There are hundreds of small villages, and even if we narrowed it down to the closest ones, we won't be able to find her in time. And she'll need to be in place early anyway."

"So maybe we need to focus on mitigating damages." No one wanted to say it, so I did. "But if she uses Benito like I think she's planning, I'm hoping we can secure him without killing him . . . it's not his fault."

Ritter's touch on my waist was gentle. "That's probably not going to be possible. I'm sorry."

The others nodded, while Mari whispered, "That poor man."

They were right, but it didn't make it easier. "Just remember he's one of the innocent victims we're trying to save today." They already knew, and I didn't feel any better saying it.

"We'll stake out the ruins," Keene said. "I'll stick with the senator and relay anything I see from that vantage point." He looked at Ritter for approval, though I knew he had every intention of doing exactly what he wanted regardless.

Ritter studied him for a moment, his black eyes dangerous. Finally, he nodded. "We brought two-way radios with earbuds and mics. Range is about three miles. But everyone needs to keep in mind that Justine will be expecting us and will have warned Benito to stay low. He may not come in plain view until the very last minute. That means we check out everyone. Even the Maya. Benito might be taller than most natives, but he could pass." His gaze shifted to Dimitri. "You take Jace and Mari to the ruins and get everything scoped out. Erin and I are going to scan the nearby hotels. See if she catches anything. We'll join you as soon as possible."

Dimitri nodded. "Maybe we should leave Mari here with Cort. We can't stop to get those bullets out of him now, and he might need something."

"I don't need a babysitter," Cort muttered. "With or without your help, my body will eventually get rid of the bullets. It's just a matter of how long."

Dimitri and Ritter shared a look, which told me the idea had been more for Mari's safety than anything.

"Oh, no, you don't." Mari jumped up from the table. "I might not be able to handle a weapon all that well yet, but I can at least keep an eye out and report what I see. Besides, I can shift if I get into trouble." She could, but would she? Already she might be too assured of her own immortality.

Ritter arose and began digging through one of the duffels. "You can go, but you're carrying a pistol. Keep your vest on." He tossed an extra vest at Keene, who took it without question. "We may have to draw Benito's fire in order to gain control of the situation."

"A lot of good a vest did me," Cort muttered.

"Actually, your vest did save you from a couple more hits," Dimitri said. "And it was a good thing you were standing between Jace and the gunman, or they might have hit him as well and we could have crashed."

Cort rolled his eyes. "Glad to be of service."

Dimitri and Ritter began giving Mari a quick lesson with the pistol—much better than the one I'd given her with the Smith and Wesson back at the hotel. I motioned Keene over to Cort's bedside. "Look, there's something you two should know." I sank down on the edge of the bed.

Keene cocked his head and Cort struggled to sit up. I pushed him back down onto the pillows. "It's Tom. Justine said he's your brother. Tihalt is his father, too."

"No." Keene shook his head, his green eyes vivid. "There's no way. Tihalt was with my mother then. They were—" He scowled. "He loved her."

"I have to agree with Keene," Cort said. "While Tihalt was responsible for his wife's death in the end, he would never sleep with Justine. She's not his type."

"He was involved in gene manipulation," I said. "She didn't ask permission."

Keene and Cort's eyes met for a long moment. "It doesn't change anything," Cort said finally.

"It does to me." Keene frowned. "I have to at least try to get him out and away from them."

Not exactly the reaction I'd hoped for. Or was it? Had I wanted them to help Tom? Maybe.

"Not now," Cort said.

"Of course not. The mission comes first." Keene started for the door.

"There's something more," I called after Keene. "He's unbalanced. I think Delia did something to him."

Keene's step faltered briefly, but he continued to the door, where he turned to face us. "I'll keep that in mind. Look, Ritter, I have a way to the ruins already with some men the senator hired, so you and Erin can take the rental I got this morning." He tossed Ritter a set of keys. "The rest of you can walk. It's not far. It'll be better if you can get in without using the entrance. They'll be checking for weapons because of the senator."

Ritter nodded. "They'll go in from the jungle. There's no use in announcing our presence to the Emporium agents who are bound to be watching the main entry. Their people will have had time to arrive from the jungle, same as us."

"I'll call if anyone I bribed spots her or anything strange." Keene yanked open the door and vanished.

Cort sighed. "I wish you hadn't told him about Tom."

"What?" I shook my head. "Why not?"

"Because he's been hurt enough by my family, and we already know where Tom's loyalties lie." Cort shut his eyes, leaving me to chew on that.

"It's not like he wouldn't find out. Justine plans to make issue of it very soon." I believed Cort was wrong, but it was his family. Wouldn't I want to know if I were in their place?

That made me a big hypocrite because my own brother was unaware of who his birth father was, and I certainly wasn't in a hurry to tell him. As for myself, I knew Dimitri had other children, and a lot of descendants, but that didn't mean I was going to rush out and introduce myself. Most of the descendants didn't even know who he was.

"I'm sorry," I said to Cort.

He opened one eye and smiled. "It's okay. I just worry about him. Take care of yourself."

"I will." I laid a pistol on the bed within his reach. "Just in case."

He nodded, his fingers sliding over the gun.

Keene's rental turned out to be a motorcycle, which wasn't exactly low profile, given our attire and weapons. We had to pull shirts over our vests, and stash Ritter's FAL, his sword, and the extra magazines in a duffel. It wasn't ideal, but it would do.

We were already at one of the hotels closest to the ruins, so we backtracked, driving along the small road as quickly as traffic allowed, slowing whenever we neared a building or settlement. Trusting Ritter with the navigation, I shut my eyes as he drove slowly around the parking lots, reaching out with my mind. Bright life forces of tourists and natives assaulted me, along with the less noticeable ones of various Maya. No mental shields. But for all I knew, Justine was in a barn out behind someone's trees, out of my range. Or even in a hotel room that didn't border a parking lot. Besides, I'd been at high awareness for hours already. What if I was too exhausted to sense anything of value?

For Benito's sake I had to keep trying. Focusing, I began absorbing nutrients from the air, bolstering my physical reserves. I caught a hint of something fruity and some kind of protein, followed by something with a slight moldy feel, which made me glad I wasn't using my taste buds. If my body found something useful, I'd trust it to take what was needed to repair itself.

Straining my mind, I could feel animals in the rainforest that bordered the road. No Justine. No blocked minds. "They're just not here," I called to Ritter. "Or they're out of my range. So unless we're going to go inside each hotel, this is useless."

Ritter slowed down. "We'd better go back. I'll need to get these weapons inside the park."

I'm sorry, Benito. I kept searching as we retraced our path.

We hadn't gone far when Ritter pulled over to the side, braking hard and reaching for his phone. "Ritter here." He paused. "Where? Got it." He hung up and put the bike into gear. "That was Keene. One of his moles reported seeing three men with poorly-concealed guns at our hotel. They were heading toward our room. Justine must have her own spies in place."

He punched the gas and the scream of the motor filled all the parts of my senses that weren't overcome by shock. We'd left Cort in bed, alone and unprotected. Better that he had stayed in the Pinz than to be found there by Justine's henchmen. Ritter drove heedlessly, darting around busses and taxis and other vehicles on the road. Honks and more than a few fingers followed us, but we plunged on. My mind pushed out, searching for dark mental signatures.

At the hotel parking lot, Ritter stopped so abruptly that I would have vaulted off if I hadn't been holding on tight. "Four," I muttered, as we hurried to one of the doors. "Four people who are shielding, not three." Two were completely blocked, but the others radiated anticipation. I couldn't sense Cort, though he could be unconscious or one of those blocking.

Even as I tried to pinpoint them, the mental signatures were outside the hotel, and moving away fast. "I think they're leaving!" Panic enveloped me.

Ritter turned on his heel and hurled himself toward the bike. I hurried after him.

The flash of a thought slowed my step. Someone calling out in bright pain. Someone I knew.

I whirled and started running the other way. Ritter was at my side in an instant, a gun appearing in his hands. "Behind that car," I said, pointing in front of us.

Without hesitating, Ritter sprang around the vehicle, his weapon ready. A second later, he blew out air, relief softening the tense lines of his face. I peeked around the car, still afraid of what I might find.

Cort lay between two parked cars, his brown hair matted to his forehead with sweat and his clothes stained with the fresh blood seeping from under the bandages. "Keene called," he said, lowering his own weapon. "I climbed out the window before they got in. Think I broke something falling out." He gave me a crooked grin. "Better get after them."

"You stay here with him." Ritter was already turning.

I shook my head. "You won't be able to find them without me."

"Go—both of you! I'm okay, though I think someone gave me a little too much curequick. I'm feeling quite a buzz. Go on. I'll wait for you in the Pinz. I can make it that far." As if to prove his point, Cort pushed himself to a seated position. He looked like he'd fallen from a cliff.

Ritter's jaw worked for a few seconds, but we both knew we had no choice, not really.

Seconds later, we squealed from the parking lot. The traffic this close to the ruins had increased while we'd been at the hotel, the usual thousand daily visitors augmented by the natives coming for the celebration. Ritter zipped in and out, often passing on the side of the road. Several angry shouts followed us.

"I've lost them," I shouted to Ritter. We'd reached the parking lot near the entrance to the ruins, brought to a standstill by several busses and a streaming crowd of people. No way to pass with all the cars and pedestrians.

I looked toward the flow of people heading to the park's entrance, sensing a shuttered mind. I found the owner easily, a blond mortal who studied each passerby intently. His bulky overcoat despite the heat warned me he was armed. Another fainter signature was closer to the entrance. "Keene's right. They're watching," I told Ritter. "Not the ones we were following, but at least two others. Should we grab one of them instead?"

"Too many people around." Ritter guided the bike into the slight opening between a bus and a taxi. He turned before the parking lot on a small dirt path, heading off road. Deep into the jungle we went, the foliage growing thicker with every passing minute. I held on tightly, pressing my cheek against the hardness of Ritter's back to avoid being slapped in the face by stray branches.

Finally, we could go no further, and he killed the engine. We wasted a few precious moments covering the bike with branches, though it was unlikely we'd ever go back for it. "We should be in range now." Ritter pulled an earbud from his pocket, attached to a thin cord that also held a tiny microphone. Ingenious in that it could pass as an earbud for any musical device or cell phone. "Dimitri, Jace, Mari, can you all hear me? We're here and preparing to enter the park now. Any sign of them?"

I put in my own earbud in time to hear Dimitri's response. "Nothing. They've roped off one of the larger monuments.

Apparently, they're going to use it for the celebration as a sort of stage. They've got a group of about two dozen children here, all dressed in native gear. We've got to find Benito in time." Worry filled Dimitri's voice, a rare occurrence in the two months I'd known him.

I turned on my mic to speak. "I can't sense him." In fact, I couldn't sense anyone at the moment, only Ritter, whose thoughts were as dark as they came. Not even Jace or Mari appeared on my radar. "Any eyes on Keene?"

"He doesn't seem to be in the park yet," Jace said. "So he's probably not in radio range."

"The senator isn't around either," added Mari.

Ritter frowned. "Well, it's a big park, and if I were Justine and her cronies, I'd stay out of sight until the celebration began. Keep searching—and keep your radios on." He switched off his mic and added to me, "Let's go."

Ritter and I fought our way through the jungle, finally managing to reach the part of the ruins that had been uncovered and reclaimed from the jungle. It seemed ludicrous to me to check people at the entrance when anyone who was seriously intent on attacking the senator and his sister would have done enough research to find another way inside.

We stayed in the trees, moving in a circuit around the open area. I pushed outward, trying to sense what I could, but the only thing coming through was the occasional burst of an unshielded mind. So much confusion and excitement radiated in those bursts that I felt nauseated.

I checked the clock on the GPS Ritter had distributed to each of us. "We're nearly out of time."

Ritter held up his tiny microphone to his mouth. "Dimitri, we're coming up empty. Which structures still need checking?"

"We've gone to all those inside the reclaimed area, but there are at least a thousand structures in the jungle that haven't been uncovered yet. She could be in any of those. The locations are on your GPS, but there's no way we can search them all in time."

"It can't be too far away," I put in. "Justine will make sure she's not in danger, but she won't want to miss all the fun."

"She'll also have to be close enough to keep her shooter hidden until the last moment."

"Uh, excuse me," Keene's voice crackled. "Just to let you all know that I've arrived with the senator. He's enlisted the local authorities, but they won't be much use against a mad man with an assault weapon."

"Stay with him," Ritter said.

"Yes, sir." There was a slight mockery in the words.

"We'll have to separate," I told Ritter.

"Keep your mic on, then." He hesitated, and for a moment the thing between us was there, alive and eager. "Be careful."

"You, too."

He turned and ran into the trees.

I followed my GPS to the structure nearest us, sending out my thoughts to see if I could feel any life forces. Nothing. Still, I ran up the stairs to check for signs of their equipment, but there were only ruins inside a collapsed center. Nothing we needed, so I marked it off on the list of places and continued on. The next building was similar, and I pushed deeper into the jungle, probing with my mind. A dull throb filled the base of my skull.

At the third ruin, I hit pay dirt. One life force. Dark, so the person was shielding. My pulse picked up. It was a smallish structure, covered completely by vines and brush, but the roof was intact and the tall, thick columns holding it managed to let in light despite the thick foliage. It reminded me of a huge gazebo made of crumbling stone.

"Got something," I said. "One person at my current location. Not in view yet. Checking it out now."

No one was inside, and that puzzled me because I could feel the life force close. I scanned the area carefully, wondering if they'd managed to breed back the gift of invisibility, or if they'd managed to create a material that rendered the wearer invisible. Cort had been working on such a thing for years, and while he was sure he'd eventually succeed, so far he could make only small, stationary objects invisible—or at least *appear* invisible as the surrounding light bent around them.

Then I spied the stone staircase. *Great.* This gazebo had a second floor, or had at one time. Maybe it had been some sort of ancient restaurant with open-air seating on the roof. Either way, I didn't want to climb those stairs. But I had to. Before I could change my mind, I started up, taking two stairs at a time, slowing as debris from the eroding stone became thicker at the halfway point. I didn't want to alert whoever was up there.

A stone archway marked the top of the stairs, and I slowed further, pressing my body against the wall. From what I could see the second floor had once been walled in, but those walls now lay in ruins, which was why I hadn't noticed the second floor from below. Clenching my jaw, I edged closer to the arch and peered around.

There she was. Only feet away from the steep drop to the jungle floor, Justine knelt on a tarp next to a laptop, two rifles, and Tom's black bag from the hotel. My stolen machete stuck into an opening between the huge floor stones. Next to it was a bottle of red wine, and a half-eaten loaf of bread lay nearby on a folded tablecloth.

I stepped out into the open, my gun sighting her. "Hello, Justine." My stomach flip-flopped as my acrophobia crashed down on me. The weight stole my breath and threatened to crush my chest.

Her hand stilled, poised over the computer. I didn't see the thumb drive that had held the research, but I'd seen them transfer it to the laptop earlier, and Stella could use it to retrieve the cure information.

"Don't move," I ordered.

"You're too late, Erin. The celebration is beginning. Though if you hurry now, you might be able to save a few children."

"Where's Benito?"

"With Edgel. There's no way you can stop it now. The drug is in his system." Her hand dropped to the computer keyboard.

I staggered forward, and the weight of the sky felt like a thousand tons. Each step was like pushing through heavy mud. My stomach lurched sickeningly. I wanted sink to the rock and throw my hands over my head. *One foot in front of the other. Keep going.* After what seemed an eternity, I reached Justine and kicked the laptop away from her.

She laughed. "Always too late, Erin. You'll never get that research back."

The screen now showed a list of rapidly vanishing files. I pointed the gun at Justine. "Stop it now!" I hated the desperation in my voice. I didn't want to need anything from her.

"I don't think so."

"I'll shoot." I wanted to pull the trigger so badly, I was shaking. I'd have done it already if I didn't want to save Bronson. Or maybe I was waiting until I could see again. And breathe.

Justine laughed again. "Poor, poor Erin. It's the height thing, isn't it? Why do you think I chose this place? I was worried that you might find me—you've become quite resourceful lately. But so much for that, eh?"

I pushed back my fear into a corner of my mind, locking it into a little black box I imagined there. *I can do this. I've prepared for this.* Making my expression hard, I took three solid steps toward her, my stomach barely quivering. "Listen closely, Justine. Give me the research now, or I will shoot you. And then I'll kill you for good."

"No, you won't."

I turned at the new voice. Tom. He'd appeared at the top of the stairs behind me, breathing hard, a pistol in his hand. He wore an expensive black suit as if he were about to leave for the office.

"Put down the gun, Erin."

CHAPTER 22

I'D BEEN SO INTENT ON FIGHTING MY FEAR OF HEIGHTS THAT I HAD forgotten to stay on the lookout for more life forces. Justine had probably signaled Tom the minute she'd seen me, and our brief chitchat had given him time to return. Worse, the laptop screen had gone completely blank. Did that mean everything was erased? Knowing Justine, the answer was yes.

None of it mattered. I could get off at least one shot at Justine before Tom pulled his own trigger. I'd have that much at least. She wouldn't win completely.

I glanced at Tom and back to Justine. Catching sight of the blue sky and the tops of the jungle trees made me dizzy, and my fear peeked out from the black box. "Walk away, Tom," I said, holding my aim at Justine.

He strode toward me. I fired. Once. Twice. Justine screamed and fell backward, but the holes in her blouse didn't turn red. Too late, I realized that like me she was protected with a vest. She coughed, a hand going to her ribs.

Tom's gun jabbed into my neck. "You shouldn't have done that," he growled. "She'll just be that much angrier." His hand reached for my earbud, dropping it to the stone floor and crushing the tiny mic under the heel of his black dress shoes. My guns and knives were next to go, tossed over the edge into the jungle.

"Shoot her!" Justine ordered. When Tom hesitated, she arose unsteadily. "Oh, you're useless. She doesn't love you. Don't you understand that? She never will. I don't blame her either, not with that Renegade in the picture. He's so much more than you'll ever be. You've always been a disappointment."

"Shut up!" Tom's fingers bit painfully into the flesh of my upper arm.

I knew Tom would eventually cave in, and I would be in a world of pain, not to mention on my way to the Emporium as a wounded prisoner. Maybe even temporarily dead. But I still had a card to play. "Why don't you tell him the whole truth, Justine?"

Justine reached for my gun. "I'll do it myself."

Tom's hand moved, and he fired into the floor in front of Justine. The bullet ricocheted and hit the arch above the stairs, sending a small shower of stone to the ground. "Tell me what, Justine? What does she mean?" His gun was back at my throat, but his eyes riveted on her.

"Nothing, dear." Justine's voice was soft and she'd begun exuding pheromones. I choked back the need to go to her, to help her any way I could. Unable to hold it in longer, my fear burst from the black box. It was all I could do not to sag against Tom.

"She's your mother," I said, clinging to sanity. Gritting my teeth, I took a deep breath. "She's been lying to you all your life. Now you have to let me go. I need to save the senator and those kids."

Tom stepped away from me, his gun lowering slightly, his eyes fixed on Justine. "Is that true?"

She tossed her head. "What difference does it make?"

"You lied. Again."

"Oh, Tom, don't be like that." She slid toward him. "Honey, everything I've ever done has been for you."

His head swung back and forth. "No, it's for you. I've always known that. I'm just a means to an end. Don't think I haven't seen the pattern in the way things are and what you've planned. That is my ability, after all. I should have known it was you who put me in that foster home all those years ago. It's so clear now. You came to visit me only twice in eighteen years. You said our mother died and that you had no choice."

"I didn't have a choice. What would I do with a baby?" Her hand went up to caress his neck. He didn't lean into her touch, but he didn't move away, either.

Not a good sign. I'd have to make a break for it. Not easy when the sky weighed a million tons. *Calm. Just focus. Push it back.* I could do it. I *had* to do it. I slid one foot over the stone, going slowly until I was sure I could make a final leap for the cover offered by the stairwell.

"Tom, darling," Justine purred. "I came back. Isn't that the important thing?"

"Not really." Another voice, sounding rough and out of breath. Ritter. Relief flooded me. I knew he and the others had been listening until the instant Tom destroyed my mic, but I had no way of knowing if any of them would make it to me in time.

Tom turned slowly. "You." An odd note had entered his voice, one I recognized as belonging to the unbalanced side of him.

"Put it down," Ritter said, edging forward. "I can shoot you before you start to aim that gun, but there's no need for this to get violent. Just call off the attack."

"Don't listen!" Justine stepped to Tom's side. "He'll tell you anything. They kidnap our people and brainwash them into hurting the Emporium. You can't believe anything they say. The only way we'll leave here is in three pieces."

"I said call it off." Ritter's eyes glittered as he took moved closer to the pair, the barrel of his rifle pointed at Tom.

Tom didn't put down his gun. "It's too late. But before we shoot it out, there's something you should know, something Erin's been keeping from you all this time. Justine was there with our agents that day when your family was killed."

"Shut up, you idiot! Shut up, shut up, shut up!" Justine launched herself at Tom, but he pushed her away.

Tom laughed at Ritter's hardened expression. "She told me all about it in detail—your poor little sister, your parents, the girl you were going to marry."

Ritter's nostrils flared and his white-knuckled grip on his rifle was so tight, I was surprised the metal didn't shatter. He leapt at Justine, knocking her to the ground, pushing the length of the rifle against her throat. "Is it true?" he grated. "Did you kill my family?" Justine tried to shake her head, but his hold didn't budge.

I had to stop this. If he killed her, the rage might swallow him whole. "Stop, Ritter! Don't do it like this."

"Why not?" I didn't recognize his voice. "She did it to my family." His eyes left Justine for an instant, finding mine. "Why didn't you tell me? Why are you protecting her?" Without waiting for an answer, he looked back down at Justine. He leaned into the gun, and she whimpered. "Did my little sister cry?" he asked softly. "Did you laugh when you cut her apart?"

Tom brought up his pistol, the barrel pointing at Ritter. I started to lunge for it, but a flash from Justine's mind stopped me. A woman crying out. Not Ritter's little sister, but the mortal fiancée who had sat by Ritter's bedside during his recovery. I saw Justine's sword slice into her. She'd been helpless, confused, weak—and Justine had happily taken her life. My stomach churned acid.

Tom fired and the force of the bullet rammed into Ritter, knocking him off Justine. The image from Justine's mind vanished, freeing me. I jumped at Tom before he could fire again. He'd hit Ritter in the back, the brunt of the bullet absorbed by his vest, but I didn't want to risk another shot. We tumbled to the hard floor, knocking over the half-full bottle of wine. Red leaked over the pale gray stones.

Justine was reaching for one of the rifles, but she didn't fire at me or Ritter. She aimed at Tom. Ritter was already rising, murder on his face. Swooping up the machete, I launched myself between them, swinging with all my force. At the woman who'd killed my sister-in-law and who would have used me in her attempt to take control of the Emporium. At the woman who had caused a man I was beginning to love so much pain. A woman who'd murdered so, so many. But also at the woman who'd given me a reason to live after my failure in law school. A woman who'd been my friend. Who'd helped me find Tom and what I'd thought was love.

The machete hit its target and Justine crumpled, her head half severed from her body. More red, deeper this time, gushed over the thirsty stones. Her blank eyes and horrified expression stared up at me.

"Do you want to finish it?" I yelled, thrusting the machete under Ritter's nose. He'd drawn his sword and was already lifting it. "Is that what you want? You'd finally have your revenge. Your whole life has been about this moment, hasn't it? That's exactly why I didn't tell you about Justine. You can't live for revenge. That's no kind of a life. So, tough. I'm not going to let you kill her. I'll do it myself." The rest of her head would be easy to detach, but I had no idea how I'd make the machete go through her body in order to sever the final focus points. I only knew that Ritter had suffered enough. If I didn't do it, he would, and maybe I would lose him forever.

"No." Ritter's hand whipped out and caught mine. We stared at each other, both of us clutching our weapons and each other. I didn't know if I was right to ask him to choose me over revenge. Maybe I'd never know. It didn't matter. I cared about him too much to make a permanent mistake.

The fury drained from his face, and his sword clattered to the stone. I let go of the machete, sagging against him. I hated Justine for what she'd done, but I didn't want this to be personal. I didn't want her death to come between me and Ritter. I wanted her taken to the prison compound where she could stand trial for her murders—and I didn't want to be anywhere nearby when that happened.

"The senator," Ritter said. "Let's go."

"Wait. What about Tom?"

He was lying motionless where I'd left him on the stone floor, horror registering on his face as he gaped at Justine. Ritter grabbed him by the shoulders, shaking him. "Where's Benito?"

Tom didn't even look in his direction, his gaze still fixed on the blood, pumping over the stone.

"Tell me!" Ritter shook him again. "Or I'll kill you right now."

Tom managed to tear his eyes away from Justine. "Near the children. Edgel had your guy replace one of the teachers. But you're already too late. Way too late." Wild laughter bubbled up from his throat, dying abruptly as he looked past us again to Justine.

Ritter drew back his fist and punched hard. Tom's eyes rolled up in his head. Dropping him, Ritter grabbed at his mic. "Did you hear that everyone? The children's teacher. Get to the teacher!" As he spoke, he swept up his weapons and began pulling me toward the stairs. "We'll come back for them later."

I grabbed the machete and the scabbard lying on the stones near the spilled wine. There was surprisingly little blood on the blade, and I swiped it once over Justine's tablecloth before shoving it into the scabbard and tying it on.

We ran from the ruins, jumping over vines and brush and skirting piles of stone. After only a few minutes, my breath choked in my throat and my step slowed. "Go on ahead," I panted. With his ability, Ritter could run much faster without me along.

"I'm not leaving you."

"Yes, you are." Then I remembered. "Open your mind. I can use your ability."

That he didn't question how showed his trust, which almost made me sit down right there and have a good cry. I'd told myself repeatedly that I didn't really know him, that our time together had been too short, but I knew him better than I thought. Or part of me did. The connection in our minds ran deep.

I reached out to him, channeling his ability. Together we ran. Trees rushed by so fast that my stomach threatened to heave. In the next instant euphoria settled in. I felt powerful. I knew where to place my feet without looking. I knew exactly how high to jump.

I brought out the machete and used it to slice through the foliage blocking my path. If I could use the combat ability, could I use the talents of others as well? The thought was both frightening and intoxicating.

We reached the cleared part of the ruins and heard Senator Bellar's voice over a loudspeaker, though it was still far enough away that the words were garbled. We continued to run, my mind linked to his. He jumped over a backpack someone had set on the ground, and it seemed as if I were the one jumping. Several people stopped and stared, but they were blurs, hardly registering on my consciousness. I slid the machete back into the scabbard.

"Three teachers are talking to the children," Jace's voice said in Ritter's earbud. "They're standing in front of them. All wearing masks. Which one is he?"

"He won't be talking," Ritter said. "He doesn't know Mayan."

Dimitri answered. "Well, they're all talking. I doubt these children use the same Mayan dialect. It's probably Spanish."

"Grab them all," Ritter barked. "The senator's men will probably hold off shooting since you're near children."

"I'm not quite in range." Jace sounded out of breath. "Got a little hung up with one of their guys. But I'm almost there."

"I'm close," Keene said, but the next minute he swore. "Stupid policemen pulled their guns on me. Going to take longer than I thought. The senator must have told them I was a danger. Idiot."

"I see them," Mari's voice crackled with static. "I'm shift—" Her voice cut out on the last word.

Ritter and I rounded a stone building, and a crowd of people came into sight. Halfway up a temple, the senator stood holding a microphone attached to a portable speaker. At his side was solid, stern-looking woman with graying hair. The Maya children sat in several rows along the stairs below them, and farther down three Maya adults in native dress stood several stairs above the crowd.

"Out of the way, out of the way!" Ritter shouted brandishing his rifle. The back of the crowd parted. A child cried out and a woman screamed.

One of the teachers reached for something under his cloak. Mari appeared beside him, jumping onto his back, her arms around his throat. The crowd at the front gasped and then began to clap, thinking it was part of the program. The man, with Mari on his back, fell down the stairs, pinning her beneath him. Another teacher jumped down the stairs to help, while the third reached for something in a canvass bag on the step next to him.

I knew before I saw it that it was an automatic rifle with enough bullets in the magazine to kill half the crowd. The mask fell away as the gun came out. It was Benito, though I almost didn't recognize him. His face was covered in dark bruises and ugly red gashes. He hadn't given in to Justine easily in the end. Like us he wore an earpiece. His eyes were wild, frantic. More shouts from the crowd as people began to flee.

We weren't going to make it. The only way was to shoot. Ritter had his gun up, but two men stumbled into him. He shoved them aside. I felt his frustration. Impossible to shoot Benito without wounding one of the children, but taking time to aim meant more people who would die under Benito's gun.

I reached out with my mind, searching for the life force that was Benito's. I knew it well enough, as I'd been blocking his thoughts for the past few days. There, I had it. "Kill, kill, kill 'em all." The words came through his earpiece. "Just like you planned."

Benito gave a shout of glee. *Finalmente*, he thought. Beginning with that stupid windbag with the microphone and that hag next to him. I didn't understand the Spanish words but the images were clear, his anticipation palpable.

Stop! I pushed out as hard as I could, reaching deeper. Focusing on his hand. Forcing it still. *Benito, you will stop!* I shoved harder, felt something shatter in my mind. White-hot agony. I was drowning, but I held on.

Benito paused, his face grimacing with effort. In his mind I felt his fingers start to squeeze the trigger. In the next minute, Jace reached him, ripped the gun from his hands, and bashed him in the face with his elbow. Benito sprawled on the stairs.

Long enough, I thought.

Then I was falling, falling. I never seemed to reach the bottom. Hands grabbed me. "I got you," Ritter said.

Blackness filled my sight. I was blind.

"Stop them!" someone yelled into a microphone.

"No, you idiot! They just saved you!" Keene's voice from nearby, so the first must have been the senator.

A gunshot cracked through the air. The senator cried out, and people around us fled, screaming. Ritter slung me over his shoulder.

"Help me get the senator inside!" someone shouted. "And find where that shot came from." Had to be the bodyguard, given the American accent.

The Emporium must have fired the shot, trying to make the best of a situation gone wrong. I couldn't see how badly the senator was wounded or if the shooter might have another clear shot, but for the first to have missed, the shooter would have to be at a significant distance. Even so, I doubted it was Edgel or anyone gifted with combat.

More frantic shouts in Spanish, sounding like orders, but I didn't understand the meaning. Nor had my vision cleared so I could see who spoke. I couldn't even sense the life forces of the people around us. Or feel the connection that had been open between me and Ritter.

"Move!" Ritter barked. "Into the jungle!"

My head banged into his back as he ran, sending more white flashes through the darkness.

"No! The entrance!" Dimitri countered. "Cort's there. He's got the Pinz."

Ritter changed directions. "Mari, shift over there. Distract them at the gate. Be careful. The Emporium has watchers there. Back her up, Jace. Give Benito to Dimitri."

I couldn't see anything besides the occasional searing flash of white, but I knew Ritter was speaking to Mari through his mic, and I could imagine her appearing at the gate and distracting everyone there long enough for Jace to clear the path with a few well-placed punches.

More screams and shouting as we joined the crowd leaving the park. "There!" Ritter picked up speed and my head banged harder. I'd always appreciated Ritter's well-muscled back, but this was ridiculous.

The next thing I knew I was lying in the Pinz with something nasty shoved under my nose. I jerked my head away.

"Sorry, Erin," Dimitri said. "But we may need you awake. We barely got out of that park. We seem to have dodged the Emporium agents, but the local authorities are hot on our tail."

My head felt like someone had squeezed it between a vise, but I pushed myself to a seated position on the hard bench, my mind struggling to make sense of the information sent by my eyes. At least they were working again, though the images were blurry and distorted.

Jace and Ritter hunched near the back, rifles drawn, Mari tying Benito's hands. He lay face down on the other bench, his exposed flesh looking worse than I remembered from the park. Ground beef came to mind.

Dimitri tossed her something I couldn't see. "Better give him this. Can't take any chances until that drug wears off."

She made a face. "I don't know how to give shots."

"Figure it out," Dimitri said. "I have to help Cort. He looks ready to pass out. After I take care of him, I'll see what I can do to counter the effects of the drug, but I don't know how successful I'll be with the supplies at hand. Probably better to keep him unconscious."

I glanced up front to see Cort at the wheel. His face was flushed with determination, but the blood gushing down his neck didn't look promising.

"I'll give the shot." I crawled over our equipment, one knee banging into a gas can that didn't budge. *Full,* I thought. Cort had been busy. No wonder he looked so terrible.

I took the needle from Mari and eased it into Benito's arm,

more by feel than anything else. If he'd been Unbounded and unconscious, I wouldn't have taken such care, but he'd feel the injection site when he awoke, unlike an Unbounded whose body would heal the area before he regained consciousness.

Mari's face zigzagged in front of me, and I shut my eyes. "Is everyone okay? What about the senator?"

"He was hit in the thigh," Mari told me. "He should be fine, if they get him medical attention fast enough. His sister will probably take care of him. Everyone else is okay." Her voice lowered as she added, "Well, I don't know about Keene. He wouldn't come with us. I heard him say something about going after his brother. I think he meant Tom."

I sighed. "I shouldn't have told him."

"No. You did the right thing." Mari squeezed my shoulder.

But I hadn't really. Not in everything. I'd had the opportunity to rid the Renegades of a woman who had brought repeated damage to us over centuries, but I'd selfishly hesitated when finishing the deed or letting Ritter finish it. Now Justine's people would dump her in a tub full of their version of curequick and her neck would heal or her head would regrow. She'd be the same as before—every bit as conniving and amoral. That I wouldn't have made it to Benito in time to stop him if I'd dealt with Justine didn't matter. Anything she did in the future, any lives she took, the responsibility would be mine.

Mine and Ritter's. How did he feel about letting her go?

"We can't leave Keene," I said.

"Jace already tried to go back for him when you were out, but Ritter wouldn't let him. Said his first duty was to protect us." Mari leaned closer and I cracked my eyes just a little to see her expression. "Right now we're trying to get back to Chris and the plane. Cort's plane is closer, but he's in no condition to fly after driving around. You should have seen him. When Dimitri gave him the signal, he crashed through a couple of police cars to pick us up."

"Sorry I missed it." It was hard not to appreciate her enthusiasm.

I spent much of the three-hour trip back through the jungle dozing. Jace was driving again, while Ritter stood guard and Dimitri took care of his patients, including me. He injected Cort with more curequick and a sedative. No one mentioned Keene, but I worried about him every time I awoke, and I knew the others worried, too.

I also thought about what I'd done at the park. Preventing Benito from firing had taken great effort, but I had succeeded in controlling him with my thoughts. That meant it was only a matter of time and practice until I could master the ability. Ava had been right all along about my talent being strong. No wonder Delia from the Emporium wanted to keep me her little secret until she could use me as a pawn in her war. How many other minds had she messed with besides Tom's in order to keep that secret? It didn't really matter, because I was going to be ready for her when we did meet again.

Chris met us at the airport. He had a split lip and a bruise on his cheek, but he was in good spirits. "Had a little run-in with some local bandits. Tried to steal our plane. Apparently, they were upset over some deal they made with the owners here. Not sure exactly what kind of deal, but some of their guys died, so they wanted retribution—or our plane for payment. We managed to hold them off." He cracked a grin. "I did have to take the airport owner's sister hostage to make him fight the bandits with me, but it all worked out."

"You'll have to tell us all about it," I said, linking my arm around his neck so he could help me into the plane. What was it with my brothers and trouble? I'd never dare leave them alone again.

Benito stirred as Ritter settled him into one of the bunks in the back of the plane. "No," he moaned, pushing our hands away.

"It's okay, Benito." I tucked a blanket around him. "We stopped you in time. You didn't hurt anyone."

"I didn't?" The words came out a sob. One eye fluttered open, the other too swollen to even crack. "So you got the drive?"

I sighed. "I didn't see the drive, and Justine destroyed the information on her laptop." We didn't even have the laptop to see if Stella could retrieve the information, but I didn't feel like discussing that with him or anyone else.

"I have eet."

"You're hungry?" Was it his accent? Or was my brain still playing tricks?

"I have *it,* "he emphasized. "They were punchin' me and kickin' me, and I was there on the floor anyway, so I took the drive from the laptop. Look in my shoe."

I stared at him. "You have the research?" My voice rose loud enough that the others stopped what they were doing and hurried over.

"My shoe." He moved his foot and groaned.

I pulled off the shoe as the others crowded around, spilling a blue thumb drive onto the thin mattress. I gave a disbelieving laugh as I swept it up. I couldn't imagine how he'd had the courage and presence of mind to take it, bloodied and half dead as he was. "Oh, Benito," I said, stroking his bruised forehead. "You're a hero just like your grandfather. He would be so proud of you. I know I am."

"So you trust me now?" His ruined face twisted in a gruesome attempt at a smile.

"Yes, I do." I had from the moment he hit Justine over the head with that rock. "You've more than proven yourself. This is going to help a lot of people." One in particular.

I met Ritter's eyes and saw the same relief I was experiencing. He turned and strode down the aisle. "Let's take off, Chris. Now. Every minute we waste is a minute the Emporium might show up to stop us."

Spirits rose as Chris guided the plane into the air. We hadn't saved the lives of the two scientists, and we didn't know what had happened to Keene, but our mission was no longer an utter failure. We had brought back the cure for Bronson. We hadn't let Stella down.

I sat next to Ritter, my aching head resting on his arm. "You still worried about Keene?" he asked me.

I couldn't tell if there was a hidden innuendo in the question, if he was really asking whether I cared for Keene as a man, but I chose to take the comment at face value. "He's a big boy. He can take care of himself. I think I'm more worried about how mad Cort's going to be when he wakes up and realizes Keene didn't come back with us. He'll blame me for telling him about Tom. And then there's Justine. What about her?" I had to say the words. Would saving her stand between us every bit as much as killing her would have?

Ritter stared at me for several long seconds. "There's something you should know. Keene wanted to go back for Tom, but that's not the only reason I let him."

I stared at him. "He asked permission?"

"Not exactly. You know how he is. But when I knew he was going back, I ordered him to get Justine. We'll have to wait to see if he succeeds."

"If he doesn't, it's you Cort will be mad at."

He shook his head. "I know, but I had to make a decision based on the entire picture. Keene's good at what he does, and for what it's worth, I don't believe they'll kill Tihalt's son."

I wasn't so sure about that, but in the headiness of the moment, I would let myself believe.

Ritter closed the gap between us. "I never told you thanks," he whispered in my ear, his breath spreading delicious heat through my body.

"For what?"

"Watering my plant while I was gone."

"I noticed you'd brought it from the palace. I should have let it die."

He grinned. "But you didn't."

No, I hadn't, and of all the personal things he could have rescued, he'd chosen that stupid plant. Both things probably said a lot about us, but I didn't care what.

So much left to say. So much to decide. Relationships were never simple for Unbounded. Yet for the moment none of it mattered. It was enough to feel Ritter close. I'd deal with the rest later.

I fell asleep then, waking up only to check periodically on Benito and Cort, though Dimitri was on the job. He and Mari played cards, apparently too keyed up to sleep. We'd barely passed into U. S. air space when Jace stumbled from the cockpit.

"We just talked to Ava," he said, looking pale and ill. "It's Bronson. He's dead."

CHAPTER 23

As the sun rose over the freezing city, our subdued group arrived at Stella's apartment. A moving van sat out front, and Mari, who'd shifted the moment we landed in Portland, was helping our mortal guards carry boxes from the apartment. Time to leave. It had been inevitable, but coming so soon after Bronson's death, the idea made me weepy.

I kept my mind tightly closed now that my headache was gone because whatever had sent that white-hot pain through my skull when I'd stopped Benito had also unlocked something else in my brain. I felt the others differently now, as if their shields were not as strong as before. Or at least not strong enough to keep me out for long. As soon as everything calmed down, I'd test the theory.

Inside, Ava met me with a hug. "Where is she?" I asked.

"The bedroom." She hesitated before adding. "Bronson's still in there. She thought you might all want to say goodbye, especially Chris's kids. She says it helps children deal with death if they can spend some time with the body." Her eyes filled, but she blinked the tears away. We lived with death every bit as much as we lived with life, and it never seemed to get easier.

Dimitri was behind me and she turned into his arms. "Thank you for bringing them all back safe." Her words hinted at what it had cost her to stay behind.

"Always, Ava." As he kissed her cheek, I moved away. Whether they were still oblivious to each other's emotions, or simply too afraid to act, I might never know.

I went into the bedroom, my shoes quiet on the soft carpet. Stella lay on the bed next to Bronson, her head on her own pillow, one arm thrown across his chest. He looked at peace for the first time in months, and I let out a breath of relief.

Stella jerked and opened her eyes, coming to a seated position. "Erin," she whispered.

"I'm so sorry." I went around the bed to sit on her side, away from Bronson.

She caressed his cheek. "Isn't he handsome? Even now?"

"Yes."

"I'm going to miss him." Tears started down her cheeks.

I took her other hand and murmured, "I know."

"All these years I didn't have a child. I saw the pain other Unbounded endured when their children grew old and died, or when they were murdered by the Emporium. I buried all my sister's children, who were as close as my own. I knew the risks—I've always known the risks—and I did it anyway. I was glad. But now . . ." She paused, a loud sob escaping her throat. "I'll never have anything of Bronson's. He's gone, and so is my baby."

There was nothing I could do but hold her. Hold her and help her say goodbye. Help her bury her husband.

"You have Mari," I reminded her. "She's incredible. You should see her shifting in and out like a pro."

Stella gave a short laugh, which surprised me. "So I hear."

"Then there's Oliver and the rest of us." I blinked through my own tears. "I can never repay you for saving Kathy and Spencer, but I'm going to try. I know Chris feels the same. He . . . Kathy and Spencer . . ." What more could I say? She'd exchanged her baby's life for theirs.

She hugged me tight. "I don't know if I'll ever be okay again," she whispered, "but I will *never* regret saving them."

How could she know how much I needed to hear those words? I'd come to comfort her, but in the end, it was she who gave me what I needed.

A soft popping came from behind me. I turned, reaching for a pistol that was probably still lying somewhere in the Maya ruins. "It's just me," Mari said.

I shook my head. "You're going to have to stop that."

"Sorry, but I thought you'd want to know right away. Keene's here, and he's not alone. He's got that Unbounded with him. You know, the black man who was with Justine. Ritter almost killed him right outside! Anyway, the guy's asking to talk to Ava. Ritter called her and she said to bring him up."

Stella dived for the drawer in her nightstand, bringing out a gun and racking it. I grabbed another one and did the same. We hurried down the hall to the living room, where Keene was coming through the outside door into the apartment. He nodded at me, his eyes running over my body as if checking for signs of injury. "Good to see you all made it out."

"We could say the same to you." Warmth spread in my chest at his stare. I told myself it was because I hadn't caused his death by revealing his relationship with Tom, but the tiniest part of me wasn't exactly sure. Keene edged further into the apartment, giving me an infuriating grin, as if he knew exactly what I was thinking. I returned this with a scowl as Edgel and Ritter appeared in the doorway, Ritter's gun pressed against Edgel's head. Jace and Chris were close behind, weapons also drawn.

"Why have you brought him here?" Ava demanded of Keene. She didn't have a weapon in her hands, but the sharpness in her voice cut deep. "How dare you compromise our safe house."

Keene shrugged. "You're leaving anyway. So that makes the point moot."

"I know for certain none of my people gave you this location," Ava pressed. "How did you find us?"

"I'm not without resources." Keene's gaze didn't waver.

I wondered if he'd followed Ava and the others here the night after the attack on the palace, or if he'd planted his own tracking device.

"Anyway," he added, "I brought Edgel because he has a request to make."

"What do you care about his request?" Cort lurched up from the couch where he'd been recovering. "I can't believe I've been lying here consumed with anger at Ritter for letting you go after Tom and Justine on your own, and here you waltz in with this murderer."

"I gave him my word. He helped me get away from the Emporium at the ruins when I went to find Tom."

Cort blinked, slowly sinking back to the couch. "What happened?"

Keene's expression flashed pain, but it was gone again just as quickly. "I arrived at the ruins where Erin found Justine. Tom was . . . he was—" He broke off.

"Spit it out, man!" Jace said impatiently.

It was Edgel who answered. "He killed Justine."

Mari gasped. "Really and truly killed?"

He nodded. "When our men found Tom and Justine, they revived him. She was still unconscious, of course—probably would have been for several days—and somehow in the excitement Tom got hold of a sword. He went crazy, screaming something about patterns and how he wouldn't let her destroy his plans. Her men were too late to stop him, but they're loyal, so they turned their own swords on Tom. vive."

I could imagine the horror all too well, though the reality of what it meant to me was hard to comprehend. Justine and Tom were permanently gone. I'd never have to worry about them reappearing in my life. I'd never have to worry about them murdering my friends or feel guilty for all the lives they would have taken. I didn't know whether to scream with happiness or weep for all that we had lost. I glanced at Ritter, who surely must be experiencing a similar disbelief and shock, but his face was impassive, his attention riveted on Edgel.

"That's when I happened on the scene," Keene said. "Too late to stop his final blow or the resulting anger from her men." The tightness in his voice was painful to hear, telling me he felt he'd failed Tom. "Fortunately Edgel stopped them from killing me as well. In exchange, I agreed to bring him to you. I also gave him my word that you would let him go."

"Yeah, right," Cort said. "The only place he's going is to our prison compound."

Ritter lowered his gun. "Don't be too hasty. I suspect he's rigged himself."

"That's right." Keene flashed Ritter a bland smile. "It was my idea. I don't like to be made a liar."

Edgel held up a small mechanical device in the palm of his hand. A thin wire snaked down his wrist and disappeared into the sleeve of his coat. "Sorry that it's necessary. There are enough explosives here to take out this building and several of the nearby ones as well, though I do assure you I'm not suicidal."

So he said. I wanted to strangle Keene, but at the same time I was curious as to why Edgel was so intent on seeing Ava. The explosives indicated that he wasn't trying to defect to the Renegades.

"Go ahead," Keene said. "I believe you, but they might not."

Edgel wet his lips with his tongue, the first indication that he was nervous. "I'm here to ask for a copy of the research from your Mexican lab."

"What makes you think we have it?" Ava glanced at Stella and then back at Edgel.

"Justine put it on her laptop. She may have had it elsewhere, but that was the only place I saw it, and now that she's gone, I don't know where it is. No one does. I was depending on that research." Edgel's gaze went to me. "You guys obviously took it when you found Justine, but the laptop was empty. I figured you erased it, and that means you must have a copy."

"You think we're just going to turn it over?" Dimitri took a step closer. "Do you know what that research almost did to all those school children?" He snorted. "There's not a chance in a thousand worlds that we'd ever give it to you. You're as insane as she was to even think it."

Edgel shook his head. "That's not the part I want. I want the other research, the cure for autoimmune diseases."

"Why should we believe you?" I asked.

Again Edgel's gaze shifted to me. "It's my mortal daughter. She has an autoimmune disease. She's already bedridden. The doctor gives her less than three months before her body destroys itself." His gaze went back to Ava. "Please. She has two young children. The Emporium was going to suppress the cure, but they were going to let me have it. They didn't know why I wanted it, but that was the promise. They don't know about my daughter." His brow furrowed. "Now, I have nothing." No mistaking the misery in his voice.

I pushed hard at his mind shield, and almost immediately his surface thoughts became apparent. He was telling the truth. "You killed that scientist," I retorted. "You murdered him in cold blood. If you hadn't, he could have helped you. But after what you did to him, you don't deserve it."

His jaw tightened. "I was a soldier following orders. I *always* follow orders. Besides, we had the research. What did I need him for? Killing him meant no chance of it being duplicated. For us it was the right thing to do."

"He was innocent!" I almost lunged for him, but Ava's hand on my arm stopped me.

Edgel lifted a brow at the gesture. "Maybe you're right that I don't deserve it, but my daughter does. Please. I'm begging you. She knows nothing about the Emporium or Unbounded. Please." His dark eyes searched mine and then each of the others in turn. No one spoke. His was a dilemma we all understood only too well. Yes, his daughter was innocent. Should she pay the price of her heritage like so many of our descendants? The Emporium would say yes.

Ava and Dimitri exchanged a long look. Finally, Ava spoke. "I personally don't believe you deserve this, and while your daughter may be innocent, she could have more children who might become Unbounded and eventually work for the Emporium. Of myself, I would say no. But the decision is not mine alone. I will let Stella decide. Your interference in Mexico has cost her the most. As a technopath, she is also the only person who can make sure that we give you only the final recipe and none of the actual research, in case you try to recreate the other drug." Ava looked around at us. "Do you agree?"

We all nodded. I was sure Stella would send him away, and maybe Ritter could even get rid of him permanently by detonating his explosives when he was far enough from the apartment. The man was never going to switch sides, and we'd have to face him again in the future. So what if he loved his mortal daughter and kept her a secret from his leaders? It didn't mean much in the face of our own loved ones.

Or did it?

Stella released a long sigh. "Let him have it. No one—not even him—should have to feel this pain."

I choked back a gasp. We all stared.

"Erin." Ritter nodded at me.

I pulled the thumb drive from my pocket where it had been since I'd taken it from Benito on the plane. I handed it to Stella. Any way I looked at it, Justine's and Tom's deaths meant our mission had been more of a success than we'd known, especially after losing Bronson, but giving the cure to Edgel seemed to diminish everything we'd achieved.

"Will you get the laptop from my spare room?" Stella asked me, moving toward a box of equipment salvaged from the palace. By the time I returned, she'd found one of her headsets and put it on. Plugging the drive into the laptop, she began transferring files. One minute. Three. Six. We all waited. A single tear slid down Stella's cheek.

In ten minutes she was finished. She took out the drive and

handed it to Edgel. “I swear to you that this is all we have. I’m really sorry about your daughter.”

Edgel’s hand closed over the drive, swallowing hard, his jaw clenching and unclenching with his emotion. “Thank you. Thank you so much.” He backed toward the door, and we all let him go, watching until he jogged down the road out of sight.

Ritter’s voice broke the silence. “Fifteen minutes and we’re out of here. It’s too dangerous to stay. Leave whatever we can replace. I’ve already sent Marco and the others to the storage unit to get what we need there.” He strode to a box of electronics, hefting it. “Grab something, Keene. You owe us.”

“Owe you? Ha. I’ve done enough of your dirty work the past few days.” But Keene grabbed a box and followed Ritter outside. Dimitri, Jace, and Chris lifted more boxes and hurried after them, Chris with an uneasy glance over his shoulder at Stella.

Stella’s arms wrapped around her stomach. She looked lost and alone. “I’m sorry,” Ava said, going to her.

“Poor man.” Stella’s voice was scarcely a whisper.

“I don’t see what’s poor about him,” Mari retorted. “He’s getting what he wants.”

“My thought exactly,” Cort said from the couch.

Stella sighed. “No, he’s not. He’s going to have to reap what he has sown. I only let him believe I gave him the research so he didn’t blow us all up.”

“You mean . . .?” While I hadn’t wanted to help Edgel, this cruelty seemed unlike Stella.

“I mean the drive didn’t contain the cure or any medical research, and I knew he’d never believe that.” Her arms dropped from her stomach and her shoulders straightened. “However, the drive did hold numerous Emporium files, which together may be the single most important piece of intel we have ever managed to recover. Names, dates, locations. It may even be enough to turn the tide permanently in our favor. There were too many for me to analyze in such a short time, and some are encrypted so I’ll need to break their codes, but even the unencrypted files should prove useful. At least one is clearly related to us." She paused, her expression less somber now. "It tells the location of our people they took prisoner in the New York raid."

A smile lit Ava's face. "Where?"

"They're still in New York."

"Ritter's going to flip," Mari said.

I nodded. "Better tell him *after* we finish loading the van."

"No," Stella said. "We'd better get someone out there now. I transferred all the files from the thumb drive and reformatted it, but by now they're going through all of Justine's personal effects and recovering what they can from her laptop and any other computers she owns. Depending on where she kept her files originally, or where she copied them from, they might figure out exactly what information was on that thumb drive. I'd be able to. They'll change protocols and identities and whatever to mitigate their losses, and it won't matter because we'll still be able to use much of the information. But if they suspect we know where the kidnapped Renegades are, they'll move them again, and we can't allow that to happen. Two months is a long time to be held by the Emporium."

Even two days was too long in my opinion. "I'll get Ritter."

I hurried out the door, passing all the men except Ritter on the stairs as they returned for more boxes. Keene's grin grew wide when he saw me, but I didn't stop to give them the news—Ava and Stella could fill them in. Knowing how much it meant to Ritter, I wanted to tell him myself.

I found him organizing a mound of boxes and duffels piled inside the back of the van. My shoe hit the edge of the metal opening, clanging loudly as I pulled myself inside. Ritter turned, his hand going to his pistol, stopping short when he saw me. He looked strong and powerful and dangerous—and incredibly sexy, though I probably shouldn't have noticed that at the moment.

Our eyes met across the dimness. I felt the burning in him and the echoing fire in my own veins. Before I could get out a word, he dropped the box in his hands and crossed the space between us.

Pushing me up against the interior wall of the van, his mouth fell on mine, a heated contrast to the cold metal at my back. Flames ignited everywhere we touched, and he pushed closer, or I did.

"Told you it wasn't over," he whispered hoarsely against my lips.

"What makes you think that?" My mouth opened to his, my hands going around his body to pull him even closer. I wanted to forget the thumb drive and lose myself in him, but we were in every bit as much danger as we had been in the jungle, now that Edgel knew our location. The thought brought me back to my senses, and I pushed him away.

He uttered a muffled groan, casting a quick glance at the opening of the van, where there was still no sign of the others. His black eyes returned to my face, glittering in the weak light. "You didn't bring a box," he said, his voice still rough. "So either you came out here to drive me crazy, or something happened."

Leave it to him to figure it out. "It's good news. Drop all this and grab your bags—we're going to New York. We have some prisoners to save."

THE END

Be sure to catch more of Erin's story in *The Escape,* book three of the *Unbounded* series.

TEYLA BRANTON GREW UP AVIDLY READING SCIENCE FICTION AND fantasy and watching Star Trek reruns with her large family. They lived on a little farm where she loved to visit the solitary cow and collect (and juggle) the eggs, usually making it back to the house with most of them intact. On that same farm she once owned thirty-three gerbils and eighteen cats, not a good mix, as it turns out. Teyla always had her nose in a book and daydreamed about someday creating her own worlds.

Teyla is now married, mostly grown up, and has seven kids, including a one-year-old, so life at her house can be very interesting (and loud), but writing keeps her sane. She thrives on the energy and daily amusement offered by her children, the semi-ordered chaos giving her a constant source of writing material. Grabbing any snatch of free time from her hectic life, Teyla writes novels, often with a child on her lap. She warns her children that if they don't behave, they just might find themselves in her next book! She's been known to wear pajamas all day when working on a deadline, and is often distracted enough to burn dinner. (Okay, pretty much 90% of the time.) A sign on her office door reads: DANGER. WRITER AT WORK. ENTER AT YOUR OWN RISK.

She loves writing fiction and traveling, and she hopes to write and travel a lot more. She also loves shooting guns, martial arts, and belly dancing. She has worked in the publishing business for over twenty years. Teyla also writes romance and suspense under the name Rachel Branton. For more information, please visit http://www.TeylaBranton.com.

Made in the USA
Lexington, KY
28 November 2014